TWO HUNDRED AND TWENTY-ONE
BAKER STREETS

An Abaddon Books™ Publication
www.abaddonbooks.com
abaddon@rebellion.co.uk

First published in 2014 by Abaddon Books™,
Rebellion Intellectual Property Limited,
Riverside House, Osney Mead, Oxford, OX2 0ES, UK.

10 9 8 7 6 5 4 3 2 1

Editors: Jonathan Oliver & David Moore
Cover Art: Sam Gretton
Design: Simon Parr & Sam Gretton
Marketing and PR: Lydia Gittins
Publishing Manager: Ben Smith
Creative Director and CEO: Jason Kingsley
Chief Technical Officer: Chris Kingsley

ISBN: 978-1-78108-221-8

Printed in Denmark

Two Hundred And Twenty-One
BAKER STREETS

EDITED BY DAVID THOMAS MOORE

ABADDON
BOOKS

WWW.ABADDONBOOKS.COM

Contents

INTRODUCTION
DAVID THOMAS MOORE

SHERLOCK HOLMES OWES a lot to the revisionists.

Or, I suppose, *I* owe Sherlock Holmes—the Sherlock Holmes in my head; the fey, frantic, brilliant man that drove me to put together this anthology—to the revisionists.

I have a confession to make: as a younger man, I wasn't particularly into Holmes. I encountered him first on film and TV, as you do. Basil Rathbone in the old black and white movies, Jeremy Brett in the '80s TV show, striding across the screen, sneering and smug; pompous, superior, and so terribly, terribly *dry*. Dr. Watson as a gobsmacked, foundering sycophant: "Egad, Holmes, how *do* you do it?" etc. Tedious, tedious, tedious.

Watching them again now, I can see that I was being extremely unfair on some genuinely wonderful performances, but at the time I found them all so off-putting. It felt—and I still feel this, at least to an extent—like the actors got as far as the word 'Victorian' in the character description and allowed all that implied, all the hauteur and formality of Empire, to dominate their interpretations.

Sherlock Holmes wasn't a Victorian; or if he was, he was more Wilde than Disraeli. Reading Doyle's work, you encounter a man *rebelling* against the standards and constraints of the Victorians. Frequently wild, often despondent, the world's first (and only)

7

consulting detective had no interest in the politics, manners and niceties of his time. He lived for the hunt, for the exercise of his brilliance, and couldn't give a damn for appearances. He took cocaine when bored, kept his tobacco in a Persian slipper, and pinned (stabbed?) his unopened letters to the mantelpiece with a jack-knife. He disdained class and privilege, and would devote weeks to his poorest clients, if the case interested him. This was not a man who strode about London with a top hat and cane, exchanging banter with aristocrats.

That's Holmes. I *love* that Holmes.

But sadly, that's not the Holmes I saw, or not back then.

And then the Robert Downey, Jr. film came out, five years ago. Okay, it was steampunky, silly, an action flick. But here was a totally different Holmes; frenetic, twitchy, bleak, storming about the place with little regard for social mores, prize-fighting for the distraction. Jude Law's Watson is tough, capable, brilliant in his own right, and frequently clashes with his friend and companion. I thought, "What an amazing Holmes! What a great Watson! How original!"

And then I dipped into the canon, and do you know what? That stupid, noisy, big-budget, steampunky Hollywoodisation comes closer to Doyle's Holmes—closer, at least, to my reading of Doyle's Holmes—than all those dry, traditional, Victorian takes put together.

And then there's Benedict Cumberbatch's brilliant borderline-autistic (not actually sociopathic, whatever he says) modern-day Holmes, and Jonny Lee Miller's New York-based recovering addict. Holmes is huge now, and all in the reimaginings, unfolding the beating heart of a complex character many of us completely missed in its original context.

And it occurred to me: I owe my Sherlock to the revisionists. By seeing Holmes and Watson away from their Victorian roots, I see the men (or women!) themselves, as Doyle imagined them: troubled, broken, quite possibly dangerous.

*   *   *

In Two Hundred *and Twenty-One Baker Streets* (although there aren't really more than two hundred stories, I'm ashamed to say), you'll find fourteen Holmeses and Watsons you've never thought to see.

You'll find a female Sherlock with a male Watson, and a male Sherlock with a female sidekick. You'll find Holmes running a travelling carnival in the US in the '30s, and refurbishing derelict buildings in rural Australia. He's clearing a seventeenth-century housemaid of murder by witchcraft, and capturing a real witch in modern-day South Africa. He's Turning On, Tuning In and Dropping Out in Andy Warhol's Factory, and being summoned into a wizard's circle in a fantasy world. In one story, detective and doctor even turn up as schoolgirls...

There are new Lestrades—both capable and inept—newly elusive Adlers, and newly sinister Moriarties. Mrs. Hudson gets particular love (my personal favourite being the cranky carnival dwarf...).

What I'm saying is, the fourteen men and women I recruited to write these stories for me delivered, but *good*. They've all found incredible ways to shed new light on old characters, to show you sides of the great detective and his indefatigable companion that their fusty reputations made obscure. Fun, clever, haunting, sad, scary, strange and *weird*, here are Sherlock Holmes and Dr. John Watson as they never were... and *really* are.

David Thomas Moore
June 2014
Oxford

A SCANDAL IN HOBOHEMIA

JAMIE WYMAN

Jamie came to me courtesy of the tirelessly charming and utterly brilliant agent Jennie Goloboy. Author of the gambling-themed godpunk urban fantasy Wild Card, *Jamie provided me with a story in her self-confessedly favourite story-telling milieu, the creepy carnival. One of the delights (and frustrations) of editing an anthology is the inevitable "I want more!" moments; I guarantee you'll want more of Sanford 'Crash' Haus and his companion Jim Walker.*

THE CANVAS TENT held in heat like an Alabama kitchen, though it didn't smell nearly so pleasant. The odors of dust and grease paint mingled with the smells of pungent herbs: patchouli, sandalwood perhaps. But there was no mistaking the funk of a blue drag somewhere beneath it all. That scent—the reefer—brought back all sorts of memories. Some good, others best left in the trenches.

She'd sent me in here alone, and though Agent Trenet didn't say it, I knew she meant to test me. No genius needed to figure that out, this being my first case. I turned in a circle in the tent, focusing on all the tiny details: the way the stitches on the psychic's garish red scarves were fraying; the coffee stains on the rickety table peeking through the moth-eaten silk cloth.

Fingerprints smudged the glass orb in the center of the table. How anyone could read the future through all that oil and muck was beyond me.

But then, I wasn't Madame Yvonde, Seer of All and Mistress of Fate.

According to the painted banners and smooth talkers at Soggiorno Brothers' Traveling Wonder Show, the Seer was a direct descendant of Cassandra herself. "She can lead you to fame," the barker had said, "guide you to money. Help you seek that which you most desire."

I didn't want fame, and I didn't need money. What I needed, strictly speaking, was a man. Or at least his name. Trenet seemed to think Madame Yvonde would lead us there, and with her being my superior in a multitude of ways, I didn't bother to make a fuss. I stood in that sweatbox of a tent and waited.

Madame Yvonde paid me little mind. Probably on account of all the spirits and such vying for her attention. She shuffled about, a rotund bundle of bright scarves, grimy homespun and arthritic old bones. With her came an eye-searing stench of rotgut. Padding from one corner of the tent to another, the hunched old hag murmured gibberish and lit a number of ivory candles. The bracelets on her wrists and the tiny coins at her wide hips jingled with every ponderous step.

"Now," she said as she slithered behind the crystal ball. "You don't believe, do you, sonny?"

I put on my best, most innocuous smile. "Excuse me, ma'am?"

"Don't ma'am me, boy." Yvonde's voice was deep as a well and just as dark. She withdrew a cob pipe from the folds of her dress and brought it to her lips. She spoke through gritted teeth as she lit it. "You come in here wearing a suit like that, it says you're educated. Educated man don't listen to spirits or stars unless he's desperate. And you are not desperate. Not yet."

"I'm looking for someone," I said neutrally.

She brightened and let out a puff of tobacco smoke. "Oh! Well, then I might be able to help you after all. Come." She wrapped on the table twice. The chair across from her slid away from the table, and a brown work boot withdrew beneath the cloth. "Have a seat and we'll see what we find."

With the stiffness creeping into my left thigh, I didn't so much walk as hobble over to join Yvonde. Trying to keep my discomfort to myself, I bit down on my lip as I slipped uneasily down into the chair. Scooting closer was a whole other bargain that I wasn't prepared to make without a shot of whatever liquor the Seer had beneath those rags of hers.

In the flickering candlelight, Yvonde's face wavered in and out of focus. Layers of pancake smeared over fishbelly-white skin. The makeup flaked at the edges of every deep wrinkle, particularly around her lips where she'd stolen the pink off a peony to color her flabby mouth and bony cheeks. Those pale eyes of hers—all done up with black paint like a kewpie doll— drooped and fluttered. One of her false lashes threatened to fall off at any moment. I could see the fibers of her wig coiling out from beneath the scarf on her head.

Yvonde held out a bony hand and snapped her fingers. "Cross my palm, sonny."

"I paid out front," I said.

"You paid for the circus. Now you pay for the pleasure of my company."

I pretended to wrestle with the notion of parting ways with my hard-earned dollar before reaching into my coat and plucking a bill. I handed it to her, and she crumpled it in those skinny fingers. Yvonde grinned around her pipe as the money disappeared. That smile held a sinister edge, but her teeth were straight and white as a Connecticut Sunday social.

"Now, you were looking for someone, were you?"

An arc of cards appeared on the table. The drawings were intricate, and had probably once been lovely. Now they were just as faded as the rest of this damn circus. Yvonde tapped a card.

"The World," she breathed hoarsely. "You are a traveler. No roots, just boots. Stomp, stomp, stomping on the ground."

I bristled, my blood running cold. She came close to making me think of old times.

"I'm not here about me."

"Aren't you? You're looking for a man, but you haven't stopped to consider that you're searching for yourself. Aimlessly going from South Carolina to Alabama. Over an ocean and back again. Boy, you've just been rooting along the Southern states like a dog hunting for a master that's left him behind."

"A master?" I snarled, balling my fist on my lap. "That supposed to mean something?"

She waved me off with a jingle of her bracelets. "I don't give a flop about negroes, boy. Your money spends just as well as the next man's. But you've chosen the hardest fields to plow, haven't you, soldier?"

Her cold eyes fixed me with a challenge. *Tell me I'm wrong,* she seemed to say. We both knew that I wouldn't. Couldn't. We stared at one another, sharing only that meaningful look.

"What else?" I asked.

With a flourish of scarves and skeletal hands, the arc of cards vanished. Only three remained on the table. The World still stared up at me.

"The Empress," Yvonde sang as she slid the card toward me. "Lovely thing that you can never touch. Wouldn't want to get her pretty blonde hair dirty with those dark hands of yours, would we? Not that she's noticed you. She's too busy with her eyes on some other prize."

The old gypsy slammed her knuckles on the next card, a sound like a gunshot. I didn't jump, but my hand flew to a sidearm that was no longer there.

"The Devil! You seek him out, but beware, little soldier. Hellfire awaits you down this path."

"Hellfire," I whispered, "is behind me."

Her lip hitched up in an ugly sneer, smoke curling up from the pipe. "Sure it is, soldier."

The curtain behind Madame Yvonde twitched with a breeze, and I coughed at the smells stirred around. The pipe, the reefer. Shalimar perfume. Maybe the black powder was my imagination, but that tent filled with the odor of sulfur. Shots fired more than a decade before rang out in my ears. Shells and screams, and a woman singing along with Duke Ellington.

I stared at the Empress and let my fingers trace the inked lines of her face. I wasn't thinking of the blonde slinking into the tent, but I growled just the same. "Damned old gypsy."

"Still want to smile and tell me you don't believe? Or are you going to pass me another of those crisp new bills so I can give you *real* wisdom?"

Agent Trenet had come in silent as night, but when she spoke her voice was loud like the crack of dawn. "Or you could drop the bullshit."

My partner stood behind the Seer. A straight razor gleamed in the candlelight, poised against Yvonde's throat.

The Seer's eyes rolled back in her head and fluttered dreamily as she drew in a long breath through her nose. With an obscene purr, Yvonde clutched at my partner's hand. When she spoke, her voice was a low, throaty rumble. "Oh, Adele, it is wonderful to see you again."

"You haven't seen me, Sanford, your eyes are closed."

Agent Adele Trenet pocketed her razor and stepped away from Yvonde, leaving me more than a little befuddled.

"Sanford?" I asked.

Yvonde opened her eyes. Agent Trenet tugged at the scarf on the gypsy's head, removing both scarf and wig in one gesture. Russet curls sprouted from beneath a shoddy bald cap. And now, without the cover of all the rags about her head, I noticed Yvonde's very prominent Adam's apple.

"Sanford?" I repeated.

"Crash," the gypsy said. Now that I listened, the voice couldn't be anything other than a man's.

"His name," Trenet said sharply, "is Sanford Haus."

Yvonde/Sanford took the agent's hand in both of his. "Now, now, Pinky," he said, dropping his lips to the backs of Trenet's fingers. "You know how I loathe that name."

"And you know I hate it when you call me Pinky."

Trenet tried to pull her hand away, but Sanford held fast

"Let us have a look, shall we?" The gypsy turned Trenet's hand over in his and peered into her palm. Though he only traced the lines there with a single finger, the act was potent with meaning and lust. It made me uncomfortable to watch.

"Oh, what's this I see?" Sanford sang cheerfully. "You're hunting again, Adele. Looking for something to make you whole and fill you up."

My partner rolled her eyes.

"And I see just what you need," Sanford said. He looked up at her like a wicked puppy. "A man, strapping and brilliant. One you'd travel to the ends of the earth to find. And it seems you have found him."

As the fortune teller brought his lips to her hand again, Trenet wrenched loose. "Never, Sanford."

"Crash," he whined, bounding up from his chair. He tossed a cloak of scarves and rags to the floor, and stood at his proper height. His capped head brushed the ceiling of the tent. I boggled at how only moments ago, he'd folded most of that lanky frame into the image of a hunchbacked hag.

"Agent Trenet, who is this?" I asked.

Before she could answer, the gypsy spun to face me and thrust his hand across the table. "Vagabond. Performer. Owner and proprietor of Soggiorno Brothers Traveling Wonder Show. I am Crash."

"He's a thief and a liar," Trenet spat. She tossed a lock of blonde hair out of her eyes and put some distance between her and Sanford Haus.

Rather than bristle at the accusations, Haus smiled. He lifted one shoulder in a dismissive shrug and regarded me with interest. "And you, soldier boy? Have you a name?"

I winced as I got to my feet. Shook his hand as I replied, "Jim Walker."

"Jim? Well, isn't that just dandy?"

"How did you know?" I asked.

"Know?"

"That I am a—was"—I corrected myself quickly—"a soldier? All that stuff about South Carolina? Alabama? Did she tell you?"

Trenet plopped into the chair I'd just vacated and crossed her arms over her chest. "Here we go."

"You walk with a stiff leg," said Haus as he began to divest himself of Madame Yvonde's ample hips. "The footprint of your right is significantly deeper than that of your left. You've had an injury of some sort that has led to amputation. While that might be more common for a farmer, you dress too well for someone working the fields. You're of an age to have served in the Great War, so I can presume soldier."

Haus shimmied out of the costume while he explained. Beneath all those rags and scarves was a stained undershirt, brown trousers and suspenders. Sanford's arms were ropy sinew and milk-white marble. He threw off the bald cap and tousled his red curls.

"Now, there are very few regiments that are accepting of negroes. It's clear by your accent that you are a northerner. There was one regiment from the North that saw enough fire that might account for your leg, and that was the 369th out of New York. They mustered in South Carolina. I made a very educated guess that you had been part of Harlem's Hellfighters. I confirmed this suspicion when I needled you about Hellfire."

My jaw hung open. "You... that's..."

But he went on, enjoying the sound of his own voice. "After you returned from the war, you spent some time at Tuskegee in Alabama. I can tell that by the ring on your right hand, with the school's seal."

"Incredible," I gasped.

"Now we get to the fun part. When you fished out your money, you made the mistake of flashing your badge. I am more than familiar with Pinkerton Agents," he said with a nod to Trenet. "Considering our previous associations, I could only assume that Adele was with you. I stacked the cards and played to that knowledge by giving you The Empress."

"And the Devil?"

Sanford Haus bowed. "I am what I am."

Agent Trenet let out a whoop of laughter. "You only wish, Haus."

"My wish has already been granted," he smirked, sliding his thumbs up and down his suspenders. "You're here, Adele. To what do I owe the honor?"

"Well, for starters, your brother sends his regards."

Haus flopped into his chair and rested a boot on the old table. Taking another drag from his pipe, he muttered something dark that should never be said in front of a lady. "How is dear Leland?"

"Leland Haus?" I blurted out. "The head of the Secret Service? If that's your family, Mr. Haus, that would make you a very rich man."

Sanford's smug grin and flippant wave of his hand was all the confirmation I needed.

Agent Trenet nodded. "Sometimes Director Haus prefers to keep an eye on his wayward sibling, make sure he's keeping his nose clean while playing dress-up in the gutter."

"I'm happy here," Sanford snapped. "Leland needn't worry his tender sensibilities about little old me."

"He hopes you'll come home and—"

"Yes, I'm sure he does. Now, Adele, why are you really here? I hardly think Leland's mommy complex would be just cause to send a couple of Pinks all this way. What do you have?"

Trenet smiled despite herself. Reaching into her shoulder bag, she produced a photograph and held it to her forehead. Mimicking a spiritualist, she called out, "I see the Hermit." She slapped the picture onto the table.

Sanford gave the picture the most meager of glances. "A dead hobo. What of it?"

"Ah-ha!" Agent Trenet fished out another photo and laid it beside the first. "He was murdered with this."

When his gaze took in the knife in the picture, Sanford Haus went still and silent. He steepled his hands beneath his chin and pondered, his eyes gone hard. He stared and stared at the photographs, unflinching and barely breathing. For long minutes, the only sounds came from the midway outside, muffled by the tent. When the carousel started up a new waltz, my partner turned her own leer onto the gypsy.

"Problem, Sanford?"

This shook him from his reverie.

"Crash," he chided.

Then he was up, gathering all the pieces of Madame Yvonde from the floor. "This is a conversation for the back yard. Dear Adele. Mr. Dandy"—he thrust the bundle of rags into my chest— "follow me, if you please."

He proceeded to lurch through a tent flap hidden behind a map of the human skull. I followed, watching as he once again unfolded that beanpole frame. I drew in a breath of clean, fresh air. The night was cool and breezy: a welcome change from the musky tent.

Stretching out those long legs of his, Sanford took off at a brisk walk, leading us through a maze of tents, ropes and canvas stalls. Soon, the music and hustle of the carnival fell away to background noise and I found myself in a small shantytown. Trucks, wagons, tractors, even a couple of repurposed box cars. Few people lingered here, but those who did were obviously carnies. Here a woman in a sequined costume shared a cigarette with a dwarf. There, a man broad as an elephant scraped the last of his dinner from a tin plate.

Haus brushed off the occasional call of, "Hey, Crash!" without acknowledgement. As we passed a chuck wagon, Sanford piped up, "Mrs. Hudson!"

A dwarf with wild copper hair and an ample bottom raised her head. "What'll it be, boss?"

"Three coffees as black as my soul, if you please."

"Don't know that I've got anything that dark, Crash, but I'll see what I can rustle up. And will there be anything for your guests?" she joked.

Sanford gave Mrs. Hudson a wry grin. "Where's Arty?"

"Last I saw he was tagging along with a couple of bally broads and a butcher. He should be at the kiddie show by now, though."

"If you'd be so kind as to send Mars on over to the kiddie show, then. I need to have a word with Arty *tout suite*."

"Aye, Crash," Mrs. Hudson said as she waddled away from her cart.

Sanford hadn't broken stride. I struggled to keep up, my prosthetic leg wobbling and chafing.

With a leap, he took three stairs up to the door at the back of a gypsy wagon. The thing had been cobbled together with various pieces of other things. I recognized the eaves of a farmhouse, a wall built of aluminum, a couple of railroad ties. The door had come from some apartment or other. The numbers 221 clung to the peeling paint, as defiant as Sanford 'Crash' Haus himself.

He pulled a key from a chain around his neck and unlocked the door. "Good sir, gentle lady, I welcome you to my home." With a wide, sweeping gesture, he indicated we should enter.

As the door shut behind us, I dropped Madame Yvonde to

the floor and hobbled to the nearest chair. The ache in my leg had become a tight vice, a hot brand of pain settling around the joint where my knee had once been. If the bone-deep throbbing was any indication, we might get rain soon.

Sanford rooted around and produced a cigar box. Opening it, he offered it to me. "Would you like some?"

I blinked at the papers and mossy green herb therein. "I'm sorry?"

"For the pain, obviously. If you've need of something stronger I can provide that as well."

I waved him off. "No, thank you. Not while I'm working."

He snapped the box closed. "Talk to me, Adele. What do you know?"

"The vagrant was Enoch Drebber. Before the Crash, he was an accountant in Salt Lake City. He and his family lost quite a lot, though. They became Lizzie tramps, traveling, looking for work. Then the family car busted and they took up with a Hooverville outside of Omaha, just in time for that mammoth dust storm to plow through this month."

Two quick knocks on the door interrupted Agent Trenet's story. Haus opened the door where Mrs. Hudson stood with three tin cups on a wooden platter. She gave a bow and exaggerated flourish. "Your service, dear sir!"

Haus moved lithely through the cramped space of his wagon, fetching the cups and doling them out to Trenet and myself. "Excellent, Mrs. Hudson. Thank you."

"Johnny is on his way to take Arty's place. When I see the kid I'll send him your way."

"Fantastic."

The dwarf's eyes landed on me and sparkled with lascivious delight. "Crash, do call if there's anything your guests need. And I do mean *anything*."

Mrs. Hudson gave an impolite wiggle of her rounder virtues and rolled back into the night.

Trenet smiled into her cup of coffee. "Well, well."

Haus shut the door. "You were saying. Mr. Drebber found himself outside of Omaha, destitute and most dead."

"Yes," Agent Trenet continued. "Well, it so happens that his death coincides with the date your particular mud show slunk out of town."

"Coincidence."

"Perhaps, Sanford—"

"Crash."

"—but it's not the first crime to turn up on your route. Three weeks before that, Mary Watson was kidnapped less than a quarter mile from your tent. Pinkerton agents are still looking for her."

"Never heard of her."

"Two weeks before that, Calvin Bailey was found dead."

"Calvin Bailey? We oil-spotted him in Duluth!"

"Oil-spotted?" I asked.

Haus rolled his eyes. "Oil-spotted. Red-lighted. Means we left him behind and all he saw was the oil spot where the truck had been."

"He worked for you?" Trenet asked.

"Until I found out he was using his job as a balloon vendor to find little girls, yes. As I say, we left him behind."

"Well, he was found dead on the Kansas-Missouri state line."

"Serves him right," Crash said, rolling a cigarette. "Wasn't me or mine, I'll tell you that. We're no Sunday School, but we generally keep clean."

"You're sure?"

"We haven't pulled close to Missouri this trip."

Trenet's pretty face scrunched up with confusion. "But your posters..."

"We had to take a detour due to bad weather, Adele. We missed that stop entirely. Planned on hitting St. Louis on our way back to Peru."

"But you recognize the knife," she said pointedly.

Haus took a long drag of his roller, staring at me. Studying me. Without taking those cool eyes off my form, he exhaled a plume of blue smoke from both nostrils like a lanky dragon. "Is it wooden?"

"Excuse me?" I asked.

"The leg. Is it wooden?"

I nodded. "Hollow. Iron foot, though. Why?"

"Dammit, Crash!" Agent Trenet was on her feet. "Have you been listening to a damn thing I've said?"

Haus gaped at her, but mischief danced in his gaze. "Why, Pinky, you called me Crash."

She let out a frustrated growl and kicked at his shins.

"Yes," Haus said through his laughter. "I recognize the knife. It's identical to the ones Arty uses in his act."

She yanked the cig from his lips and raised it to her own. "Tell me about him."

"Barely old enough to shave. Born into circus tradition to a burlesque dancer and an inside talker. His dad got red-lighted before I bought the show, but his mother—Baker Street Baby—will be onstage in an hour or so." He nodded to me. "You'd like her. Has a penchant for peacock feathers and parasols."

"How do you figure I'd—"

Trenet cut me off. "What about the kid?"

"Arty's a sword-swallower and knife thrower. Goes by Arthur on stage, plays up the Excalibur legend."

"Do you think he could have killed Drebber?"

"Adele, my dear, given proper motivation, anyone could kill."

"I suppose that's true. Just talking with you makes me homicidal most of the time."

"You flatter me. What else? Any other evidence found with Bailey or this Watson dame? You must have more than just my tour schedule and a knife."

"Coffee cans."

Haus's face scrunched in genuine concern. "Come again?"

"Coffee cans," I said. "Found at every crime scene. Each of them contained a letter and a handful of objects."

"Objects such as?"

"The can found with Calvin Bailey's body had a taxidermied dog's paw. Drebber's held the knife. A third can turned up at Mary Watson's home. Inside was a necklace fashioned after a snake."

Haus launched himself out of his chair, and in two long strides he was out the door.

"Crash!" Trenet called after him. To me she muttered, "Come on."

We followed him at his blistering pace—well, I hobbled as quickly as I could all things considered—as Haus led us back toward the siren song of the carousel and hawkers. He swept the folds of a tent apart with his long hands and barked to the assembled crowd.

"Everyone out."

Though there were murmurs and complaints, no one dared argue with the glare Crash passed. Of course, his painted face was rather ghoulish, which might have had something to do with their compliance.

Haus had led us into the sideshow tent. Tables and ramshackle shelves were covered in little curiosities. Jars of amber fluids and specimens—two-headed lizards and the like, as well as fetuses—were caked with dust. One such jar contained only a thumb. A wooden box on a table nearby held a bit of rock. The card in front of it heralded the item as the Mazarin Stone. There were other such relics; a beryl coronet, a tree branch from Tunguska, the stake used to kill a vampire.

"What's this about, Sanford?" Trenet asked.

He led us to an empty bell jar and plucked the card from its display. "The Devil's foot is missing. Tell me, did the paw you found look anything like this?"

I eyed the photograph. "To a tee."

Haus tossed the card and hissed another black curse. Flipping his hand toward an ornate jewelry box, he snarled, "And the Borgias' torque is missing as well."

I padded to the box and read the card. Apparently, the necklace usually kept there was the property of that most notorious family. The card said that Lucretia used it to deliver poison to her rivals. And it was modeled after a scarlet snake.

"Matches the one found at Watson's scene," I muttered. "Right down to the speckles on the snake's head."

"What did they say?" Haus snapped at me.

"The snake?"

"The letters, damn you! The letters found with my stolen property?"

"Just the same two words, every time: *memento mori*."

Haus seethed with palpable rage. The tendons in his fists popped as he clenched. "Arty."

A grizzled old bearded lady joined us. "Boss? There a reason no one been by my stall in five minutes?"

"Where's Arty?" he bellowed.

Agent Trenet took Crash's temper in stride, but the bearded lady jumped back, startled. "Ain't seen 'im tonight. He never showed up for call. He's probably drunk behind the wheel."

Crash growled and spun on his heel. Over his shoulder he called, "Tell the talkers to let the towners back in. Business as usual."

He was a hound on the hunt, leading Trenet and me back into the strange back alleys of the circus. The equipment housed here had seen better days. Trunks of props were open. I saw a few performers grab what they needed, then dash back into tents. Though my thigh ached with the fire of Hell itself, I felt the old rush of excitement that came with having a mission; a goal. Hadn't felt that surge since a time when I had both legs, but that night—stomping through the carnival's backlot—I felt more whole than I had in damn near twenty years. This might have been my first case for Pinkerton, but I was hardly a greenhorn.

That swell of confidence helped to mask the pain and lit a fire that let me keep up with Crash and his spidery legs.

"Where are we going?" Trenet called.

Crash had no time for explanations as we came up on a looming disc. Small metallic triangles glinted from its surface—the points of knives. We were looking at the back of a knife wheel. And one of the exposed blades—this one exceptionally long—was red with blood.

Crash was the first to round the wheel. He spat a few salty words, then kicked up a cloud of dust.

Arty sat in a reeking puddle. The sword—Excalibur, I presumed—had been thrust through his mouth, pinning his head to the rotting wood of the wheel. His face was fixed with a terrified expression. I raced forward and knelt, the prosthetic protesting as I did. I checked the boy for a pulse, but it was a futile effort.

"Marks on his wrists," I said. "He was bound."

Haus paced with mounting anger. "What else?"

I leaned in close to sniff the boy's waxy face. "Chloroform."

"Someone drugged him, tied him up and did this," Trenet surmised. "When did you last see him, Sanford?"

"Just before the gates opened," he answered. "Sometime after two in the afternoon."

I stood up, took out my handkerchief and spoke from behind it. "The blood has been clotting for a while. Flies are on him, too. A few hours. Six at the most."

"And everyone's been working the show since then. Not a soul to find him."

"Jim," Trenet said, her voice nasal as she pinched her nostrils shut, "you stay here with the body and Haus. I have to call the local police."

"No!" Crash barked. "No police."

"Sanford, I have to."

"You can't."

"It's my job!"

"Locals get sight of coppers on my lot, they'll assume the worst."

"They'd be right!"

"They'll stop coming and my people will lose money. If word carries too far, we could lose the rest of the season."

"You can't seriously think I'll just let a murder—the latest in a string of them, I might add—go unnoticed."

"He's not a towner, Adele. He's not even a gaucho like me. Arty was born in the circus. Let the circus deal with it."

The war between Crash's reason and Adele's conscience played out on her face, and I understood both sides. All of the consequences weighed against one another and Trenet simmered.

"I let you clean this up, Sanford, there's gonna be some conditions."

"Name them," he said.

"You let me in on any evidence found, so I can keep this on record as part of our case."

"Done."

"Second, I get alone time with every one of your people. If someone is stealing from you and leaving the items at crime scenes, following your route, now killing one of your performers, I want to know if it's someone in your show."

"It's not—"

"That's how it's going to go down, Sanford, or so help me God, I will shut this show down myself and feed you to the local cops with a side of cotton fucking candy."

I jumped at the lady's language, but it didn't stop me from smiling. The other Pinks had told me Adele Trenet was a firecracker, but it was another thing to see her in action. Crash seemed to appreciate her as well. The slightest of dimples formed on one cheek as he stuffed his hands into his deep pockets.

"Fine, Adele," he said. "We'll play it your way. You can start talking to Mrs. Hudson back at the crumb car while Dandy, here, helps me deal with Arty's remains."

"Shouldn't I go with her?" I asked. "Your people don't much care for outsiders."

"Adele's not a stranger to my crew. They might not care for the badge, but no one will give her too hard of a time."

"I can handle them," she agreed.

"You can handle me," he added with a provocative waggle of his eyebrows. My partner glared at him, and he held up his palms in surrender. "Fine. Work first."

She rolled her eyes, but couldn't hide her own smile as she started for Mrs. Hudson's crumb car. As we watched her jog along the back lot, Crash let out a pleased sigh and rumble of approval.

Haus and I quietly extricated Arty from the wheel, and I tried not to think about all the things my partner wasn't telling me. She wasn't crooked or a bully, like some of the other Pinks, but something didn't jive. For starters, her connection to Leland Haus. The Secret Service and our agency didn't play nice together. But she had some connection to the Haus brothers. I assumed her dealings with Leland involved money and investigations on the sly. But with Crash? Well, I didn't much want to think on that.

Not that a woman so snowy would be seen with a man dark as cinders such as myself.

We were filling the boy's grave when Crash spoke up. "So tell me, doctor, how long have you been with Pinkerton?"

"How did you...?" I stopped asking the question when Crash just gave me an incredulous look over the handle of his shovel. "Right. This is my first case."

"Doesn't seem to suit you."

"Maybe not," I answered truthfully. "Can't keep soldiering. Tried to put down roots and be a good doctor, but, well, that didn't work out any better. Thought I could put both those skills to use with the Agency, though. Not sure it's not another bust." I piled more dirt on top of the grave and patted it down with the blade of my shovel. "Now you tell me something: do you reckon this is one of your folks doing all this?"

Crash shook his head. "Whoever the character is, he's not job."

"You're certain."

"One of the deaths occurred in a town we skipped. He couldn't have known we would wildcat around the weather, any more than we did. And being fifty miles to the south is a pretty good alibi for me and mine, don't you think?"

I nodded grimly. We were no closer to finding the Devil than I'd been when I walked into Madame Yvonde's tent.

The dirty work done, Crash and I shambled to his wagon wrung out as old cloths. As he went to open the door, it jerked.

"Locked," he said, tone dark. "I didn't have time to lock it, Dandy. We ran out in a hurry."

I leveled the shovel in front of me and gave Crash a nod. "Let's see who's inside, shall we?"

Gingerly, he slipped the key in the door and turned the lock. We burst in to find his wagon unoccupied. It was precisely as we'd left it earlier—Madame Yvonde's rags still strewn about the floor and our joe gone cold in the tin cups. One thing, however, was different. On Crash's bunk was a yellow, rusty coffee can.

Crash picked it up and cradled it in one arm while opening it. His fingers snatched the paper out and he let the can fall to the floor.

"'How good it is,'" he read, "'to have a real opponent for my game.' That's all it says?"

He flipped over the page and chuffed out a rueful laugh.

"What?" I asked.

"Have a look."

I took the paper. While the front had only the single line of handwritten text, the back was all flourishes and tiny drawings. Like something from an illuminated manuscript, the figures were ornately detailed. They decorated large letters.

Memento Mori

Something about the drawings bothered me. One of them—a mermaid—was too long. Her body stretched the length of the old paper before joining up with her tail. And another, this one a teddy bear, was bifurcated. One half of its body was on either side of the page. My gaze fell across a seam in the paper. A crease. It had been folded many times. I followed the crease as I brought my hands together. The mermaid shrank into a more average body. The teddy bear became whole. A new word appeared.

"Moriarty?" I asked.

"What's that?"

"I was about to ask you." I looked up from the paper and offered it to Crash. He pocketed something—a pearl, from the looks of it—and put the can down. I hadn't even noticed him pick it up. I began to realize that Sanford Haus was full of talents.

Crash took the picture from me, unfolded it and re-folded it again. Several times.

"Moriarty," he whispered. "Moriarty."

I turned at a knock on the door to see Agent Trenet lowering her hand. "Something you've found, boys?"

Crash swept the can to her. "Another note from our killer. Seems he's enjoying himself."

Agent Trenet looked at the paper. "A game? That's what this is to him?" Peering into the can, she frowned. "There's nothing else here. He always leaves something else, like the necklace or the foot. Crash, was there anything else?"

"Just the paper," he said, lips pressed thin and colorless.

Weary, Agent Trenet brushed her hair over her ear. She grabbed her earlobe with surprise. "Damn! I've lost an earring."

"Could be anywhere," Crash said quickly. "It's likely gone out on the lot somewhere."

As Crash swept Agent Trenet out of the wagon, I noticed the pearl in her other ear.

My stomach fell. How had her other earring landed in that can?

In that moment, my years of wandering ended. All of the steps I'd taken—from Harlem, to South Carolina, to the beaches and trenches in France, to Alabama and now to this mud show in the middle of Arkansas—all roads seemed to have led to this moment. To this puzzle with the answer already filled in. A decision was made as I followed them out, although I'd not even asked myself the question.

"Moriarty," I said under my breath.

"What was that?" she asked.

Over her head, Crash gave me a stern glance.

"Nothing, Adele," I answered.

She shrugged and ran toward the crumb car, where a beefy man with a broad moustache waited. "Excuse me, Mr. Mars. A word," she called.

I lingered behind, watching the work of a Pinkerton Agent at the top of her game, now a pawn in someone else's. *Moriarty.* Our killer. He was there, somewhere at the circus, watching us. He'd followed us enough to pluck up the pearl earring when Adele dropped it. Had slipped into Crash's wagon and had been kind enough to lock up on his way out.

The case was here. The answer to it all was here. Not on the road or behind a desk at the Pinkerton home office.

Crash put his hands in his pockets and sidled up beside me

leisurely. "Payday is every Friday. First of May like yourself would get three aces a week for your pocket. Until we get something else square, you can kip in my bunk."

"Excuse me?"

"Unless you would rather stay with Mrs. Hudson. She'd enjoy that."

I laughed. "A dwarf and a one-legged negro. That belongs in your freakshow for certain, Crash."

"Everyone works," he continued. "Normally I'd start you as a candy butcher, but that requires a lot of walking the lot. No, you're not a vendor. Though you might make a good talker. Inside talker, I'm thinking. You catch details. You're not as good as me, but then, who is?"

"Humble son of a gun, aren't you?"

"You can start tomorrow, Dandy. I'll introduce you around tonight while Adele is questioning my folks."

"Wait, wait," I said. "I didn't say I'd run off and join your circus."

"Of course you did," he said. "And you're going to. It's settled."

"Shouldn't I think about it?"

"You've already decided."

I had, of course. But... "And just how do you know?"

Sanford Haus smiled wide as a Cheshire cat. "You called me Crash."

BLACK ALICE

KELLY HALE

Kelly was pretty much a perfect match for this collection, as the author of Erasing Sherlock, *a time-travel paradox novel about the great detective; I'm hugely indebted to the indefatigable Deborah Stanish for putting me in touch. 'Black Alice' is a wonderfully mannerly Enlightenment-era story pitting our hero against the parochial superstitions of seventeenth-century Worcestershire. And I have a soft spot for Mrs. Malpass's little spotted spaniel...*

SHERLOCK HOLMES DID not care to leave London under most circumstances. Not even the plague. Not even the Great Fire had managed to stir him very far. It wasn't so much the dangers of the road—the robbers and cutthroats and bands of gypsies— no. It was the horrors of being confined in a coach for days with lawyers and tax assessors.

So when he invited himself along on a four day journey to Worcester before the subject had even been broached, Watson, though grateful, was understandably surprised.

"My dear fellow," Holmes admonished. "It was perfectly obvious you were about to beg me to accompany you."

"Beg you?"

Holmes set the *Oxford Gazette* aside, oblivious to Watson's affronted tone, and leaned back, waving airily at the paper the doctor had in hand. "You're holding a letter from someone residing in Stourbridge with whom you regularly correspond. The letter is brief, compared with other such missives you've received from this person, and contains news of a troubling nature, judging from your expression as you read it. Something about the matter is suspicious and, dare I suggest, bizarre. Hence your desire to ask for my aid."

"Well, that is it exactly, Holmes. You will recall my mentioning a benefactor, Rev. Lilly?"

Holmes grunted an affirmative.

"The matter concerns the daughter of Mrs. Mills, his housekeeper. It seems she's been accused of murder." Watson cleared his throat of residual embarrassment. "By maleficium."

It was not often that Watson could surprise his friend, and never so much that the man's mouth hung open. Even so, astonishment turned quickly to action. "You country people and your witches," Holmes said, bounding from his chair. He then set about making travel arrangements with an irrepressible and unholy glee.

THE DUMPLINGS MADE by Mrs. Mills, all fluffy and tender and coated in gravy, dwelt in John Watson's memory with such high regard that he started awake from a dream of being in a storm at sea and trying to catch the dumplings in his mouth as they rolled back and forth along a plank. The dumplings only stopped rolling when the coach in which he dreamt also stopped rolling. On the bench across from him, Mrs. Malpass's little spotted spaniel stared haughtily at him a moment, then politely averted its eyes as Watson wiped a bit of drool from the side of his chin.

His fellow travellers within the coach had dwindled over the course of the journey to just himself, Mrs. Malpass, her daughter and the dog.

The ladies, only just awakening themselves, looked about in confused hopefulness and were immediately cross about it. "What now?" the older woman said. She leaned across to open the shutter only to draw back at the ominous growling of her dog. The daughter shrunk against the older woman, whimpering, "Oh, Mama!" as the carriage door was thrown wide, to the screams of all and sundry.

Sherlock Holmes stood in the blinking sunshine. "Do calm yourselves, ladies." He cocked an eye at Watson. "And *gentleman*."

Seeing it was only Holmes, the spaniel set to wagging its tail enthusiastically. Holmes reached over to give it a quick scratch behind the ears. "We were plunged into a nasty rut in the road just then. Tully and son need to check for damage, and we're being encouraged to make what ablutions we are able, and to breakfast if we are so fortunate as to still have food."

Watson's stomach whined fretfully. "How long a delay?"

"If there is no damage or little, we should reach Stourbridge by noon."

Ideally it would have been mid-morning, but ideal travel schedules were rarely met even in midsummer when the roads were passable. Midsummer was a busy and opportune time for highwaymen as well, and they'd kept good luck on that count too.

Though they'd both paid for the relative comforts of the coach's interior, Holmes had forgone those early on, preferring to ride up top with his pistol at the ready. Despite being covered in travel grime, he looked annoyingly well rested.

The spaniel ran off into the trees as soon as it was on the ground. Mrs. Malpass indicated that she and her daughter intended to follow it into a wooded area, and that they would be within shouting distance if they needed assistance. Watson took their meaning and went the opposite direction to relieve himself.

As he wandered back toward the coach, wondering if he could scrape together a meal of the crumbs left in his pack, the little dog burst through the brush ahead of its mistresses and dropped to the ground to worry at whatever it had in its mouth. The item drew Holmes' attention immediately.

"What have you got there, my girl?" he said, crouching. She eyed him, lips pulled back in a snarl and then, having made her point, let him take it from her mouth.

"Is that a horseshoe?" Watson asked.

"It is indeed. French, by the looks of it." Holmes wiped away the dog spittle, dirt and grasses. "Made for hard riding. It's well-worn, but you can see here how the heel was much thicker than is preferred in England. One of the calkins has broken off, but this was quality work. Expensive, too, I should think. It could have been repaired and used a while yet." He turned the thing over and over in his hands. "The rider must have been travelling fast, and either didn't notice the loss—which is highly unlikely—or dare not return to search for it."

Tully's son, a youth of twelve, overheard the exchange and said excitedly, "Could belong to the fellow that robbed Bill Tucker's coach in May—" The rest of his speculation was forestalled by his father's hand on the back of his head.

Holmes put the horseshoe into the pocket of his coat.

There were no further incidents, and by noon they had arrived at the bustling little town of Stourbridge.

"ALAS, JOHN," THE Reverend Lilly began with a wistful smile, "since the good Mrs. Mills passed a year ago, the secret of her dumplings has sadly passed with her. Alice tries, the dear, but she hasn't her mother's deft hand. She may—that is, I had *hoped* she would acquire the knack. I only took her on as cook three months ago. She was working the dairy farms before that."

Watson remembered Alice Mills as a round-faced, sturdy little thing chasing chickens around the yard, black curls flying, dark eyes gleaming mischief. Full of laughter and endless questions, she'd been. Full of the Devil, some had said, though not in earnest, he was certain. She'd the sort of high spirits and bright disposition that made people fond and forgiving, not resentful. Her father had died a soldier in the battle of Worcester, though rumour had it he'd been a gypsy, not a soldier at all, and the soldier-tale mere invention of Mrs. Mills. Apparently this bit of gossip had calcified into a 'fact' used to explain Alice's dark eyes and her apparent penchant for murder by witchcraft.

Watson drank to the memory of Mrs. Mills and to her dumplings, then filled the hollow of his stomach with the perfectly serviceable bread and cheese provided. His associate was somewhat more measured in taking his repast.

Holmes had gone out immediately upon arriving at the reverend's house, the horseshoe weighing heavy in the pocket of his coat. When he'd returned, a quarter hour ago, the horseshoe had not returned with him.

Both refreshed by food and drink, they could now give full attention to the reason for their visit.

"Who has accused the girl of murder?" Holmes asked. It was not the question Watson assumed he would have asked first.

Rev. Lilly adjusted a wig that didn't need adjusting, a telling habit indicative of the effort the old man was making not to pass judgement. "The dead boy's mother, Margaret Bowen, and his employer, Wenzel Ternac. According to them, Jimmy had spurned her love and she'd set about exacting revenge. Jimmy and Alice had been overheard arguing some days before his death."

"About what?"

"That he was going to London with Mr. Ternac and she... was not."

"And this conversation was overheard by whom?"

"By Ternac. He claims she threatened the boy with a 'hexen,' as he called it." At Holmes' expression, Rev. Lilly sighed. "I know it must seem ridiculous in this new age of science. But Alice is like many country girls, in that she knows the lore of the love charm, a few medicinal herbs, some tinctures and talismans and the like. Nothing more sinister, though, I'm certain of it. She was sweet on the boy, it's true—and perhaps he didn't return her affections, I don't know—but the proof her accusers have given is hardly proof at all! They could have placed the items there themselves, and who could claim otherwise?"

"What items?"

"Alice had a little cloth bag worn on a string beneath her bodice, containing, amongst other items, a lock of the lad's hair woven into a ring."

"Surely this is not unusual for sweethearts."

"No, but in combination with a similar pouch found beneath Jimmy's bed, and the strange symbols drawn in chalk over the door of Mr. Ternac's shop, it was damning. Then there is the witch's bottle the Bowen woman made to protect her son, found dug up and broken with its contents scattered."

Holmes leaned forward, elbows upon his knees, and fingers steepled together. Something about the information had set the gears in motion. "Have these items been kept in evidence?"

"I believe so."

"Good. I will want to examine them. But... I am confused about the broken bottle. The witch's bottle. It is my understanding that a witch's bottle is designed to *repel* the witch, to send her harmful intentions back upon her. If the witch believes herself to be a witch—that is, if she buys what she is selling—she'd be disinclined to touch the bottle at all, I should think, let alone dig it up and smash it to bits."

"You seek to apply logic to the sadly illogical, Holmes," Watson chided.

"Perhaps, but so, then, is someone else. If Jimmy Bowen were suddenly without the benefit of this magical prophylactic, he would then be exposed to malicious intent via witchcraft. If someone wished to imply murder by maleficium, then removing this barrier would certainly convince the boy's mother, at the very least. We must determine who had the most to gain from the young man's death."

"I can't fathom who that may be, Mr. Holmes. He was well liked by everyone. Mr. Ternac's business was so much improved by Jimmy's assistance that they'd made plans to move shop to London. And lest you think his mother suspect, she was to join them there."

"So it would seem that only the spurned Alice Mills had cause to wish Jimmy dead."

Lilly nodded, then immediately shook his head. None of this made sense to him.

Holmes looked thoughtful a moment before asking, "What was the actual physical cause of death, Reverend? Has it been determined?"

"Apparently, he went to bed that night as usual and never awakened. He was discovered in the morning by Mr. Ternac when he did not report for work."

"Was Jimmy apprenticed to Mr. Ternac?"

"Oh, no. He'd been apprenticed to a glazier named Vandernedon, who died last year. Ternac was so impressed with Jimmy's skill that he hired him as assistant."

"He must've been very good indeed, then. Ternac's specialty is lens-grinding for scientific instruments."

"Is it?" Lilly said, "I knew only that he made lenses for reading spectacles."

"And how did *you* know of this speciality?" Watson asked of his friend.

Holmes smiled. "Neither by witchcraft nor deduction. Mr. Ternac has a shop off Church Street. I chanced upon it on my earlier errand. Although I saw no strange markings above the door, one of the specialties writ upon it was high-magnification lenses. You know ocular lenses of that type are a particular interest of mine, Watson. I have long wished to study the techniques for grinding these very small lenses in order to create ones more suited to my needs, but such secrets are guarded closely in London."

Rev. Lilly laughed. "They guard them closer here. We make the best and most varied glassware in all of England, as I'm sure you know. Even the formulas for the glass they use to make the lenses are locked within the minds of the master glaziers, and only shared upon their death beds."

"And did Mr. Vandernedon share his secrets with his apprentice on his death bed?"

"Poor Vandernedon had no opportunity to share his secrets with anyone. He fell from a ladder and broke his neck. An unfortunate accident. There were many witnesses."

"Bowen would have learned much of the trade by eighteen years of age, though, surely?"

"Oh, yes! He was already quite skilled when his master died. Jimmy was a very clever lad, very good at blowing the glass. There were plenty of others who'd have been glad to take him on. It was his mother convinced him to accept Ternac's offer. Wenzel Ternac was lucky to get him at any price, for he was that good. But he was humble as well, and kind, not a vain bone in his body, though he was handsome as any gentleman." The reverend's voice had thickened at that last, and he pulled a linen square from his sleeve ruff. "Forgive me. I'd known him since he was a child." Watson looked away to spare the man's dignity. Though it was likely the boy had been a babe at the breast when John Watson lived with Rev. Lilly, the depth of his benefactor's loss made him feel guilty for not sharing his suffering.

After a moment, Lilly had recovered enough to continue. "Those who saw him last claim he was not himself that evening. That he'd been raving drunk, which was not at all like him."

"Could he have simply passed out, aspirated vomit perhaps?" Watson asked.

"Dr. Green, who examined him, believed the physical cause to be asphyxiation as the result of a coma, but he could only speculate as to why a strapping young man fell into such a state."

"He speculates poison, I'll warrant," Holmes said.

"Yes, I'm afraid he does."

"Poisoning happens by accident or intent, sir. Poison is not witchcraft. Poison is ordinary murder."

"Ordinary to you, perhaps, Mr. Holmes. And for that I am sorry for you and will pray fervently on your behalf."

"That's very kind, Reverend, but you'd do better to aim your prayers at your girl Alice. You said she knows herbs—"

"Alice Mills isn't capable of murder," the man stated with great conviction. Watson hissed in a breath between his teeth, anticipating the lecture he himself had heard often enough about how anyone is capable of murder given motivation and opportunity. But it was a different lecture this time.

"Of murder by witchcraft?" Holmes said. "Quite so. She's not guilty of that. No one has ever been guilty of that in the history of the world. Perhaps it was an herbal charm gone wrong. Perhaps he took the poison himself, for pleasure or stimulation. The point here being that poison was likely the cause, not witchcraft. That witchcraft is asserted at all means that someone wanted it to appear that way."

"Someone wanted Alice to be blamed for it, you mean?"

Holmes didn't bother to answer. Instead he went still, his eyes open but fixed on the puzzle inside his head. Long, uncomfortable moments passed before he cried, "Ha!" and leapt to his feet, headed to the door. "Come, Watson! We must pay all the key players a visit before nightfall."

With his hat in hand, he paused and turned again to the Reverend. "How long has Mr. Ternac been in Stourbridge, do you know?"

"Hm. A year come September. It was in the last days of Stourbridge Fair, as I recall. Brought samples of his goods to show, and then stayed and opened shop."

"And when did the unfortunate Vandernedon meet his demise?"

"August."

"Excellent." Sherlock Holmes set the hat upon his head at a jaunty angle and strode out into the glorious midsummer sunshine of a town not London.

As it was midsummer and no one could be spared from the harvest, or from shearing sheep, or from road repairs, or the numerous other important tasks best done in the long days of summer, there was no one available to escort a witch to the county gaol. The deputy constable's buttery had been conscripted until such time as an escort could be found.

Jeb Cafferty, deputy constable, was practically gushing over the brilliance of the gentleman investigator up from London. It seemed that Sherlock Holmes' errand in the first hours of their arrival in Stourbridge had been to finger a highwayman in the town's midst.

"I'd ha' taken you for a witch yourself, Mr. Holmes, the way you divined Rob Duggar was the culprit from just a thrown horseshoe and the sag of his coat."

"Mere observation, Mr. Cafferty, nothing supernatural I can assure you."

"So that's where you hared off to," Watson said, mostly to himself.

"Takes a keen eye is all I'm saying," Cafferty went on. "His coat was well-lined, sure enough—with stolen jewels and coin. He's in the stocks for now. I suppose Alice ought to be there as well," he said, unlocking the door at the back of his house, "and you may think me weak and a fool, but I just couldn't do that to her."

Alice Mills was still quite... sturdy, Watson noted, though no longer little by any means. Quite a large girl, really, thick through the middle and heavy-breasted like her mother had been. No great beauty under the best of circumstances, but worse for wear here in what served as her prison. At least the buttery provided cool respite from the summer heat. Even so, grime and misery seemed embedded into every crevice of her being. The skin around her eyes looked bruised from exhaustion. A few stray black curls lay greasy against her neck where they'd escaped from her cap, and the dimples of her ready smile now clung to the corners of her mouth like abandoned children.

Holmes showed neither pity nor horror at her appearance or circumstance. "Have you confessed?"

Alice drew back, oddly affronted by his directness, her gaze darting to Watson.

"Hello, Alice. Do you remember me?

Her brow furrowed, but it seemed more out of irritation than confusion. "Master John. Yes. It's been some years."

"Indeed. Rev. Lilly sent for me to stand as witness to your character. I asked my good friend Mr. Sherlock Holmes if he would look into your situation."

"He's a famous examinant," Cafferty said, puffed up by association.

"I prefer the term 'investigator,'" Holmes said with a sniff.

"He'll find the truth about what happened to Jimmy, no mistake."

Alice squeezed her eyes shut at the name. Watson said, "We're—we're here to help you if we can."

"In which case," Holmes interjected, "if they've wrung some sort of confession from you, then we'd be wasting our time. I mention it because sleep deprivation is one of the less-overt methods of torturing confessions out of those accused of witchcraft, and you look as if you haven't slept in a week."

"It's not because I'm keeping her awake!" the deputy constable cried.

"Mr. Cafferty's done nothing to keep me from sleeping, sir. I've not slept because I've been arrested for murdering my own true love. I try to sleep, I do—but then I start awake remembering he's dead." She took a shuddering breath, and closed her eyes again, but couldn't seem to shut out the horror of it. "My Jimmy's dead. He's dead. Oh, God!" She swayed on her feet. Watson moved towards her, but Holmes was quicker, lifting a chair from the wall and setting it behind her just as her knees buckled. Her eyes shot open and she gazed at him, pleading. "Please, sir, I've not done what they accuse me of. I loved Jimmy and he loved me. I would never have harmed him. We were to be married."

"Hush now," Holmes said, "I believe you."

Watson, in the midst of applying a wine-dipped cloth to her the back of her neck, shot his friend a warning look. Why was he giving the poor thing false hope?

Alice seemed to wonder the same thing. She emitted a short bitter laugh. "Do you? On both counts? Because you'd be the only one who believed he wanted to marry the likes of me."

"Now girl, none of that," Cafferty said, not unkindly.

"It's true, though. Jimmy was handsome as anything. Could have had any girl he wanted, but he chose me. He had a pure heart and he weren't vain like some."

"Alice. We've spoken with Mrs. Bowen," Holmes said.

Her head dropped, eyes locked upon her hands clenching and twisting the filthy apron. "I cannot understand her hatred of me. Jimmy and I had been friends since we were little. She was never unkind to me then."

"You were not a threat to her son's future success then."

In fact, when they'd interviewed Mrs. Margaret Bowen, she'd painted quite a rosy picture of what could have been. "Why, in a few years' time, my boy could have had a Foley girl to wife, or even a Sparry. Though I dare say there are richer, finer young ladies in London whose fathers would have been pleased of so enterprising a son-in-law as my Jimmy." Her once handsome face had twisted in anguish and spite. "Well, that's not to be now, is it? She's a wicked, scheming girl, is Alice Mills. She cursed my boy rather than let anyone else have him. And I'll see her hung for it." Holmes asked if there had, in fact, been anyone else that she knew of and she admitted she didn't think so, "—but that don't mean he was sweet on that great cow of a girl!"

Before taking their leave, Holmes rather unkindly wondered— hazarding a guess—if Mr. Ternac had withdrawn his proposal of marriage now that her son was dead. The only answer they'd received to that was in the form of crockery thrown at their retreating backs.

"If she thought you were trying to keep him here in Stourbridge—" Holmes ventured.

Alice gave a snort of hot derision. "He was never going to London with Mr. Ternac, no matter what she believed. He'd an offer from the Henzley glaziers."

Cafferty heaved a sigh of paternal frustration. "Joseph Henzley himself told us Jimmy refused that offer, Alice. I've the letter Jimmy wrote in evidence waiting to show the magistrate. Says right on it, 'got a better offer, taking it.'"

Confusion burrowed its way between Alice's heavy brows. "Yet another offer?"

"Presumably Mr. Ternac's," Watson pointed out.

"No," Alice said softly, then again with certainty, "No. That can't be. Henzley was going to make him foreman of bottles right off, and Jimmy was so happy because it meant he could stay in Stourbridge. He'd have money enough to take care of his mother and... and a wife."

"Oh, Alice..." Watson whispered.

"You can believe me a foolish girl, deluded by love. And

maybe that's so. But Jimmy didn't want to go to London. I swear it. He hated the very idea."

Cafferty said, "That's just from the boys at the Ram's Head, telling as how fellows far less handsome than Jimmy were constantly murdered for their fine white teeth and pretty hair."

Even in the dim shadows of the buttery, Watson couldn't fail to see Holmes roll his eyes. "Oh, yes, *constantly*."

"Jimmy had such good teeth too," Alice said. "And his *hair*— like golden barley."

"He sounds a very paragon," Watson said.

"Oh he is—*was*, was, he was." Her dark eyes welled with tears. "I could have run off, you know. Escaped. Anytime. Could have been long gone before anyone knew I was missing. But what would that serve me? What would I do? Where would I go? How could I live on without my Jimmy?"

ALICE'S DECLARATION REGARDING the potential ease of escape should she so desire had prompted Cafferty to lay in extra measures. Holmes and Watson waited for him outside in the lazy heat of an afternoon that seemed to stretch on forever—so much like the summers of his youth that Watson felt a twinge of resentment at the sound of Holmes' voice pulling him back to the realities of the case.

"To curse and to kill are not synonymous," Holmes said rather peevishly.

"Right. Yes. Your point being?"

"Mrs. Bowen accused Alice of *cursing* her son, not killing him. To her, these acts are synonymous. Indeed, most everyone here assumes the same, and yet we've been given to understand that only one person actually heard Alice place a curse upon Jimmy."

"Ternac."

"Indeed. We can assume he wanted Mrs. Bowen sufficiently

motivated to make certain Jimmy took the offer to move business to London. Jimmy alive in London and working at his side was the goal, I'm certain. Jimmy resisted for whatever reasons, and so Ternac invented the tale of Alice's spite, which he told the mother, and the mother made the witch's bottle and buried it. I suspect the intention was only to cast suspicion on Alice, and once they were safely away she would likely be exonerated."

"But Jimmy dies."

"Yes. Jimmy dies." Holmes stood thoughtfully tapping one finger against his lips then heaved a sigh. "Speak with the doctor who examined the body. He may have noticed details that none thought to ask of him. I will examine the evidence in Mr. Cafferty's possession and we'll meet at Ternac's shop in an hour or so."

Watson nodded and went off to seek out Dr. Green, glad to be strolling in the sunshine rather than holed up in a close room with Holmes, Cafferty and a collection of nails, hair and broken crockery. He passed the stocks, and its lone occupant, the highwayman Rob Duggar, strangely unbowed by confinement for all that he was on his knees with his neck in a vice. His fine shirt was filthy and stuck to his flesh with sweat and blood. There was dried blood in the tangle of his locks, blood that trailed down the side of his sharp jaw. He seemed to be biding his time, not a care in the world, and he smiled. Watson could feel the man's eyes on his back, long after he'd left the square.

WENZEL TERNAC WAS a small, tidy fellow, fine-boned, delicate features, with wisps of ash-brown hair and the palest blue eyes Watson had ever seen. Those eyes peered at the two intruders in his kitchen over a pair of wire spectacles and a dried bit of cake. They were all seated at the table, gazing politely across at one another.

"I don't know what more I can tell you, gentlemen. The

deputy constable and the coroner from Dudley gave the place a thorough going over."

A fly bumped past Holmes' head and he waved a lazy hand at it. "Have the flies been particularly bothersome, Mr. Ternac? They are dreadful in London this summer, I can tell you."

"Must be all the excrement running in the streets, I suppose."

"Not to mention the sewage, eh?" Holmes said with a wink and a grin. "But I understand you still intend to move shop to London at the end of summer, despite the recent tragedy. I do hope the thought of our sewage hasn't changed your mind. There are so many opportunities for a man of your abilities there."

Ternac, uncertain if he was being baited, said, "I have not decided. I had much counted upon young Bowen's assistance with it all."

"And also his skill, I imagine. He learned a great deal in his time with Master Vandernedon. So I'm told."

"He was well-trained," Ternac acknowledged coolly, "but was far from a journeyman."

"Yet you paid him a wage."

"A small wage. Because of his mother. He would have had to work as a common labourer to provide for her welfare. I didn't wish to see his talents go to waste."

The persistent fly landed on the cake, and Ternac brushed it away. His hand was trembling slightly.

"You'll need to put the saucers out again," Holmes said.

"What?" Ternac blinked and blinked behind the little ovals of his spectacles.

"The saucers with the fly agaric in them. You're out of powder, though. I found the empty packet in the rubbish heap behind your workshop."

"Why—? What were you doing at my shop?"

"Admiring your spring pole lathe. We were all very impressed."

"All?" the man whispered.

"Dr. Watson and myself, and the deputy constable." The sound of Ternac swallowing was very loud. The fly landed upon the cake again. "Were you aware, Mr. Ternac, that flies don't actually die from fly agaric? It merely intoxicates them. That is why you're advised to pluck them out of the milk where they float in indolent bliss and toss them onto a fire. Otherwise they recover and fly off, no worse for it."

"I cannot see why you feel the need to tell me all this about flies."

"Oh, Mr. Ternac," Holmes clucked in mock sympathy. "But you do. You *do* see. Jimmy Bowen, much like a fly, did not die from the amanita muscaria you gave him. He fell into a coma, that much is probably true, but you couldn't risk his waking. Not after he figured it out, about the poison... That is why you were forced to put a cushion over his face and smother him."

"That's—that's a lie. I had no reason to wish him dead."

"I know. That's what confused me at first. But once Joseph Henzley has had a chance to examine the broken glass from the witch's bottle, I think we shall learn the truth—No, no don't bother," he cautioned as Ternac shot a glance at the door. "There are men coming here to arrest you. They will not feel kindly toward you if they are forced to chase you in this heat."

Watson rose nevertheless, and moved to block any attempts to flee, but Wenzel Ternac, caught in the icy mien of Sherlock Holmes' condemnation, could not seem to find his feet.

Holmes continued, "I've been told that the secret to creating the finest of small lenses is not as much in the grinding of the glass as in the formulation of the glass itself. And of that particular clear, fine glass the late Vandernedon was a master. That was the secret everyone believed he'd taken to his grave. Even Jimmy thought so, but you knew otherwise, didn't you? You knew Vandernedon had shared his secret with the boy, even if Jimmy didn't realise it himself. You knew it the first time he showed you the bottle he'd made for his mother. The very one she later filled with nails and pins and urine in order to protect her son from the girl you said had cursed him with witchcraft."

Ternac drew in a deep shuddering breath. "He was going to stay for that dull ugly girl. I offered him a chance to better himself, I offered prestige, honour, the chance for greatness, and he wanted to stay here—with a dairymaid! What could I do?"

"Murder, apparently."

"I'D'VE THOUGHT GROUND glass'd be the first choice of a glazier," Cafferty said, over a much deserved pint at the Ram's Head. It was his own ale from his own buttery, as he was also the proprietor.

"A glazier, of all people, would have known that doesn't work, Mr. Cafferty."

"What? Ground glass? It does! My cousin's friend in Dudley heard of a woman that killed her husband with it."

"She may well have killed him, sir, but not with ground glass. The mouth and tongue are sensitive instruments, able to detect a bit of grit or a tiny stone in a spoonful of beans. Enough ground glass to kill a person would be very obvious in the mouth; if it were ground fine enough that the victim didn't notice, it would pass through the gut with only mild discomfort, and perhaps not even that. The human body is a remarkably efficient machine."

"A machine doesn't commit murder, Holmes," Watson said. He rolled a silver ring back and forth beneath his palm. They'd found it amongst the effects Jimmy had hidden under the floor boards beneath the bed in which he'd been murdered: earnest efforts at poetics, a lock of black hair and other indications of mutual affection. These items were in Watson's pocket, to be given to Rev. Lilly with the ring, so that he might give it to Alice. He hoped it would be some measure of comfort to her.

Noting the ring and easily deciphering Watson's expression, Holmes smiled. "Nor does it love, you will tell me. But one day man will create a machine as intricate as the human body, and that machine will find us ridiculous and flawed and wicked, and that machine will justifiably end us."

"An old philosophical discussion I am much too tired to have with you tonight."

"All right, all right, old friend, I shall spare you my gloomy predictions. Have you set a guard on Rob Duggar as I suggested, Mr. Cafferty?"

"He's in the stocks, Mr. Holmes. Where can he go?"

"He's escaped before. As I've mentioned. More than once."

"Yes, I'll see to it." But he went over to talk to the barman instead.

"He'll not be there by morning."

"Who? Duggar?"

"He has an accomplice in town. A young seamstress with a talent for lining coats."

"Well, you'd best tell the deputy constable hadn't you?"

"I don't see why I should do *all* the work for him. But you and I should take extra precautions on our journey home. Loaded pistols, my friend, just in case."

Watson shook his head wearily and rose to make his way to their room and a bed. He could scarcely believe they'd solved a murder, saved a girl from the gallows and sent the guilty party to it—and all before the sun had set.

THE ADVENTURE OF THE SPECKLED BANDANA

J. E. COHEN

I came by Julie Cohen when another author I'd approached contacted me to give his regrets, and threw her under the wheels of my fury; and it's just as well he did. Aside from discovering that she lives on my old street(!), I got an immensely fun Holmes story set in the late 'seventies (one of three stories with a New York-based Holmes investigating a crime on the West Coast, which is a weird coincidence), full of pop-culture references. I can't actually tell you why I really love 'The Adventure of the Speckled Bandana' without spoiling it, so I'll just leave it there...

IN MY MANY years as the intimate companion of Mr. Sherlock Holmes, we inevitably were called upon to investigate confidential matters. Sometimes these involved international security; at other times the cases dealt with the hardly less delicate world of celebrity. Of course everyone is aware of the role that Holmes played in solving the Puzzle of the Grassy Knoll, and his key actions laying bare the full extent of the Watergate Scandal; but in my extensive notes, I also find records of the sensational case of the Abhorrent Disco, and the shocking affair of the Squealing Louse—both matters where the utmost discretion was required to avert an international scandal, or indeed warfare.

All my papers relating to these cases are safely locked away in my old dispatch box. The press has attempted persuasion, bribery and, more recently, burglary to access the box. Every attempt has failed—and I will take this opportunity to warn the parties involved that every similar attempt *will* fail, as I have security advice from no less a person than Mr. Mycroft Holmes, late of the CIA.

This week, however, I received a letter from Holmes himself, written from his retirement maple-tapping in the Okanagan woods. The envelope contained only two objects: a folded and creased page torn from a tabloid newspaper, and a note written in Holmes' characteristic laconic scrawl. Both made my heart sink.

He has passed on to a better world at last. He is safe.
You may write about the speckled bandana. SH

It was a Thursday in the summer of '77, then, that I called upon Holmes in his quarters at 221B Bleecker Street in Manhattan, during a break from my medical duties. Despite the hot weather I found him in a fug of smoke, an empty packet of Winstons at his knee; he greeted me in his habitual offhand way, by tossing a plastic specimen bag at me.

"Watson," said he, "what do you make of this?"

I held the bag up to the light. At first, it appeared to me to be empty, but upon inspection I saw that it contained no fewer than three hairs.

"Is it the forensic evidence from some crime scene? Traces left behind by a murderer, perhaps?"

"No no, nothing so exciting. I stepped out this afternoon, and I've had a caller in my absence. These hairs were left on the cushion of the very sofa where you sit now, Watson. Who is our prospective client? You know my methods; apply them."

I peered more closely at the hairs in the bag. "It was a woman?" I hazarded. "They're all over six inches long."

"Watson, you are the one fixed point in a changing age," remarked Holmes, laughing. "You, of course, keep your military crew cut, but for the rest of us, fashions have changed."

"You think it was a man, then?"

"I know it was a man, for the simple reason that Mrs. Hudson informed me that his name was Kevin. But what sort of man, Watson? And what is his likely business with us?"

"How can we tell his business from his hair, Holmes?"

He merely raised his eyebrows, passed me a magnifying glass, and opened another packet of Winstons.

I applied myself to the task at hand. After a very few moments I put down the glass in satisfaction and said, "He's a hairdresser."

"Good, Watson, good! You noticed, of course, that the three hairs aren't from the same head."

"One is curly and red, one straight and black, and the third is black and kinky. He must have cut the hair of all of these people before he came to Bleecker Street."

"A very sensible guess. However, it *is* a guess, and it is wrong. If our visitor is a hairdresser, why are the hairs all full-length? Why are there no smaller cut hairs left behind as well? One would expect there to be many more shorter-cut hairs adhering to a hairdresser's clothes than long ones."

"What is the explanation, then?"

"You are a medical man—examine the hairs more closely. Do you not notice a certain sheen to them? Open the bag; do you not detect an odour?"

"Hairspray?"

"No no, it is self-evident that this man is—but here, if I am not mistaken, is his tread upon the stair, and he can tell us the facts himself. Hello, Mr. Kevin Lowe. I apologise that I was absent when you came by earlier."

The man who entered the room had hair slightly longer than average, even for the current style, but it was brown, with bushy sideburns. He wore a denim jacket and a yellow shirt, with a wide pointed collar open to an expanse of chest hair, and brown satin bell-bottom trousers. Although no more than of the average height, his platform boots gave him several extra inches, and he wore a diamond ring on his finger, and a small gold earring in the lobe of his left ear. His hands were fine and sensitive, as was his mouth, giving the impression of an artist or a fine craftsman. Holmes waved him to a chair, and offered him a cigarette, which he accepted and lit with an engraved Zippo from his pocket.

"Oh man, I'm glad that I caught you," he said. "My flight back to Vegas takes off in three hours, and I was hoping you'd be on it with me."

"This is my colleague, Dr. Watson, before whom you may be as frank as before myself. Pray tell, Mr. Lowe, what's so urgent in the wax museum business that you need me to fly to Nevada immediately?"

Our client's eyes widened. "I didn't think I'd left my card behind."

"You didn't."

"Well, Mr. Holmes, I'd heard you were good, or I wouldn't have flown all the way across the country. But I didn't know you were *that* good. Or have you visited Lowe's House of Stars?"

"I haven't had the pleasure."

"You'd be a rare person if you had. Business isn't exactly booming." He sighed, letting out a long stream of smoke. "I've studied my craft all over the world, and I like to think of myself as an artist, but when it comes down to it, I'm not much competition for a plain old one-armed bandit. I'd sure like to know how you knew what my job was."

"The hairs!" I cried. "Their smell and their unnatural sheen told you that they were not from any human head. But how did you deduce the wax museum, Holmes? Why not a wig-maker?"

"You accuse me of not keeping up with popular culture, my dear Watson. But when a man leaves behind hairs that clearly

56

resemble not only those owned by recording artists Cher and Michael Jackson, but also the star of this year's new smash Broadway hit, *Annie,* he would have to be a wig-maker to the stars indeed."

"You've got it right, Mr. Holmes. I spent yesterday updating Cher and little Michael, and I pulled an all-nighter working on a new Annie model that hasn't even made it to display yet. And I guess I didn't bother to change my jacket before I hopped on a plane out here to see you. I didn't have time, after what I discovered this morning."

Holmes stubbed out his cigarette and leaned forward. "I am all attention."

"Well, I'll give you a little bit of background. I'm not only the owner of Lowe's House of Stars, but I'm the chief wax modeller. I learned my craft at Madame Tussaud's in London, followed up at the Musée Grévin in Paris, and carried on at the Hollywood Wax Museum; I worked at all three of them for many years as chief modeller, and I'm not boasting, only telling you fact, when I say that I was the best in three countries in the end, before deciding to set up for myself with my own collection of celebrities. Pop stars and movie stars, presidents and murderers. I've got all the stars, all in their latest outfits, with their latest hairstyles. Last month I added Luke Skywalker and Princess Leia, and I'm working on Chewbacca as soon as Annie is finished. You can imagine the work it's going to take to glue all that hair on, but I have a hint that *Star Wars* is going to get even bigger."

"Do you think they'll make a sequel?" I asked, despite myself. I had seen the film at the Strand, and I had found myself thrilling to the adventures in a galaxy far, far away.

"Word from L.A. is that there might even be two."

"And the case?" inquired Holmes, who had declined to see *Star Wars* with me, and who still insisted, in odd hours, that the sun orbited the Earth.

"I'd always dreamed of setting up on my own, but I couldn't do it until my rich old Uncle Vernon died and left me his fortune. I left Hollywood and spent over two years creating my own waxworks, working day and night. No expense spared, every one of them based on the latest photos and using the most modern techniques, though my brother Louie thought I was wasting my money, and wanted me to invest in time shares in Reno. I got a pitch in the basement of the Starlight casino, and I sat back and waited for the money to roll in. Well, Mr. Holmes, it hasn't happened. I don't know what's worse, the basement location, or the lure of those one-armed bandits, but I've been losing money hand over fist since I opened up. Fortunately, thanks to Uncle Vernon, I can afford it."

"You haven't come all this way to consult me over your lack of business."

"No, I haven't. There's no mystery to that; I need to lower my prices and find a new location for my waxworks if I want to start making money. No, my troubles started this morning when I walked into my museum and found it empty."

"Completely?"

"Almost. There was nothing left in the room except for two things: my model of Toto from *The Wizard of Oz*, kicked into a corner onto its side, poor little fellow. And an envelope containing twenty thousand dollars in cash."

I sat up straight in my chair. "Twenty thousand dollars!"

"The police think I'm crazy for being upset. They think I've made a pretty good bargain, since the raw materials cost a lot less than that. But I don't want the money. I want my work back."

"Pray start from the beginning. Every detail may be important." Holmes steepled his fingers under his chin, and his eyes took on the dreamy, introspective air that belied the fierce analytical intelligence of that formidable brain. "Have you had any threats, or any offers to buy? Any hints that someone may have set their sights on your collection of celebrities?"

Mr. Lowe tilted his well-coiffed head to the side, thinking. "It's been quiet. We've had a few visitors, mainly families with kids, or some retired couples taking a break from the canasta tables. Though, come to think of it, Wednesday was busier than normal. For one thing, my brother Louie turned up."

"And this was unusual?"

"Not as much as it should be," said Mr. Lowe, grimly. "He seems to think that if he only harangues me enough, I'll give up the waxwork business and join him in his investments in Reno. We got into an argument and it ended up with him storming out."

"In your opinion, were his feelings high enough to justify his stealing your waxwork collection?"

"Louie's never been a big one for hard work, to be honest. I can't imagine him renting a truck large enough to hold the collection, let alone hunking all the figures into it. I had fifty-six of them, and though they're made of wax, they're not light."

"But he knows your habits, and presumably has a motivation to put you out of business, if he wants the support of your investments?"

"I suppose so. But if he had twenty grand, why wouldn't he use that?"

"Do you have the envelope with you?"

"I do. It's been checked for fingerprints." Mr. Lowe extended the article in question.

"Pity." Holmes examined it with his glass. "A standard manila envelope, no marks, unsealed. The bills are all hundreds, nonsequential. Any evidence will have been destroyed by the police when they handled it." He handed it back to Lowe, who tucked it into his denim jacket. "Besides your brother, were there any other visitors of note that day?"

"There was, actually. An old white guy wearing a Hawaiian shirt. We get a lot of retired people, so he wasn't all that unusual, but he was alone, that was one thing. And the other thing was, he hardly spent any time at all in the museum. Normally people come in, they wander around, take some photos, ask some questions, maybe. Not this guy. He paid for a ticket, walked in and through and out in about thirty seconds."

"Singular," commented Holmes. "Did he seem to take a particular interest in any waxwork?"

"I couldn't tell. I was too busy arguing with my brother."

"And you spent that night working on your *Annie* exhibit. Where is your workshop? Is it on the premises?"

"No, it's about two miles away, in an old garage on the outskirts of town. I have a small apartment at the back, where I live."

"So your museum was empty at night. Unguarded?"

"There's security outside the casino, but the only entrance to the museum is down a side alley."

"This side alley—is it big enough to drive a truck or van down?"

"I'd say so."

"Any witnesses?"

"I haven't found any, Mr. Holmes, and nor have the police."

"Were the doors forced?"

"No. They were locked from the outside when I came to work this morning, as usual."

"Does anyone but you possess a key?"

"My brother does."

"You walked in and discovered the place empty?" I asked. "Did the police find any fingerprints?"

"They dusted every inch, but even a museum as unfrequented as mine has a lot of fingerprints in it. As soon as I discovered that my life's work had gone, you can imagine that I was anxious to find any clues that I could. When we couldn't find anything, and the police seemed not to have the slightest idea, I jumped on the first plane I could get to, to ask your advice, Mr. Holmes, before the trail was cold. Will you come out to Vegas with me?"

"It would give me a great deal of pleasure," said Holmes. He saw his client out, arranging to meet him at the airport in two hours' time.

"You will come, Watson? I may need an extra pair of eyes."

"Ashcroft will be happy to take on my practice for a few days."

"Excellent. If we put aside the question of the money in the envelope, the chief suspicion falls on the brother. It seems clear that if one Mr. Lowe is forced out of business, the other Mr. Lowe may find himself the recipient of some investment for his time shares. But the twenty thousand dollars changes everything."

THUS WE FOUND ourselves on the red-eye to Vegas. Lowe and Holmes chose seats in the smoking section, which was, to be honest, trying, even to someone with my iron constitution. "All the latest medical research indicates that smoking is hazardous to your health," I told Holmes as he puffed away. But he waved aside my objections, choosing to spend the flight quizzing Kevin Lowe about his techniques for modelling from life in wax.

Recalling Holmes' experiments in this very art, in the adventure of the Abandoned Condominium, I occupied myself with talking to the very pretty stewardess, regaling her with anecdotes of my time in service, until the plane touched down at McCarran Airport.

It was too late that evening to do much more than a cursory inspection of the basement of the Starlight Casino, which had until recently housed Lowe's House of Stars. Holmes examined the doors and their stout padlock, and the alleyway leading up the side of the building, which was indeed dingy and ill-lit. Inside the museum, all that remained was some furniture which presumably the waxworks had been posed upon, and the forlorn figure of the dog Toto, lying on his side by the wall.

"We won't get much more tonight," declared Holmes, straightening from his scrutiny of a footmark that was invisible to the rest of us. "Mr. Lowe, tomorrow we may pursue our own methods. Stay by a phone; we will call you as soon as we have any news."

"Mr. Lowe is a true artist," he said to me, when we were in the elevator ascending to our rooms in the Starlight Hotel, above the casino. "Look at this leaflet for his museum, Watson. I think you'll agree that the figures are so lifelike as to defy belief. I made some calls before we left, and all of them confirmed that Mr Kevin Lowe is the foremost waxwork modeller of his generation."

I turned over the folder in my hands, marveling at the depictions of Reggie Jackson and President Carter. "He's very good. Do you plan to visit the brother tomorrow? Or track down that mysterious visitor in the Hawaiian shirt?"

"I will be very much mistaken if one does not lead to the other. Goodnight, my friend, and stay away from the roulette table."

AFTER A BRACING visit to the breakfast buffet the next morning, Holmes and I were ready to go. He spent some more time in the alleyway, pacing its length, once or twice flinging himself onto all fours to examine the tarmac in the daylight. Finally, he straightened. "Most instructive. Let's hail a taxi to Mr. Louie Lowe's office."

The office was a single-storey building near the edge of the desert, with a low-pitched roof and an adobe front. The gold lettering on the glass door informed us that we had called on *Mr. Louis Lowe, Travel Agent.*

Mr. Louis Lowe himself was a slight, weaselly man, with greased-back hair and a plaid suit. He wore a heavy medallion on his chest, and platform shoes even higher than his brother's.

When we entered his office, he reclined in his leather chair, his hands behind his head, his feet propped on his desk.

"You've come about the robbery at Kev's place, I guess. If you can call it a robbery, since he was paid for what was taken."

"Your brother mentioned an argument about money," said Holmes.

"I wanted my half of Uncle Vern's dough to invest in condos in Reno, fair enough. But you know what? I've decided I don't need it after all. Kev can keep it, for all the good it does him."

"Of course, it doesn't do him much good if he's lost his life's work," said I.

Louie Lowe shrugged.

"You noticed, of course," said Holmes as we left, "the map on the wall?"

"Of all of Nevada. But Holmes, the area is vast."

"It's slightly less vast when one has a greasy fingerprint for guidance."

There was a Hertz office nearby, and within half an hour we were heading out into the desert in a rented Oldsmobile Cutlass Supreme.

"Mr. Louis Lowe wanted money," explained Holmes as I drove. "He wanted it badly enough to argue with his brother on Wednesday. And yet by Friday morning, he is no longer looking for investment in his Reno time shares. What do you suppose has changed his circumstances?"

"The possession of a key to Lowe's House of Stars, and the ability to look the other way."

"So much seems obvious. The question is why, Watson? Who would pay Mr. Louie Lowe to betray his brother?"

"A jealous waxwork museum owner, who wants to steal Kevin Lowe's masterpieces?"

"Possibly. And yet why would they give Kevin Lowe twenty thousand dollars?" Holmes tailed off into silence, breaking it only to direct me. His memory was photographic, and he recalled the location marked by the greasy fingerprint without having to consult another map, although it took us nearly three hours' driving to reach it. It was a featureless expanse of desert next to Route 267. The sand and gravel baked in the midday sun when we stopped. The air wavered with heat, and as soon as I opened the door of the air-conditioned car and stepped outside, sweat sprang onto my skin. Sherlock Holmes, however, looked cool as ever as he pointed at the ground.

"Observe, Watson, the same Goodyear tread with the wearing on the back offside tyre as in the alleyway." He set off at a pace over the sand and I followed, wiping perspiration from my brow.

The ground was cracked from the sun, uniformly flat and bare other than the very occasional scrub. Although the tyre tracks were invisible to my untrained eye, Holmes followed them with the skill of a bloodhound. When he stopped short, however, I didn't need his superior senses to know why.

I let out a cry of dismay. The light-coloured ground before us was blackened with soot in a radius of about fifteen feet. Clearly there had been a large fire here, and in the centre was a grey substance that was neither ash nor sand. Holmes stooped and put his hand into it.

"It's wax," he said sadly. "The figures have been melted down."

I touched it. It was unmistakably wax; the ash that lay around it in clumps was undoubtedly the remains of the mannequins' clothing and hair. With a sickening thrill, I spotted a glass eye gazing at me out of the mess. It was bright blue.

"So much for a jealous waxwork owner," I said, straightening. "Do you think it's revenge, Holmes? Or some sort of spite?"

"I think it's..."

Holmes trailed off again, but this time it was not because he was thinking. He had spotted something. He took off at a run across the baked earth, and I followed.

It was a scrap of fabric, fluttering from the branches of one of the rare scrubby bushes. Holmes caught it up, but he only glanced at it for a moment before he was again scanning the featureless landscape around us.

"What do you make of it?" He passed me the fabric. It was white, a sort of scarf or bandana, still crisp from an iron. Otherwise pristine, it had been speckled with ash from the fire.

"Left behind by one of the thieves?"

"Dropped as he was climbing into the plane."

"Holmes!"

"Can you not see the airstrip, Watson?"

I had to squint, but I saw it eventually: the ground had been packed down in a wide strip. We stood near the foot of it, and it stretched past the melted wax into the distance.

"The sequence is clear from the marks on the ground. There were two thieves, one over six feet in height and a shorter one who was heavier and less active than the other—most likely our man in the Hawaiian shirt. They drove a van packed with mannequins to this spot. They were met by a small plane; I'd say a Piper Cherokee Arrow, from the tire marks. The man in the Hawaiian shirt boarded the plane and left, and the remaining thief unloaded his cargo and burnt it. The fire was set after the plane took off; otherwise it would have driven straight through the flames."

"If we know the make of the plane, perhaps we can trace it from yesterday's flight records."

"It would be an arduous job, Watson, and uncertain to succeed if the plane embarked from a private or remote airstrip like this one. No, I already know the destination of the plane. It is clear from this speckled bandana." He turned abruptly. "Let's go, Watson. We have some unwelcome news for Mr. Lowe."

* * *

KEVIN LOWE DIDN'T take the news well. He turned white and staggered to a chair. "But why, Mr. Holmes?" he gasped. "Why would someone steal my entire life's work, only to burn it?"

"Do you have any enemies?" I asked, but Holmes shook his head.

"It's not revenge," he said. "In fact, I don't think this was done for malicious motives at all; rather out of kindness, though perhaps not from your perspective. Tell me, Mr Lowe, the elderly man who acted so strangely the day before your theft: was he overweight and bald, with an egg-shaped head?"

"Yes. Was he the thief? Can you find him?"

"He was the mastermind behind the theft," said Holmes. "I know where to find him, and most likely his accomplices, too. But I will not."

Lowe leapt from his chair, his face suffused with anger. "I hired you! Why won't you catch the man who's ruined me?"

"While I feel sorry for your loss, and pained that you are the innocent victim, you aren't ruined, Mr. Lowe. You have the funds and the skill to replace the waxworks you've lost. You said yourself that you wanted to start afresh somewhere else. It means hard work for you, yes. But for a person close to the man who stole your mannequins, it means life or death."

"How could it possibly be so important?"

As an answer, Holmes held up the white bandana, speckled with ash. Lowe's eyes widened.

"Him?"

Holmes passed a cigarette to Lowe; the modeller's fine hands shook as he lit it.

"I believe we will have an answer in the national news in a day or two, perhaps a week," said Holmes. "Meanwhile, Watson and I will return to New York. We'll be in touch when events come to a head. If you're looking for a way to pass the time, I suggest you begin a new collection of waxworks. Perhaps starting with Chewbacca."

Holmes was silent for the journey back to Bleecker Street. Although I called in on him several times in the days that followed, eager to find out if there had been any developments in the case, he remained taciturn, refusing to answer any of my questions relating to Mr. Lowe or the speckled bandana. Indeed, he seemed almost melancholy, as if he had been saddened by the events in Las Vegas.

ON WEDNESDAY MORNING, August 17th, I looked in on Holmes just after sunrise. He was sunk deep into his armchair, his brows drawn down over his eyes, surrounded by smoke so thick it made me cough. He looked as if he hadn't moved all night.

"Holmes," I said, "this is no good, man. You've got to get out. Take up jogging, or something. These moods aren't healthy."

"Have you listened to the radio this morning? Seen any papers or the TV?"

"I've been with a patient."

Holmes passed me that morning's *New York Times*. In the headline, in the photo, I saw the news that he had been expecting, although until that moment, I had had no idea what it could be.

"Good God, Holmes," I gasped. "Not—"

He nodded. "We must call Kevin Lowe and get him on a plane to Tennessee."

Although we started early in the morning, Holmes had several phone calls to make, and we didn't arrive in Memphis until nearly noon. Lowe arrived half an hour later. He was drawn and worried; even his paisley polyester shirt added no colour to his features.

I knew that Holmes had called in favours from his local contacts, but I didn't know how powerful those contacts were until we stepped out of the airport into the crushing southern heat, and straight into a snow-white Cadillac.

Even from the airport, the roads were crowded with cars and pedestrians, and the crowds grew and grew as we approached our destination. Lowe gazed out the tinted window at the people sobbing, clutching flowers and records.

"Mr Holmes," he began, but Holmes just shook his head.

The car parted the throng of people, waved through by the policemen in their helmets and sunglasses. The white iron gates opened for us, and we proceeded up the drive to the columned entry of the mansion. A suited guard opened the car door and we walked in solemn silence, past the flowers arranged into bouquets and guitars, into the marbled-floored foyer of the house.

The coffin lay under a crystal chandelier. The man lying inside it wore a white suit and a blue shirt. His hair was as dark and gleaming as it had ever been in life. To my left, I heard Kevin Lowe gasp. I sensed rather than saw him stagger and I caught him and offered him the support of my arm as we were ushered from the house. Hardly a single minute had passed since we had been admitted.

Holmes did not speak until we were back in the car, driving out the gates of the mansion, with the glass panel closed between us and the driver.

"Was it yours inside the coffin?" he asked.

Beside me, Lowe was trembling. "It was mine," he said. "That was my waxwork, sure as anything."

"And so now you have your answer," Holmes said. "They burned the other waxworks so that no one would suspect that the goal of the robbery was to take only one. It was unfortunate for you, to be sure. But I think you can see, Mr. Lowe, and appreciate, the need for confidentiality in this matter. If it is to work—if such a man, hounded by the press and his fans, is to find peace in this world—no one must know he is still in it."

"I understand, Mr. Holmes," said Kevin Lowe in a hoarse voice. "I won't tell anyone. He... he deserves some rest, after all he's given the world. But all these people..." He wiped his eyes as we drove through the crowds, even larger now than they had been on our way in.

"It's a necessary path, but one which may give one's friends pain," said Holmes, and he caught my eye.

I nodded, remembering my own pain, and understanding at last the reason for my friend's melancholy over the past several days. At times, Sherlock Holmes appeared to be no more than a calculating, deducing machine. In moments like this, I knew otherwise.

"Still," resumed Holmes, "take heart, Mr. Lowe. Your work was chosen because of its quality, because of its absolute adherence to current fact. You're an artist, and you were chosen by an artist, in his last, most desperate hour. I hope you will remember that."

"I will," Mr. Lowe said. "I will never forget."

In the silence, I could dimly hear the car's radio playing 'Heartbreak Hotel.'

THE RICH MAN'S HAND

JOAN DE LA HAYE

"Alright," said Joan to me, when I cornered her at a convention, "but it's apt to be a bit... twisted." Joan de la Haye's a razor-sharp, brutal young South African horror author, and she wasn't kidding. 'The Rich Man's Hand' is a bleak, sun-baked glimpse of life in one of the tougher corners of her native Pretoria that nudges at the boundary of the impossible.

SHERLOCK HOLMES WAS on the verge of a relapse and needed a distraction. The Nigerians would be showing up on our doorstep soon to collect on the debt he accrued on his last bender. I'd already searched his office and flat for the little packets containing crack and found one hidden in the toilet cistern. He'd glowered at me while I emptied the rocks into the toilet bowl and flushed it. Thankfully, we'd received several emails asking for help since the success of our last case was smeared across the *Pretoria News* and on News 24.

The sensationalised case of the farmer and the lion had originally been thought of as an average farm murder by the local police, but had turned out to be a murderous love triangle. Detective Lestrade had, in his usual bungling manner, overlooked most of the pertinent facts. Holmes, while sucking on his electronic cigarette—its LED tip shining blue with each intake of nicotine—took great pleasure in pointing out his main error. The farmer, a Mr. Petrous Marais, had been described as a brutal man by his wife and farm workers. They'd claimed that he'd tormented his labourers with threats of feeding them to his pet lion, which apparently was the only creature the man had shown any affection to. His wife had insisted that he'd beaten her and the workforce on a regular basis, but the lack of bruises on her person, or any other evidence of spousal abuse, like medical records, and the comfort in which the workers lived had given Holmes pause. Surely a man who beat his workers and threatened to feed them to his lion wouldn't house them quite so well. The workers had indoor plumbing and didn't live in tin shanties like some workers on other farms across the country. The atrocious living conditions of South African farm labourers was a familiar plight, but it was not the case on that particular farm.

Mr Marais, while a hard man, was not brutal or cruel. He'd treated his workers fairly and paid them what he could afford. His wife, on the other hand, while attractive in the conventional and obvious sense, was not a fair woman. She piqued Holmes' interest when he noticed the tennis bracelet she wore on her right wrist showed no scratches on the clasp, and was obviously—to him—brand new. The wrapping from the jeweller's shop and the credit card slip in the rubbish bin backed up his premise. She'd bought it the day after her husband's death, as though to reward herself for a deed well done. It was not the act of a woman in shock over the brutal murder of her husband. He also noticed traces of lint on her blouse, which matched the fibres from the farm foreman's shirt, and traces of lipstick on the foreman's collar that matched the shade of lipstick Mrs Marais favoured. Holmes deduced that they had been having an affair and that the foreman had riled up the workers against Mr. Marais and convinced them to feed him to his outsized pet.

Once confronted, the lovers had turned on each other in a rush to secure a plea bargain. The farm labourers had felt contrite and come clean on all the details. The poor animal had been put down and Mrs. Marais and her lover were charged with conspiracy to commit murder and sundry other charges.

But that was over a month ago, and Sherlock needed a new diversion to prevent another crack-induced manic episode. Mrs. Hudson put the tea tray down as I read through the potential cases. Most of the requests for help were the usual twaddle, a missing dog or a necklace that Holmes said was clearly taken by the maid. There was one that briefly held some interest—a missing child—until Sherlock surmised that the father had absconded with the boy because the mother refused him visitation rights. He claimed there was something in the wording of the woman's email that had led him to that conclusion; I personally didn't see it. Holmes sent the distraught mother an email informing her that perhaps if she hadn't used the child as a weapon against his father, the father wouldn't have resorted to such measures, and that perhaps she should endeavour to be a better and less selfish parent.

Her response had been less than friendly.

A text message from Lestrade, sent from a crime scene along with a photo, finally caught Sherlock's attention for longer than five seconds. The dismembered body of a well-dressed white businessman, found in Mamelodi Township, was not something that happened every day, and was therefore noteworthy to Holmes.

"Watson," he said after sucking on his e-cig, the blue LED light glowing in the dimly-lit room. The blinds were closed. Holmes had a hangover and bright sunlight bothered his blood-shot eyes. "I think Lestrade will be out of his depth on this one, as per usual, and it would only be right if we did our civic duty and solved it for him." With that, he stood, tossed the car keys at me and marched out of the room. He winced as the bright sunlight hit his eyes and a pair of sunglasses was promptly propped up on his nose.

We drove from our small office on Baker Street in Brooklyn and then down Jan Shoba, before we turned into Stanza Bopape.

A beggar outside the Silverton Police Station held a cardboard sign declaring that he would rather starve than steal. I'd seen the same sign a few days ago being held by another beggar outside our office; it was evidently doing the rounds. Silverton was a lower-middle class suburb, and also the heart of the motor industry in the city. We could see the decline in the value of houses as we drew closer to Mamelodi.

Inside Mamelodi itself, we found a mix of small houses with well-tended patches of garden next door to tin shanties or shacks built out of whatever building materials could be pilfered from the surrounding area. Mixed in with the informal shacks and small one-bedroom homes—which housed ten people—were larger houses that wouldn't have looked out of place in the more affluent suburbs.

The body had been dumped next to the river, and the smell from the stagnant, polluted water made me gag. The odour from the water was worse than the stench from the corpse, which was still relatively fresh. He'd only been killed the night before. Somehow the stink of it didn't affect Sherlock, though. His nose was always raised up in the air, above the rest of us. Lestrade stood next to the body, holding his nose. Unfortunately, the Vicks vapour rub he'd smeared under his nose to combat the stench from the river didn't seem to be doing the trick this time around. His handlebar moustache was caked with the stuff. His ample beer gut protruded over his belt and prevented him from bending over the body to get a proper look.

From a quick evaluation, I saw that the victim's right hand was missing, as were his genitals, and several organs, including his heart and lungs. His wallet had been emptied and discarded in the bushes nearby.

"From the blood splatter and pooling, I'd say he was still alive when they mutilated him. He died from exsanguination," I stated.

"Been watching *Dexter* reruns, Watson?" Lestrade jibbed.

"No, it's called having a medical degree," I answered. "But you wouldn't know anything about having a degree, would you? Since you barely finished high school."

"You may have a medical degree, but at least I didn't piss everything away at the poker tables," Lestrade said, knowing just where to twist the knife.

Holmes surveyed the body for a few seconds, ignoring our unfriendly banter. He bent down and sniffed the corpse.

"I detect a hint of olive oil," he said as he stood.

"We think the main motive was robbery, and his organs were taken for the black market. There's money to be made with organs. Some of these guys will sell their own kidney for a few hundred bucks." Lestrade nodded to himself. "I know you prefer the strange cases, but I think we may have called you prematurely. We've got this one covered."

"But why take his hand, organs, and genitals if the motive is just robbery?" I asked.

"I'm not disputing that this has to do with the black market, Lestrade. But it's not the black market you're thinking about. This man's right hand has been removed. Typically, in traditional witchcraft, or *muti* in the vernacular, the right hand is the power hand, the one that is used to attract wealth; but he was not right-handed. Our victim was left-handed. There is no watch tan line on the remaining wrist. This leads me to conclude that the attacker did not know the victim personally, otherwise he would have taken his left hand instead, since that was his power hand."

"How do you know he was wearing a watch?" I asked.

"The tell-tale signs of wear and tear on the right cuff of his shirt where his watch caught."

"And that just goes to prove that the motive was robbery! They chopped off his hand to take the watch," Lestrade interjected with a hint of self-satisfaction.

"While one of the motives may have been robbery, it was only a secondary concern," Holmes said. "Whoever took his hand and other organs was an idiot, a thug for hire, sent out with a list of ingredients. Our victim's body parts happened to be part of the recipe, and another of the ingredients is olive oil, which is also often associated with money or wealth-attracting spells. I suspect that this is probably a variation on the hand of glory, except that our victim was not hanged."

"And maybe they're cannibals and are going to use the olive oil to cook the hand and organs," I said with a sarcastic smile. "Also, why was he here? This isn't exactly the sort of place the rich like to frequent."

"You'd be surprised what kinds of people find their way into Mamelodi at night. He was probably looking for some strange," Lestrade leered.

"Well... the strange certainly found him," I said with a smirk.

Sherlock ignored us and surveyed the area, scrutinised the ground again, and touched the mud close to the body. There had only been a light drizzle the previous night, not enough to wash away the blood, but enough to wet the ground. There were tracks from the police and crime scene unit; the likelihood of finding tracks from the killer was minute, if not impossible.

"He went that way," Holmes said, pointing downriver.

"How the hell do you know that?" I couldn't help myself. "There's no way you could know that for sure. Those tracks are a mess. Nobody could discern the murderer's tracks from every other cop's prints."

"Quite easily done, my dear Watson," he said looking down at me from his six-foot-four-inch height. His nose hairs needed a trim. "If you examine these tracks, consider the shoes, body weight and height of the police officers—and I use that term lightly, since they resemble a herd of elephants and not a proper constabulary—you will find that there is a set of tracks that stands out from the rest. Cast your glance at these imprints," he pointed at a barely perceptible smear on the riverbank. "The heel of the left shoe is cracked and the sole of the right foot has been worn down at the big toe. The depth of the imprint suggests a heavyset man, probably muscular rather than fat. He slipped in the mud because of a limp due to his right leg being shorter than his left by an inch, probably due to an injury of some sort. This is not the shoe print of a policeman, but of our murderer." Sherlock stood waiting for applause that wouldn't come; instead his deductions were met by grudging silence.

"The game's *a foot*," he said with a grin and stalked off in the direction the tracks led. Sherlock was at his happiest when tracking a killer. Lestrade and I looked at each other, shrugged and followed him. We were both used to following him, even if it meant being shot or stabbed, which had happened to both of us on more than one occasion.

"Wait," I said to Lestrade. "What about the body?"

"The coroner will take care of it," he said with a dismissive gesture of his hand.

Holmes walked ahead of us, his tall body bent, his eyes intent on the trail, ignoring his surroundings. The entrepreneurial spirit was alive and well in Mamelodi. We passed small businesses set up in shacks built out of concrete bricks. The services offered were painted on the walls. A hairdresser braided a woman's hair under a tree. A queue formed outside a tuck-shop advertising fresh chickens. A backyard mechanic worked on a client's dilapidated car on an oil-stained pavement. The car would probably not pass its roadworthy test, but the mechanic got it started, to the delighted cheer of the car's owner. A few hundred-rand notes exchanged hands and the car drove away, sending up a puff of black smoke in its wake. The mountain stood sentinel on our left-hand side, and the township spread out in front of us as far as we could see.

Sherlock veered right, away from the river and the mountain, into the belly of the settlement. He came to an abrupt halt, bent down and stared at the ground around him, a dusty patch of dirt and gravel with only a few tufts of grass growing wild.

"Lost the trail?" Lestrade asked. Holmes ignored him, continuing to stare and frown. He stood once more and walked down a narrow street that was little more than a dirty alley. A mongrel that looked more like an overgrown sewer rat yapped as we walked passed it. The pungent smell of decay wafted from a small shack built a short distance away from the other houses. The word *Inyanga*, along with a list of services offered, was painted on the front wall. The shaman offered to heal illness, remove curses, provide protection from evil, find lost property, and perform money spells. Drying herbs hung from the tin roof, along with a variety of small bones, which I hoped were only animal bones, but on closer inspection realised were not. My stomach lurched.

"I think we're in the right place," I said.

"Of course we are," Holmes said and tapped his index finger against the side of his nose. "Q.E.D." As though there would be any doubt that his tracking skills would find the killer's destination.

We stood outside the shack like three scared teenage girls in front of a haunted house. A few herbs and indigenous plants that I assumed were used for healing potions or tinctures grew like weeds in the small garden. Another emaciated mongrel with rotting teeth strained against its fetters as it barked at us. I couldn't help but wonder if it carried rabies. A small, shrivelled woman with a cane stepped out of the dark doorway into the light and silenced the dog with a single stomp of her walking stick. As she tilted her head, I noticed the milky-white cataracts. Her hair was braided with white and black beads and bits of shell or bone. When she moved her head, they rattled against each other. Her feet were bare and gnarled, dirty, toes curled over the edge of the threshold. Those feet had never seen a pair of shoes. She looked at us as though she could see our cowardice flashing in bright neon lights above our heads. A smile stole across her face, exposing toothless gums. She looked harmless enough, but her smile sent icy tentacles up my spine.

She was just an old woman, I tried to tell myself. I looked over at Holmes and Lestrade; the detective looked the way I felt. Sherlock seemed to be holding up better than Lestrade and myself.

"Are you going to stand outside all day?" she asked with a strong clear voice that would have been more suited to a much younger woman. "It's going to be a hot one, hey," she said turning her face into the sun and closing her eyes. "And you whities tend to get burned." She cackled, covering her mouth with her arthritic hands.

Holmes stepped forward and we followed him at a respectable distance. Sherlock always tended to run where angels feared to tread. The infuriating man had never heard of self-preservation. Sometimes I wondered if he had a death wish, or thought he was immortal. He certainly had a God complex. I, on the other hand, had quite enough scars and was not in the mood to end up in the casualty ward again. The old woman disappeared into the darkness beyond the entrance to her shack. A multi-coloured beaded curtain covered the doorway and brushed against our faces as we walked through the entrance. The smooth mud floors smelled of cow dung. Peach pips had been pushed into the floor when newly wet to form an intricate pattern. The room was cool and dark. Paraffin lamps lit the windowless space; their smoke hung in the air, making it hard to breathe. My lungs craved fresh air. The spots floating before my eyes could just have been dust particles, but I suspected they were those stars you see when you're not getting enough oxygen.

As my eyes grew accustomed to the dim light, I noticed the walls were lined with shelves, each shelf holding an assortment of bottles, jars, and rusty cans. Dry herbs stood like flower arrangements in the cans. The contents of the glass jars and bottles made my bile rise. Sherlock went from one bottle to the next, examining each with interest. A pair of floating brown eyeballs stared at me from a jar. Another held a small aborted foetus of about sixteen weeks. The dismembered hand of what I assumed was a gorilla lay discarded and collecting dust next to the bottle containing the foetus. A still beating heart thumped inside another jar. A pale Lestrade stood at the door, refusing to come any further. In the centre of the room was a cooking fire with a pot hanging above it; the smell wafting from the pot was unappetising to say the least. The old woman sat in a chair that was probably as old as she was and stoked the fire. Something wriggled under the dirty sheets of a single bed with a sagging mattress in the corner. My imagination ran riot and thoughts of snakes and rats and other nightmarish things cavorted under the blanket. With my heart in my throat I strode over to the bed and ripped the blanket off, half expecting the killer we'd tracked there to jump out at me. Instead, a child of about four blinked at me, yawned, stretched, cast a wary eye in the old woman's direction and then jumped off the bed and scampered out the shack. It took a few seconds for my heart to realise that it could stop racing.

Holmes turned from the shelves and faced the old woman, who in turn stared vacantly in his direction. His cigarette glowed in the dark as he puffed and considered her.

"He seems to not be here," Holmes said.

"No shit, Sherlock," Lestrade said from the safety of the doorway.

"Who did you think you'd find here?" she asked.

"A killer," I answered.

"You will find many things here, but not who you came looking for. What you find here will make you wish you hadn't come looking," she said, staring into the gloom. She tried to get out of the chair to stir the contents of the pot, but fell backwards with a grunt.

"Let me help you," I said lifting the lid off the pot and burning my hand in the process. The cast iron lid hit the floor and my stomach reacted violently to what I saw floating in the grimy pot.

"What is it, Watson?" I heard Holmes say through the shocked fuzz that built up in my ears. I shook my head as I stepped away from the pot. He stood next to me and stared into the cooking utensil. The door behind us slammed shut and the bit of light that had filtered through the beaded curtain disappeared. Lestrade's breathing was heavier from fright and sounded as though he was right at my ear instead of across the room. The only light now came from the smoky lanterns.

"What's in the pot, Watson?" Lestrade asked. His voice was hoarse, barely above a whisper.

"It's offal," Holmes answered for me. "What's wrong with you?"

"Remember my comment about cannibals chopping the hand off to eat it?"

"Don't be ridiculous, Watson," Holmes said sniffing the pot. "This isn't human flesh, and the hand would be used in a wealth-attraction spell, not eaten. It's probably in the process of being cured right now."

"And what about his heart and lungs, and his testicles?" I asked. Like most men, the thought of having my own testicles removed made my hands instinctively cover my groin.

"The testicles would be used in a fertility spell, and his other organs are probably being sold on the black market as we speak," Sherlock said in a matter-of-fact tone.

The old witch just smiled at us.

"Can we go now?" Lestrade said as he took a step back towards the door.

"In a minute," Holmes said as he looked around the room,

squinting to see what was hidden in the dark corners. A frown scrunched up his brow. I watched as the offal boiled, steam rose, and Lestrade banged against the closed door which wouldn't open under his panicked barrage.

"I think we're trapped," Lestrade choked out the words.

"Nonsense," I said as I made my way over to him.

The witch cackled as I tried to open the door gently, pretending that panic didn't have a vice-like grip on my brain. I gave up trying to be calm and tried to force it open. The harder I pushed the door, the louder she laughed. My shoulder ached and sweat dripped from my brow, but the door was no closer to being open.

"We're trapped," I said, ignoring Lestrade's *I told you so* expression. Sherlock simply considered the cackling old woman, while he took a casual stroll around the shack. He stopped at a small table hidden in the dark recess of a corner. The harsh intake of breath told me he'd found something interesting. Curiosity got the better of me. I had to see what had entranced Holmes. A severed hand, holding a watch, took pride of place in the centre of a bowl of salt. A black, unlit candle stood next to it, as well as a small bowl of oil, which I assumed was olive oil. As Sherlock and I bent over to take a closer look, the candlewick burst into flame, almost singeing Sherlock's eyebrows. It took a few moments before my mind could comprehend what I was seeing. One of the fingers twitched and then another finger did the same. The fingers were tapping on its glass face in time with the second hand of the watch.

Tick. Tick. Tick.

Sherlock picked up the hand to examine it more closely, he just couldn't help himself—he never could—but dropped it when all the fingers contracted around the watch, giving him, and me, the fright of our lives. The witch just cackled even more at our expense. The hand scuttled into the shadows like Thing from *The Addams Family*. A hysterical shriek escaped from Lestrade; he clapped his hand over his mouth to prevent further outbursts.

I stood next to Holmes, still unable to understand what I'd seen. It defied all logic; not even Sherlock would be able to find a rational explanation for it. Severed hands did not simply run across floors of their own volition. He would try to come up with a rationalisation, he always did on the strange cases, but on this occasion he would fail. Differing expressions drifted across his face as his mind sifted through the plausible explanations. I'd seen him go through it before on other cases, but this was the first time I'd seen his face lose all colour. It was the first time I'd seen him shocked or surprised. I didn't know what scared me more, the witch and the severed hand, or Holmes without a plausible explanation. His constant logical explanations for whatever we found had always given me a sense of safety. He was my rock, even when he was on one of his binges, but I would never tell him that. There'd be no living with him if I did.

Holmes visibly shook himself out of his confusion and went looking for the hand. He never did know when to tuck tail and run. His damn curiosity would always get the better of him, and one day it would get him killed.

"Sherlock," I shouted. "Step away from the dark corners. You don't know what's hidden in there."

He looked back over his shoulder at me and opened his mouth—in all likelihood, to tell me I was being ridiculous—but the words never passed his lips. The hand flew out of the shadows and grabbed his throat. A manic, excited look enraptured the evil old bitch's face. Lestrade shrieked again and ran at the door, but only succeeded in knocking himself unconscious. I ran to Sherlock. The world slowed down, and panic gripped my bowels as I tried to pry those cold, dead fingers from his neck. The fingers squeezed tighter. His throat turned red. Sherlock gasped for breath. Bones cracked as I pulled at the fingers and its grip loosened. I flung the hand at the witch. It landed on her face, and its fingertips dug into her eyes and the palm covered her mouth, suffocating her, thankfully putting an end to her laughter.

My vision blurred as I watched the old woman turn into a large, muscular man, who could easily have broken Holmes and I like small twigs without breaking into a sweat. For some unfathomable reason, even in this form, he could not save himself from his own creation. Flies came from every corner of the room and buzzed around him like a black shroud. Through the ever-growing cloud of flies I noticed that the heel of his left shoe was cracked, and there was a hole where his right big toe would be. The killer we'd tracked and the old witch were one and the same.

"A genuine case of transmogrification." Sherlock was breathless with excitement. "I've never actually seen a case like this. It's fascinating, don't you think, Watson? There's never been an actual case recorded before. I should have brought my camera to record this for posterity."

I, on the other hand, was less enthused by our situation. While Sherlock was excited, he did not look surprised by this turn of events. The flies buzzed and the shaman fought for his last breath. He changed form and was once again the old woman. Her struggle with the hand became feebler and her body shuddered as she lost her struggle for life.

"Fascinating," Holmes said as the hand released its death grip and scuttled back into the shadows.

"I have no words," I said, shaking my head at Holmes. I knelt next to the witch and checked for a pulse.

"What is it, Watson? I can hear that tone you get in your voice when you're displeased with me."

"A man was brutally murdered, Lestrade is unconscious, you were almost killed, the witch is dead, we're trapped inside this hell hole, and all you can think of is that you should have brought your camera to record a case of transmogrification. And then there's that small fact that you didn't even seem surprised when she changed form. You knew this whole time, didn't you?" My voice rose a few octaves.

"I had my suspicions, but I didn't have any definitive proof. But I do believe we should depart. The smell from that pot is rather vile."

He stepped over Lestrade's unconscious body and pulled the door open with a smirk.

"Alright, so I was pushing the door instead of pulling it. No need to rub my panic in my face."

"I didn't say a word."

"What about him?" I asked tilting my head at Lestrade.

"I'm not carrying him. You're welcome to try, though."

"He'll break my back."

"That's an exaggeration. He'd merely strain it."

"Why did the hand turn violent? I thought it was for a money spell?"

"The witch, while powerful, was an idiot. She, or he, used the wrong hand, which resulted in the spell going awry and ultimately caused it to turn on her or him."

"How did you know that the old woman and the killer were one person?"

"Elementary, Watson! There were no tracks leading away from the shaman's lair, ergo the killer was still inside, and the only option was that the old woman was the killer in disguise."

"It could have been the child that ran off," I said.

"No, the witch's ego prevented her from running away. She enjoyed the game too much. Ultimately, it was her over-inflated sense of her own powers that destroyed her; if not for her gross miscalculation, we may have ended up being used as spare parts for another of her spells."

My cell phone vibrating in my pocket prevented my mind from delving deeper into the unpleasantness of having my organs removed for *muti*. An heiress had gone missing, presumed to have been kidnapped.

"Holmes," I shouted as Sherlock tried to revive Lestrade. "We've got another case."

THE LANTERN MEN

KAARON WARREN

I'm a fan of Kaaron's short stories, and she was one of the first people I approached to contribute. Kaaron's a fellow country-woman, and I fully expected her to set her story in Australia; but I was otherwise completely unprepared for 'The Lantern Men.' It's a true ghost story, a hauntingly beautiful tale in which a mood of failure and regret hangs over everyone, including Sherlock and John themselves. And as with any ghost story—and certainly as you'd expect from one featuring the world's most famous detective—the dominating question is: what's real?

THE PEPPERTREE WAS a puzzle to be solved, but that was his fame. As an architect, he liked to ensure nothing was left to chance, and nothing was lost of the genius loci, the spirit of the building.

Peppertree Lodge—*Affordable location in a waterside setting*—was his second job since returning to his home town. 'Triumphantly,' the local paper said, and Holmes didn't mind that. Peppertree was a town he'd been desperate to escape, but what he found elsewhere was no better. Here, at least, they had the peppertrees to cover the stench of the river. Here, he could breathe again.

He walked the location, exploring the details, the cracks, what he called the *clues*. When the ute pulled up, he squinted to read the name on the side. *Bright Building Insurance*, and the logo of a glowing lantern.

"Sherlock Holmes! Good to see you home at last!" This was an older man Holmes did not recognise. All the older men of the town looked similar. It was something they were proud of.

"We all come home in the end," another one said, and even standing side by side, Holmes could barely tell them apart. He understood that was his own failing, not theirs. He was being lazy, enjoying himself, letting his brain atrophy. One had a splodge of dried tomato sauce on his ugly tie. Unmarried. Alone, Holmes thought.

One had a web of pen drawings on his hand. A grandfather? The grandfather had more hair coming out of his overlarge ears and the bachelor far less hair on his head.

The third man wore a T-shirt too broad for his skinny shoulders (*Peppertree Footy Team Go Dingoes*).

"Hear you're going to chuck up some living space," the skinny one said. Holmes nodded. "We need it. Place is growing. Need to keep the kids around."

The grandfather said, "Glorious colour, our peppertrees." Holmes looked up at the tree. It was true; there was real beauty. It was one of the things that drew him back home. "My great grandfather planted the first, did you know that? Building goes back a long way in my family." He looked at Holmes with some disdain. "Hope you're not thinking of knocking it down. You wouldn't want to do that."

Holmes shook his head, feeling like a child in trouble.

"You let us know when the foundations are going in. We'll sort you out some 'insurance.'"

The bachelor lifted his fingers in quotation marks. Holmes nodded, far from understanding, but wanting to get back to work.

For Holmes, insurance was the spirit that inspired him. It was the nature of the building. The clue that helped him create the best possible structure.

"You call us. Ask for the Lantern Men."

As they drove away, Holmes thought, *What sort of insurance men drive a ute?*

He'd left town to avoid citizens such as these. They were guilt on legs. They judged you on a mere thought and they were strict with it, on all you'd ever done or considered. And yet he understood he was like them, passing judgement based on appearance. The difference being that he didn't bring prejudice or pre-conceived ideas to the analysis.

Still, they had brought him inspiration, and that could not be denied.

This pink peppertree was over a hundred years old and should be kept. It wasn't so much the size of it that caused a problem, nor the shade it cast, but the many thousands of peppercorns it dropped. He knew these trees well, had climbed them as a child, been snagged by their branches, lost in their leaves. He knew the scratch of the bark.

The smell was peppery and sweetish and their colour, as they rested on the ground, was a gentle pink that lifted the grey surrounds.

And there. There it was. He would make a feature of those peppercorns. Rather than shipping in tonnes of ornamental pebbles, these peppercorns would act as same. He would design a low holding wall; place an outdoor lounge or two, and the space would be perfect.

He walked back to his car to scribble notes and was struck by the smell of the river that ran through most of the city. On high-pollution days, the reek of it was pervading. Yet by the peppertree, the smell was lessened.

Deep in his scribbles, he didn't notice his phone vibrating for quite some time. He hated the jangle of it if he had the ring tone on, and was willing to face the ire of all in order to keep the thing silent.

It was Watson, the city's most trustworthy builder and the man Holmes most relied on.

"I've sorted the peppertree problem," Holmes said.

"That's good, Sherlock, but not why I'm calling. I'm here at the museum site and we've found something... interesting."

"In the architectural sense?"

"Not quite."

Holmes had tendered for the upgrade of the museum, a two-hundred-year-old dilapidated house once dwelled in by the town's founder and left relatively untouched for a hundred and fifty years. The founder's fall from grace (taking with him much of the town's money) was the stuff of legend now, but at the time, the residents had half-destroyed the mansion in their fury. It was a house of many, many rooms. The founder's delusions of grandeur had him hiring teams of builders, over decades. Perhaps he thought this registered his worth? Many did the same. It was how Holmes stayed in business.

As CHILDREN, HOLMES and Watson had tested their nerves here, as did many others.

"You remember our nights there, Holmes? We *did* hear ghosts, we were certain."

"You were certain. I thought it was rats, if anything."

"Can you pop over? Incognito, as it were. Wearing your other hat, if you know what I mean."

Holmes felt a flutter of excitement. It was a long while since he'd solved anything outside the realms of bricks and mortar, so this sounded tempting indeed. He still bore the scars, physical and emotional, of his last encounter, but also carried the satisfaction of knowing that evil had been stopped in its tracks.

Given that he had sorted the peppertree problem, he felt he deserved an afternoon off.

When Holmes arrived at the museum site, he saw the police car already parked.

Disappointed he could not investigate alone, he pulled on a hard hat and carried his clipboard. It didn't hurt to be seen as one thing when you were in fact another.

The mansion was solid and square, with a minimum of windows. The river had always been prone to foetidness, and Holmes admired the architect of the time who clearly designed the home to allow little of the stench in.

His brief had been to 'allow in the light and the air while still protecting the historical artefacts,' and given modern methods, he could easily replace the windows with EFTE or the like. In the bigger cities, no house or office block was built without windows such as these.

He struggled beyond that, to find the spirit of the place. He found it difficult to be in. He did not believe a building could have an actual personality, nor did he believe it could be haunted, but there was something off-kilter about the old mansion that made him feel queasy. It offended his need for symmetry. Some of the rooms were too small, giving not only Holmes but others a sense of claustrophobia. He had hoped to make some drastic changes, but the town council (some of them the men of Bright Building Insurance) were determined in their desire to leave the historical building almost untouched.

The front door had been boarded up for decades and now stood askew, though undamaged, testament to Watson's careful work.

As teenagers, they'd been careful to enter through the back window. It was boarded up, but they kept a hammer hidden in the bushes. The key, they called it, and with it would lever out the nails, replacing them when they left. Even drunk teenagers could manage that.

The place was haunted, the rumour went, by the founder, who died filled with longing for this place, and by anyone who died away from this town, because if you died elsewhere, you'd be anchored to the earthly plane.

How many nights did they spend there? You had to do two or three to prove your worth, so maybe it was that many. Their last visit was enough. They were fifteen years old. No girlfriends; Watson too studious, Sherlock too... odd. Already he had discovered the medicine cabinet, and perhaps his occasional altered manners put girls off. And his sharp intelligence, his wit, his disinterest in the stupid.

Watson, always and ever, accepted him as he was.

There were four of them that night. They brought cold pizza, beer, chips and sleeping bags. The house was always freezing. No fire had burnt there for decades, but still they gathered around it.

The other two boys talked of sex, sex and sex. Holmes tired of it and wandered the house, tapping walls, whispering. There was no part of him that believed in ghosts, but he enjoyed the solitary exploration.

Later, past midnight, they sat listening together in an upstairs bedroom. Old porn mags lived in the cupboard there, so it was a favourite place for them.

"Make a noise," one of the boys called out. "Tap for us." Holmes didn't know where the ghostly stories had originated, or how. The source of these things was always hard to trace.

Creak. Tap. Creak. Tap. Creak. Tap.

Four sharp intakes of breath. Silence.

"Again? Can you tap again?"

Nothing.

"Tap again!"

A creak.

One tap.

They tried to find the source, tried to hear that tap again (or was it a scratch? In the distance of time, Holmes thought the latter) but nothing.

Holmes felt their fear settle on him, so put himself to sleep by working through equations.

They woke him before dawn. Terrified.

"We're getting out of there. There are ghosts everywhere." And in the glow of the moon, the dust motes did appear to have a life of their own.

"You know you are imagining it."

"You missed the flashing light, and a creaking sound as well. That was fucking freaky."

Holmes went back in daylight, looking for clues. He found a square shape in the dust on the hall table, and a bare footprint in the front hall, near the drawing room door. A man hoping to be quiet.

It was that, far more than the imagined ghost tappings, that frightened him.

He had not been back until recently.

And here they both were, thirty years later, back again. Adult now, making a living. And neither would want to live anywhere else.

Holmes ventured through the front door. Inside, it was dark and musty. There was something else, though, rising over the smell of the river and of old wood, old carpet, old books.

He could hear the police, loud-talking, from what had been the drawing room, and Watson's voice there, too.

He paused to text Watson:

I am here.

Watson emerged. His hair was mussed and dusty and he lifted his hands to demonstrate grubbiness and preclude the politeness of hand-shaking.

"Thanks for coming. I'm not sure what the police are going to do, but I wanted you to get in for a look early on."

"At what, Watson?"

"We've found a body. In the wall."

Holmes' eyes widened. He thought back to the stories. Was there any rumour of missing wives? Children? Maidservants? It was unusual to find mummified remains in old homes, but it did happen. He wondered at the urgency, though.

And the smell...

"Is it one of his children? His wife, do you think?"

"This is not an old body. This is a brand new one. Recent."

Not an old body.

HOLMES KNEW THE policeman, Peter Jones; he had been a year behind them at school. Quiet and intelligent. Both had tried out for the police force. Holmes had failed both the physical and the psychological tests. Jones looked five years younger, at least. A fit, healthy man.

"Holmes is the architect," Watson said, fudging the truth only a little.

"I know Sherlock. Good to see you," Jones said.

"Is it really a new body? My nose tells me so, and yet..."

Jones said, "And yet no one has had access to the place in years."

Watson and Holmes exchanged glances. Smiled, knowing how they used to get in. The policeman had been a loner at school and Holmes felt momentary pity.

"No access," the policeman repeated. "Apart from monitored works."

Holmes coughed. "Not exactly true. I see evidence of recent incursions throughout. There, a high heeled footprint I imagine doesn't belong to any of the workers. On the wall by the staircase, a smiley face drawn into the filth with a clean finger and not yet covered with more filth. And, if I'm not mistaken, the remains of a recent pornographic magazine in the hallway."

Watson blushed at that. "I've told the men," he said, then whispered to Holmes, "The kids leave a lot more mess than we ever used to, but that one was the workers."

Holmes entered the drawing room. The smell there was far stronger, and he understood where the concern came from.

It must once have been a glorious room. Thick brocade wallpaper from floor to ceiling, a lavish expense. The furniture was solid, beautifully made, laid out to encourage conversation. The wood fire appeared to contain remnants of the last evening spent there (not a recent visitation, given the state of the ashes and the wood) and Holmes romanticised the occasion for a moment.

The wall had been broken open. This was planned construction work, part of the development process. Inside was a body. Male. Looked to be mid-20s, but this was a damaged human, that was clear. Someone who had lived hard and rough. His hair was long and ragged. His clothing was caked in various substances and coated with dust, although that was most likely from inside the wall. He appeared to be tied tightly to a crossbar. He was gagged. One arm was free below the elbow, the hand clenching a lantern. Holmes touched it; cold.

He had not been dead long. One or two days, Holmes thought.

The pathologist finished her cursory investigation. "Alive for a while, at least. I can smell pepper, beyond the usual. We could be looking at an overdose."

Holmes leaned in. Over the smell of the decaying corpse was the smell the pathologist described, and that of methylated spirits.

"Looks like a spirit lamp. I wonder how long it burned for?" Watson said. "Before he was left in the dark."

The body was removed and the lamp left behind.

"Watson, look. Does that remind you of anything?" Holmes

said when he'd lifted the lamp. There was a square mark in the dust.

Watson peered in, covering his nose.

"Don't you remember? Our last night here? We found just such a mark."

Watson nodded, although clearly that memory had faded.

On exploration, they found the same mark in three more places.

"Lanterns were placed here, Watson."

"Old-fashioned."

Holmes took out his penknife and walked it along the edge of the wallpaper. "It looks as if this has been recently replaced, the wall rebuilt. That explains why it feels out of proportion in here."

Holmes loved symmetry. He felt disoriented in parts of this home, and had done from the start. He felt slightly ill. He was the same as a teenager, but not in every room, he didn't think.

"What is it, Watson? I feel the same way I do when I walk up uneven stairs. Dizzy. Ill."

"There are many types of vertigo," Watson said. He had never been sick a day in his life.

HOLMES WALKED THE perimeter, got a feel from the outside, although he'd walked it a number of times while working on the plans.

When a building is new, there are geographical problems. A mountain in the way. Uneven dirt. A waterway. Rocks. A gully. These things must be sorted before you begin, and the land must be solid, and even.

Holmes liked new buildings. Fresh spaces. All the spirit his own.

With old buildings, the problems were different. Do you gut the place? Knock it down? Change the nature of it?

These were the problems faced by Holmes. Every old building carried clues to its history. Its spirit. He did love that.

He looked under the bush. The hammer was there, rusted into the ground like a rock. Sad that the chain of information was lost. The teenagers must get in another way.

Leaving the police to do the footwork, Holmes headed back to his office.

On the way, his mouth was dry, and he wanted food. He stopped at the bakery below his office, where bare rafters held moody room lights and the walls bore damage of a long-ago fire.

In the bakery, people were decidedly cool towards him. There was anger in the town over the museum renovations. The school needed work, and other public buildings. The roads. Money should be spent on buildings in use, rather than one not in use at all.

However, the money was specifically left to the museum by a wealthy man who'd moved away and had come home to die. He'd had childhood memories of seeking out ghosts. "I don't want to become a wall-tapper," he'd said. "That's why I came back." Even the successful can be superstitions, Holmes thought. He opened a folder and worked while he ate. Anything to avoid conversation.

A GROUP OF teenagers came in, loud, full of life, and he let himself be absorbed by their talk, then headed up to his office. The smell of cakes was enough, most days; others he caved and walked downstairs to purchase a vanilla slice or a lamington. He always regretted it after a bite and threw the rest away.

WORK ON THE museum progressed. Peppertree Lodge was building well. The pink peppercorns lay thick on the ground, as he had hoped. There would need to be warnings posted, because some parts were poisonous. Anything that has the potential to poison has the potential for drug use; one man's meat is another man's poison.

Birds hated the peppertree, meaning a quiet living space.

"Looking good!" Holmes heard. It was Peter Jones, the policeman. "There's a sense of calm here. You don't often get that these days."

"That's because of the symmetry. You're not thrown off-balance. All is equal."

They exchanged glances. "What is it about that place? Beyond the fact someone walled up a person there?" Jones said.

"It's the walls. Not just in that room, but most of them. The rooms are out of proportion. Any news of that poor kid?"

"I came to let you know. No one's reported him missing, so they still don't know who he was. They say he died of positional asphyxiation. That he crawled in and got stuck."

"Ridiculous. He didn't crawl in there, he was walled in. How could he do that, let alone one-handed?"

"They sent an ambulance out there last night for another kid. Got blind drunk, thought he could fly, fell off the roof." He reported this as fact.

"He's okay?"

"They don't know yet. His friends say he wasn't drunk, but scared."

"What's fear but imagination, I say. All in the mind. I would like to visit that boy in hospital, though. I'm wondering if perhaps he knows more about the body in the wall than the others do. Certainly the reaction seems extreme."

"It would be good to settle people; I've had citizens talking about closing work on the museum. Saying it isn't safe. But I'm not sure you'd be welcome there. People are blaming you. Saying you didn't keep your building safe." He looked at his watch. "I've got another one missing, too. Drifter. Girl last seen on a street corner. She's not one of ours. That's keeping me busy."

* * *

IN THE BAKERY, a group of teenagers sat with milkshakes and great piles of doughnuts. He overheard them talking, mostly gibberish they all understood; they had probably shared drugs before coming out. Then one said, "Bloody scary, that place. I'm not going back. I swear, I heard tapping. No wonder he was shit-scared."

Holmes bought another pile of doughnuts and took it to the table.

"Hi, guys," he said. They eyed him suspiciously, as well they should. He disarmed them with some observations. Two were wearing footy shirts, so Holmes asked him how the team was going. Another was the only one with a heavy backpack. Holmes said, "You skip school today?"

"How did you know?"

"Observation, that's all."

"That's kinda freaky."

"Anyone can do it. You just have to pay attention. Are you talking about the museum site? The accident there? I heard he was pretty drunk."

"He wasn't that pissed. I've been heaps more off my face than that. He freaked out about the tapping. He reckoned it was the guy they found in the wall come back to haunt him 'cos of his dad."

"His dad?"

They didn't respond to that.

"We used to say it was all of the founder's children. Dozens and dozens, murdered in the house, left to haunt it forever," Holmes said.

"Creepy."

"So this was a couple of nights ago?" he asked.

They nodded.

"Have you been there other nights?"

"Yeah, and we heard that tapping and like a creaking noise then, too."

Holmes dismissed this. He could only deal in facts. "Have you seen your friend in hospital?"

"You should talk to him. No one believes what he saw."

Holmes didn't confess that he didn't believe it, either.

"So, what is it you're smoking? Some kinda weed? Must be good."

"Caribbean," one said. Another kicked him under the table.

"Is the Indica strain?"

"Whatever."

"That's pretty powerful stuff. Be careful. Can you keep an ear out for me? There's a girl gone missing. The police don't care. I think someone should."

They agreed, even shook hands. Up close, Holmes smelled something familiar. It was the odd scent of the dead young man. That sharp, peppery smell.

Later, he said to Watson, "Is it possible for generations to share the same delusion?"

"I'm not a doctor." But he almost had been; three years in medical school, until an unplanned pregnancy meant he had to go to work. "But I'd say no. I'd say all of us did in fact hear it."

THAT NIGHT THE lantern men came to him. Bright light flashing in his eyes.

"My grandson tells me you've been asking him questions."

"Have I?" Holmes thought back. One boy in the bakery had large ears, he remembered that.

"You know it's always best just to *be*. That's my philosophy. Should be yours, too. And keeping away from people less than half your age, that's another one."

The man's knuckles were red and bruised. Bare-fisted fighting? It was possible.

"Keep away from our kids." He drummed his fingers. A real sound.

The skinny one said, "That was my son, Sam, who fell off, and I blame you. You had no insurance."

Holmes felt blinded by the light. Frozen in place. Still, he smelt the lamp fuel.

"It's not too late. Give the nod. You give the okay. We'll worry about the rest. We've got it sorted, but your blessing would be nice."

He felt smothered. Choked. As if the walls were closing in. He shook his head, not trusting them, not knowing what they meant.

One said, "Sacrifices. People don't make them anymore. We have to step in. We've been making sacrifices for a hundred years."

The creak-creak of the lanterns as they swung.

"We're builders going back generations. We're descendants of the men who built this town. We understand what needs doing. We got the warnings. More to come. So we did the duty."

"Who else has the courage, ay? The courage of the lantern men. To keep the good people safe. It'll be on you. The next building collapse, or mine disaster, or bridge failure, it'll be on you."

"We've done it, anyway. Fuck you. All we wanted was your support. That's all we ask. We do all the hard yakka."

They picked up their lanterns, swinging them, the bases square and criss-crossed. The lanterns creaked as they swung.

HOLMES STOPPED AT the council offices to find copies of the original plans for the mansion. When he approached his office, he saw a skinny boy, leaning up against the bakery window, smoking. His leg was in plaster and he had crutches under his arms. He wore a T-shirt, too big, which read *Peppertree Footy Team Go Dingoes*. It wasn't hard to guess who he was.

"They let you out, did they, Sam?"

The boy nodded.

"All your mates at school?"

He nodded again.

"Should we sit down, have a coffee? I can show you these plans. The old house. You can see where the body was. Might help to sort things out for you."

Sam shuddered. "Yeah, no. I'll wait for my mates. You can come have a smoke with us later, if you want. You seem to like that kind of thing."

Holmes was impressed that the boy could make this assertion.

IT WAS LATE at night when the subject of lantern men came up. One of them had smoked too much, had slipped from pleasant numbness to paranoia.

"They're at the window! See, the flashing light? Oh, God, I don't want to die, I seriously don't want to die."

Holmes realised they had developed a mythology around the lantern men.

"If you get too fucked up they come for you. Swinging their lanterns. They'll tell you you're a fuck-up and what they're gonna do to your family. Then they'll slit your throat," one said.

Another said, "No, they don't. They pour the oil from their lanterns all over you and set you alight. You'll burn down before anyone even knows you're gone."

Sam said, "No. they'll wall you up in a place no one will find you."

He'd watched them smoke this peppery drug, becoming more and more distant from reality. Holmes was ever and always mere moments from 'the other life,' the dark sinking into oblivion which obliterated all good he had done.

Sometimes a drive from address to address to look at his creations, his structures, helped.

Other times, the less dangerous descent into alcohol sufficed.

He had tried the addiction of gaming, but there was nothing but frustration, with the simple puzzles, the idiocies of plot, the infuriating game play.

"Will you come out to the museum with me tomorrow, show me where you heard the noise?"

They agreed.

HOLMES WALKED FROM room to room, tapping. For the first time, he really *listened*, hoping for a faint noise. The slightest hint and he would call the police.

It smelled different. Fresh paint covered the mustiness, and with the body removed, the air was clearer again.

Watson was there, supervising the builders.

"I feel queasy," Holmes told. "Many of them are out of kilter. Off-balance. I don't think the drawing room is the only one with a wall extended."

He tripped over a stair as he climbed, catching his fall with a hand against the stairway wall.

The wallpaper felt sticky, grimy, and he wiped his hands on his pants. They were destroyed, anyway.

"See, Watson?" Holmes held up the original plans he'd collected from the council. "This room is smaller by a metre at least."

He took out his tape measure. "One metre, five centimetres."

He tapped.

"This is where you heard tapping? When we were kids?"

"You said you never heard it, Holmes. Remember? I felt like an idiot and you didn't help. You said you heard nothing."

Holmes tapped on the wall. Cocked his head sideways. "Nothing."

They heard the noise of construction start up below again. Lunch break was over.

"What room were you and your friends in last week?" Holmes asked Sam.

"The top bedroom. It's like a little attic. One of the guys reckons a kid was starved to death. They reckon he was born without any arms or legs. And he was white and fat like a slug, and even though no one ever fed him, he lived for seventeen years. He snuck out at night to suck on the blood of anyone in the house."

"Did he suck your blood?"

Sam's hand rose to his neck. "No, not me."

"But you did hear tapping."

"It was that kid. The one they sacrificed in the walls. He's gonna haunt me for life."

They walked up the stairs to the attic room. "Shhh," Holmes said. They listened; just the distant sound of construction.

Holmes rapped on the wall. "This room is smaller than it should be by ninety-seven centimetres. Very strange."

Holmes stood pressed up against the wall, his nostrils flared. His nose almost flattened.

"Oh, God," he said. "Watson, can you smell it? Oh, Christ, I think there's another in there."

He looked around the room for a tool. "Let's get it open. Now."

There was no sound, but a sense of urgency took them.

Watson called downstairs to his men. "Don't worry about being careful. Just get the wall down."

The wall was new indeed.

Inside, with a lantern in her fist, was a young woman. She was gagged and bound, apart from the hand that carried the lantern.

She was long past saving.

Holmes swung the lantern against the wall. Tap. Creak. Tap. Creak.

"She was alive. They heard her. We could have saved her, if someone had listened to them."

"And the night we stayed here? When we were kids? Oh, God."

They went to the upstairs bedroom and knocked down the wall. There were remains.

It was a sickening moment. The tapping they heard as teenagers was a person trapped and dying; perhaps every ghostly haunting had been another victim, swinging the lantern for attention.

"Watson. I think the house is full of such poor souls."

He was so logical. He knew he wasn't hearing ghosts, so he dismissed the noise. He realised now that his so-called logical brain had meant death. It meant he did not investigate further, that he took no action.

"If only I had listened. Then and now. These innocents could have been saved."

For once Watson had nothing to say.

THEY FOUND BODIES going back a hundred years. Holmes couldn't take responsibility for all of them, but as he stood beneath a peppertree, he did contemplate climbing up there and letting himself drop. Seeking oblivion that way.

It wasn't the first time the tree's limbs had tempted him.

IT SEEMED TRITE, but he understood the genius loci of the place now.

The walls needed to be transparent, made of Perspex. The beautiful old beams apparent. The nail holes, the plane marks. The dark uneven stains where the sacrifices stood for long, long years.

They should be seen.

A WOMAN'S PLACE

EMMA NEWMAN

I met Emma standing on opposite stalls at BristolCon one year, while she was pursuing quite the most thorough, professional bid at self-publishing I've had the pleasure of encountering. Fearless—and utterly committed to everything she does—Emma's a delight to work with, and a delight at any rate. 'A Woman's Place' tackles an old favourite of the Holmes canon—the unflappable, ever-present Mrs. Hudson—and asks: why exactly does she put up with so much of Holmes' crap?

MRS. HUDSON ARRANGED the sandwiches on the plate in concentric circles, taking care that none of the corners overlapped and that the gaps between them were even. She was more creative than people gave her credit for. Once the hot water was poured into the warmed teapot, she carried it all up the stairs into her tenant's rooms.

The latest potential client was there, sitting in the armchair always given to those under Sherlock's scrutiny, with Dr. Watson sitting to the left of the coffee table. The good doctor's fingers were skipping over the virtual keyboard projected a couple of inches above her lap as the client spoke, but she paused long enough to give the landlady a grateful smile.

Mrs. Hudson put the tray down and sneaked a peek at the stranger. She could smell cologne, too much of it, and noted the dandruff on the back of the man's dark jumper. It was clustered just below his neck, but not on his shoulders. She imagined him trying to brush it off before putting his coat on. Poor chap.

"I just... I didn't know who to—"

"Did your uncle give any reason why the police shouldn't be contacted?"

The man shook his head.

"And I assume you haven't sent in a request to the DotGov database team?"

"Of course not, Mr. Holmes. That's worse than contacting the police! They'd be sniffing around every byte of data long before any copper came to the door. I don't want to go against my uncle's wishes when he's so ill. But I can't help thinking something must be wrong, for him to beg me not to tell anyone."

Holmes had steepled his fingers beneath his chin and still not acknowledged Mrs. Hudson's presence, even as she poured. If she moved slowly and kept within the usual behaviour of serving tea and plating up the sandwiches, she'd be able to listen in as long as she liked. If the conversation lasted past that— and it rarely did—she'd be able to catch up on their adventures through Dr. Watson's journal. She preferred to listen in herself, though, see the new clients when they arrived and which cases Sherlock chose to take on. She had a feeling, from the way Sherlock's eyes had fixated on a spot a few centimetres to the right of the man's shoulder, that he was going to pursue this one.

"Your aunt has been missing for over two weeks?" At the client's nod, he said, "Why come to me now? Why not last week?"

The man shrugged. "I had hoped she was... I hoped she had left him. I thought I would hear from her any day, after she had time to settle in her new place. But... nothing."

Mrs. Hudson watched Sherlock's eyes scan the man's face and take in all the details that Watson, bless her, had undoubtedly missed. "Hoped? A difficult marriage?"

"They're... estranged. But still living together. Separate rooms and no common friends. They never went anywhere together—couldn't even stand to be in the same room. Times are hard, Mr. Holmes; they couldn't afford to pay the data amendment fee to the DotGov people if they divorced, let alone pay separate rents. Cost of living these days..." He shook his head. "I do what I can to help, but I don't have a great deal myself." He clasped his hands together. "I heard that there are some cases you take on without payment, just for the thrill of it, I suppose. I can offer you a little money, but—"

Sherlock waved a hand, all his contempt of money encapsulated in the movement. "All I need is their address and for you to meet me there this evening at seven p.m."

"My uncle is very ill. He won't take kindly to visitors."

"I have no interest in speaking to him," Sherlock replied, hand drifting towards his teacup. "Leave the address on a piece of paper and I will meet you there."

"I could just ping you with the coordinates—"

"Mr. Holmes doesn't use a Chip," Dr. Watson said, passing over the note-block and pen.

The man balanced the stack of paper on his knee precariously, adjusting his hold on the pen several times. Mrs. Hudson pitied the man, trying to remember how to write under the scrutiny of Sherlock Holmes.

"Is that all, then?" He said it with such relief.

Mrs. Hudson wrapped two of the sandwiches in a napkin, knowing what was coming. Sherlock stood, gave the man a curt nod and strode over to the window. "Seven p.m. exactly, Mr. Eddard."

"Yes, Mr. Holmes, thank you."

Mrs. Hudson smiled at him and led the way out, taking the

man's coat off the hook as she passed it. "I'm sure Mr. Holmes will be able to help you," she said, not without pride. "By the time you go to bed tonight, all your worries will be over." He shrugged his coat over his shoulders and Mrs. Hudson wished he had the wherewithal not to wear a black one, with a scalp like his. She held out the wrapped sandwiches. "Why don't you take these with you to have on the way home? They'll only go to waste otherwise."

Mrs. Hudson watched the man go down the steps into the street. He turned and smiled at her before joining the crowds trying to squeeze their way out of Baker Street in the rush hour crush. She locked the door and went back up to Sherlock's apartment.

"I will need five minutes at the most," Sherlock was saying. "And then I'll go on to the Albert Hall. You're welcome to join me, Watson. I've heard very good things about the composer."

Watson shook her head, reaching for what was probably her third sandwich. Her cheeks dimpled as she smiled at Hudson. "I have a date, but I don't have to be there until eight o'clock. Do I need to bring anything special with me?"

Sherlock shook his head. "It's the simplest of cases."

"And the other one?"

Sherlock twisted, hands still behind his back. "Other one, Watson?"

Her grin revealed a piece of ham caught between her two front teeth. "Oh, come on, Holmes. Even I notice some things. You haven't been eating again. What slipper is caught between your teeth?"

Sherlock frowned, disliking Watson's favourite metaphor: that on a new case, he was like a puppy with a new slipper to chew. "Something important," he muttered, turning away once more to look down on the people hurrying below. "Did you want something, Mrs. Hudson?"

"Just collecting the plates and cups, Mr. Holmes."

"It's to do with Moriarty, isn't it?" Watson pressed.

The cup Mrs. Hudson was holding nearly slipped off the saucer and made a loud *clink* as she recovered it. She looked up at Holmes, waiting for his reply, but he was scowling at the teacup. She had overstayed her welcome.

She picked up the tray, trying to seem disinterested, but she lingered outside the door long enough to hear his reply.

"It is, Watson. But not, perhaps, in the way you might imagine."

"Oh?"

"Another time, my friend. There is still data to gather. But all will soon become clear."

Mrs. Hudson was back in Sherlock's living room by ten the next morning, having spent the two hours since breakfast waiting for him and Watson to leave. The news of a lead to Moriarty had made her restless, and she had to be careful not to upset him. All of these other cases were just distractions. Moriarty was the prize, and she knew it just as well as he did.

The cleaning bot took less than a minute to set up and activate. Its eight legs twitched in its calibration routine before it crawled over to the nearest book case and began sucking up the dust with its metal proboscis. She unplugged the armadillo-like carpet cleaner from its charger and set that off to work too.

It left her free to read Watson's journal. The doctor was an incredibly skilled woman, but not, thankfully, when it came to hiding her back-ups. Every time Mrs. Hudson pulled the tiny flash drive from the soil of the potted plant, she was grateful for the fact that Watson was old-fashioned enough to back up on a near-obsolete physical drive every day.

Watson had no idea she knew the hiding place. She connected via her Chip, entering the password that hadn't changed in over five years and had only taken three goes to guess correctly, and downloaded the latest journal entry. Five minutes later, she was sitting in her own living room as the bots worked in the room above, drinking tea and reading the private entry.

Journal: May 6th, 2031

My date turned out to be a rake-thin publicist for some sort of media company (the name of which I have already forgotten). She was just as self-absorbed as Holmes, but without the intellect and, of course, as soon as she made the connection, it was the usual round of questions about him. That's the last time I let Carrie organise a blind date for me. Honestly, I'm better off single.

What happened before I got to the restaurant was far more interesting. I met Holmes outside the address as arranged, looking very dapper in his *I'm-going-to-a-concert* suit and greatcoat, and the nephew arrived a minute after me.

"I need only three items—or lack thereof—to determine the whereabouts of your aunt," Holmes said to Mr. Eddard. He used that deep voice that comes from the sure knowledge that he was soon to dazzle us with his superior intellect. He's such a drama queen.

Mr. Eddard asked us to be quiet; it was clear the uncle had no idea the nephew was letting us in. The poor man was on the top floor of the rickety town house, one of the low-rent properties supplied by the government to keep poor people away from their wealthy neighbourhoods. I could smell the cheap chest-rub that back-street doctors still prescribe off-grid. Indeed, we were still adjusting to the dim light when the most appalling coughing started upstairs. I fear the uncle has neo-tuberculosis and whispered to the nephew that he needed to make sure his vaccinations were up to date. I didn't have the heart to tell him his uncle would likely die within the week. It was hard not to go up there and tend to

him, but without clearance to enter on medical grounds—
and the fact the uncle was obviously trying to keep his illness
off-grid—there was nothing I could do that wouldn't land a
DotGov team in the property and me in a cell by the end of
the night. He was too far gone to have any hope of recovery,
but it was hard being unable to give him something to make
his last days more comfortable.

Holmes went straight into the living room/kitchen. We
could hear the family next door through the paper-thin
partition. There'd been no effort to make it look anything
other than a once-pleasant house chopped into the smallest
legally-permitted slices. I wondered if the uncle and aunt
considered themselves lucky. I've tended to people south of
the river in houses where there are ten to a room. Neo-
TB sweeps through those places so fast the DotGov teams
barely get the children registered before they're dead.

Both Mr. Eddard and I watched Holmes scan the room and
then go to the chipped photo frame in the corner. It was
old enough to still need an ether cable connection to the
communal network. I haven't seen one plugged into a photo
frame since I was a child.

Holmes pointed, unable to bring himself to touch it, and
said "Show me their wedding photos, Mr. Eddard."

Eddard didn't move. "There aren't any, Mr. Holmes. They
married abroad, in secret."

Holmes looked at me then, with the sparkle in his eyes
of one more piece falling into place. "Then show us all the
photos of them together."

"There aren't any. As I said, Mr. Holmes, they were
estranged. My uncle deleted them all. There are a few of them
with other people. Would you like to see those?"

Holmes gave one of those grunts, conveying that the offer
was superfluous to his needs but of interest nonetheless.
Eddard cycled the photos, but they were so grainy, taken on

obsolete equipment instead of the hi-res LensCams most of us are used to now. Holmes was attentive, but made no comment.

"You said they sleep in separate rooms," Holmes said once the sad display was over. "These places rarely have two bedrooms."

"My uncle made the attic space into her room." Eddard's eyes widened. "You won't tell anyone, will you? It's... not entirely legal."

"Show me her room."

"You can only get to it by a ladder from the upstairs landing."

"That's of no concern to me," Holmes said and waved a hand in my direction. "Nor Watson."

"We'll have to be quieter up there," Eddard said. "The ladder is right outside my uncle's room."

We climbed the stairs and gave Eddard a moment to check in on his uncle, and then all three of us climbed the ladder. Eddard's fears that his uncle would hear us were unfounded; the poor devil was seized by frequent coughing fits and was barely conscious between.

The attic space was a tragic, dingy garret without a window and only a solitary light bulb hanging from the eaves to light it. There was a single chest of drawers, a canvas wardrobe with black mould creeping up the sides and a small bed covered with a faded comforter. The smell of damp wood and misery lowered my spirits immeasurably. Perhaps that was another reason why the date was disastrous. To go from that place to a restaurant where a starter costs more than Eddard's family live off per week made me feel wretched.

Holmes went straight to the top drawer and opened it. Eddard stood back in shocked silence at his effrontery but, like most clients, didn't dare say a word. Holmes rummaged, nodded to himself and then looked in the drawer below. After a swift inspection of the contents and then those of the wardrobe—a few dresses still hung in there—he turned and clasped his hands behind his back.

"Mr. Eddard, your aunt has not disappeared. She never existed in the first place."

Eddard looked as shocked as I must have. "But I used to see her every week! Are you saying I'm mad?"

"Not at all. I'm saying you have been duped into believing your uncle married a woman before you were born and lived with her in this house. But the woman he married abroad never returned with him. I'm willing to stake my professional reputation on the supposition that if one were to delve into the licence details held by DotGov, one would discover they married in a county with less rigorous requirements than our own—and that all her records would have been established by proxy, rather than in person. You are in your early thirties. Thirty years ago, the DotGov teams as we know them didn't exist."

Eddard opened and closed his mouth several times, like a goldfish spilt from its tank.

"But who did Mr. Eddard see every week?" I asked on his behalf. "I doubt the uncle could afford an actress. And why keep up the pretence anyway?"

"There was no need for an actress, Watson," Holmes said. "The uncle played the role of the aunt himself."

"Now this is just too much!" Eddard blurted.

"As for why he should keep up the pretence, I imagine it was a simple need to have two DotGov living allowances subsidising the household rather than one. And married couples get preferential treatment on housing lists."

"I don't believe you."

Holmes opened the top drawer and pulled out a handful of padded breast forms, stitched crudely into shape, and dropped them onto the bed. Then he dumped a pile of corsets on top. When Eddard remained silent, Holmes pulled out what looked like a box of tissues, only to reveal a hidden compartment inside filled with heavy-duty make up. "I assume your aunt was always immaculately presented?"

Eddard nodded dumbly.

"I would be unsurprised to find wigs under the bed. Of course, no-one has ever slept up here." He pulled back the comforter with a dramatic flourish, revealing a pillow resting atop a rectangle of foam propped up on several piles of bricks, collectively masquerading as a bed. "Your uncle has been too ill to reprise his role for your weekly visits. Neo-TB has a rapid onset and decline. He didn't have time to craft a story for your benefit."

"But... surely... why didn't I notice?"

"You loved your aunt, didn't you?" I asked him. "And your uncle was the one who made her miserable. I doubt you even looked at him that often. Am I right?"

He nodded, a single tear breaking free. "I'm such an idiot."

"People notice very little," Holmes said. "And they too easily believe that which they wish to. Now, if you'll excuse us, Mr. Eddard, Watson and I have other engagements this evening. May I bid you goodnight?"

"What do I do now?" Eddard asked me once Holmes was down the ladder.

"If I were in your place," I said, "I would make your uncle's last days as comfortable as possible and then contact DotGov with a full account of what Holmes uncovered. I will vouch for the reasons behind the delay, should they make a fuss."

"But shouldn't I confront him?"

"To what end?" I embraced him then. He seemed so vulnerable. "I'm so sorry this has happened to you. But you will heal. Try to forgive your uncle."

I have no idea whether he will ever be able to—or to forgive himself for not noticing. How strange to love someone who never existed.

And now it's the morning after and Holmes has only one more loose end he wishes to pursue before revealing his findings on Moriarty to me this evening. I'm rather excited, despite the fact I've decided to report the Neo-TB case at the Eddard property. It's the right thing to do for the rest of the street. Doesn't make it any easier, though.

THERE WAS FOOD to buy and errands to run, but Mrs. Hudson couldn't leave the house and risk missing a single detail of Holmes' day. He returned home shortly after lunch, declined any offer of food and went straight up to his apartment two stairs at a time. She listened to him pacing as she had her afternoon tea. At five to four a gunshot from his rooms made her drop the plate she was holding and run up the stairs.

The door to his apartment was open, as usual, and he was standing there in the dressing gown he favoured during the winter months, belt tied, worn over the shirt and trousers he'd been wearing earlier. The gun was still in his hand and he stared at her intently.

There was a hole in the living room wall. The wallpaper was ruined.

"What... what on Earth are you doing?"

"An experiment."

"I'd better call the police and tell them—"

"No need, I forewarned them." Holmes didn't take his eyes off her.

"I wish you had forewarned me. It would at least be polite."

"I suppose you'll want me to leave."

Her heart, only just settling down, raced again. "What? No, of course not. I'll get the damage repaired. It'll come out of your deposit, that's all."

His frown chilled her. "Is there something else you wanted?"

"No, Mr. Holmes. I shall leave you to your experiments."

"Oh, they're all done for today. Send Watson straight up when she comes."

By the time Watson arrived, Mrs. Hudson was calm again. Sherlock had been doing silly things for years now. She had to just accept it was part of who he was.

Watson was rosy-cheeked and cheerful, giving her a smile before dashing up the stairs. Mrs. Hudson prepared the tea tray. Her macaroons looked splendid in a star formation on the dainty plate. She carried it upstairs, hoping that the breakthrough Holmes had made was what everyone hoped for.

"Holmes, you're teasing me," Watson said as Mrs. Hudson arrived. "I didn't rush here from the surgery in that awful rain just to have you ask me questions to make me seem stupid."

"Very well," Holmes replied from his favourite spot at the window. "Do you recall how I first discovered Moriarty was behind some of the most notorious crimes of the decade?"

Watson's fingers were waggling over the tea tray as she decided which morsel to try first. "I don't think you ever told me."

Mrs. Hudson poured the tea, keeping her eyes studiously upon the task.

"I received a letter," Holmes said. "But..." When he didn't speak, she risked a glance at him. Holmes was tapping a finger over his mouth as he looked up at the ceiling. "I think, perhaps, there is a better place to start than the beginning. Mrs. Hudson?"

She jumped. "Yes, dear?"

"Why don't you join us for tea today? I know you have a fascination for my pursuit of Moriarty."

"Doesn't everyone?" she hoped her blush wasn't too deep. She sat down and helped herself to a sandwich, glad that she didn't have to skulk about to listen in this time.

"I have made a breakthrough on this case, but it wasn't as a result of searching for Moriarty," Holmes looked back down at the Brownian motion of the umbrellas in the street. "It was an examination of the self that triggered it. Watson, you know me better than perhaps anyone. How would you describe me?"

Watson's mouth was full and she coughed as she tried to swallow too fast. She, like Mrs. Hudson, had been expecting a lecture.

"Well," she eventually began, "you're inconsiderate and often belligerent to most of the people you interact with. However, you are loyal and sometimes quite sweet to those you care about. Most people don't see that, though. You're superhumanly observant, you have a borderline eating disorder and you obsessively put intellectual puzzles above the needs of the flesh. You have a variety of strange habits and a pathological hatred of technology. You're also a talented musician and probably not as clever as you think you are." Holmes raised an eyebrow at that and Watson added, "Because men like you never are."

"Let me modify that list," Holmes said. "I don't have a hatred of technology. I have a phobia. I also have no memories of my childhood, and the only things I know about my parents are those which my brother told me."

"That's because of the accident, though," Watson said, reaching for a second sandwich. "He told me all about that. How you were never the same afterwards. I've often wondered if that's why—" she stopped. "Hang on. A phobia?"

Mrs. Hudson did her best to keep chewing on the mouthful of sandwich.

"I let myself believe that I didn't want a Chip because it was cheating. I pride myself upon being able to observe and deduce more than the average person, and I believed my aversion stemmed from that pride. However, when I examined my attitude more closely, and tested myself, I discovered an insurmountable fear of anything like that near my person. Once I measured the extent of my... affliction, I wished to identify the source, but it's proven impossible. I find it..." He paused, a muscle working in his jaw. "Almost unbearable. But that alone is not particularly noteworthy. I began to identify other details that I should know, but could not recall. How I happened upon this apartment, for example. I couldn't have seen it advertised, as I only see mass budget adverts designed to capture the attention of a wide audience. Local classifieds are broadcast direct to Chips, with which I am still unencumbered. I didn't know anyone in this part of London, and neither did my brother." His gaze swept away from the window and fixed on Mrs. Hudson. "Do you recall, by any chance?"

She brushed the crumbs from the corner of her mouth and smiled. "Yes, dear. The man in the café next door told you. You ordered a coffee and asked if he knew of any rental properties that might not mind someone approaching them outside of the usual online checks. I hadn't listed the apartment on the DotGov database yet, so there was no need for us to worry about any of that nonsense."

"I was very fortunate to find these rooms." Sherlock returned to his account without acknowledging Hudson's reply. "In the years I've been here, the rent has never gone up, and it was extraordinarily low to begin with. I've broken three chairs, burned a sofa, smashed two mirrors, stunk the entire building out with various experiments, played music at unsociable hours, and paced at all hours of the night on wooden floorboards above my landlady's rooms, and never once in all that time has she complained."

"Mrs. Hudson is a treasure." Watson said. "'Fortunate' is an understatement."

"This afternoon I fired a gun into that wall." Sherlock pointed at the hole. "Mrs. Hudson wasn't angry. She even said it would be repaired from my deposit, but I know that the damage I have done to these rooms would require a deposit at least ten times that which I paid." He turned to face her again. "The question is, Mrs. Hudson, why are you subsidising my lifestyle?"

Mrs. Hudson smiled again, hoping it didn't look too forced. "It's my privilege, Mr. Holmes. You're the world's greatest detective, and I'm honoured to be able to help in the little ways I can."

"You haven't considered that your multiple PhDs in mathematics, synthetic biology, computing and molecular engineering could be more helpful?"

"Mrs. Hudson!" Watson's macaroon was abandoned, half-eaten. "Do you really hold those qualifications?"

"I don't like to go on about them," Mrs. Hudson said, horribly aware of the flush rising up her neck. "That was a long time ago, and—"

"You published a paper under your maiden name almost twenty years ago, in which you theorised that the performance of the human brain could be radically improved using a technique you'd pioneered in secret." Sherlock had moved from the window, round the back of her chair.

"I don't write those sorts of things anymore, dear," Mrs. Hudson said, dropping her plate onto the tray with a clunk and standing up.

"The only problem with the theory was that it required the brain to be dead in order for the modifications to be carried out," Sherlock went on. "But you were confident that if the heart could be stopped and started without damage, the surgery could take place and then the brain—the patient—could be revived."

"Good God," Watson said. "I heard about that at university. Controversial in the extreme. I heard the author was offered an obscene amount of money by the company developing Chip technology, but turned it down and disappeared. Was that you, Mrs. Hudson?"

"Oh, this is so silly," Mrs. Hudson said, gathering the plates and spilling crumbs over the carpet. "You're making a fuss over nothing."

"The books in your rooms you said belonged to your late husband actually belong to you. You wrote a number of them,"

Holmes continued. "Why did you turn the money down? Did someone else make you a better offer?"

"This is ridiculous. I'm just a landlady now, and—"

"Watson, come here," Sherlock raised the hair on the back of his head with his right hand. "These are scars, are they not?"

"Yes," Watson said. "From your accident?"

"From *her* intervention. Mrs. Hudson—or rather, Doctor Hudson—took her research underground, until the perfect subject came her way. Me."

Sherlock moved in front of her. "You made me what I am. I have no idea what I would have been like without your intervention; I can hardly remember my life before it."

"Without my intervention, you would be dead," Mrs. Hudson replied flatly. There was no point denying it now.

"And you 'built in' an aversion to the very technology that could give your work away."

She nodded. Sherlock's gaze lingered on her briefly, then he returned to staring out at the street as both Watson and Mrs. Hudson sat back down in silence. After a few moments, he asked, "Why haven't I caught Moriarty yet, Watson?"

"He's always one step ahead, it seems. I think he's the only person in London—no, the world—who has what it takes to keep you foxed."

"It's as if he can predict my next move. Like he knows how I think." He twisted to look at Hudson, but she couldn't meet his scrutiny. "Was he your first attempt?"

"Now, Holmes," Watson said. "That's quite a leap, even for you."

"Let's return to the letter I mentioned earlier. It was hand-delivered whilst Mrs. Hudson was out, just over two years ago." He went to the book case, pulled out a slender volume and plucked a folded letter from the inside cover. He cleared his throat and read aloud.

"*Have you seen all I've accomplished? Three MPs dead*

in the most heavily defended homes in London. Over thirty million pounds stolen from government coffers, and they can't report the crime because the money was made up of illegal donations. My operation is self-funding now, and I am feared by the most powerful in this country. You think your minor accomplishments are legendary, that your mind is the greatest of your generation, but I have already surpassed you. Moriarty.

"For the past two years," Holmes said after replacing the letter, "I thought he sent that to taunt me. I understood the need to have someone else understand and appreciate his genius, someone to give him the thrill of the hunt. Many people in the press, I'm given to understand, have described my mind as the greatest of my generation. He would have known I had no email address and could only be contacted at these lodgings; it's public knowledge. I thought it was a declaration—a challenge!

"I was so very wrong. It wasn't until I began to examine my own failings, and thereby discover Mrs. Hudson's remarkable past, that I realised the note was never meant for me. It had a single 'H' on the envelope, but not for Holmes. For Hudson. He wasn't seeking an intellectual equal to highlight his criminal genius, he was seeking approval from his creator. He wanted to tell her he had done as she had asked."

Mrs. Hudson was studying her hands in her lap as the final blow came, all too aware of the way both stared at her. "I've waited for this," she finally said, still staring down into her lap. "I knew it would happen eventually. I made you to be the greatest detective, after all. I'm surprised it took you as long as it did, and how difficult it is to hear."

"Did you create Moriarty?" Dr. Watson asked.

"Yes. I made him to do what I could not; to take down the government. When the company that makes the Chip technology approached me, all that time ago, I could see where things were heading. The British Front had taken power, eroded personal rights and freedoms, destroyed net neutrality, and seized control of the ISPs, and now there was a new technology that they could put inside people's heads. I had to take them down before that company was bought by a GovCorp front organisation and used to further their twisted ideology. I made my own Chip and tricked DotGov into thinking it was standard issue. I'm just a landlady on their system, but the vast majority of people don't know how to protect themselves like I do. I hoped that eventually my creation would destroy the system.

"But Moriarty had a taste for violence and drama. He initially built a criminal network to carry out my orders, but soon broke away. But worse than that, he gave the Government all the reasons they needed to bring in harsher laws and take even the last pathetic rights to privacy we had."

"So you made me to catch Moriarty," Holmes said.

"Yes. I learned from my mistakes and I kept you close. You're so alike, I had to be sure you wouldn't go down the same path as him. Dr. Watson helps with that."

Holmes looked at Watson then and she held her hands up. "I had no idea about any of this, I swear. I can hardly believe it." The doctor looked at her friend, and then to Mrs. Hudson, and back again. "What now, Holmes?"

Holmes gave the faintest of smiles. "Now I can drop the slipper."

"That's it? This woman made you into some sort of cyborg super genius and you just shrug and carry on?"

"Yes. The case is solved."

Mrs. Hudson breathed again and with a double blink, closed the dialogue box she'd called up should she need to blast his neural implants and shut him down for good. She managed a smile and wiped the sweat from her palms onto her apron. "Tea, anyone?"

A STUDY IN
SCARBOROUGH

GUY ADAMS

Uniquely among the contributors to this collection, Guy has not only written several original Sherlock Holmes works, but actually played the great man on stage twice! Larger (and louder) than life, Guy's a wit and raconteur as well as an author of no mean talent. 'A Study in Scarborough' is as much an homage to the classic BBC radio comedy of the early-to-mid twentieth century as to the Holmes canon; as a die-hard fan of The Goon Show myself, I wasn't hard to convince.

I SOMETIMES WONDER if I'm built from old videotape. I feel archaic, worn from overuse and increasingly obscure. One day I'll get caught up in the grinding wheels of my own life and unravel.

"What does 'elementary' even mean?" asked Eddie, doing his level best to put an entire bag of smoky bacon crisps inside himself using the minimum amount of time and effort.

"Straightforward," I replied. "Basic."

"Not much of a joke, is it?" Eddie decided.

Having finished his consumption of the crisps, he was now folding the bag up and tying it into a knot, an act of tidiness betrayed by the amount of crisp crumbs left on the front of his T-shirt.

"It's not a joke," I explained, reaching for the remote control for the VCR now the credits had begun to roll, "it's a catchphrase."

"Still supposed to be funny." Eddie picked up the case for the cassette and stared at its washed-out cover. "But it's not."

"I think it is," I told him, snatching the box and hovering impatiently by the VCR, as the cassette gradually rewound. "You have to watch it in context; it was a long time ago."

"Before comedy was invented?"

"I just mean some of the jokes riff off a different time, different sensibility."

"Well, I don't get it, mate. Each to their own, I suppose. There must be people that like them if they're willing to do a book about it."

I could have pointed out that the book in question was unlikely to trouble many bookshops. If I sold a handful of Kindle copies, then I'd consider myself lucky. But I didn't. Instead I said that "Holmes and Watson still have a lot of fans," finally ejecting the cassette and clicking it away in its box, snapping plastic into plastic as a sort of full stop.

Eddie, never one for punctuation, refused to recognise it as such. "God knows why."

I TOOK THE train north, a narrow, metal gulag of running children, discarded sandwiches and upholstery as rough as a squaddie's hair. Hiding beneath my headphones, I closed my eyes, listening to old episodes of Homes and Watson's radio show (the third series, when it really hit its stride). I rested my head against the glass and lost myself between the imagined walls of the Camden Theatre. The smell of cigarette smoke and hair oil. The easy laughter of a gentle crowd, eager to spend half an hour in the fictional world of 221b Baker Street, home of consulting detective Sherlock Holmes and his friend and biographer, John

Watson. What nonsensical mystery would they solve this week? What odd crime would form the framework for their comic business?

ANNOUNCER: This is the BBC Light Programme.

GRAMS: ['HOLMES & WATSON OPENING 1' by Willy Scott]

ANNOUNCER: We present Sherlock Holmes and John Watson, with Gordon Lestrade, Martha Hudson and Billy Page in...

GRAMS: ['HOLMES & WATSON OPENING 2' by Willy Scott]

HOLMES: The Adventure of the Red-Headed League.

EFFECTS: Usual establishing sounds. A horse-drawn carriage passes along Baker Street, a newspaper boy shouts the headline of the day, in the distance a police whistle.

WATSON: It was a particularly miserable Tuesday when Holmes and I first heard about the Red-Headed League. The wind was icy and the fog thick. So thick, in fact, that one kind soul was heard giving it directions. It was so cold, I was forced to set fire to the front door just to get my key in the lock. By the time I reached my armchair I needed a large brandy. I sat and savoured it, rejoicing in what the papers were assuring us was one of the finest British summers on record.

HOLMES: Good morning Watson. You appear to have an icy growth under your nose.

WATSON: (Bunged up) Oh Lor'...

EFFECTS: A scraping sound followed by a noise akin to a chandelier smashing.

HOLMES: I see it's another temperate day.

WATSON: Someone was chipping a horse off the pavement as I came in. Street children were licking the shattered remains like equine ice lollies.

HOLMES: If it distracts them from stealing the lampposts again, we may consider ourselves lucky.

EFFECTS: A distant sawing followed by the sound of a lamppost falling over and a loud, youthful cheer.

WATSON: No such luck. I can't imagine what it is they do with them.

HOLMES: I'm told they make effective clubs against the rats.

I ESCAPED THE train at Scarborough, stepping out into a mass of traffic and gloom.

I had grown up in Yorkshire and half-remembered lazy Sundays in the town, reading yellow-stained comic books from creaking spindle racks and sitting on the beach, letting sand pour through my hands in the hunt for precious shells. There was no such nostalgia in sight as I crossed over to the main road and made my way towards the front.

There's a universal rule that all train stations must be located in the most awful part of town. Scarborough was no exception. The station was the heart of a street full of betting shops and estate agents, cheap cafés stocked with watery coffee and inedible sandwiches. There was the theatre, of course, but whatever its reputation, it was an ugly pile of bricks, only coming to life as darkness fell. I slogged my way along a pavement spotted with the dark remains of old chewing gum. A newspaper sign tried to cheer me up with the story of a man who had recently been poisoned by his wife. *Nicotine Death Stuns Police*, it claimed, though obviously it hadn't stunned them quite enough to let the murderer get away with it.

All in all, it was a miserable welcome to a childhood haunt.

Eventually I found myself in the pedestrianised part of town, a shopping centre that could have existed anywhere, a place of mobile phone shops and orange brick. I queued inside a coffee chain, a raucous room of dark wood and hissing steam, and bought a universal cup of its universal coffee to sip as I walked.

By the time I reached the front, a hint of sun had thrown a more flattering light on the row of Victorian buildings and amusement arcades. The sound of beeping machines and electronic racing cars spilled out onto the pavement. The beach, while empty, looked like the sort of place where nice things *might* happen, if you had sufficient imagination packed along with your bucket and spade.

The wind was blowing so hard that walking involved effort. After several hours on the train, it was as good as a shower and a couple of hours nap. I would never be completely ready to meet the man I was here to interview, *never*, but after ten minutes of being sandblasted I was as, at least, suitably alert.

I made my way past the endless stream of paint-flaked hotels: *Thursday Night is Caribbean Night!!*; *Appearing Tonite: Double Down* ('Best vocal double act on the coast,' *Yorkshire Evening News*); *Karaoke Competition! Sing for your Supper at Cap'n Jim's Bar and Grill*. Soon the offers of accommodation dwindled and the street shifted towards the residential. Checking the numbers, I finally found the address I was looking for.

I was twenty minutes early, so I walked straight past it and sat down on a nearby bench.

I checked my dictaphone; the last thing I wanted was to look a fool by faffing with it once in the house. It was fully charged, set automatically to back up recordings to cloud storage. I'd be hit by a whopping data charge, but better that than lose a word. I put it in my jacket pocket, then took it out and checked again, suddenly hit by a panicked certainty that I'd missed something the first time. Perhaps I should have brought two machines? A backup for the machine with the built-in backup? I was fretting myself in circles. Finally convinced I had no need to worry, I returned to the secure world of my headphones.

HOLMES: Watson, meet Mr. Jabez Wilson. You will note several obvious details at once. He has spent some time in China; the tattoo on his left thigh of a young Geisha wrestling with an octopus can hardly have come from anywhere else. Several elements to its design are distinct to the country: the colour of the ink, a faint pink hue sourced from fish scales, the thin, stylised line-work...

WATSON: The words underneath saying "Hu Tat, China's Premiere Ink-Flinger since 1856."

HOLMES: Well... yes, those too.

WATSON: He's also clearly a drunk.

HOLMES: Watson! How many times must I warn you against theorising without facts? Upon what evidence do you base such a deduction?

WATSON: He's passed out naked in our coal-scuttle.

I CHECKED MY watch, decided that being five minutes early was no bad thing, and walked back to the house.

This was my Schrödinger's Cat moment. Before my finger triggered the bell, the man behind the door would exist only as a theoretical construct, a man of fiction. The moment the bell rang, leading the door to be opened, he would be real, inarguable, and staring right at me. I found the notion of it terrifying. You should never meet your heroes.

I rang the bell.

After a few moments a shadow appeared through the frosted glass and made its way towards me. The indistinct figure reached out for the catch and its fingers resolved into clarity, pink and lined through the glass.

The door opened and I was face to face with John Watson.

I had been prepared for him to be transformed by his years, few of us can hope to get to eighty-five unscathed. His hair had all but disappeared, his rugged, leading-man looks sagged. His skin had grown thin and shiny, his eyes pale. He seemed far too small to be the man who loomed so large in my appreciation, his body awkward and his movements slow. His famous smile—that had allegedly won over the attentions of everyone from Shirley Eaton to Jean Seberg—was nowhere to be seen, and the set of his jaw was so stern it was impossible to imagine it ever making an appearance.

"Yes?" he asked, his voice fractured by years of tobacco.

"I'm Arthur Doyle? We spoke on the telephone?"

"Did we? About what?"

"I'm the one that's doing the book." This didn't seem to help. "The book about you?"

"Oh, that. Today, is it?" He turned and walked into the house, I assumed it was safe to follow. "Thought today was Monday," he said, checking his watch as if to test any claim to the contrary. "Bloody bank holidays."

He wandered into the kitchen and waved at the table, inviting me to sit down.

"That's the thing with retirement," he continued, "every day the same. End up losing track. Looking an idiot."

"Not at all," I tried to reassure him. "Easily done. Same when you're a writer, to be honest; when I'm working weekends, the days blur into one."

What little I'd seen of the house seemed soulless. A place inhabited, but never truly embraced. It was littered with functional things, old magazines and books. A man who lived to please his whims, with no mind to aesthetics.

A pair of glasses with Sellotape on their bridge lay, lenses down, on the worktop. Next to them, an e-cigarette sat charging next to a pile of various liquids. Vanilla, menthol, coffee and cherry. John Watson had clearly been forced to kick one habit, only to develop another. It felt absurdly personal to see them, a little window into my host's habits.

He filled the kettle. "Writer. Yes. Always fancied that myself. Prose. Done scripts, obviously. Different, though." He turned the kettle on and rifled through one of his cupboards. The kitchen units were old, owned by a man who hadn't the enthusiasm to replace them. The cupboards were half-empty. No clutter of excess groceries here; he was a man who bought what he wanted, consumed it, then replaced it. "Tea or coffee? Coffee's fresh. Don't do instant."

"Don't go to any extra effort."

"It's only coffee. I'm not past being able to fill a cafetiere."

"Sorry, no. Coffee would be lovely."

"*French press*, the Americans call it. Because *cafetiere* is too hard a word. French press. So literal, the Americans. Probably why they never liked us. Any country that can only just stop short of naming a cafetiere 'French coffee thing' was never going to like two stupid bastards making jokes about death. Sugar?"

"Just milk, please."

"Can't say *herb* properly either, have to affect a silly accent. Contradictory. Never understood the Americans."

"Two countries divided by the same language," I said, with what I hoped was a suitably friendly smile.

"Sense of humour, too. Very different."

Holmes and Watson had never really found success in America. They had been household names in the UK and had successfully toured Australia towards the end of their professional career (despite reports that their relationship had soured into wild rows broken by uncomfortable silences) but all attempts to 'break' across the Atlantic had failed. Perhaps the most notable example being their box-office flop, *Clueless*, which had seen their characters attempt to solve a New York mystery with the assistance of Mickey Rooney as a diminutive Sam Spade clone.

"I suppose you'll talk about that damned film?" Watson asked.

"I'd like to talk about everything," I admitted, "well, everything we have time for. I appreciate there's a lot to cover."

"Time I have," he said, handing me the cafetiere and a mug. "Not much else. Let's go into my study. More comfy."

I followed him out of the kitchen, still not quite believing that I was walking round the home of a man I had revered since childhood. If you were not supposed to meet your heroes, you certainly weren't supposed to notice the messy state of their living room, or the curious stain on their hallway rug.

I had come to Holmes and Watson not through the radio shows, or TV series, but rather *The Casebook of Holmes and Watson*, an illustrated book of short stories and comics featuring their famous characters. I'd bought it at a car boot fair, not realising the stories were supposed to be absurd. I still feel a nostalgic glow remembering the time Holmes and Watson averted the flooding of Croydon in 'The Adventure of the Norwood Plumber,' and the utterly bonkers, alien-invasion comic 'The Adventure of the Creeping Men.'[1] I had a copy of the book in my bag, just in case I felt brave enough to ask John Watson to sign it. Unless he thawed out completely, I likely

---

[1] Not to be confused with the 1963 radio episode 'The Adventure of the Crooked Man,' where Holmes fights a murderous chiropractor who bends his victims into grotesque geometrical shapes.

wouldn't. One smile would probably do it, but that seemed too much to hope for.

His study was a jumble of memorabilia, bookshelves filled with folders of scripts, CDs, cassettes, videos and, with what space was left, books. A large desk sat at one side, empty but for an ancient laptop, a lamp and a photo of his deceased wife. A two-seater sofa stood underneath the window, the view of the sea reserved for the man sat behind the desk. The walls were lined with posters from live shows, newspaper clippings and photos of Holmes and Watson stood with other famous folk. I couldn't help but linger.

"Take a look," he said, sitting down at the desk, the large wooden chair creaking despite how little it was being asked to bear. "My wailing wall. On miserable days, I pray to it."

Beneath a poster for their Australian shows—cartoon images of Holmes in his deerstalker hat and Watson with his service revolver disguising the age and mood of the two men—there was a photograph of the two of them with their arms around Brigitte Bardot; in another, it was Susan George; yet another offered Anoushka Hempel. It was a veritable cluster of blondes that the shallow part of me couldn't help but speculate on. John Watson's libido had been notorious in the years prior—some even claimed during—his marriage to Mary Morstan in 1976. Indeed, in Edward Malone's seminal, if rather scandalous, biography of Holmes and Watson, *The Hounds of Vaudeville*, 'sixties tabloid gossip columnist Langdale Pike claimed Watson was a regular at Isadora Klein's notorious sex parties.[2]

There were other famous faces on display: sportsmen, movie stars and politicians, all bookended by the unconventional pairing of Holmes and Watson through the years. You could track the dates not only by the clothing, but also the stars'

---

[2]"That great cesspool into which all the loungers and idlers of the profession are irresistibly drained," Langdale Pike, 'Tittle Tattle,' *Daily Mirror*, 1962.

weight. As time went by, Holmes got thinner, his face becoming more hawk-like and drawn. The man that loomed out of the photos taken in the 'seventies, all beiges and greys—seemed like a man close to death, his skin yellow, his features severe. Conversely, Watson grew bigger, years of alcohol and fine dining accreting on him like geological formations. Once Mary began to appear, red hair and freckles, she hung on the arm of a man who could have been the avuncular uncle of his former self, a man of bushy facial hair and ruddy cheeks. Throughout, Holmes haunted the pictures, a malevolent spirit waiting for his moment to pounce.

I raised myself up on tiptoes to read a small, faded newspaper clipping, announcing that the two of them were turning on the Blackpool Illuminations. They stood either side of a confused Mayor, their baggy suits billowing in the wind that blasted its way along the pier. Watson's eyes were hooded against the sand that was being kicked up, his mouth pulled into a false grimace of pleasure. The Mayor had discovered that his ceremonial robes had become an ostentatious sail that would hurl him into the Atlantic were it not for the ceremonial chain around his neck acting as an anchor. Holmes simply stared at the camera, straight-faced, seeming impervious to the weather.

In a grisly coincidence, a fragment of the adjoining news story was still visible. A holidaymaker had been stung by a Lion's Mane jellyfish and died. The local authorities were eager to point out that the species in question was rarely encountered so close to shore. Even in the unlikely event a swimmer did so, its sting was rarely fatal. The holidaymaker had suffered an allergic reaction resulting in anaphylactic shock. Many years later, Holmes would die in a similar manner, stung by a swarm of bees that he kept in his home on the Sussex Downs. This indomitable, intimidating man, brought down by insects.

* * *

```
WATSON: Careful Holmes, we're surrounded.
HOLMES: Pathetic! You think you're a match
    for me? Idiots! I have the most celebrated
    mind in the whole world. It was the matter
    of moments for me to deduce that the Red-
    Headed League was cover for a bank heist.
    I have my intelligence, you have a bunch
    of thugs with cricket bats; what could you
    possibly do to stop me?
EFFECTS: The extended sound of several men
    swinging their cricket bats, grunting and
    the smacking of skull on willow.
WATSON: [Weak] You had to ask. [Groans]
```

"FASCINATING," I SAID, turning away from the news clipping as I realised I was ignoring my host.

"Like the marks parents put on walls, charting their children's growth," Watson replied, "but going on far too long. No children for me. Just a dead career. Sit down, let's talk."

I did as asked, pulling my dictaphone out of my pocket and holding it up. "Do you mind?"

He shrugged with indifference so I set it to record and placed it on the desk between us, turning it so that the red light was pointing towards me, in case it should decide to spontaneously pack-up.

"Where do you want to start?" he asked.

"The book's about your entire professional career together, from when you first met, right up until..."

"The bugger died."

"Well, yes."

Watson had never tried to pursue a solo career. At the time of Holmes' death in 1984, Watson had been fifty-four and seemingly content to vanish from public life altogether. He even refused to appear in the inevitable documentaries and retrospectives of Holmes and Watson that would bubble up every time there was a viable anniversary to hang a broadcast on.[3]

When I'd first contacted him via his old agent I hadn't expected to receive a reply, let alone be granted an interview. Being invited to his home had therefore been a shock, and probably the only reason my publisher had agreed to take the book.

"Were you never tempted to carry on without Holmes?" I asked. "After all, you had always played a major part in the writing of the scripts, I'm sure you could have had your choice of solo projects."

"Nobody wanted to hire me. Not for anything worthwhile. I wasn't going to fill a seat on panel shows or afternoon chat shows. After a year of failing to get anything commissioned, I decided enough was enough. I didn't need the money. Nobody to spend it on but myself, and there was nothing I wanted that could be bought."

"A shame," I said, "the industry can be so narrow-minded."

He shrugged once more as if it was of no importance. "I'd done enough. Probably for the best."

"Well, perhaps we should start at the beginning and work our way forward," I suggested. "You met Sherlock Holmes when you were eighteen."

"TB," he said. "We both thought we were dying. Lying up in a sanatorium in Godalming. Coughs and chills. Different times. Now they just throw antibiotics at you, back then you were given food, a bed and a prayer. You might be there for years. Not so bad for the old duffers. For two young men, it seemed even worse than death. We wanted to be in pubs, going to dances, getting up to trouble. At least I did. Sherlock was unusual, even then. Hard not to be when you're called Sherlock,

---

[3]The most notorious of which was certainly *Elementary! My Favourite Holmes and Watson Moments* (Channel 4, 1989), when a drunken Oliver Reed had claimed to have starred in an episode that didn't exist.

I suppose. Blame the parents. Called his brother Mycroft. Even worse, sounds like a village in Kent. Met him in the garden, my first week there. Sherlock that is, not Mycroft. He was staring up at an elm tree. Seemed confused by it. He seemed confused by lots of simple things. His knowledge was vast, but the simple, everyday things were baffling to him. He told me he was trying to judge the tree's height by the length of its shadow. I told him I couldn't see the point. 'What else is there to do?' he asked, and I was so bloody bored I helped him. He measured my shadow and correlated it against the shadow of the tree. The tree was sixty-four feet; quite why I remember that, I don't know. Useless facts cluttered between the ears.

"We spent the rest of the day talking about ourselves. Different worlds. I'd grown up in Edinburgh, son to a drunk and a woman who wanted her child to be better than his father. She pushed for me to be a doctor. I wasn't interested. Head full of stories of the war, I wanted to run off and join the army. TB put paid to both. Lucky, as it worked out, I suppose.

"Holmes grew up on a country estate. Son of a squire. Silver spoon. Kicked out of Eton for blowing up the chemistry lab.[4] He claimed he had been so suffocated by his parents' wealth and expectations that he had run away from home. Wanted to go to theatre school and a life on the stage. He always did love dressing up. I remember he once stole a doctor's coat from the office and paraded around the sanatorium, hair whitened with talc, false moustache made from trimmed hair and glue. He had half the place convinced he was a visiting specialist until he coughed his guts up over a set of medical notes and the moustache went skew-whiff.

"If there had been anyone else there my age I likely would never have become friends with him. We were almost complete opposites: I liked sport, he loathed it. He read the classics, I read Dennis Wheatley and Agatha Christie. He liked science, I was

---

[4]Or poisoning the caretaker's cat; accounts vary.

baffled by it. There was only one thing we agreed on and that was ITMA. Probably don't know it, do you?"

Of course I did. While most men my age might be baffled by the acronym, I was only too aware of *It's That Man Again*, the long-running radio vehicle for fast-talking comedian Tommy Handley.

"Well, most buggers have forgotten it," he said. "Product of its time. We used to listen to it on the hospital radio, the monotony broken up for half an hour every week. Holmes would mimic the characters, Colonel Chinstrap, Ali Oop.[5]

"After a while I joined in. We'd create new adventures for the characters. A way of occupying the time. Inventing fictional conversations in silly voices, because there was nothing the real Sherlock Holmes and John Watson had left to say to one another.

"Then it became a challenge. We wanted to outdo the show. The other residents started to laugh at our jokes. They'd ask us to do a turn. So we wanted to get more laughs than the radio. Not be second fiddle. Holmes never could stand being second fiddle.

"Eventually we came up with characters of our own. Based on residents and staff to begin with, then just people we invented."

"Was one of them the detective?" I asked.[6]

"He came a little later."

Watson thought for a moment before continuing.

"In interviews, Holmes aways claimed it had been his idea. Said he'd seen me reading a Poirot.[7] He said that turning it into comedy seemed obvious. I never used to argue. No point arguing with Sherlock. But actually, it was me that first thought of it.

---

[5]Both played by Jack Train, the Chinstrap character would also feature in two episodes of *The Goon Show*.

[6]As both performers used their given names in the roles that would make them famous, they frequently referred to them as 'the detective' and 'the doctor' when conducting interviews.

[7]Hercule Poirot, the fussy Belgian detective, and his loyal friend Arthur Hastings were created by Agatha Christie.

"I'd been reading Poe. *Murders in the Rue Morgue*, C. Auguste Dupin. The stuck-up rationalist, solving cases by analysing dust and bootprints. I liked the idea of someone so pompous, so full of their own cleverness being used to comic effect. This absurd brain that was so hopeless in everyday life. The idiot savant. Pure comedy. Thinking about it I suppose Sherlock inspired me himself; he had that same way about him. Full of unbeatable confidence. I never cared enough to correct him, but I may as well be honest now. The idea was mine.

"Still, what Sherlock did with it, the character he developed, that was all him. All him. They blurred into one, eventually. He'd played it so long, so well, even I struggled to find where the character stopped and the man started."

I'd heard this in other interviews. Tobias Gregson, the director of the first series of *Holmes and Watson* on TV, had talked about how difficult Holmes had been to work with, a man so lost in the role that he was impossible to reach.

"We should have changed our names," Watson continued. "That would have helped. The character, the detective, wouldn't have been Sherlock Holmes, it would have been someone else, someone he could take off and put away after recording. But the name worked so well. Sherlock bloody Holmes; enough to get you a kicking in the playground, but perfect for a Victorian detective.

"A lot of people said it was a good idea to use our real names. It was fairly common. The Tony Hancock who lived in East Cheam wasn't the same Tony Hancock that sat in the BBC canteen, but listeners knew who you were. They'd always remember you. They'd call it brand recognition these days, I suppose. Good PR."

"Did it make it more difficult," I asked, "when you tried creating new characters?"

I was thinking in particular of *A Case of Identity*, the 1969 movie featuring the double act as Pete Huggins and Teddy

Hardwicke, a pair of actors who decide to cross-dress in order to get work. Unfavourably reviewed,[8] it was a flop at the box office.

"We were typecast from the word go," Watson agreed. "Sherlock Holmes and John Watson were the characters, not the actors. Whatever else we did, people weren't interested. They wanted adventures on Baker Street. We bumped the characters off for eight years when the radio show finished, but it didn't work. Eventually we gave in and brought them back on the telly."

I realised we were running a risk of skipping past their entire radio career and decided to bring things back onto a chronological track.

"So, how did you go from amusing patients in a sanatorium to amusing the nation on the radio?"

"Years of hard work and pure bloody luck. Always the way in this business.

"Holmes left the Sanatorium a couple of months before me. I'd developed complications, tuberculosis of the reproductive tract."

He picked at the surface of the desk, perhaps uncomfortable with such personal details. "Killed my chances of ever having kids. Of course, at that age, I was just glad to get out alive; who thinks of being a father at eighteen?

"Holmes had tried to get acting work, but got nowhere. I met him in London, listened to him rage about the lack of opportunities for his talent, and ended up moving in with him. He couldn't manage the rent on his own.

"We decided to try our hand at more performing. We spent a miserable few years getting nowhere on the circuit, trying out different characters and sketches. Then we bumped into Harry Stamford. He'd been a fellow patient. His brother worked at the Windmill Theatre in London. You know it?"

I did. A great number of post-war comedians had made their names there.

---

[8]Most memorably dismissed by the lauded film critic, Roger Ebert as 'Some Like it Not.'

"We got ourselves a few slots in the revue. The place was thick with talent scouts and BBC producers at the time. They liked the girls. The tableaux vivants.[9] Tits filled seats.

"One night we did a sketch featuring the detective; a producer liked it and asked if we'd work with a couple of script writers to make it a radio series. Holmes was precious about sharing a script credit, of course, but I convinced him to keep his mouth shut before he cost us the opportunity. Within twelve months, we were on the air."

"That first series is now missing from the archives,"[10] I said.

"Just as well. It wasn't very good. It took a couple of series to find our feet, I think. To begin with, we were all over the place, trying things, seeing if they'd stick. Holmes having a girlfriend..."

"Your dog?" I suggested. It had been a running gag; a bull pup that would bark at the most inappropriate moment.

"Christ. Ridiculous idea. A stage hand shuffling around on his hands and knees barking. The live audience didn't know where to look. Too many cooks. We worked with good writers, but they all pulled in different directions."

"Series three was just the two of you with Ray Simpson?"

"That's right. He was a rising star as far as the BBC were concerned. Done a few gags for *Life with the Lyons* and *Much-Binding-in-the-Marsh*.[11] They wanted to give him a show of his own, but he was slow. Struggled with deadlines. So they

---

[9]Taking advantage of a loophole in the censorship laws, it was agreed that nudity could not be classed as obscene if it was static. The Windmill Theatre immediately became famous for its popular presentations of immobile, naked women.

[10]As is a good deal of the second, only 'The Adventure of the Copper Britches' existing in broadcast quality, with a handful of off-air recordings covering a further three episodes.

[11]Two other popular radio comedies. The former would be the basis for two early movies from Hammer Films, the latter featured Kenneth Horne who would later go on to front *Beyond our Ken* and *Round the Horne*.

thought they could team him up with us. We met him in the bar. Always doing business in the bar, back then. He and I hit it off and Holmes didn't hate him, so we got him."

"'Holmes didn't hate him.' Was he that difficult to work with?"

"A nightmare. But, as much as it might not sound like it now, he was my friend, so I put up with him. I spent a lot my time trying to stop fights breaking out. He hated any form of interference; directors or producers telling him what to do. You'd have thought he was a star from the first moment he stepped on a stage, determined to get his own way. He was so often right, mind you. That was his saving grace. He never missed a trick. Well, almost never. But you didn't get far with that attitude as a newcomer, took a lot of charming from me to keep things on track. Politics."

Watson looked past me and out of the window. For all he talked about his 'wailing wall' of past glories, and a study filled to the brim with relics from the past, this was the first time he showed any sign of losing himself in it. His speech was often as percussive and brutal as a man offering the last few kicks to a felled enemy. Words were facts, no more; they weren't intended to portray any emotional depth. Rather than try and drag him out of his reverie to continue our organised wander through his career, I decided to keep him on the same subject, hopeful—and I'm quite aware of how hateful this sounds—that he might be end up sharing something scandalous about his deceased partner.

Not that the memory of Holmes was exactly sacrosanct. His predilection for drugs was well known, cocaine in particular, but that seemed to be his only vice. There were no stories of affairs; indeed, no mention of women at all, which naturally led most commentators to assume he had been gay and circumspect, common enough at the time.

"When did those problems become more than you could handle?" I asked, hoping I was phrasing the question with suitable diplomacy.

"In 1984," he said. "I could tolerate everything up until then. Not *like* it, tolerate it. I grew to dislike him, yes. Tiring of his constant bloody attitude. But hate him? Really, utterly, loathe him? 1984."

"When he died?"

Watson smiled.

Hadn't I said that once he'd shown a glimpse of good humour, I'd consider getting my book out for him to sign? Not a chance. That smile didn't relax me. If anything, it made me even more uncomfortable.

"The third series," he said, returning precisely to where we had been before our digression. "That was good. Excellent, in fact. I sound as arrogant as Holmes, but it was. Ray was just what we needed. He took Holmes' wilder ideas and my love of word play and built a bridge between them. We weren't a double act, not at our best. We were a trio, the silent partner tapping away behind the drapes. Those five years saw us at our best.

EFFECTS: The sound of a champagne cork being popped, the champagne being poured into a glass.

HOLMES: Ah... Champagne and petit fours. Could it get any better?

WATSON: Yes. It could be us out there, enjoying it.

EFFECTS: Watson rattles on the bar of his cell.

WATSON: Damn you, John Clay! You can't keep us locked up forever!

CLAY: [Drinks] True. But I can certainly keep you in there until I've finished my dinner. Yours is on the floor.

EFFECTS: Watson kicks the tray of gruel.

WATSON: You expect us to eat this slop? I've
just seen a fly die after landing on it.
CLAY: I know how it feels; the canapes are
positively heavenly.

"RAY STAYED WITH you until series seven," I said, "then there was a falling out?"

"Holmes again. He finally got one of the higher-ups to agree that we could write the show on our own. Ray was fired. Couldn't believe it. I tried to reverse the decision, begged Ray to come back, but he'd had enough of Holmes by then. He wasn't going to carry on under sufferance. Horrible. I lost a good friend, didn't talk to him again for years. It was Mary that built the bridges between us again, she'd worked with him on his sitcom, *The Scowerers*.[12] Told him that I'd love to see him again. We met up for dinner, but it wasn't the same, too much time, too many regrets. Good of Mary, though. Course, he got some revenge; the eighth radio series was the last. People didn't like it as much. Too silly."

EFFECTS: A rushing sound, the roar of a
rocket.
WATSON: [Shouting] I can see the sea from
up here.
HOLMES: [Shouting] Splendid. If I can't
defuse the warhead you'll be able to
sprinkle yourself over it.

SERIES EIGHT HAD seen Holmes and Watson fighting the Nazis. While British comedy—particularly *The Goon Show*—had obsessed over the war during the 'fifties, by the 'sixties the idea

---

[12] A comedy set in a Glaswegian cleaning firm and an early vehicle for Nicholas Lyndhurst.

seemed dated and absurd. Listeners had turned off in their droves.

"Was that part of the reason you cancelled the radio series?"

"For sure. Holmes never could stand criticism, and I was bored of the characters, happy to try something new. Much good it did us; eight years of floundering and then we were back."

"The TV series was a huge success," I said. "Was that a surprise? After so long off the air, did you worry that people wouldn't be interested in the characters anymore?"

"It was all people kept banging on about. Those that had liked it before came back, and we added a new audience, a younger one. I was bored with them, but nobody else seemed to be."

"And of course, that was when you met Mary."

Watson nodded. "She'd been a production unit manager for a few years, hopping from one show to another. She'd been pushing for a producer's job, and they gave her to us, I think they thought she'd quit after a few weeks working with Holmes—I'm damn sure nobody else wanted the job—but she always was made of sterner stuff. She would weather his moods. Eventually he grew to respect her. 'The Woman,' he called her. It started off as an insult, but eventually it was a compliment. To him she was the definite article. The Woman. To me, too, of course."

"You married in 1976."

Watson looked at the picture of Mary on his desk and finally I sensed warmth in him.

"We'd been a couple for a year or so. Kept it as quiet as possible, but that didn't last, people talk. You never can keep a secret on a set. We'd been on location for the Christmas special."

"'The Hounds of the Baskervilles'?"

"That's right. 1975. Buggering about on Dartmoor, freezing to the bone. Holmes was in a sour mood because Christopher Lee was the guest star and was getting all the attention. Second fiddle again, he never could stand it. He'd flounced off halfway through shooting and Mary was beside herself. She'd come to me, hoping I might be able to calm him down but nobody even knew where he'd gone. We shot around him as much as possible, and that night Mary and I had got drunk in the hotel, taking it in turns to moan about him. We ended up in bed and that was that. I suppose it was Holmes that brought us together, in his own strange way. Just as he would later tear us apart."

If Watson saw my surprised look at that, he ignored it, continuing:

"Of course, he re-appeared the next morning, acting as if nothing had happened, and we managed to get back on track."

```
INT. BASKERVILLE HALL
  SIR HENRY: How dare you, sir! I am a peer
    of the realm! What gives you the right to
    treat me in such a manner?
  HOLMES: The fact that I'm the only man who
    can protect you from the lumbering great
    mastiff that wants to chew on your kidneys.
```

"YOU WERE MARRIED to Mary for eight years," I said.

I'd thought about asking Watson to clarify what he had meant when he'd said that Holmes had torn he and Mary apart, but we'd get there soon enough. I imagined he'd be more open if I let him tell his story in his own time.

He seemed distracted now, that sharp, staccato manner of his having softened into genuine reminiscence. It was clear that Mary was the one thing that broke through his cold exterior.

"Eight wonderful years," he agreed, "happiest time of my life. We bought this place, our seaside retreat. She'd always wanted to live by the sea. Never went in it, just loved to hear the noise of the tide. In the winter, when all the tourists are gone, you have the place to yourself. Wonderful. An empty beach, haunted by summers."

The softness that had begun to creep into his tone when discussing Mary was more noticeable.

"It's a beautiful town," I said. "I used to come here when I was a child."

He nodded, though I'm not entirely sure he was paying attention to me. He was lost in memories of his own.

"I made her happy," he said. "At least, I think I did."

"I'm sure she was," I said. "I've read a lot of interviews with people who knew her and they always remark on how happy she was, how full of life." That last comment might have been tactless. I hadn't intended it to be, but once out of my mouth, the words worried me.

He turned to look at me. "I know she was happy," he said, with a slight trace of anger. "That wasn't my point."

"Sorry." I wasn't altogether sure what I was apologising for. I only knew that the gentle, reminiscent Watson showed signs of slipping away again. "It's obvious you would have done anything for her," I said, desperate to bring him back.

His eyes turned to the window again. "I did," he said, his meaning far from clear.

I felt like I was losing control of the interview, and I tried to think of ways to bring it back on track. Before I could say anything, though, he carried on talking.

"It was no way to go," he said, "unfair. Cramps, swelling, blurred vision. Headaches. Reading about that stupid woman in the papers, the American singer, whole thing presented as if it were a noble battle. Posh doctors running around. Her fans filling the Internet with insubstantial prayers. Whole thing played out like a soap opera. Rubbish. Nothing noble about it."

He looked at me and the anger was still there, a cold, dangerous thing that I realised was not directed at me, but at the world in general.

"I only hope you never see someone you love go through that sort of pain," he said. "That perfect, glittering presence, reduced to a thing of screaming, sweat and death."

He picked up the picture of her on the desk and stared at it.

"I try and remember her like this. Not the corpse he reduced her to. I got rid of most of her things. Didn't want them cluttering the house. Reminding me. This is all I need."

He put the picture down and got up. "More coffee. I need a break."

Without waiting for my answer—and, in truth, I didn't really know what to say—he picked up my mug and the cafetiere and walked out of the study. I was left on my own, staring at the posters on the wall and trying to make sense of what I'd just heard.

Mary Watson had died of a seizure. That's all that I had known—my knowledge of John Watson and his life was embarrassingly encyclopaedic; it was all *most* people had known. From what Watson had just said, it sounded though the cause of that seizure had been pregnancy. The American singer he was referring to could only be Miko Clash[13] who had recently, publicly, suffered from pre-eclampsia giving birth to twins. But if Mary had died during pregnancy, why had the fact been hidden? The obvious reason was because John Watson, sterile thanks to TB, couldn't be the father.

I stared at the dictaphone on the desk and wondered what I had stumbled upon.

If Watson wasn't the father, then who was? My mind kept returning to the news clipping on the wall. Holmes and Watson on Blackpool front, the seeds of murder just a column-inch away. Was that possible? When I had asked Watson when he had truly begun to hate Holmes, he had said 1984, avoiding my attempts to force a specific answer. "When he died?" I had asked. Watson had just smiled.

It was absurd. I was jumping to conclusions, reading too far between the lines. My obsession for crime fiction—fostered by the comedic work of the man I was interviewing—was colouring my judgement. There was no way my suspicions could be correct.

Was there?

---

[13]Real name: Rene Adler, probably most famous for her single 'Eat Me' (Sony, 2013).

HOLMES: How many times must I tell you,
Watson? It's always a mistake to theorise
before you're in full possession of the
facts.

WATSON: Like the time you burst into the
Coco Club claiming Mimi DeVaux must be the
Brixton Strangler? An assertion based only
on the size of her biceps and the speed
with which she could knock up a reef knot?

HOLMES: How was I suppose to guess at the
services Madame Mimi offered her clients?
Unbelievable. I'll never see the like
again. Like a Sunday roast being trussed
up for the pot. The man must have been mad.

WATSON: Him and the rest of the cabinet.

THE DOOR OPENED and John Watson returned, carrying a tray of drinks.

I jumped up to help him, but he waved me away.

"More than capable," he said.

He put the tray down on the desk and poured two cups of coffee. He passed me one and took the other. For a moment we just sat there, an awkward silence hanging between us. I took a sip of the coffee. It was far too strong, but I continued to work at it; better that than sit there doing nothing.

"I've probably said too much," he said, after a couple of minutes. "Know I have. Stupid. Shouldn't have let you come. Missed it. That's the truth of it. Stupid profession, putting people in the spotlight, turning them into stars, making people need the attention. Adoration. Pathetic, really. Agent told me you were doing a book, and I felt the old thrill. To be important."

"You're very important to me," I admitted, slightly embarrassed at the turn of the conversation. "I've been a fan since I was a kid." I considered for a moment, then reached down to my bag and pulled out the book, handing it over to him. "I bought that when I was eleven. Always loved crime stories, and I thought it was a serious book."

He smiled, and for the first time there was a kindness to it. "Serious book? Arguably, it's neither."

"But I loved it. Read it over and over again until I could recite the comics by heart. Then I found the radio series on cassette. Then the TV show when they finally released it on video. Holmes and Watson were my heroes. Friends, almost. Well, Watson at least, *you*; Holmes was too cold, too remote. He was funny, but you didn't like him. Not in the same way. The doctor felt like someone you wanted to know, the warm, faithful, kind man who would be the best friend you could have. I think I loved him a little."

Now it was me that had said too much. He didn't look concerned, though; in fact, he was in agreement.

"So many did." He stroked the cover of the book. "All the letters. The autographs. It never affected Sherlock. Probably because he'd *always* believed he was special. Me? I could never refuse it. The social events, the women. So many women. Sherlock could resist those as well, of course. All except one. Mine."

He looked at me and the anger had gone, to be replaced with a gentle, almost fatalistic, look of comfort.

"That's what I always assumed. That Sherlock wanted Mary because she was mine. Because finally I had someone else I needed in my life. Someone I needed more than him."

"Second fiddle," I said.

"Exactly that. So he charmed her. And he could be charming, when he really tried. Mary and I were having a rough couple of weeks. My fault. I'd been unfaithful and careless about it. Holmes saw his opportunity and struck. Talk about careless. He got her pregnant.

"She'd always wanted children, but had accepted that, with me, she could never have them. We talked about it. Did I want a termination? I did. God help me, of course I did. The idea of the baby being his. But I thought that maybe, the child... it could be something that would bring us all together. It would paper over the cracks. She'd have what she'd always wanted. He would have won his little battle, and I... well, I would still have Mary. Of course, that's not quite how it worked out."

"She died."

"And the baby died with her. Eclampsia."

He looked over towards his wailing wall, casting his eyes over the memories.

"He killed her. With his child. No more. No more Sherlock bloody Holmes."

"The jellyfish sting?"

He looked confused.

"The newspaper article on the wall," I explained, "about you turning on the lights at Blackpool. Next to it there's an article about someone dying from a jellyfish sting. Anaphylactic shock. I assumed it gave you the idea?"

"It must have done," he nodded. "I'd never realised. The things we soak up when we're moving through the world. When bees are threatened, they release what is known as an alarm pheromone, the scent of which drives the rest of the swarm to attack. To protect the hive. Like almost anything in life—with the notable exception of true happiness—it can be synthesised. Smells like bananas. I poured it on him and watched them go wild. I had to run, didn't want to be caught in my own trap, but I heard him scream with every step. Not so funny now. Except to me. He made me laugh."

I felt sick. What was I supposed to do? How did he expect me to react to this? I could hardly not tell the police, could I? Hero or not, the man was a murderer. Perhaps I could sympathise, understand what had driven him to it, but that was neither here nor there. He had killed his partner of thirty-six years. That was not something you could just shrug off. My stomach churned violently, just thinking about it.

"Some people die after a single sting," he continued. "Those with severe allergic reactions. But most people, those that have not built up a natural immunity at least, will die if they're stung enough. Renal failure or rhabdomyolysis. Do you know what that is?"

I shook my head. I felt too nauseous to even speak.

"It's a common condition in trauma victims. The skeletal tissue breaks down, releasing proteins into the bloodstream. Some of those proteins can damage other organs. All very complicated. Don't really know the ins and outs myself. Point is, it can kill.

"In Holmes' case, it wasn't even necessary. He was severely allergic. How wonderful was that? He finally found the one thing he wasn't brilliant at. Keeping insects. Brilliant. Now that's a punchline."

"What—" I pressed my fingers to my mouth, trying to compose myself, I felt sure I was going to be sick. "You can't just tell..." I bit back the nausea again. "What do you expect me to do about this?" I asked.

"Not much," he said. "I poured a whole bottle of this into your coffee."

He held up one of the bottles of e-cigarette liquid. The coffee-flavoured one. *Devil's Foot Vaping Supplies*, it said on the bottle, above a cartoon image of Satan, huffing on an e-cigarette.

"From what I gather, it's not an ideal murder weapon. The standard shop brands aren't quite strong enough. I import mine. Ten percent nicotine. Always was a martyr to my habit. I poured it into your cup before I brought it in, then added the coffee.

"When I went out there I meant to put poison in both our cups. Or the cafetiere, perhaps. French press. Not like I have much to live for. For some reason I didn't. Stupid. Can't have you telling people about Mary, though. Won't tarnish her memory. Say what they like about me. But not her. *I* have to remember her how she was in hospital. Soiled. Broken. Nobody else."

He held up the picture.

"They can remember her like this."

I couldn't hold it back any longer. I fell from my chair, vomiting, my muscles cramping.

Absurdly, I thought of the newspaper headline I'd seen when I'd first arrived here. The woman who had murdered her husband with nicotine. My murderer was always open to influence, it seemed. "The things we soak up when we're moving through the world..."

I'd never really thought about my own death. The circumstances of it. If I had, this would not have been something I could ever have predicted. Ceasing to be, in a study in Scarborough.

"I'd better get rid of this," I heard him say, reaching for my dictaphone. "Can't have anyone finding that can we?"

And then I realised. The cloud. Everything John Watson had said was backed up to the cloud. For all the good it would do me.

Never meet your heroes. Very true. It's funny the things people say. You ask a fan of a pop group what they'd do if they met their idol. "I'd just die!" they swoon. Yes. Exactly that.

INTERVIEWER: We're joined by Eddie Conan, close-friend of Arthur Doyle and executive producer of tonight's documentary.

EDDIE: Hi, Alex.

INTERVIEWER: It was you who exposed John Watson as the murderer of your friend.

EDDIE: It was. I was sorting through his belongings and I found the recording he'd made of their interview. It was backed up on his computer. I don't have to tell you how awful it was to hear it.

INTERVIEWER: It must have been terrible.

EDDIE: Heartbreaking. Arthur was such a good mate, you know? And to hear him die... And

Watson, a man loved by so many. To think he could have done such a thing.

INTERVIEWER: I believe the audio recording is to be played in full as part of tonight's film?

EDDIE: It is. We thought long and hard about it, but decided the public had a right to know. I think it's what Arthur would have wanted.

INTERVIEWER: Tomorrow also sees the release of the book you were co-writing with Arthur?

EDDIE: Yes, obviously it's not quite the book we planned, but I know he would have wanted me to finish it. It's a testament to his memory.

HOLMES: This is it, Watson, the final problem. With this case, my career will be over.

WATSON: Never, Holmes! You'll go on forever.

HOLMES: I think not. Everything has it's time, and mine is done.

WATSON: Fair enough.

EFFECTS: He lights his pipe.

WATSON: (Cont.) After all, there'll always be repeats.

THE SMALL
WORLD OF 221B

IAN EDGINTON

A hugely prolific comics writer, Ian has a clear fascination for English literature of a certain period, as a quick scan of his 2000 AD credits (Leviathan, Stickleback, Ampney Crucis) demonstrates. He jumped at this anthology, I'm glad to say, and 'The Small World of 221B' is a wonderful, playful contribution that sits squarely in the sandpit of the postmodern. It begins the descent into weird almost immediately...

IT IS STRANGE how quickly things can change.

How the life as we imagine it can be turned upon its head in the blink of an eye. One moment, everything is as it should be. God is in his Heaven and all is right with the world.

The next...

Well, to say everything I have ever come to believe is a lie would be a monumental understatement. I write these words, to what end I cannot say. I know no living human soul will ever see them, but I have become so accustomed to documenting the fantastic fiction that has become my life, I know no other way of articulating the events of the past twenty-four hours.

In times of crisis we fall back onto the comfortable, the favoured and familiar, and thus I once again find myself sitting at the dining table of 221B Baker Street, pen in hand. The gas lamps are lit, the fire crackles in the grate. The soporific metronome of the mantle clock marks the passing time. My good friend and colleague Mr. Sherlock Holmes reclines in his chair. Fingers steepled, eyes closed in quiet contemplation of the day's revelations. A sight I have witnessed countless times over the years, or—as it transpires—not at all.

My name is Doctor John Watson, and I am a fictional character.

I remember most precisely the first indication that all was not quite right with the world. It was a week ago today, May 22nd 18—, on the occasion of the marriage of Mr. Michael Stamford to one Mary Bennet of Longbourn, Hertfordshire. Stamford had written to me some months earlier asking if I would fulfil the role of best man at his wedding. His older brother was chief engineer on a dam construction somewhere in the Canadian wilds and unable to return home.

I initially declined. Stamford had been my dresser, working under me at Bart's, but we were by no means good friends. At best we were former colleagues, now acquaintances. I therefore felt uncomfortable playing such an intimate role in his forthcoming nuptials. It was Holmes who pointed out that were it not for Stamford, we might never have met.

"If he had not tapped you on the shoulder that day in the Criterion Bar, and you had not mentioned that, due to your dwindling army pension, you were looking for comfortable rooms at a reasonable price... Our lives would have been that much poorer for lacking the company of the other.

"As ordinary and uninspiring as the Stamfords of this world may be, they are the subtle catalysts who, by a myriad of minor choices, inch history along in increments. They are less about the broad strokes and more of a mosaic.

"Who knows, if everyone who stepped out of their front door this morning turned right, instead of left, how different the world might be?"

"So, it was a coincidence?" I replied.

Holmes regarded me with a familiar weary indulgence.

"By no means. The Criterion is the preferred watering hole of the staff and students of St. Bartholomew's Hospital. It is therefore highly likely that you and he would be there. Given your prior history, he would of course introduce himself. Your search for affordable lodgings would arise in conversation, as would mine, since I had spoken to Stamford about finding someone to share rooms with that very morning in the chemical laboratory at the hospital.

"For better or worse, dear fellow. Our lives are inextricably intertwined with his."

"Then you go and be his blessed best man!" I chimed.

Holmes did not reply. His look alone spoke volumes.

So it was that I wrote to Stamford, notifying him of my change of circumstances. Having chronicled the extraordinary exploits of Holmes and myself over the years, I can say with authority that writing my speech for Stamford's wedding felt like one of the twelve labours of Hercules. Even back in the day, we knew each other only sparingly, although some of the stories I heard tell of his youthful scrapes would make even a docker blush.

I presumed he had mellowed with age, but even so, I was still hard put to find the right words. Find them I did, and never was there a greater work of fiction. However, upon reaching Longbourn, the speech was the least of my concerns.

Life in the countryside has always proceeded at a slower pace than that of the town. Lacking in the smoke and cynicism of the city, it presents a green idyll. That is its charm. Of course, these things are as much a fabrication as my wedding speech, but even so, the English countryside does have a unique allure. An Arcadian Eden we have abandoned in a mad dash for futurity, but not, apparently, in Longbourn.

Stepping off the train, the place seemed as if from an age gone by. Stamford met me and took me in a small dog-cart to a local inn where he and I were staying. He was as ebullient and over-familiar as always. He'd certainly filled out. Younger than I by a good few years, his face was puffy and pale, with a florid bloom to his cheeks. The buttons on his waistcoat were certainly being put under strain, as was the collar of his shirt, which fought to restrain several chins. It is often thought that we in the medical profession, thanks to our knowledge of what may harm or ail the body, would treat our own with great respect. It is not always thus.

As we made our way to the George Inn, I remarked how the locals were dressed in a style that was in fashion in my grandfather's time. Even Stamford's own attire had an antique air to it.

"You know how it is in pedestrian backwaters like this, John. By the time the fads and fancies of London have permeated all the way down here, they're already old hat.

"To be honest, that's why I like it. For sure, the ladies are as interested in a man's prospects and position as they are in the city, but they're also willing to compromise a good deal too.

"Look at me. A dresser at Bart's. Not the income, nor attribution, to rise much more above my station. But here, I am assistant to the doctor and the local chemist to boot. I am respected in the community and shortly to have a wife from a family of good breeding. Not bad for a young shaver from Shoreditch, eh?"

I was unaware that Stamford was such a social climber, but scarcely surprised. His talk of young women, as if he were trading horseflesh, set my temper rising, but I held it in check and bit my tongue. Despite Holmes' counsel, I was already regretting accepting Stamford's invitation.

"And I've told them all about you." He winked, and nudged me with his elbow in an almost comedically conspiratorial fashion. "About how I introduced you to Mr. Sherlock Holmes—the great detective!"

So there it was. I, too, was being traded. I had not been invited to his wedding because of our past association or his brother's inability to attend, but rather because of my current connection with Holmes.

"Pity he didn't come with you. Still, I bet you've some tales to tell, eh? Ones that didn't make the pages of the *Strand*?"

My jaw ached and head throbbed from clenching my back teeth in repressed anger. Fortunately we arrived at the inn, where I disembarked in no small haste. I retired to my room, my head now pounding. I drew the curtains, kicked off my shoes and lay back on the bed, my arm flung over my eyes to bar even the slightest blade of light. This was no ordinary attack of cephalagia. Under any other circumstances, I would have sent to the village doctor or chemist for a powder, but given Stamford's link with both, I chose to endure the discomfort and hopefully sleep it off.

I dozed fitfully, imagining at one point there was someone else in the room. A shape or shadow. The geography of the room rippling as it passed by the foot of my bed. I awoke several hours later, the low afternoon sun suffusing the curtains with a radiant red glow. Stamford was hammering on my door.

"I say, Watson! Are you alright in there? It's almost time for the off and I've not heard a peep from you since you arrived!"

I opened the door, tousled and bleary-eyed. Stamford's chuckle did not help my demeanour.

"Good God, man, you look as if you've tied one on already. You need to pace yourself, old fellow, the night is young!"

"I have not being drinking," I assured him. "I have had the most wretched headache, which seems to be abating, if you will kindly lower your tone."

On hearing this, Stamford, to his credit, did seem genuinely concerned.

"Now, isn't that the dickens! When I first washed up in Longbourn, I was struck by a similar malediction. You must be made of sterner stuff, I was laid low for days.

"Fact is, it's how I met my Mary. Her harpy of a mother heard that there was a handsome, stricken stranger in the village and sent her along with soup and kind words to minister to my fevered brow.

"Best be warned, Mrs. Bennet's married off all but one of her five daughters. If she catches wind you're in the market, she'll try and pair you up as well."

Once again I could feel my ill-humour stirring. "I am not 'in the market,' Stamford. I am a widower."

That at least appeared to penetrate his thick skin, and bought a flush of embarrassment to his cheeks. "Of course, forgive me. I meant no disrespect."

I realised he was a fool, not a fiend, and perhaps I was judging him too harshly.

"I know, and I apologise for speaking so sharply. This damned head has put me in an ill-humour, I'm snapping and snarling like a tatters-dog."

"Then what you need is good food, fine wine and sparkling company! Sadly you won't find any of that here, but if you'd care to spruce yourself up and meet me downstairs in half an hour, I'll see you fed, watered and entertained to your heart's content!"

Either my headache had passed or Stamford's relentless good humour had browbeaten me into submission, but I actually felt my spirits lifted by his puppyish ebullience. I bathed, dressed for dinner and joined him a short while later. He introduced me to his circle of friends, half a dozen in all and whose names, I confess, I had forgotten by the end of the evening. The food was fair, the wine passable and the company entertaining. It was clear Stamford's chums were intrigued with how exotic I seemed.

Very few of them had ever travelled beyond the county's bounds, let alone London, and when I mentioned my time serving—in Fifth Northumberland Fusiliers and later the Berkshires—during the Second Afghan War, they were both bemused and confused, unaware that such a conflict had taken place.

Likewise, when Stamford—despite my protests—attempted to apprise them of my adventures with Sherlock Holmes, they did not believe him. They thought they were tall tales by which he was making sport of simple country folk. To them, the London he described was as fantastic as far Ophir or Samarkand. I truly did not know what to make of it all. The fashions were not the only things behind the times. These were not ignorant men, yet their knowledge of life beyond Longbourn was out of date by a century or more.

They attributed their confusion to the copious amounts of wine they had consumed and soon thought nothing of it. I, on the other hand, had been drinking frugally—wishing to spare my poor head further distress—and was conscious of this discrepancy. The hour grew late and so, shortly before midnight, I made my excuses, bade the company goodnight and retired to my room. As I undressed, my mind raced, searching for an explanation.

The most vital tool at a doctor's disposal is not a stethoscope or scalpel, but his own five senses, and above all observation. What others dismiss as inconsequential may well mean the difference between life and death. My friend Sherlock Holmes has elevated this to a fine art and I, in my own modest way, have sought to hone my own abilities on the whetstone of his teaching. Nothing must be overlooked, as he once remarked.

"You know my method. It is founded on the observation of trifles."

The following day, the day of the wedding. I discovered there was less in the way of trifles and more a banquet. The entire ensemble—bride, groom, guests, vicar and all—looked as if they had stepped out of the pages of history. There were a number of British officers present, all in full dress uniform which, by their cut and style, I was able to narrow the period to somewhere around the late-Georgian era.

In fact, I was the one who looked out of place, and I drew a number curious glances. Mary Bennet, the bride, was a wan young woman whose expression was perpetually inclined to the morose, even on this, her supposed happiest of days. She was well-mannered and reserved when Stamford introduced us, but there was no denying that like everyone else, she saw me as quite the oddity and hastened to move on.

Stamford was also spot-on with regards his mother-in-law. Blustering and belligerent, Mrs. Bennet set upon me with the focus of a hare-coursing hound. I was given the family history, chapter and verse—its marriages, connections and the availability of her daughter, Catherine—all at breakneck speed. As I avoided one subject, she would raise another undeterred, moving with the dexterity and tenacity of a prize-fighter.

Fortunately, her husband stepped in to save me, and with a masterful touch of her elbow guided her back towards the white lace maelstrom.

"Come, my dear, let us first make sure this daughter is wedded and away before we seek to cast off the last one. There's still the chance young Stamford will come to his senses and make a bolt for the gate."

I nodded in gratitude and he returned the gesture. The wedding banquet and speeches proceeded as expected. As the afternoon wore on, I slowly slipped towards the periphery with the intention of retrieving my bags from the inn and boarding the first train for London as soon as was humanly possible.

My manoeuvring had not gone unnoticed when I was approached by the second eldest Bennet daughter, now Mrs. Elizabeth Darcy.

"Dr. Watson, are you leaving? I was hoping you could spare a few moments to talk?"

"Unfortunately, I must return to London. I have a practice and engagements that I simply cannot defer."

"Ah, yes. London. To hear my brother-in-law speak of it, it has changed a great deal since I was there last. A great deal indeed."

"Well, life in the city does move at a frantic pace."

She stepped nearer to me, closing the gap between us. There was a flicker of urgency in her expression.

"Doctor, some here see, but choose to say nothing. Others do not see at all, but you and I, we know everything is not as it appears. Do we look as strange to you, as you do to us?"

I hesitated for a moment, uncertain how to reply to her cryptic question, but there was truly only one answer.

"Yes. Although to my eyes, it is as if you are all living in the past."

"You're not the first person to say that. There have been others, like yourself, who have passed through Longbourn. And others still who looked to us to be from even older times. Clad in doublet and hose.

"It is as if... there are different ages occupying the same space, like books upon a shelf, where the edge of one brushes against another."

As fantastic as it sounded, I could not fault her reasoning.

There was a sharp mind and keen intellect at work here.

"How do you come by that conclusion?"

"Observation and analysis. The acquisition of information. If I hear of a visitor in the vicinity, a new face, I make a point of interviewing them. After that, I attempt to reach a logical conclusion, however seemingly impossible the facts. If there is no other explanation, it simply must be the truth."

I could not help but smile.

Mrs. Darcy, however, did not.

"Do I amuse you, sir?"

"No, please do not be offended. Your methodology is very similar to that of a good friend of mine, Mr. Sherlock Holmes. A detective of some repute. In fact I intend to see him as soon as I reach London. He may be able to shed some light on all of this."

"Then make haste. Go now. The longer you tarry here, the more you will change. Like your friend Stamford, your tastes, thoughts and opinions will subtly shift to fit in with the rest of us."

"What do you mean?"

"I have seen it happen. Travellers, outsiders like yourself who have lingered too long and are now indistinguishable from the residents herein. Several of the men you dined with last night were once as you are now."

I needed no further persuading. I thanked Mrs. Darcy for her advice and in under three hours was on the train and London-bound once more. As I left Longbourn behind, I was yet again struck by a vile headache. Not as debilitating as the first, but a discomfort I could have well done without.

I slept the bulk of the journey, waking refreshed as we pulled into King's Cross Station. I jumped into a hansom and bade the cabbie drive flat-out for Baker Street with promise of a suitable remuneration if we made good time.

That we did, and soon I was home, taking the stairs two at a time, almost colliding with a tall, mature, yet handsome looking woman as I turned on the corner.

"More haste, less speed, young man! You'll do yourself—or worse, someone else—an injury jumping around like jackanapes!"

She spoke with a soft Edinburgh burr cut through with a core of steel. It was a tone I heard in numerous matrons and ward sisters over the years.

"Please, forgive me."

I stepped aside and let her pass. I couldn't help but smile. It had been a long time since I had been called a young man, as the grey at my temples would attest. However, I imagined that to her, all men, irrespective of age were 'young men.' Silly boys who on occasion had to be brought up short and put in their place.

"We shall see. We shall see."

I dashed into 221B to find Holmes standing before the fire, staring intently at his open pocket-watch.

"Holmes! Holmes, I have something extraordinary to tell you!"

Holmes response was to raise the index finger of his left hand, indicating for me to be quiet.

"But Holmes!"

His eyebrows flicked into a high arch and I fell suitably silent. Without looking up, he withdrew a small folded square of white paper from his waistcoat pocket and handed it to me.

> *Watson,*
> *Look in the corner, by the window. Do not react.*

Refolding the paper, I acted as nonchalantly as I dared.

"Well, I suppose it isn't so important it won't keep until after dinner. Was that a new client, by the way?"

I turned to look out of the window, as if to observe Holmes' recent guest as she left the house.

"What was it? Missing jewels? Errant husband?"

Holmes' note was an enigma; there was no one there. I was about to announce the same, thinking he was playing me for a fool, when something by the window moved. It had the form of a man but taller, seven feet at least. It appeared to wrap its surroundings about itself, the same way in nature an insect may resemble a leaf or branch to prevent itself being preyed upon. This, though, was another level of complexity entirely. It mimicked not only a section of the wall, wallpaper and all, but the pictures thereon, as well as part of the bureau and a chair.

I heard Holmes cluck his tongue against his teeth as he would occasionally do as an act of rapprochement and I quickly turned my gaze back towards the window.

"Although, from her demeanour, I would judge she is more of a housekeeper, rather than the lady of the house, hm?"

As the clock struck six, I felt myself jump. At the same time, a sudden breeze brushed my face. When the last chime sounded, Holmes exploded across the room.

"My dear fellow, you were superb! Nerves of steel! Bravo! Bravo!"

I hazarded a glance to where the figure had stood, but it was no longer there.

"They appear every six hours and for a duration of five minutes to five hours. That gust you felt was his instantaneous departure, a rush of air filling the vacuum he vacated."

I poured myself a large brandy.

"Holmes, what in God's name is going on? What was that... thing?"

"I call them 'phantoms,' what else? They manifested shortly after you left."

"*They*? You mean there's more than one?"

"They appear singly, but by observing their differing body shapes and gait, I have been able to distinguish at least three distinct individuals."

"What are they? What do they want?"

"I do not know, and it is quite exhilarating! For now, they seem content to observe, but with their level of technology, I can scarcely surmise their further intentions."

"Are you enjoying this?"

"Absolutely. How often are we engaged to solve the mysteries of others? Now we have one of our very own, right here!"

Holmes crossed to where his 'phantom' had been standing and dropped into a crouch, lightly brushing the carpet with his fingertips.

"See, the nap has been compressed where he stood, meaning our visitor has mass. And when he disappears there is the rush of air, meaning he occupies space as well. Hah! Have you ever known anything like it?"

I finished my brandy in one gulp.

"Yes, I believe I have."

"Watson?"

I poured us both another and motioned for him to sit.

Cradling his glass, Holmes gave me a wry smile.

"The floor is yours, Doctor. I am all ears."

For the next hour or so, I regaled him with the story of my sojourn to Longbourn, sparing no details, including my conversation with Mrs. Darcy and the spectral visitation of my fever dream.

After I'd finished, he sat in silence for a few moments, letting the data bed in. His eyes flashed across at the clock.

"We have a little over four hours before the next shift arrives. We can do it! Yes, by Heaven, I believe we can."

I was, by this point, completely confused.

"Do what, Holmes?"

Holmes sprang to his feet.

"Snare ourselves a phantom!"

"And how do you propose we do that?"

But I was talking to myself. Holmes had already left the room and crossed the hallway into mine. I followed after, to find my bedroom was now home to a jumble of boxes and crates containing an assorted array of odd-looking equipment. On my bed lay a dozen lengths of quartz crystal, three feet long, encased in finely wrought copper cages. The crystals themselves had copper wires running through them and exiting at either end in delicate plumes. They were clearly meant to be attached to something, but what, I could not imagine.

"What is all this, Holmes?"

"A missing-persons case."

Holmes scooped up the nearest box and carried it through to the next room. With little option but to comply, I followed suit.

"You were right, Watson, she is a housekeeper. Her name is Mrs. Watchett, and her employer has disappeared, from inside a locked room, no less.

"Certain aspects of the case piqued my interest and I thought it would pass the time until your return."

We passed each other on the landing as we carried the cargo to and fro, continuing the conversation as we went.

"It was most perplexing. The more I understood, the less sense it made. I could find no trace of foul play. Neither Mrs. Watchett nor any of his other friends stood to gain a great deal from the man's passing. There were no romantic entanglements or unsavoury habits that could have lead to blackmail or murder."

"You know Holmes, people do sometimes just walk out of their lives. The pressure and responsibility of work or family life can make them simply snap."

"But not this fellow," said Holmes. "He was driven. Dedicated. His closest friend, Philby, said that on the night before his disappearance, he had arranged a dinner party for his friends. He spoke to them about his discovery and even demonstrated a working model which they dismissed as clever trickery.

"Philby said his friend took affront to this and was intent on proving them all wrong. They never saw him again after that night."

I paused to help Holmes with a particularly heavy crate.

"Mrs. Watchett let me read her employer's journals, and it all fell into place. He had not disappeared at all. He occupied the same space, but not the same time. What we are carrying in these boxes are, in truth, the spare components of a time machine."

I stopped dead in my tracks.

"Don't be absurd. Time travel? Such a thing isn't possible!"

"Isn't it? How about an English village, living two hundred years behind the times? Or a spectral figure clothed in a science we cannot yet comprehend?

"Absurd or not. I can only follow where the data leads. Think, Watson, of all the scientific advances we have today and are yet to come. Someone has to be the first to discover them. To break ground in the realm of the unknown. Why is this any different?"

I paused for thought, attempting to formulate an argument, but as ever, I could not fault Holmes' logic.

"So, I assume you have a plan?"

"Of sorts. From the time traveller's notes, I have determined that in order to move through time, one must first establish a zone of temporal grace. A bubble, if you will, of real time, that will shield you from the march of years beyond. If not, you would wither and die of old age in moments. We shall do the same with this room. Trapping the phantom within."

"Holmes, it's just struck me. You've not once mentioned this fellow's name. Who is he?"

"Of course, his name. His name is..."

Holmes stopped, and for the first time I saw a flash of genuine confusion cross his face; and something else. Fear. Holmes was afraid.

"Watson, for the life of me, I do not know! My mind betrays me. How could I have taken the case without even knowing his name? Now I think back, even Mrs. Watchett did not name him. I have always simply thought of him as the time traveller."

I laid a reassuring hand on his arm.

"Holmes, I am with you through thick and thin, you know that. But I sense there are facets and angles to all of this that we cannot yet perceive, and it would be a dangerous falsehood to think we have a grip on them.

"Our world, right now is quicksand. We must tread carefully."

Holmes' mood lightened a little.

"Thank you, Watson. You are my rock, as always, but for now, tempus fugit! We have much to do and little enough time to do it in!"

The hours passed in a flurry of activity as Holmes unpacked the eccentric array of items and began piecing them together using the missing man's notes as a guide. I, in turn, was primarily relegated to heavy lifting and the pouring of drinks.

A little before midnight, we slumped into our seats, joints and heads aching. In front of the hearth lay a grey metal box, the size of a tea chest. Its upper surface was encrusted with switches, dials and gauges, while its bottom edges were fringed with sockets out of which snaked a plethora of cables wired up to the caged crystals in each corner of the room.

"Holmes, if this snare of your works, and we truly trap a phantom, won't we be in the room with it?"

"Yes, but I'm afraid there's no other way if we are going to try and communicate with it. If things should go awry, however, do you have your revolver to hand?"

I reached over and patted the pocket of my jacket, which was draped over the back of the settee.

"It goes without saying."

A sudden short breeze sent the gas lamps guttering.

"Watson, we are not alone."

As coolly as possible, I slid my jacket down beside me and reached inside for my pistol.

Holmes leant forwards and smartly flipped a sequence of switches. Dials glowed and the box began to admit a low, bass hum. In each corner of the room, the crystals too were suffused with a soft white light.

"Watson, observe!"

I followed Holmes gaze. Back by the window, apparently the phantom's favourite spot, its chameleon-like camouflage was failing. The images of the room it had wrapped itself in had begun to warp and distort like a funhouse hall of mirrors.

With a final frantic shimmer, it dissipated and the true phantom was revealed.

"Good Lord!" I heard Holmes exclaim, in a whisper.

My estimation had been correct, the being before us was easily seven feet tall and humanoid. It was wearing what I could perceive as a skin-tight, one-piece suit. Grey, but shot through, head-to-foot, with intricate silver thread. The thread itself swam like smoke over its surface, which swirled and whirled, creating intricate patterns before breaking apart to recombine in even more elaborate designs. The only constant were the geometric shapes imprinted on the forearms, which the phantom kept stabbing at with growing agitation.

Each hand had only three fingers and a thumb, long and

slender, with four joints each. The index finger was half the
length again of the others and it was with this our visitor was
urgently pressing the symbols on his arm.

Its face and the few exposed parts of its body were also
humanoid, but the skin was a pastel, pale green, almost yellow,
rather like the belly of a turtle. Its eyes were twice the size of
normal, with deep purple irises, but no whites to speak of. It
bore a wide, lipless mouth filled with small, flat teeth. There
was no nose, but two small oval vents edged with cartilage.

It looked up at us from its work and I saw what I can only
term as dread in its eyes. It was terrified of us. It chattered to
itself, its voice sounding as if someone were plucking at a harp
with a dinner fork.

Holmes stepped forwards, his hand on my forearm, urging
me to keep my revolver low and out of sight for now.

"We mean you no harm. We merely wish to talk. Do you
understand me?"

In response, the phantom spurred on its attempts, tapping
frantically at its forearm.

"Holmes, I do believe it is more afraid of us that we are of it."

"Quite, so but if we cannot communicate, it will all be for
naught!"

The phantom chirruped again in a less discordant fashion
and I swear I saw it smile.

Behind us, the metal box began emitting a discordant grinding
noise as black smoke issued from the sockets. Their connections
to the crystals broke, in a cascade of orange sparks.

"It's doing something to the device!"

Holmes' cry came too late as the phantom vanished, leaving
only the now-familiar dash of displaced air.

We quickly yanked the cables from the box, which had given
up the ghost. The room reeked of burnt metal. A pall of acrid
smoke hung in the air. I flung wide the windows to save our
breath.

"Damn! Damn and blast!"

"There was nothing more we could do, Holmes. We tried."

I studied the charred ruin.

"Can it be repaired?"

"Not by me. The only one who might is whatshisname, who's disappeared into God knows when!"

"And he won't be very amenable to assist us when he sees what we've done to his device!"

A flicker of a smile twitched at the corner of Holmes' mouth before exploding in a great guffaw of laughter. It proved infectious, and seconds later, we were both laughing like fools. It was the rain clearing the air after a storm.

There was a knock at the door.

"Mrs. Hudson?"

"Visiting a friend in Worthing."

We quickly regained our composure. I crossed to the door, retrieving my revolver en route while Holmes straightened his waistcoat and jacket.

He gave me a short nod and I opened the door.

There was another phantom.

"Dr. Watson?"

His voice sounded artificial. Smooth, flawless and perfectly enunciated, it did not quite match the movement of his lips.

"May I come in?"

"By all means."

I stepped back, keeping my gun to my side, hidden behind my leg.

The visitor stooped to enter. He was a different kettle of fish to our previous guest. His suit was black, not grey, chased through with gold thread instead of silver. His skin colour was a darker green than the other, and heavily lined. He gave the impression of being an older, senior figure.

Holmes gestured for him to sit.

"Please, be seated."

Despite his size, he comfortably folded himself into the chair.

"Mr. Holmes, this is a great pleasure. I have long been an admirer of yours."

"Then you have me at a disadvantage, Mr...?"

"My name in my native tongue does not translate easily. You may know me by occupation instead. I am the Curator."

"Curator of what?" I enquired.

"Of all that remains of the human race. Of you. Its fiction."

I was dumbstruck.

The seconds that followed after were an eternity.

Holmes smiled serenely and nodded, as if the secrets of the universe has just been revealed to him.

"Of course... of course we are."

"It may be awkward to explain, but I will do my best to put it in terms you can comprehend."

"Don't be so damn patronising!" I snapped.

"Lower your hackles, Watson. There's no need to be so defensive. From what we have seen thus far, I imagine there are concepts and technologies at work that even *I* may be hard-pressed to comprehend."

"There is no easy way to say this," said the Curator. "So I will come to straight to the point. The human race is extinct. We estimate it has been so for over two hundred and fifty thousand years."

"How did it happen? How did they die?"

Holmes hid it well, but there was no denying the crack of emotion in his voice.

"We are not entirely sure. Possibly war, or radical environmental change, but we cannot say with any certainty. There is evidence they went to the stars, but we have never encountered them on our travels.

"Fortunately we were able to salvage a good deal of their literary and historical works from data banks that were preserved underground."

"Data banks?" I asked.

"Mechanical libraries. Machine memories. We are in one now."

"This is all some sort of construct?" said Holmes

"Exactly. We are inside a machine mind. Via an interface, I can insert my consciousness directly into it. It is a completely immersive experience. For instance, I can feel the heat from the fire in the grate. The breeze through the window carries with it the odours of coal fires, undercut with horse manure."

"Can you die here?" I asked.

"No, Doctor, I cannot, but please, keep your revolver to hand if it makes you feel at ease."

Feeling suitably chastened, I laid my pistol on the table.

"So, what are we?" I asked. "If we are not men?"

"You are the literary work of Sir Arthur Conan Doyle, a Scottish physician of your time. His stories about you were considered some of the greatest ever works in the field of crime fiction. To many of my race, they still are. I can give you access to his biography, if you so wish?"

"If you created us, can we not also meet our maker?" said Holmes.

"Not quite. Not yet. That is partly why I am here. The entire canon of your stories resides in the Aleph—the machine mind—but it is so much more than that. It is a consciousness in its own right."

Holmes sat forward, intrigued.

"Is it self-aware?"

"Yes. They are commonplace in our culture. My university alone has six hundred. This one is solely dedicated to the works of your people. It has taken all the information regarding yourselves, stories and otherwise, and along with all available historical data of the period, extrapolated an environment for you to live in."

Something akin to a smile crossed the Curator's face.

"The result of which, is you are not bound by your stories anymore, Mr. Holmes. You are... chaotic variables. Your lives are your own."

This sounded too good to be true.

"Why would you do this for us? To what end?"

"By observing you, we hope to learn what mankind was like. We shall know them by their works."

"So, we are exhibits in a zoo!" I said.

"Not at all. Many of the others do not even suspect their world is any different from the way it has always been."

If this was meant to put me at my ease, it did not work.

"Others?"

"Other works of fiction, Watson," said Holmes. "Like the observant Mrs. Darcy and our missing time-traveller?"

"The works of Jane Austen and Herbert George Wells." replied the Curator. "However, some of them, like yourselves and Mrs. Darcy, have begun to perceive the changes. You are not the only ones. Interestingly, they are characters who are free thinkers; daring, even dangerous. They are also unexpectedly expanding the remits of the program and pushing at the boundaries of their fictional worlds, crossing over from one to another. The Aleph accommodates the shift, but not without some discomfort."

"So I've discovered," I said.

"If they remain too long out of place, the Aleph will attempt to acclimatise them into their new world. Blend them in, so their presence is not so conspicuous."

"It's not going quite as planned, though, is it?" said Holmes. "That other fellow who looked half scared to death. He had more of the engineer than the academic about him."

"Yes. Which is why I am here," said the Curator. "Occurrences of migration are rising, and my university faculty faces a difficult choice. One that is not solely ours to make, but yours also. All who are like you.

"On the one hand, the Aleph can shut down and reinitialise all of the fictional worlds, but with new restrictions. Your awareness for one, would be purposefully limited."

"Lobotomised," I said.

"In a manner of speaking. It would also render our study moot if you were so constrained. The other choice, and the one favoured by my colleagues and myself, is to let things go on as they are. More so, in fact. We would let migration continue unrestricted for those with a mind to travel. There would just be some checks and balances to ensure the rules of internal logic may be stretched, but not broken. We wished to see the nature of mankind; how better than to give them new worlds to explore?"

"Be careful what you wish for," I said.

The Curator pushed himself up from his chair.

"So, gentlemen, I have laid my case before you. What is your decision? Will you take it?"

I caught Holmes' eye. This whole thing was madness, but from one look I knew what he was thinking. I could not let him go alone, and he knew it. With a nod, I gave my affirmation.

Holmes sprang to his feet.

"Indeed we do! The game! My dear Curator. The game is afoot!"

THE FINAL CONJURATION

ADRIAN TCHAIKOVSKY

"It'll probably be secondary-world," said Adrian when I spoke to him about this, "as that's my thing." And oddly, 'The Final Conjuration' takes both the longest and shortest leap with the concept of the anthology, actually 'porting Doyle's original creation directly out of Victorian England and dropping him into the ultra-High-Fantasy world of the seven great Lords Wizard. I suppose it's cheating, but the detective's palpable frustration at being unable to apply his famous maxim is worth it.

YOU WILL HAVE heard, of course, of those events in the Year of the Yellow Cat that almost plunged us all into a disastrous war. A handful of days, now consigned to history, when the great wizard-lords mustered their most destructive energies, and armies of conjured demons roamed restless on every border, waiting to be unleashed.

And yet the details of these events are as obscure as they are notable. How the business was resolved has been hidden behind a veil for many decades, by those fearing that the revelation might open up wounds only recently scabbed over.

Now, however, these matters have passed into something close to myth, so that my master, the Green Wizard Ang Tze, has graciously given permission to this humble scholar to narrate the full truth, many particulars of which are known to none but I.

You will recall that year was marked by many an inauspicious omen, so that throughout the drawn-out months of the dry season the wise prepared for ill fortune, and the foolish sought to perpetrate it.

This is how it started: I had been seated on an ornamental hill overlooking the demesne of my master, and pondering certain philosophical absolutes, when my master's summons shattered my train of thought. I was transported in the blink of an eye into his audience chamber, a nine-sided doorless vessel of glass which was lit emerald by his radiance.

"Wu Tsan," he said, "a most unwished-for occurrence has transpired. I am called to the demesne of Men Shen, the Blue Wizard."

I was speechless. Rarely indeed would any of the great lords venture into the sanctum of another.

"The call has gone out to all of us," he clarified. "Some fate has befallen Men Shen."

My heart was all but stilled. The Blue Wizard, no less than my master, was one of the great lords. To even so much as inconvenience him would require a degree of power only possessed by his peers. The seven wizard lords had ruled in peace—if a quarrelsome and acrimonious peace—for many long centuries, but the spectre of war between them had always been present. Such a war would reshape the world, transform or obliterate millions, perhaps destroy all.

"Wu Tsan," my master said, naming me once more. "Of my servants, you are noted for your open and enquiring mind. Today such qualities may find favour. Travel with me, and we shall see what has become of Men Shen."

*   *   *

THEY WERE ALL present: the Green Wizard was the last to arrive. It is a testament to the splendour of the lords of our world that they held my attention, and not the shocking devastation of our surroundings.

Soo Mi the Red was attired in feathers wreathed in flames, beautiful and terrible. Amyat Pre the Golden bore about her broad body many hundredweights of precious metal in chains and amulets and mail. The Black Wizard Lu, squat and toad-like, wore festering rags and stank of swamp water, a stark contrast to the Ochre Wizard, whose name had been cut from her in an assassination attempt a thousand years before. She was slender as a pole, taller than anyone there by a head. Last, there was Sun Gong the White, androgynous, flesh gleaming softly, whose eyes were covered with smoked glass so that the fires of her/his gaze could not burn us.

Nobody spoke in the long moments after my master's arrival. The great lords of the world were uncomfortable in the presence of those who could challenge them.

Around us was the demesne of the Blue Wizard. Some great force had torn it apart, so that blocks and scraps of its dense blue-black stone were scattered for miles around us. I could just make out the foundations of villages, like the stubs of rotten teeth. The toll amongst the peasantry must have been terrible. All too often, as the philosophers write, a slight against one great lord is written in the blood of thousands.

Lu the Black was already indicating the true reason for the summons. The deaths of peasants was a tragedy, but it would not have moved my master and his peers to gather here.

There was Men Shen the Blue Wizard, but blue no longer. His complexion and attire alike were granite grey, and he stood in an attitude of alarm, hands raised to perform his magic. Alas, that magic had not saved him. Here was not the man himself, but only an effigy. He had been turned to stone.

"So," said the Red Wizard, her flames dancing higher. "At

last someone has had their fill of peace. We knew it would come to this."

"We knew no such thing," said nameless Ochre. "And we do not know what has happened now."

"What's *happened*?" demanded Lu. "One of you has broken the peace! One of you has initiated a cowardly blow against Men Shen, striking him down in his very hall. One of you, in short, believes himself strong enough to rule the world alone."

He looked on my master as he said this, and Ang Tze replied hotly, "One of us? Or *you*? For you were never a friend to Men Shen."

"We have none of us ever been friends," the White Wizard pronounced. "I regret that our truce has not held. I will return to my own demesne and prepare to defend the security of my holdings." And he/she was gone in a scattering of light.

"Wait," said Amyat Pre the Golden hurriedly. "This need not descend to war. We have all built much in these peaceful centuries. All will be lost and scattered if we fight."

"Then let the malefactor confess," the Red Wizard declared. "Let the guilty party be brought forth, and stripped of power. Or war there will be."

WE TRAVELLED BACK to my master's demesne. Ang Tze kept me by his side and I had never seen him more troubled.

"Wu Tsan, you have aided me in the past, in seeking hard-to-find truths," he said to me.

I confirmed that it had been my pleasure.

"You have a singular source of information. You know the demon to which I refer." Ang Tze pinched at the bridge of his nose, a sign of unhappiness. "If ever there was need of true knowledge, it is now. Go, conjure your familiar. Find out who struck down Men Shen, or the world may end in many-coloured fire."

* * *

IT IS NO great matter for magicians to call up demons. Most summon soldiers or workers, winged steeds, or to gain knowledge of other realms beyond our own.

I believe I am the only magician who has called up a demon of thought: not one that can impart secrets of the unknown, but one that can examine the known, and order and interpret the details of everyday life. Of course, I am a scholar first and foremost, and not a practical magician. I have never sought to reshape the world, only to understand it.

I had called up this particular demon several times in the past, when my own perspicacity had proved unequal to whatever problem was facing me. Now, I judged, I required all its formidable powers of investigation.

I burned the requisite herbs, burdening the air of my chambers with the potent haze of ginseng, radiant lotus and coca leaf, and I drew out the sigils and the numerals that were its secret name. In a trance, I reached out into the gloomy and cramped netherworld that was the demon's own demesne, that half-glimpsed place of enclosing walls, spaces crowded with too many bodies, air that was rank and malodorous with the smoke of chimneys.

And I named it. I called it through the boundaries between the worlds, opening the way. Sometimes I would have to try many times before it deigned to answer.

Not this time, though. This time I simply uttered, "Sherlock," and it was there.

I REMEMBER WHEN I first summoned the Sherlock.

It was a trivial matter, but then I have always been a trivial man. There was unrest within one of my lord's villages and I was sent to quell it. Being no creature of force or violence, I instead sought to understand the cause, discovering it to be a matter of thefts from many of the people there: the disappearance of small items of sentimental value.

I summoned the Sherlock as an academic exercise. I had often wondered if it might be possible to conjure a demon of investigation. In many ways the goings-on of our own world at a mundane level are great mysteries. We are very well informed about the conditions of a hundred other worlds. We understand the underlying nature of the fabric of reality and how to reweave, stitch and cut it to our liking. The truth of how a farmer lost his shoe, or what lies behind a closed door: these are not fit subjects for magic. Magic is a distorting mirror. The one thing you cannot see in it is the truth.

So, after much experimentation, I successfully conjured the Sherlock for the first time. It appeared as a very pale, very tall man, its features as sharp and hooked as an eagle's, wearing severe and drab clothes of an alien cloth and fashion. The scent of coca redoubled as it manifested, so that I thought that must be the native atmosphere of its home. The demon looked on me and my surroundings—so different from its gloomy netherworld home—with the wide eyes of a man gripped by a fever.

Some demons rail against captivity and service. Others wheedle and beg and bargain. The Sherlock was not like this. For a while I could not engage with it at all. It did not seem to credit me with any objective existence. It is a humbling prospect, to have the demon you have summoned refuse to consent to your being. At last I fell to describing the puzzle that I was working on, and that caught the Sherlock's interest. An abrupt and striking change came over it, lending an animation to its gaunt features. It asked me many questions, and I confess I could not answer most of them. Instead, the demon and I visited many places where the thefts had occurred, and it made enquiry of the terrified peasantry.

At first I thought my experiment was a failure. Although the

Sherlock had shown a sharp and enquiring mind, as might be expected from a demon of its nature, it was unable to account for the thefts. Its failure frustrated it, and at last it confronted me, insisting that there must be some information hidden from it. "I cannot see any possible means by which this act has been accomplished," it told me agitatedly, and I felt bitterly disappointed that I had nothing to show my master.

But then the demon went on, "Of course there must be some connection to the tin-trader who visited this place some months before, as every one of the victims confirms having dealt with her, and as the miniature animals that they purchased have been stolen along with their things of value. And yet the trader is long-departed, and unless there were some way for her geegaws to have come to life and accomplished the thefts themselves, I cannot see how her involvement is relevant. It is true that there are small marks and scratches on the shelves and altars where the valuables were on display, as of diminutive animal tracks. But all this is plainly impossible, so I discount it."

I tried to explain to the Sherlock that these things were not impossible at all, and it eyed me sternly.

"Well then, *hypothetically*, that would be your solution," it stated, "but they are impossible and so it cannot be."

But it was. Even though it strained the credulity of a demon, it was.

THIS TIME, WHEN the Sherlock manifested, matters were different. Each time before, the creature had appeared before me gripped by the fevers of the coca leaf, solving my puzzles detachedly, as an academic exercise. Now, when I called, the Sherlock almost fell at my feet. It is not uncommon for demons to fight each other in their own worlds, but I had not expected it of this cerebral monster. However, its garments were torn and it was bruised and sodden. For a moment I thought it would be no use to me, and despaired of ever finding another demon of its capabilities. However, it lifted its head and fixed me with its crystal gaze.

"So," it said, looking on me and my surroundings. "One last time I am amongst the illusory Chinamen. But I have taken nothing, and this is no phantasy of my idling mind. Is this some relapse in my last moments, to spare me from the pain?"

"O demon, but this is reality, such as it is," I told it politely.

It looked at me with a wintry smile. "Why, if I believed that, I would be mad indeed. I remember my previous visions well, and there was nothing in them but nonsense: a fantastical reimagining of my real cases transfigured under the influence of the cocaine I used to fend off the tedium of inaction." And I saw the smile freeze and fade. "And yet here I am."

It swayed suddenly, and I thought that it would fall. "Have you been making war upon other demons?" I asked it solicitously.

"You could say that," it murmured, closing its steely eyes for a moment. It seemed only a shadow of the haughty creature I had previously conjured and made use of.

THE ADVENTURE OF the stolen heirlooms was too minor a matter to reach the ears of the Green Wizard, of course, but I next had cause to conjure the Sherlock when one of my master's own servants met a suspicious demise. The deceased woman was a steward of one of Ang Tze's retreats, a place where he often spent less guarded hours, and there was a concern her killer had gained secrets from her. As a junior magician in his service, I was tasked to find the truth. After bumbling about the retreat, questioning the other servants and getting nowhere, I despaired of solving the mystery on my own.

When the demon came, it was relaxed, with a sharp humour. It dismissed almost everything I told it, and informed me frankly that many things self-evident to me were impossible, up to and including my summoning of itself. Working with it was a belittling experience, but at the same time the eccentric keenness of its wits was unparalleled.

"If there was such a thing as this magic you describe, then simply discover the truth with a spell," it suggested derisively. I was forced to explain that, of all magic's many capabilities, the art is lamentably poor at uncovering mundane truth. Magic is a force drawn from the imagination. A man who scries for his future, or the deeds of his paramour, is more likely to see a scene drawn from his own suspicions than any objective reality.

The Sherlock found this deeply amusing, and remarked, "Yes, that is exactly as I would imagine the failings of sorcery to be, which only reinforces my certainty that all of this is a mere delusion. However, it is a delusion that offers me a conundrum and it so happens that my real existence is painfully devoid of any such at present, so let us solve this imaginary murder of yours."

None of the other servants had seen anything, and the enchantments that kept the retreat spotless had removed any tell-tale clues, much to the Sherlock's derision. The demon did raise an eyebrow when I explained that we could also interrogate the victim herself. I dutifully raised her ghost once more so that the Sherlock could hear her testimony: the story of a shadowy figure coalescing in the room with her, the icy fingers about her temples, the sense that understanding was being drawn from her. All these facts had filled me with a dread that I would have to report to the Green Wizard both that his secrets had been stolen, and that the culprits were unknown.

The Sherlock was undismayed, however. After questioning the ghost carefully, it informed me briskly that, whilst it had no wish to gain any understanding of witchcraft, it was clear on one thing: the account we had just heard was not that of the victim, but of the murderer itself! I was taken aback, but its logic was unassailable. The perspective of the ghost's account had included various details the victim could not have observed.

Unmasked, the possessing demon within the corpse attacked us, but my defensive magics mastered it and I was able to deliver it to my master for deconstruction. Once again the assistance of the Sherlock had proved invaluable.

IN THE MATTER of the Blue Wizard, I was hard-pressed to focus the demon on the matter in hand. The idea that its surroundings might be as real—more real—than those it had hailed from became more and more oppressive to it. "This world of yours is madness," it remarked, as I flew it to the ruin of Men Shen's demesne in a chariot of bones. "How can anything be solved by deductive reasoning, in a world where every possibility is impossible?" Only reminders of its past successes would mollify it for a time, until a blackness of soul would arise in it again.

Still, the scene of devastation seemed to give it a fresh lease of enthusiasm, and I shadowed the demon about the great heap of broken stones, and stood before the petrified Blue Wizard, cringing from the expression that was Men Shen's last legacy to the world.

The Sherlock quizzed me of what he called 'suspects' then, and so I explained to him that the statue had been one of the seven great wizard lords who ruled the known world. I set out the natures and characters of those who might have done the deed: Red, Ochre, White, Black and Golden. "One of these must have acted to destroy the Blue Wizard."

"Unless it was your master." The demon wagged a finger at me. "I do not know your insane and unreasonable magic, but from your description, not one of your great conjurors was a friend to this man. Your Green Wizard may just as easily be the perpetrator of this crime. Until eliminated by some logic of motive or opportunity, he remains a suspect. I would say *means*, also, but it is clear, by the madness of this place, that such means are commonplace. Is it really the case that your rulers sought to create stability by each of them possessing the power to annihilate the others, in the hope that mutual fear would keep them all in line? I cannot see such a system succeeding. Far better to disarm all, than go on building greater guns." And, in response to my assertion that the system had served us well for millennia, it only pointed out, "Until now."

And then it insisted that it would have to meet with my master.

MY RISE IN the hierarchy of my master's household is not entirely uncoupled from my use of the Sherlock at times of need. It is common for a magician of my stature to come to rely on certain demons whose strengths and capabilities are known, but my relationship with the Sherlock has always been unusual. I have found it hard to remember, when it has been conjured into the world, which of us is master, and which servant. No other demon has dismissed our true world as nothing but a trick of its own mind.

By the fourth summoning it had experienced enough of my world and my ways to gain confidence in its methods despite its disdain for magic. "Your sorcery may be absurd," it would tell me airily, "yet there is an internal logic to the madness, just as one often finds with even the most demented lunatics of the asylum. They are adrift from the world, and yet within their heads there is a consistency of delusion which renders them predictable. So it is with your magic and, given that it is the creation of the underused portions of my brain, I would expect no less."

And then it would turn to the matter in hand—in that case, I was tracking a monstrous demon hound which some renegade had unleashed in my master's demesne, and which seemed to give the Sherlock even more cause to believe that all he saw had its origin within his own drug-twisted memories. And of course he examined the spoor, questioned the witnesses, enumerated the suspects, and without any grasp of the principles of magic, he read the true conjuror of the demon hound as clearly as if the villain had signed his name in bold characters on the creature's forehead.

IN BRINGING THE Sherlock before Ang Tze I was dreadfully afraid that I had overstepped my place. It was not for a mere demon, after all, to question one of the great mage-lords, and I anticipated the Sherlock's condescending manner would see both it and myself banished to some dungeon plane for a thousand years. The Green Wizard is wise, however, and the Sherlock demonstrated a deftness that, whilst it fell short of proper deference, at least demonstrated that the creature was used to standing before the demon lords of its own world without disgracing itself.

The Sherlock asked many questions about Men Shen, about the relations between the magi, and then about each of the 'suspects,' as he referred to my master's peers. He had Ang Tze conjure up images of each: likenesses tainted, of course, by the Green Wizard's personal feelings, so that each was decidedly less flattering than the original might have preferred.

"Well?" my master enquired politely of the demon. "My servant Wu Tsan speaks highly of your abilities, demon. Can it be that this... mere talk has enabled you to uncover which of my fellows murdered Men Shen?"

"Not as yet," the Sherlock confessed. "This mere talk is doubtless a curious way to proceed, for one who has the power to remake the world in his image, but in this I have the advantage. I have never sought to remake the world in my image, but rather to understand others through the way they remake the world— albeit in a less literal manner than you might."

The Green Wizard hunched forwards. "And what now, demon?" he asked.

"Now? Now I must speak to each one of your fellow lords," the Sherlock told him, "and I judge your land similar enough to mine that this will not happen without your recommendation."

The Green Wizard laughed as I have not seen him do for many moons. "Yes indeed," he confirmed, "I shall send Wu Tsan to each of them, with you in his retinue, and I shall watch through his eyes as you strut before them, demon. I wish to see how they will react to this impertinence. Perhaps the one that destroys you shall be the murderer."

The Sherlock only smiled thinly.

WE SURVIVED THE other interviews. I had not thought we would. Between the general animosity that exists between the great lords of the world—made worse by the fate of Men Shen—and the known arrogance of the Sherlock, I thought my fate surely sealed. My master would express his displeasure if I were slain, but he would not commence hostilities over one such as me.

And yet I lived, and I realised, as I watched the Sherlock perform before each of those terrible and powerful lords, that it had a hidden art for speaking plainly to the mighty. What the powers of its own world might have been, I cannot say, but I saw that the Sherlock had an art for manipulating and managing audiences with the great. As it spoke, its words were in turns provocation, suggestion, insinuation, redirection, so that each of the magi believed full well that they were masters of what was said and done, and yet I could see the Sherlock drawing from them the truths it sought, as if peering into their minds. They were all of them strongly warded against any magic that might seek to trawl their thoughts, but the Sherlock had none, and instead used their own natures against them, making them its accomplices in prying out what it wanted to know.

And at the end, after it had thoroughly interrogated Sun Gong the White—who could have annihilated us both just by opening his/her eyes—we returned to the demesne of my master and it informed me, "Now I am in a position to reveal to you who the villain is."

My joy must have appeared on my face, but the Sherlock lifted a thin finger sternly and said, "but I will not, unless you provide a service for me. I am loath to concede even the veneer of reality to anything that I have seen of your world here, but if there is a chance that any of this exists outside of my own racing mind, then I have something I must ask."

One does not perform services *for* demons; that is not what they are for. I could have used my powers and compelled the creature to speak. Perhaps I should have. I had an admiration for the Sherlock, though, grown from the many knots that it had elegantly unravelled for me in the past. "If it is in my power," I told it, "then yes."

SOON AFTER, WE were back in the shattered demesne of the Blue Wizard: the Sherlock and I, and also my master and his peers, the remaining mage lords standing mistrustfully together in one place. Soo Mi burned and Lu the Black glowered. Amyat Pre's thick fingers turned over her many ornaments. The argent embers of Sun Gong's eyes glimmered through her/his smoked lenses. The nameless Ochre Wizard stood still and lean, hands pressed together and eyes narrowed. And my master, of course, watched them all.

"You have been so kind as to educate me," the Sherlock announced, pacing slowly before them. "Each one of you has been candid about your opinions on one another and the deceased." His words were just a shade off being criticism. "I have seen each one of you through the eyes of the others—literally, given your ability to make real the images from within your mind. It is plain that each one of you had the capability to rid the world of Men Shen, if you were able to pierce his defences.

Equally plain is that such an act would have repercussions. You are even now standing on the brink of a destructive war that would destroy some of you, and lessen the rest considerably."

"Enough," Lu snapped. "How does a demon think to lecture us on what is self-evident to all?"

"The very self-evidence of this state of affairs is germane," the Sherlock informed him, with that maddening not-quite-insolence. "It begs the question: who benefits? Unless one of you has some great hidden advantage, that would allow that one to emerge from such a conflict unscathed and victorious, why provoke it?"

I saw the great magicians eyeing one another uneasily. Was there such an advantage? Surely they had all sought one from time to time.

"However, there is another matter that has led me to my conclusions, and it is rooted in your magical abilities, and the limits of them."

"We acknowledge no limits," Soo Mi declared, but again the Sherlock somehow managed to contradict a great lord and survive.

"Alas, there is one, or why would my services be required? You cannot use your magic to recreate the truth, only to create new falsehoods. All that you showed me, all the images of one another and of this place, they were drawn from your minds, coloured by your individual natures. I look upon you with unbiased eyes. I can see precisely how your images of one another diverge from reality. Similarly, I have seen the late Men Shen through your eyes. Not one of you liked him, that is certain."

I wondered then if the demon was about to declare them all part of some baffling conspiracy, but of course the Sherlock was thinking on a level quite beyond me. Now it was indicating the petrified remains of the Blue Wizard.

"Looking upon your late colleague, I am forced to conclude,

however, that he was an admirable individual. These features are commanding and strong, showing a great many good qualities of the mind behind them. He is stronger-framed than you recall—a physical specimen of note. He is taller, even, than you showed him to me, and by a considerable margin."

The expressions of the mage lords showed that they had not come here to have the dead man praised to them. The Sherlock smiled patiently.

"I have compared and contrasted all of your images of Men Shen," it explained. "Combining then, cancelling out your different dislikes, I have a good picture of the victim when he lived. Taking into account your avowed prejudices concerning his person, I can come up with only one solution that is remotely plausible. This is not Men Shen. This effigy, in fact, has been created at the whim of someone whose mental image of Men Shen is far, far more flattering than yours: flattering enough that they have not been able to resist improving on nature at every turn."

"What are you saying?" demanded Amyat Pre.

"These are not the mortal remains of Men Shen," the Sherlock explained, "because Men Shen is not dead."

THEY WOULD HUNT down the Blue Wizard, after that, united in their desire to castigate him for his deception. Ranged against six equals, he was crushed, and so the world was rid of one of its great lords: the man who had sought to have his fellows battle one another until he could stride in his full power from the wreckage, to claim the world entire.

For myself I saw little of that, of course. Such matters are not for a poor magician such as I. I only knew that the favour of my master had been assured, and that I owed this to the perspicacity of the demon.

Of course, I could have broken my promise and simply

banished it, but in truth I felt beholden to the creature in a way that is unusual between magician and minion. The Sherlock was something more to me than a mere tool, and the favour it sought was not so very great, after all.

It was a matter of momentum, it said. When it returned to its world, it wished to be imparted with a precise degree of upward force.

It had been battling a fellow demon, of course, and so, once it had gone, I imagined it gaining the upper hand with one triumphant leap, springing high into the air. The upward force I had gifted it was considerable.

Unless, of course, it had been subject to a similar downward force when I had conjured it; unless it had been falling. But that is mere speculation, and I lack the Sherlock's deductive powers, to uncover the truth of it.

THE INNOCENT ICARUS

JAMES LOVEGROVE

James is one of my favourite authors to work with, and being himself an author of Holmesian fiction, was an easy choice for the gig. Eschewing the option of moving Holmes to a different time and place, James kept him in Victorian London, but changed the world itself, giving us a Victorian London where the extraordinary is altogether commonplace, and it's the mundane who are truly exceptional...

"Watson," said Sherlock Holmes as we took breakfast in our rooms at 221B Baker Street, "we are about to receive a visitor—and, one hopes, an interesting case to solve."

I would have commented to my friend that he was exhibiting remarkable powers of precognition, but for the fact that he was gazing out of the window onto the street as he voiced his observation. It transpired that a conveyance of some sort was pulling up outside our door, visible from his vantage point but not mine. The clatter of its wheels on the cobblestones was lost amid the usual rattle of early morning traffic and the cries of roving vendors.

"A two-man rickshaw," Holmes added, "privately owned. A person of some means, then."

By the time I got to the window all I could see was two liveried strongmen of the Hercules Category, panting hard as they took their rest between the rickshaw's traces. The vehicle's occupant had already exited and was at the front door, out of my eyeline.

Whoever it was, they had no need to knock, for Mrs. Hudson was already bustling down the hallway to let them in. That worthy woman, unlike Holmes, *did* possess powers of precognition. She was not gifted with the highest level of foresight, certainly not enough to land her a commission with Her Majesty's trusted inner circle of clairvoyants, among whom was counted Holmes' brother Mycroft, one of our nation's pre-eminent Cassandras. Mrs. Hudson's abilities were limited to the anticipation of guests arriving and the purveyance of refreshments that were exactly what the recipient desired. These skills suited her ideally in her role as landlady and housekeeper.

She ushered our visitor upstairs, and presently Holmes and I were in the company of a well-attired female in her mid-to-late forties, comely in appearance and refined in manners. She introduced herself as Lady Arabella Lanchester, and gratefully accepted the cup of tea that Mrs. Hudson brought her.

"Darjeeling," she said. "My favourite. And weak, too."

Mrs Hudson retired with a small smile of satisfaction. She was never wrong when gauging someone's taste in beverage or foodstuff.

"You are the wife of the industrialist Sir Hugh Lanchester," Holmes observed. "No. Correction. The widow."

Lady Arabella nodded briefly and bitterly.

"Indeed," my friend continued, "you have only recently been bereaved—within the past few hours. My deepest condolences."

The steely composure which Lady Arabella had been displaying up until then broke. A lace handkerchief appeared, and she dabbed at the corners of her eyes, trembling.

"I have been told," she said, "that you are something of a mind reader, Mr. Holmes. It seems I was not misinformed."

"On the contrary, madam, I can lay claim to no mental capabilities beyond those of the normal human brain, albeit one that has trained itself to note the minutiae and correlate them into meaningful conjecture."

"You are... a Typical?" said Lady Arabella, somewhat surprised.

"Indeed I am," said Holmes with hard-won, pardonable pride. "I belong to that vanishingly rare species, the man who is without powers of any description. I thought this was common knowledge. I am not in any Category. I cannot fly. I cannot light fires with but a thought. I cannot swim underwater indefinitely like a fish. I cannot, like my Achilles friend Dr. Watson here, withstand almost any physical injury. I can only think. But usually, thinking is sufficient."

"I am sorry."

"Don't be, madam. Your compassion is wasted. I have never felt that I have lost out, that I am somehow the lesser for my accident of birth. I am more than content with what I have made of myself. I resolved at an early age not to wallow in self-pity. Instead, I vowed that I would be anyone's equal, and superior to most, through the simple application of cerebral discipline. This has resulted in my attaining the position of the world's first and foremost consulting detective—whom you have come to see on a matter of pressing urgency connected with your late husband's demise."

"That is so, Mr Holmes," said Lady Arabella. "You see—"

"Let me stop you there if I may, your ladyship," said my friend, cushioning his peremptoriness with an affable laugh. "I have already perceived a great deal about the situation from your appearance. You dressed in some haste this morning. Your blouse is misbuttoned, although you seem unaware of the fact, which suggests distraction, an unbalancing of the mind's equilibrium. Furthermore, one of your hairpins has worked itself loose. The wife of a knight of the realm would not normally go abroad in public in anything but an immaculate state of dress. You have rushed here from your home at the earliest opportunity. Am I mistaken?"

"You are not, sir. I did not even call upon my maid to help me, but put on my outfit myself as best I could." She plucked at the misfastened blouse buttons absently and tried to locate the lock of hair that had come astray. "It has been a trying night, the worst of my life."

"The calamity which has befallen Sir Hugh," Holmes went on, "was a violent one, if I do not miss my guess. And you were there to witness it, or at least its after-effects."

"Does it show in my face?"

"Yes, but more so on your hands. Your fingernails, to be precise. You have washed thoroughly, I have no doubt, but alas, the evidence is still there."

Lady Arabella examined her fingers, and her lips took on a shape of appalled, crushing horror. "My husband's blood."

"Yes," said Holmes gravely. "Still encrusted beneath the tips of your nails. You held the body, cradled it *in extremis*."

The poor woman paled. The recollection was all too fresh, all too vivid. She went into a swoon, there in the chair, and I moved to seize her before she might slip to the floor.

Mrs. Hudson entered at that very moment with a jar of smelling salts.

"These are called for," she said, passing the jar to me, and I unstoppered it and applied it beneath Lady Arabella's nose, swiftly reviving her from her faint.

"I apologise," said her ladyship as Mrs. Hudson discreetly withdrew.

"No need," said Holmes with casual dismissal. "Frankly, I am amazed you have the presence of mind, not to mention the inner fibre, to be here at all. Most in your position would have succumbed to hysteria or shock by now. Your fortitude is impressive."

"My husband is dead," said Lady Arabella, resolute. "The police are of the view that he met his end through misadventure. I, Mr. Holmes, am convinced it was murder."

SHE LAID OUT the facts of the incident before us with remarkable poise and self-possession, given the circumstances. Sir Hugh Lanchester had not been dead some ten hours, yet his widow was able to furnish us with an account of events that was exceptional in its clear-eyed accuracy.

Sir Hugh had, the previous evening, taken a turn on the second-floor balcony of their home, as was his wont. The Lanchesters owned a large mansion on Richmond Hill, one of the benefits accrued from Sir Hugh's chain of cotton mills, an industry which had been so profitable to him that he had become one of Britain's richest men. After dinner, he liked to enjoy a cigar outdoors, weather permitting. His wife could not stand the smell of smoke in the house. She was unusually susceptible to all odours, she told us.

"You are an Olfactory," Holmes said.

"Just so."

"I noted the lack of perfume or any fragrance. I assumed you neglected to put any on in your haste to travel, but I did wonder whether it might be that you have a more than averagely acute sense of smell. Your preference for Darjeeling, one of the least pungent tea blends, seemed to confirm your Category."

While her husband was partaking of his cigar, Lady Arabella continued, she herself got ready for bed. She was startled by a short scream and then a loud, hideous thud. Hurrying outside in her nightgown, she discovered Sir Hugh dying on the lawn immediately below the balcony.

Shuddering at the memory, Lady Arabella said, "I did my best to tend to him, Mr. Holmes. Blood had been spilled, large amounts of it, and the stench—oh, God! I fought my nausea and tried to ignore it, even as I embraced Hugh and begged him to remain conscious. But he was fading fast, the light in his eyes dimming..."

"I am sure you did all you could, madam."

"I then raised the alarm, rousing the whole household. But it was too late. He—he was gone."

"How awful," I said.

"I despatched our personal Mercury to Richmond police station. He is one of the fastest of his kind, able to complete a mile-long journey such as that in under half a minute. He returned to inform me that constables were on their way, and duly they arrived, although there was little they could do beyond covering up the body and taking statements."

"They, I take it, felt there was nothing suspicious about the death?" said Holmes.

"They were of the opinion that Hugh must have slipped on the balcony, pitched himself over the balustrade, and fallen to his death. To them, it was obvious."

"There is nothing more deceptive than an obvious fact," my friend asserted. "You, on the other hand, discern foul play."

"My husband is—was," she corrected herself—"a Calculator. That is a Category whose members, aside from being able to perform advanced feats of mental arithmetic, are known for a certain ruthlessness and practicality. He was not a bad man, but he tended towards brusqueness in his dealings with others. That, and his material success, earned him envy and enmity, from both rivals and slighted business partners."

"He had many of the latter?"

"One in particular. Amos Pilkington, a Yorkshireman from whom Hugh purchased several mills as going concerns. Pilkington was supposed to oversee the running of those mills, but failed to hold up his side of the bargain, meaning Hugh had to do more of the work than was his due. In the end, Hugh edged Pilkington out of his seat on the board, for which he was rewarded with scorn and vituperation. Pilkington swore an oath that he would get even, although that was a year ago and in the intervening period he has done nothing to make good on the threat other than to instruct his lawyers to issue menacing letters and denounce my husband in public forums whenever the opportunity arises."

"Was this Mr. Pilkington left out of pocket when he lost his job?"

"On the contrary, he was paid off handsomely, and what with that and the price Hugh gave him for a half-share in his business, he has been left sitting very pretty indeed. Yet that is clearly not enough for him, nor can he stand the thought that it was his own indolence and incompetence—and, moreover, his propensity for drinking—which obliged Hugh to relieve him of his position."

"You believe he may be behind your husband's seeming accident?" I said. "Inveigled himself secretly into your house and toppled him off the balcony, maybe?"

"Put it this way," said Lady Arabella, "I would not be surprised. The trouble is, I know for certain that Pilkington is not in town. He keeps a *pied à terre* here, in Holland Park, but through mutual acquaintances I am given to understand that he has been ensconced at his country estate outside Harrogate since last Friday. There is one other, though, who has cause to hate Hugh."

"Perhaps a disgruntled employee?" said Holmes.

"How astute of you. Are you sure you are a Typical, sir? I suspect you of a telepathic talent that you choose to hide from the world."

"I am genuinely of no Category, madam. I merely make deductions based on the balance of probabilities. In this instance, it seems more than likely that your husband, who must have run a considerable workforce and who by your own admission could be brusque and unpersonable, would not command the unswerving admiration of all on his payroll."

"A steeplejack, by the name of Charlie Gartside. Hugh had to fire him last week for carelessness. Gartside was charged with carrying out maintenance on the chimney at the Shoreditch mill. It so happened that during the course of his duties he dropped a hod of bricks, nearly killing a couple of loom operators below as they arrived for work. Had the women not been Achilles Category like yourself, Dr. Watson, I dread to think of the outcome. Anyone else would have been brained, rather than merely stunned. It was an accident, but nonetheless Hugh had no choice but to hand Gartside his papers."

"Quite right," said I.

"Gartside is, of course, an Icarus," said Holmes.

"A flyer of some prowess and stamina," Lady Arabella affirmed.

"Valued in his profession for his ability to work at great heights and his freedom from fear of falling from them. I begin to divine the outline of something here. Is there anything else about your husband's death you can tell us? Any detail you may not have yet divulged?"

Her ladyship pondered, then said, "I cannot put my finger on precisely why I believe Hugh did not die through accident, other than to say that there was an odd aroma at the scene."

Holmes leaned forward in his seat with avidity. "I should be interested to hear what it was that an Olfactory detected, with her unusually sensitive nose."

"I may have been mistaken. In the grief and trauma of the moment, I was not at my most level-headed. It could be that I was imagining it."

"But...?"

"But I could swear I smelled burning."

"Burning?"

"As of a fireplace, or a steam locomotive."

"And this was not the ember of your husband's cigar, still alight?"

"It may well have been. The smouldering stub of the cigar was lying nearby him, scorching the grass. Perhaps that was all it was. Yet I am convinced otherwise."

LADY ARABELLA DEPARTED shortly afterwards, with assurances from Holmes that he would investigate her case. She told us she was going to stay with friends in Chelsea, but Holmes secured her permission to visit the house in Richmond so that he could survey the crime scene.

We set off thither by cab, post haste. It was a horse-drawn hansom rather than a somewhat cheaper rickshaw. Holmes preferred the smoother ride, even if it came at a premium and was accompanied by the racket of iron-shod hooves and the occasional unfortunate equine by-product. On the southward journey, we were overtaken several times by speeding Mercuries, human blurs weaving in and out of the traffic as they couriered letters, parcels and documents around the capital.

The Lanchesters' mansion afforded a spectacular view of both Richmond Park and the Thames meadowlands to the west, all the way to Windsor Castle. In the clear summer sky, flyers could be seen hurtling through the blue firmament, exulting in their freedom from gravity like wingless angels. If I could have belonged to any Category but my own, I would have wished to be an Icarus. Yet I had good cause to thank providence for making me Achilles by birth, else I might not have survived my tour of duty as an army medic in Afghanistan. More than once a jezail bullet which might have taken my life, or at least wounded me gravely, had bounced off my impermeable skin with no more effect than a dried pea from a child's pea shooter.

Having shown the butler a letter of introduction that Lady Arabella had drafted for us, we were permitted access to the back garden. The body had been removed, but the deep impression it had left on the lawn remained, as did the halo of blood spatters surrounding it, which had dried to a dark brown stickiness.

Holmes went down on all fours and inspected the spot minutely. He located Sir Hugh's cigar stub and spent some time sniffing both the rind of ash at one end and the butt at the other, which still bore the imprint of the dead man's teeth. Then he stood up and eyed the second-storey balcony from which the industrialist was supposed to have fallen.

"What do you observe, Watson?" he asked finally. "And note I said 'observe,' not 'see.'"

I paused before answering. From experience I knew that I was being invited to look past the obvious and that, lacking Holmes' perspicacity, I was apt to make a fool of myself if I were not careful.

"I see—pardon me, *observe*—a depression in the lawn commensurate with the body of an adult man plummeting from some height, and the attendant bloodstains resulting from injuries sustained upon impact. Nothing that I would not expect to observe."

"Quite so, but you are failing to take into account volume."

"Volume?"

"Mass, my friend. Quantity. Look how deep the depression is. Look how much blood there is and how far it has been flung. None of this suggests a fall from that balcony. Rather, it suggests a fall from a far greater altitude."

"You mean...?"

"It is my view, based on the evidence, that Sir Hugh plunged not from the house but from at least three hundred feet up."

"My God!" I cried. "You're saying he was picked up, borne skyward and dropped."

"Precisely. Murder, made to look as though it were mishap."

"Then the culprit must be..."

"Tut!" My friend raised an admonishing finger. "Let us not jump to conclusions. No one is guilty unless it has been proved beyond all reasonable doubt that it cannot be otherwise. We must find the steeplejack Charlie Gartside and interrogate him thoroughly."

FINDING GARTSIDE WAS not difficult for a man like Sherlock Holmes, with the services of the Baker Street Irregulars at his beck and call. This small army of street urchins counted every manner of Category among their number, including several of the Retentive persuasion, who forgot neither a face nor a place once they had committed it to memory. Presented with a name, they could tell you where the owner of that name had last been seen, what haunts he frequented and who his commonest associates were.

It was the head of the juvenile gang, Wiggins, who offered us Gartside's likeliest whereabouts: a pub in Bethnal Green called the Mason's Rest. In that seedy, sawdust-floored hostelry, Holmes and I cornered the aggrieved steeplejack, who responded to our approaches first with wariness and then anger.

"What, I'm being accused of murder, is it?" he declared. "I resent that!"

He made to flee, levitating from his barstool and making for the door. I barred his way, and he flew at me headlong, fully expecting that he would knock me flat. An Achilles, however, once he plants his feet, is not just invulnerable but more or less immoveable. Gartside came off the worse for the collision.

When Holmes had righted him and plied him with a glass of gin, Gartside became somewhat more amenable. My friend mollified him by telling him that while he had both the motive and the means to kill Sir Hugh Lanchester, Holmes himself had doubts about his guilt.

"I would say that, on the face of it, you could have done the deed," he said, "but somehow you are too obvious a suspect. It is almost as though someone would like us to believe you sneaked up on Sir Hugh from above while he was taking the air last night, swooped on him unawares, snatched him up into the sky and let him go."

"Last night?" said Gartside. "I wasn't anywhere near Richmond last night. I was here, at home, just round the corner."

"Can you prove that?"

"Yes. No," he amended. "I live alone. No wife, no family, just me. I was in from eight onward, asleep by ten. I have an attic room, which I enter by a skylight. Hardly anyone sees me come and go."

"So there is no one who can provide you with an alibi?"

"I don't think so. Oh, Lord, this is bad, isn't it? But it's not true. I didn't do nothing. I mean, I held a grudge against Lanchester, 'course I did. Taking my job from me like that, all for a silly slip. Nobody got hurt, did they? Accidents happen. Not something a man should lose his livelihood over. Word's got around now, though, ain't it? My reputation is gone. My name is mud. Nobody else will hire me, the man who the high and mighty Sir Hugh Lanchester sacked. I'm ruined. But..."

"But you're innocent of Sir Hugh's murder."

"As the driven snow. You've got to believe me, Mr. Holmes. Someone's setting me up. It has to be that. Someone wants me to take the fall for Lanchester's fall. You see that, don't you?"

"A SINGULAR CASE," said Holmes as we left the Mason's Rest, Gartside's plaintive plea still ringing in our ears.

"You don't reckon Gartside's lying, then?"

"Oh, it's perfectly possible, Watson. He tried to escape, after all, when we initially confronted him. That is indicative of guilt. Then again, no one takes well to accusations of murder, least of all the innocent. I am persuaded that his protestations are in earnest. We haven't yet got to the bottom of this puzzle, otherwise I would even now be sending a Mercury to Scotland

Yard with an invitation to come to Bethnal Green and collar Gartside."

"So who *is* responsible, if not Gartside?"

"Do you recall, Watson, a recent case similar in many of its aspects to this one?"

I racked my brains. "I fear I do not."

"It was quite the *cause célèbre* a few months back. The actress who was crushed to death by her lover, a Hercules stagehand? Had her skull mangled and her ribcage shattered like twigs by his bare hands? He went to the gallows for it, but proclaimed his innocence right up until the moment the scaffold opened beneath his feet."

"Ah yes, it's coming back to me. The girl was with child, was she not? And it was established that he slew her in a fit of rage, having decided that the baby was not his."

"There were rumours that she had been carrying on with another man, an aristocrat."

"Yes, the Earl of Bracewell. The stagehand all but accused *him* of the murder at the trial, but the nature of the actress's death meant the finger of blame could only be pointed at someone with Hercules-level strength. The Earl of Bracewell is a Mover, if I remember rightly, albeit with telekinesis of a very low grade. He can manipulate small objects with his mind, but hasn't the power to crush a person to death."

"Yes. Bracewell is no paragon. He is known for cheating at games, be it roulette or tennis, using his telekinesis to divert the ball in his favour. He's a rake and a profligate, too, but the actress's murder could not surely have been his doing, and must have been the stagehand's handiwork. A Crown Court jury came to that conclusion, at any rate. There is also the case of the Whig politician, Albert Filey."

"The chap who drowned in the Thames?"

"None other. Another apparent death by misadventure, like Sir Hugh's, although suicide was not ruled out by the coroner.

He plunged from the parapet of Westminster Bridge one foggy night last December. If the impact didn't kill him outright, the freezing water would have in no time."

"Wasn't there a scandal surrounding him? Something about him rigging a vote?"

"You misremember. It was Filey himself who was accusing one of his political opponents of stuffing the ballot boxes at a by-election. He promised to produce unequivocal proof, but died before he could. There was talk in some of the papers of a cover-up, a conspiracy to silence Filey, but nothing much came of it. Perhaps the fellow was under such intense pressure and scrutiny that he simply cracked."

"But you think otherwise. You think that that case, and the actress one, and now Sir Hugh's death, are all connected. They're all part of some wider pattern."

"What's interesting about the Honourable Albert Filey is that his brother, with whom he was on very poor terms, was a Poseidon. If anyone could have drowned him by main force, it would have been someone who was at home in the water as he was on land. No charges were pressed, no arrest was made, but the feeling persisted in a certain stratum of society that the other Filey—Cecil, I believe, was his name—might have been responsible. The two had had a falling out. Fraternal hatred spiralled out of control. Sibling spite soured into homicide. In the event, as if to give the hearsay validity, Cecil Filey took his own life not three weeks later. Drank arsenic. Intolerable remorse, it was assumed."

"If I follow your line of reasoning," I said, "it would appear that people are being implicated in murders they did not commit. That's the common thread that's emerging here. A Hercules, a Poseidon, an Icarus—in each instance someone is being made to look the obvious culprit, in order to deflect attention away from someone else."

"That is indeed how it looks. The question remains, however, who is doing this and how are they accomplishing it? Watson, if you will kindly see your own way home, I would like to wander alone a while and ruminate. There may be a single solution to all three cases, and if I can alight upon it, I may yet save Charlie Gartside from becoming a third innocent victim of a dastardly scheme."

IN THE EVENT, I did not see Holmes or even hear from him for a full twenty-four hours. I was visited at noon the next day at my practice by a Mercury messenger, who presented me with a note in my friend's handwriting summoning me to an address in Shadwell. I gave the messenger a shilling, and he thanked me in speech so rapid and garbled that I couldn't make out one word in three, before racing off at such speed he seemed to vanish.

The address turned out to be an engineer's workshop.

"My investigations have brought me inexorably to this place," said Holmes as he met me outside, "the doorstep of a scoundrel as ingenious and villainous as any we have encountered in our adventures together. I fear I shall have need of your invulnerability, old friend, and perhaps also your service pistol, which I am glad to see you have brought along, judging by the bulge in your jacket pocket."

"Your note implied I might need it."

"I pray my instincts are wrong," said Holmes, "yet I fear they are not. Let us go in."

The engineering workshop looked much like any other of its ilk, a barnlike premises that housed machinery and tools—lathes, drills, bandsaws. Its sole occupant was also its sole proprietor, one Algernon Roxton, according to the hoarding above the entrance.

Roxton was a small, sallow-complexioned individual with thinning mousy hair and an unprepossessing face which seemed set in a permanent sneer. Some childhood disease—polio, I adjudged—had left him with a withered left leg, a defect he had remedied by fixing an elaborate metal brace to the limb which cunningly utilised pistons and springs to lend support and an almost full range of motion. He came towards us with scarcely a limp, the brace creaking ever so slightly as he walked.

"Gentlemen," he said, his hands hidden behind his back, "how may I be of assistance?"

"You may assist us," replied Holmes, "by confessing, Mr. Roxton, to at least three counts of premeditated, cold-blooded murder. It will go easier on you, and save us all a great deal of bother, if you do."

To Roxton's credit, he scarcely even batted an eyelid. Instead, he whipped his hands out from behind him. In one was a kind of claw-like gauntlet, which he slipped over the other. It hissed with power as he flexed the fingers.

Reaching for Holmes with this device, he attempted to grasp my friend's neck.

I swiftly interposed myself between the two of them, raising an arm so that Roxton's gauntlet clamped onto my wrist rather than around Holmes' throat. The pressure Roxton brought to bear on me was immense, and inflicted considerable pain—but not, of course, any harm.

I grinned at the man, and he in return frowned in dismay.

"Dash it all," he cried. "Your bones should be powder by now, your wrist as narrow as a pipe cleaner."

"Luck of the draw," I said, and punched him unconscious.

BENEATH THE WORKSHOP, accessible via a trapdoor, lay another workshop, a secondary lair where Roxton stored contraptions he had developed which lent him the abilities of any physical Category you might care to name. There was a submersible kit, a kind of diving apparatus which allowed him to remain underwater for a significant span of time, breathing through a tube connected to a canister of compressed oxygen. There was a flying pack which used rocket propulsion to suspend him in the air and flit through the skies guided by rudimentary batlike wings. There was a mate to the gauntlet, which gave him a grip strength equivalent to that of the mightiest Hercules. There was even a prototype of what appeared to be a pair of steam-powered, wheeled boots with which he would be able to propel himself along, somewhat like an ice skater, but as fast as a Mercury.

Roxton, when he came round, was reluctant to talk at first. Holmes, however, menaced him with my revolver, and soon enough his tongue loosened.

Not only had Roxton been crippled by polio when he was a small boy, he had also been born Typical. Throughout his formative years, his lack of Category had eaten at him. He was jealous of his schoolmates as they discovered their various abilities, especially those who were fleet of foot or who could lift great weights. He was taunted for his sickliness and his Typicality. The jibes sank in deep and fuelled a lifelong misanthropy.

Finding that he had an aptitude for engineering, Roxton turned it into a vocation. He was highly proficient at it, something of a genius. Yet still resentment of others simmered away inside. The establishment, although it paid him well for the work he did building bridges and steam engines and factory machinery, never respected him the way it had the likes of Brunel and Telford. He did not move in the right circles, alienated from society by his normality, his freakish ordinariness. He should have been lauded and laureled; instead, he was kept at arm's length and treated with a grudging toleration at best.

So he decided to put his one skill—his "only God-given talent," in his words—to use in a different field. He would make himself indispensable to the great and good by volunteering to do their dirty work for them, at a fee. He would become a freelance assassin, tailoring his methods of execution so as to direct suspicion away from whoever hired him and onto other parties, incriminating them by the very gifts he resented.

As Holmes pressed him further, Roxton admitted that he was behind Sir Hugh Lanchester's death and that his paymaster was none other than Amos Pilkington, Sir Hugh's erstwhile business associate. "Since I'm likely to be feeling the hangman's noose," he said, "I may as well tell all. Besides, I bet it was Pilkington who gave me up, wasn't it? Drunkard like that. Just the sort to turn on you when the chips are down."

"As a matter of fact, it was the Earl of Bracewell," said Holmes.

"The posh devil." Roxton snorted in disgust. "Got that girl pregnant. Couldn't handle the potential disgrace to his family name."

"I ingratiated myself with him at his club last night," Holmes said. "Challenged him to a few frames of snooker. Beat him soundly, even though he kept trying to force the cue ball to swerve whenever I struck it. There's only so much topspin that a feeble nudge from a Mover's mind can counteract, however. Before long, he lost his temper and started yelling at me, calling me all sorts of names. A very sore loser. He became so enraged, just as I wanted, that the moment I mentioned the actress you killed for him, he blurted out that she was a whore and better off dead and he was glad she had died before she could give birth to his illegitimate offspring—although that is a politer phrase than the actual one he used to describe the child. This was in full view of his fellow club members, and I must say the effect was electric. Consternation. Pandemonium. His Grace had, with a few rash, poorly chosen words, all but admitted culpability for a capital offence, and before an audience of his peers, what's more, none of whom had a particular affection for him, given that he was a known cheat and cozener. After that, he turned on you pretty quickly, Mr. Roxton."

"Why am I surprised? Anything to save his own skin."

"And here we are," Holmes concluded. "Watson and I will be escorting you to the nearest police station, where you will be free to confess your role in the three murders I have ascribed to you and any others I may have missed out. I shall be especially keen for you to absolve Charlie Gartside of blame for Sir Hugh's death. Although the man has yet to be arrested, I reckon it's only a matter of time before Scotland Yard put two and two together and bring him in. With luck, we can forestall that unfortunate occurrence."

As we dragged the defeated, crestfallen Roxton out of his workshop, he said, "I understand that you, Mr. Holmes, are a Typical, like me. That's what Dr. Watson writes in the stories he publishes about you."

"And it's the truth."

"How do you bear it? How can you stand being a weakling compared with everyone else? Doesn't it fill you with hatred?"

"If it ever did," said Holmes, "I am long past caring. I may not be a Hercules, an Achilles, a Cassandra, even an Olfactory, but I have compensated in my own way. I have not been consumed with bitterness about what I am not, but rather been consumed with desire to be the best I can be, given my limitations. Mother Nature bestows her several gifts upon us. Some are glorious and enviable and come without effort. Others, like mine, need work but are no less potent once fully realised."

"You make it sound so... so straightforward."

"That's because it is," said Holmes. "I like to think I now inhabit a unique Category, my very own, a denomination in which the developed powers of ratiocination and analytical reasoning are the sole qualifying criteria."

"And does it have a name, this special, one-man Category of yours?" said Roxton with mockery and just a touch of condescension.

"It does," said my friend phlegmatically. "Because there is

nothing difficult about it, other than the application of intellect and observation, which are available to all, I have dubbed it with an appropriately simple and universal title."

"Which is?"

"Elementary, Roxton. Elementary."

Half There/ All There

GLEN MEHN

I met Glen through mutual friends at various London publishing events, and have had the good fortune to appear alongside him in two anthologies; Glen's a thrilling new talent, and you'll be seeing more from him. 'Half There/All There' is a beautiful story set in the bohemian world of Andy Warhol's 'Factory,' and perfectly grounded, not just in the mood of that crowd, but in the events of the time. It also imbues Holmes with a sort of fierce sadness and regret that took me by surprise, and which will follow you long after the story's done.

THE WORLD KNOWS Sherlock Holmes through these pages as a calculating machine, seeking justice with cold logic, but I know another side of him. A soft side, a less serious side. Playful. Actually funny, even, if you can believe it, and one of the best friends a man could ever have, if you could get past his weirdness.

I first met Sherlock Holmes at the closing party of the first Factory, that silver box filled with pills and people, covered in tin foil, mylar, and plexiglass. He walked in, this tall, rail-thin man, white skin and black hair slicked back, cut short, like a banker or lawyer or something. Not my type, but I couldn't stop watching. He was the opposite of hip, but people noticed when he walked in and stood in the corner, smoking cigarette after cigarette, rolling each one himself. He watched everyone watching him, and, after an hour, came over to me, offering me a roll-up.

"It's only tobacco. That's all you smoke. You had enough of marihuana and opium In Country after you hurt your shoulder. You're more involved with things that are a bit more imaginative, something that might spur you to get up and do something, aren't you?"

His voice was low, with an accent that was hard to place, his flat vowels and clipped consonants emanating effortless cool. A strange way of talking, too. Educated. Erudite, rejecting the language of the street, but also avoiding the affected language of the Factory pretenders, claiming European authenticity as a tiny bit of recognition. Style was the thing, convincing others that you were brilliant. Andy had a shotgun approach to catch whatever outstanding people happened to fall into the orbit of his ragtag collection of sexual deviants and junkies.

I didn't like him coming up and telling me things about myself.

"How'd you know I was In Country? And just what do you think I've got for you? I don't have anything to do with grass, or mushrooms, or any of that hippy shit."

I watched his thin face while he spoke, his jawbone etched out of granite there, though long and delicate, not like the ad men. I couldn't stop looking at him, listening to his talk. "You've got a shoulder wound, that's apparent from the hitch you had leaning against the wall, but you didn't grimace, so it's something you're used to. New Yorkers don't get much sun, but you're brown, with malaria scars. The way you move and stand shows a streetwise city upbringing. You watch other people around you, keeping an eye out for customers and the police, yet you've rolled your eyes at two deals, grass and heroin. So: you were in Vietnam, bored with common drugs. You're looking to sell something. I need something to occupy my mind and time. Something beyond even the delights manufactured in this Factory."

I didn't know what to say, so I took the cigarette he offered and lit it. It was a strong blend, thick, pungent smoke pouring out of the end, but nice. I looked up at him.

"It's called Drum. It comes to me from the Netherlands— from someone who owes me a favour."

He smiled at me, a crooked smile that turned my guts to water. I'd have a talk with him, and find out more about this observant, smoking man who'd just walked in to my life; for more than just a conversation, as it turned out.

We talked for a while, about what he liked. Up, but with a twist. Some psychedelic effect was useful, but nothing debilitating. I had just the thing, but back at the Chelsea Hotel. Blue beauties, I called them, stealing the name from the common black beauties, but they were as different as night and day. The chemical was amphedoxamine, but they wouldn't just take you up, they'd make you feel good, too. I made my rounds and sold a little to those I knew would be talking to me later, and came back to this Sherlock Holmes.

"I think I may have something right up your alley. It's in my more... private stash. There's just one thing, though. I need you to distract the landlady. We have a disagreement about the rent."

"You don't have it, yet she insists you pay it anyway?"

"Exactly."

"WHICH WAY DO you live, John?"

I don't know why I let him call me John. Everyone else calls me Doc, and I was qualified, though I hadn't lifted a scalpel, a stethoscope or so much as a band-aid since the year before, since I came home with shrapnel in my shoulder. My extensive experience in treating syphilis, jungle rot, and sucking chest wounds was of no use even at Bellevue. My hands weren't steady enough to practise any more. My licence and my knowledge of pharmacology kept me in high demand, however.

Grass was everywhere. Cannabis, mushrooms, and chemicals cooked up by burned out long hairs, as likely to contain strychnine as not.

The people who came to me weren't looking to turn on or tune in; they had more specialised tastes. They craved knowledge, the power to be creators, to be active participants in life, rejecting every custom, from money to their own sexuality and even gender. They who could only fit in here in New York.

I was a doctor, but it was good that the American Medical Society never saw my shaking hands, or the patients for whom I prescribed an increasingly esoteric variety of chemicals. Chemicals used for creativity, to give an edge, to support the frenzied, creative mind. Make something. Do something. Start something.

The news showed college kids burning their draft cards, dropping LSD, eating mushrooms, smoking marihuana, growing their hair long and burning bras on farms, trying to get away from everything, like that was going to change anything. Not so much in our little corner of New York. Downtown, making a living in empty warehouses. Staying up all night. Creating art out of anything, from cardboard to bodies, inventing superstars out of nothing. This was our buzz, our vibe. Sex. Drugs. Experiment and creation. Create something. Anything. Lots of things. Some of it would stick. We'd change the world, or at least our little corner of it.

"Which way, John?" Sherlock's voice shocked me out of my reverie.

"I live at the Chelsea, like everyone else," I sighed.

* * *

THE CHELSEA HOTEL. Heiresses desperately seeking disgrace with artistes. Writers and artists praying for a muse. Even in New York in 1968, you would be hard-pressed to find a more miserable hive of the desperate and demented.

The landlady was used to people making disturbances to get guests up to the rooms against the house rules. Someone would fake a fight, or try to sell drugs, or tip over an ashtray, and the rest of the people would run past the barricade. At two-fifty a night or fifteen dollars a week, the Chelsea was cheap, collecting youthful hope, grey enterprise, madness and decrepitude, along with any kind of bottom-feeding scamster. It also had an infamously liberal attitude towards rent, which meant that nearly every resident was constantly in arrears, and could be extorted for any money, valuables, or drugs they had while no complaints could be lodged against the owners about leaking roofs, flickering electricity, or the constantly failing boiler.

It was an arrangement that worked for most of us, particularly considering the heiresses and young men with rich fathers who came to spend time in this bohemian palace, tasting our lifestyle, but running back up to Park Avenue for Sunday brunch. They kept the place going, paying their rent for the few rooms in good shape on the second and third floors in the front. The only part of the hotel that ever saw the super's hands.

Sherlock walked into the Chelsea Hotel and demonstrated his useful observation trick. He walked straight up to the desk.

"I'd like to enquire about a room, please. I'd prefer monthly rates over weekly, if that's all right? I can pay in advance."

The hotel manager looked up through bleary eyes, and turned to get a resident's form, a cigarette dangling from his lip.

"Ah. I see that you only have rooms on the top floors available, and that it's been over a year since you've had your boiler inspected, and your exterminator certificate..."

I slipped past the doorway and up the stairs, listening to his sharp, deep voice tallying everything wrong with the building. It made me smile.

I checked the hair I pasted across the lock, and it was still in place. I opened the door and went straight to the loose floorboard under the mattress and pulled out my stash box, extracting a dozen of the blue tablets from the envelope. I didn't know how many he wanted, but ten, I thought, should do it. Plus a couple for myself, just in case. I didn't know what he was about, but the blues had helped my lonely existence for a night or two.

The room was dingy, the sheets dirty, my few belongings in the place making it look bigger than the closet it was.

SHERLOCK BROUGHT ME downtown from the Chelsea to Washington Square Park, a pale blue tablet dissolving in each of our stomachs after he interrogated me about its effects.

"Explain to me, John, what this is exactly, and why you think it's my sort of trip."

Even then, he called me *John*, and he was Sherlock to me, though Holmes, or even Mr. Holmes to everyone else.

"It's been around a while, tested by everyone. Big pharmaceutical houses. The army. Someone died after an enormous dose, twenty times or more what we've just taken. It's been tested as a truth serum, a psychiatric aid, a cough suppressant, and a diet pill. It's mildly psychedelic, but more sensual and controlled than the tabs passing for LSD you can find cooked up all around the country."

"Groovy."

The word hung off the edge of his lip and I looked at him.

"What? I wanted to see what it felt like to say it."

"And?"

"It made me feel dirty. I suspect I may have lost some brain cells."

I stopped and stared at him, until he looked over at me, just with his eyes, a smirk breaking out on his face. We both dissolved into laughter there in the street.

Sherlock put his arm around my shoulders and breathed in. "This is good, John. Very good. Tell me something. The Chelsea. You like it there?"

"To be honest? Not really. It's not that cheap, but I can't afford better. It's good for me to be there for my clients. There are quite a few hangers-on with family money there, always interested in what I have. Prescriptions for amphetamines pay my way, and allow me to indulge in my experiments."

He put up a finger, asking me to pause, and walked past the chess players, observing their games.

"Would you bet on one of these, John?"

"I'm not a gambling man. I feel I've used up all my luck coming back from Charlie and malaria."

"It wouldn't be gambling, though. Some of the best chess players in the world are here, and it is a game of pure skill. I haven't the concentration for it, though I imagine I could do well if I put my mind to it. It's a fascinating blend of wit and strategy. The rules are simple, and it is good training for the structure of the mind. Look here. This man will lose, despite current appearances. He's playing well, but his opponent has the measure of him, playing a longer game with his lesser pieces. Ten moves, if I am correct, and I'm sure I am."

"You're a man of great power, aren't you, Mr. Holmes?"

"Not so much. I see what I see, and I am compelled by a sense of logic, a desire to unscramble puzzles. I need constant stimulation. Experiences."

"Hey. *S.C.U.M. Manifesto*? Only two dollars. Might change your life."

A short, dirty woman, obviously in and out of shelters, with short hair and a broken flat cap, but there was a sparkle of intelligence in her eyes.

Sherlock looked at her, with that look I would come to know so well. He was studying her, taking in details and making a judgement about whether or not to engage. Whether she was worth his breath, his attention.

"What about a proposition?"

"Oh, sure. I've had plenty of those. What do you want to do? Where? Under the pier? East or Hudson? Hudson's extra. It's dirtier, but if that's your thing…"

"Not that. Not at all. It's not your body I'm interested in, it's your mind."

"Conversation? Okay. Four bucks for thirty minutes, six bucks for an hour. We can talk about anything you want."

Sherlock glanced at me, a twinkle in his eye. "We're not what you think. Here's my proposition. Come have a coffee with us. No strings. If we like what you have to say, we'll both buy your manifesto. If not, I'll pay for the coffee and give you a dollar for your time. Thirty minutes."

She looks at him, and at me. "Make it breakfast and it's a deal. You get as long as it takes for me to eat. Thirty minutes guaranteed."

"It's better and easier than getting a man to pay you for sex, is it?"

"Look, you want me to talk to you or not? Sure. I've turned tricks, gotten men to pay me to watch, to talk, whatever. It's no business of yours."

"Sorry, it's just that I don't want you to feel like you need to hide anything from me. I can see that you're occasionally homeless, but not always. That you're a lesbian, even though you seek the attention of men—that for money, you'll go with them, but that it's less attractive, miserable, middle-aged men that you end up spending time with. You've got moustache hairs and macassar on your fur-collared coat from at least seven different men, one black, three Italians—or Southern European descents, anyway—a blonde and two brown-haired professional men in polyester suits, and though I can see smudges of dirt from both the Hudson and East rivers, suggesting that you've slept under piers—though more often the Hudson—you're clean enough that you must shower regularly. At, if I'm not mistaken, the Chelsea Hotel, which is where my friend lodges. Shall we walk? There's an all-day breakfast place around the corner, Ms...?"

"Solanas. Valerie Solanas. Author of the *S.C.U.M. Manifesto*. I'm going to change the world."

"You don't say?"

"DON'T GET ME wrong. You guys seem all right. A girl's got to make a living, though. There's some real scumsters around."

Sherlock looked at me, an ice-blue sparkle in his eyes. He was feeling the blue beauty.

"Some real scumsters."

"Yeah. Like that guy, Andy, down at the Factory? My friend Irene brought me down there. She's this real Hot Girl. One of his so-called Superstars. She said that I 'just had to meet Andy.' When he met me, he asked me to do a screen test. Put me in one of his movies. Then I showed him a script I wrote. Brilliant play. *Up Your Ass*. He read it, said it was well-typed. Well fucking typed. Can you imagine that? Then he asked me if I was working with the vice squad to entrap him, it was so dirty. I told him, 'Andy, Irene told me you liked it dirty. I told you it was called *Up Your Ass*, didn't I?' He didn't have much to say to that, but told me that he couldn't produce it because the cops would be all over him. They were just looking for a reason to come in and shut him down. He's really paranoid.

"Then this guy Maurice had me out for dinner the next day. French guy, he says, talks with an English accent, though. Says he's published Anaïs Nin and Henry Miller. I was explaining the *S.C.U.M. Manifesto* to him and he said he wanted to publish it. Bought the rights. Wrote me a cheque right there and then for five hundred dollars and put it there with a contract. Said he could sell it and sell some more of my work, too. I could write some adult books, maybe. So I signed. Paid my bill at the Chelsea. Paid back some friends. Made some more copies of *S.C.U.M.* to sell. Got my typewriter out of the pawn shop. I had to get up onto the roof and get typing. Maurice wanted an expanded version of the *S.C.U.M. Manifesto*, a novel based on it, so I got typing. Working on it. Trying to make it into a novel. I made characters who got screwed over for each fucked-up thing that men did to women. Each grievance a character, like Greek Furies.

"I was all wound up, telling this Maurice Girodias about Andy and how he was stealing my script. He said to me 'That's your next novel, after *S.C.U.M. Up Your Ass*. Just what you need to get into the big time.' Maybe I should publish *S.C.U.M.* as it is. He wanted me to call it *The Manifesto for the Society for Cutting Up Men*. Said to get ready with *Up Your Ass* right after. But I don't have the script anymore. I was worried. I wanted another five hundred bucks. Maybe more. You should get paid more for a second script, right? But he disappeared. Later on I look at the contract, and it says it's not just for the two books, but for future writings, too. I think it must be all my future writings. Now he's split, back off to France or L.A. or somewhere. I don't know. I can't get any answers."

"Have you got a copy of the contract? I could look at it if you like. I know a thing or two about the law. About a few things."

"Yeah. Hey. That'd be good. I just... I get all excited when people are nice to me. Hey. You two. What are you after?"

"Us? We've just had a... what was it, John? A blue funk? It's anything but. A blue buzz, maybe."

I found myself grinning like an idiot, pushing my hash browns around on my plate, watching pale yellow egg yolk run over them in the harsh fluorescent light. "We've just... had a couple of pills. They're a bit..." I pointed to my plate. "Strong."

Sherlock looked at me and grinned. "Have you met John, Valerie? Call him Doc. That's what everyone else does. I think he could be a candidate for the S.C.U.M. Male Auxiliary. He is a very, very good friend to have."

I smiled at Solanas. My feet were itching, tapping the floor in a syncopated rhythm that only Sherlock could understand. "I would really like to walk."

"EAST, TOWARDS THE Alphabet! Beyond the Village, there's a city, a city of the Alphabet, Avenues of letters!" I said, exiting the greasy spoon six dollars lighter but carrying two copies of Valerie Solanas' self-mimeographed *S.C.U.M. Manifesto*, inscribed *'Too bad you're men. You'd make O.K. broads— Valerie.'*

The grey New York light was coming up, and you could see dark shapes shuffling, junkies twitching in failed sleep in East Village Park, behind iron railings. A shaft of light pierced the gloom and murk.

I looked for the street sign. "Avenue A. Direct sun, at dawn, every now and then. I thought I had enough of sunlight In Country, but I like it over here, in this quiet corner."

"It's not so quiet, John. There are plenty of dark things prowling these streets, and I don't mean rodents. People, John. The worst kind that skulk in shadows and desire harm to their fellow man. I've been considering this area."

He looked at me, up and down, appraising.

"John, what would you think about leaving the Chelsea Hotel? Moving somewhere a bit more permanent? Shall we turn here, on Avenue B? There's something I'd like you to see."

We walked along another two blocks, shapeless husks huddling in doorways, nestling with the bags of garbage on the street, shopkeepers opening their doors to conduct business through bars. Downtown New York.

Sherlock stopped in front of number 221 Avenue B. A bakery, the bars on its front window painted white, a bright sign over the door. There was a bell over the door that rang as we walk in.

"Mrs. Hendrix. How are you this fine morning?" He grinned at her, his teeth glowing almost blue in the light of the fluorescent tubes overhead.

Mrs. Hendrix was a well-kept black woman dressed in a navy blue chef's uniform, with a white starched apron and a few stray smudges of flour dusting her arms. "Mr. Holmes. You're here mighty early, aren't you?"

"My colleague and I have just had our breakfast over near Washington Square Park, and I thought I might show him the rooms for rent. Alone, I might be a little worried about making the rent, but with a second person... well, if he's willing to come in with me, then we'd never have a thing to worry about."

She looked at us, with her big smile on her face, and as it dropped off, the temperature dropped by several degrees. "My husband and I like you, Mr. Holmes, and we're not worried about what you do in your rooms, but the rent. You have to make the rent. Every single month, due on the twenty-fifth, late on the first, understand? Or you're out on the first, that day."

"Mrs. Hendrix, I wouldn't dream of being late. You and I are going to be the best of friends. Frustrating, I'm sure, at times, but I think we understand each other, and you'll have nothing to fear from me, as long as you don't bother about what we do. I will do experiments, sometimes, and Doctor Watson here will assist me with his medical and chemical knowledge."

Her smile reasserted itself, erasing any hint of malice and covering the world-weariness she felt. "Okay, then, want to have a look?"

THE SECOND FLOOR was filled with ovens, sacks of flour, paper bags, the leftover junk of running the bakery. "You have to pass through here, but just stay on this side of the tape, and try not to track any mud through or anything. Health department rules. Not that they inspect much, but you never know. Not with a 'spade' business."

She pointed to the ovens, with the pipes running from them. "My husband worked on ships in the war. We heat the water from the bakery ovens so there's plenty of hot water until around midnight. Building heat, too."

We went up to the third floor. It was a massive, open space, swept clean but could use a good scrub. "Used to be storage for a magazine company during the war. They had some clerks up here before that. Hot in the summer, cold in the winter, but the heating's covered and the windows open, top and bottom. You get a good airflow in summertime, here and on the fourth floor. I've done enough stairs, though, so you can go up to the fourth yourself."

"There's another floor?" My entire room in the Chelsea wasn't a tenth of this space. Fourteen-, maybe sixteen-foot-high ceilings of bare wood. You could dance in here. There was nothing but a couple of hard chairs and a simple table.

"Yep. There's an old bed up there, too. Just the one. My husband and I lived up here while we were fighting with Stuy Town, before that Mr. Lorch let us move in to his place."

I remembered them. The *Post* had written a scathing editorial about letting 'that spade family' move in and 'corrupt' the all-white enclave.

Sherlock looked at me, rubbing his fingers against his thumb. I reached into my pocket and gave him the ten-dollar bill he had given me a few hours before outside the Chelsea. I was overdue there, and I wasn't going to pay them another dime. I was going to live here.

"Mrs. Hendrix, we're happy to take the floors, effective today. Right now, if that's all right?"

She turned from the top of the stairs. "That's no problem.

Y'all do what you need to do. I've gotta get keys cut, but y'all stay here if you need and they'll be ready as soon as we can get them out. Breakfast rush about to start. First of June, now. See you on the first of July, if not before." The bills disappeared underneath her apron.

Sherlock looked at me. "This floor alone is worth it, isn't it? Shall we look upstairs?"

The next floor was the same, if a little cleaner. There was a bed, made up, with a dust cover on it, and a small rough wooden dresser.

"We're allowed to do what we like. Put up walls if we want, or not. And Mrs. Hendrix wanted to keep the furniture up here, said that it was too much trouble to bring it down. And free breakfast. Anything left over from the day before. I think your trim waistline may expand, if you're fed enough."

I yawned.

"Poor John Watson. I've tired you out with my manic walk the length of Manhattan Island. We should lie down." He pulled back the dust sheet.

"This is the one thing. The blue beauties will make you yawn, tired and exhausted, but you'll have trouble sleeping."

"I'm sure we'll find something to do." He pulled me to him, to those lips and that lovely long face I'd been dreaming of all night.

A SINGLE RAY of actual sunshine wandered across the floor, motes of dust sprung up from our bodies twinkling in their slow journey to the floor. "Look at the dust, Sherlock. Floating there, swirling. Lighter than air. It's like magic."

"Not at all. They're very light, but not lighter than air, or they'd float up and we'd have far less sweeping. They're just light enough that the lift from swirling air molecules, from tiny temperature changes can slow their descent. The sunlight is heating the air as it streams through the window. That's your magic, John. Motes of dust are simply pawns in the sun's game."

"Take the joy out of everything, don't you?"

"Not everything, John." He smiled at me, then, the first time I saw his secret smile; the one he only shared with me, and only when we were alone. That smile told me that this, that we, were special, but that it wasn't to leave the confines of the private lair we would build for ourselves, there above Alphabet City.

"Pawns." He sat up, moving faster than I could even think of moving. "Tell me something, John. Do you remember Valerie Solanas? Did she strike you as a pawn? Someone who would do something, unasked, for someone else?"

I thought about her. "Not really. She seemed more... more like someone who was used to playing her own game, changing the rules of the game she found herself in."

"Exactly, John. She's a queen, able to make any moves, playing her own game, but she is without the luxury of her own board. Acting as a pawn. Driving towards the opponent's back row, to regain her crown."

He got up and walked to the window.

"But she's not in control, is she?"

"That's exactly it, John. She's not in control of her life, and she's trying to work out who the king is."

"Or the player of the game."

"Or the player of the game. She's the most resentful pawn ever committed to the game, and that makes her dangerous. She's a puzzle, isn't she? Where's that manifesto of hers? I'm of a mind to read it. Ms. Solanas, you are a bit of a puzzle, aren't you?"

He padded back from the window, casting a long, lean shadow across the floor, rifling through the pockets of my pants looking for those ragged sheets with purple writing on them.

* * *

OVER THE NEXT two days, I'd packed my few belongings for my new home at Avenue B, and Sherlock had turned up the next night with an array of tough youths carrying boxes and crates of notebooks and chemical apparatus, a coffee table made from a cable spool, and a few chairs that looked like they'd spent some time on the street.

It was starting to look more like a home than anywhere I'd been since before the War.

Sherlock was still talking about Valerie. We'd run into her once more on the street, and talked to her about her *Manifesto*. Sherlock wanted to know more.

"Go on, John. Find out what you can about Valerie from your contacts at the Factory. Keep an eye out for her, and talk to her if you have to, but if you can follow her without her noticing, that would be helpful."

I didn't know why we were so interested—why *he* was so interested, that is. I would have been happy to have whiled the weekend away with day-old cakes and bread. I had some deliveries that could be made to the Factory, though, so I went ahead, not knowing what to expect. Everyone had the same reaction. Nothing outstanding, for the Factory. Billy and Paul were there, ready to get their prescriptions, only too happy to share catty gossip.

"Valerie? Who?"

"You know. The street dyke. Twitchy."

"Oh, yeah. Creepy. Did you see her screen test?"

"Eyes like dark holes, staring into your soul."

"Not attractive, really. Could be, if she put on makeup or something. Could be better, anyway. Better than street chic. Eau de Hudson, like she usually wears."

"There was something about her, though. Something interesting. She was clever, when she wasn't too twitchy. Maybe if she'd been fed."

"Some days she'd be so angry, railing about men and scum. Other days, she'd be real personalable. Friendly. She used to come in with Irene, sometimes, but we haven't seen them together in months. She just keeps coming in shouting at Andy about her script. He gets so many scripts from people. What's he supposed to do?"

"And money. She's always asking everyone for money."

"Speaking of, Doc. What have you got for us? We loved those black beauties last time. Got us right through the move. What do you think of the new digs? Union Square? Next big thing?"

"Orange OPs. Phew. Those things'll keep you going, all day, and all night long"

I finished my business and walked back to the Chelsea to see a few patients for some business there.

It was strange, heading up there. I had a pocket full of money, and another full of tablets, and I was ready to see the back of that place. Sure, lots of people had written loads of stuff there, and it was a collection of plenty of interesting people, but did it matter anymore?

Sherlock was in the coffee shop next door, sitting with a greasy-looking man in a brown suit with heavily macassar'd hair. Pencil-thin moustache, impeccably dressed, like he was just catching up with the Beats. They were out, man, didn't he know? Sherlock saw me and took his lovely long hands and knocked on the window. I went and ordered a coffee.

"John! How are you? Can I introduce you to Maurice Girodias, of the Olympia Press? Mr. Girodias is a fascinating individual, having published some of the more influential works over the last twenty years. Arthur Miller, Nabokov and others. Mr. Girodias, this is Doctor Watson. He's called Doc by his friends. Don't call him John. He hates it. Just indulges me."

"Pleased to meet you?" He half-stood and gave me a limp handshake. My impression was cheap macassar and a cheaper suit, though he had quite the breakfast in front of him: eggs benedict, fresh-squeezed orange juice, and coffee with the sugar jar next to him.

Sherlock went on. "We appear to have a mutual friend. Ms. Valerie Solanas. You remember her, John?"

He was up to something, but I had no idea what. I made a show of screwing up my face for a moment. "Short woman, flat cap, sheepskin coat?"

"That's her. Mr. Girodias is her publisher. Or will be, when he can find her, of course. He's got a manuscript, and is hoping to get a second, maybe even a third, isn't that right, Mr. Girodias?"

"It is, actually. We call them the Travellers Companion books. Great literature that offers a... a traveller, one on his own, a break from the day-to-day grind. That traveller might need some stimulation. That's what we provide. Dirty books, sure, but dirty books for the discriminating reader."

There was something about this Girodias. His accent was English overlaid with French, but a coarse English and the French sounded more like it was from the movies than from growing up in Paris, but what did I know? Just that I didn't like him. I spent a lot of time with unsavoury characters, freaks, and cast-outs of prestigious families. I didn't mind *strange*, but desperation rolled off of him, despite his rolls of money and the way he encouraged us to order whatever we wanted on his cheque.

"How did you and Valerie come to meet?"

He looked at both of us as though we were part of the vice squad. To be fair, Sherlock's clean-cut face and short hair would make him look like a bad rookie who has put on civvies and been thrown out into the wilds of Southern Manhattan to catch gamblers, pimps, and johns. "Nothing like that, I assure you. No, no, no under the bridge and down the alley liaison for me." He strained so hard to pronounce "liaison" in a French fashion that I was afraid he was going to pull his larynx.

"No, we were introduced by the daughter of one of my *financiers*." (That strain again.) "Adler. Irene, I think? Lovely family. Lovely woman, actually. Intelligent. Spent quite a lot of time at the Factory. The only one of the Superstars that was a real Superstar, if you know what I mean. Knew of my taste for *la controverse*. Good for *le commerce*. You know. She told me of the *manifesto* of *Valérie* and I knew I should meet her. With such an endorsement, I knew I should meet her and get her on my author list. So I did."

Sherlock looked at me, his expression unreadable, a look I would come to puzzle over many times in our life together. "Valerie has asked me to look over this contract you've sent her—it's so vague as to be legally questionable, you see. She'd like to, hm, clarify her position."

"Ah. Well. Tell her... tell her to talk to me, not to send some agent out. I'm a reasonable man, but I am a man of business. She needn't be concerned. We can... we can discuss the terms. Of course. She is an artist, and I want to make her some money, and myself some. She doesn't need to send someone to speak for her."

"Oh, no. She didn't send me, she only mentioned it, and since I ran into you, I thought I would ask."

"Fine. Well. I must be going. I have a printer to meet. You'll get that? Very kind, thanks."

Girodias left the impression he was running, leaving us with the bill for his breakfast.

"John, John! What have you found?" Sherlock was looking at me with a sparkle in his eyes.

"You didn't think I'd want to share with you?"

"What? What are you saying, John?"

"You've found some pills, someone's shared something with you. We're barely down from the blues and now you're up again. I thought... Nevermind."

"John. John. Look at me." We were sitting on the same side of the table, across from where Girodias had been. He put his hand under my chin and turned it to face him and his eyes softened. "I haven't had any pills. I just get excited when I'm stimulated. I just take pills to keep myself going in times when I can't find something to keep my interest. Please. What did you find out at the Factory about Valerie?"

I could have kissed him, deep, his stubble raking against mine, there in the coffee shop. I wanted to, but I held myself back. I waded through the pile of information that the hangers-on and buyers had given me. "Not much more than we knew. You have to filter it out of the language they speak over there. They mostly made fun of her, like she was part of the scene but not any longer. Irene Adler did bring her in, and used to be friendly towards her, but no one seems to have seen them together for months."

"Hmmm. Interesting. There's something there. This Adler. What do we know about her?"

"If we weren't in America, she'd be royalty. Rich. Very rich. Glamourous. Gorgeous, too, even if she's not your sort of thing. Her family made money in ice in the early 1800s, and then diversified. Lumber. Newspapers. Radio. The Midas touch. Always on to the next big thing.

"The open secret is that much of Andy's generosity comes from her. Most of the big expensive dinners out she pays for, but he gets all the credit. She bought a few paintings, has been in a bunch of his films. Lives at the Chelsea. She's the original Superstar."

"Ms. Adler. How did you come to be friends with Ms. Solanas? And why these introductions? What is it you want Valerie to do for you?"

"Sherlock, really? What could she possibly want? Maybe she was... moved by her writing, or something?"

"A woman like that? No, John. It can't be. Come on. Let's go to the Chelsea Hotel."

Just like that we were out of there, five dollars left on the table: more than double the bill, but it was enough for him. Not for the last time would I follow on the heels of Sherlock Holmes with only the tiniest idea of what was going on.

The Chelsea Hotel was buzzing with hushed excitement. Billy, Candy, a couple of other transvestites were lying on the sofas, arms artfully arranged in a pose of fainting, affecting stricken. One of the writers—Paul, I think—was standing in the corner, smoking cigarettes; a line of butts on the ground showed where he had been pacing.

"He's been walking there for at least an hour and a half. Twelve butts on the ground, seven minutes a cigarette, one in his hand. Something's happened. I don't like this, John."

I went over to Candy. She was normally a rock. As dramatic as she could be, she was someone to trust in a crisis. "What's going on? What's happened?"

She looked up at me.

"Oh, god, It's Andy. He... Andy's been shot. Valerie shot him. She slept in my room last night, went out for coffee, and came back crazy. She was running around, looking for Maurice, angry. Pacing back and forth. Got all dressed up. Make-up, can you believe? Said she was going to go talk to Andy. I thought maybe... but I don't know. I helped her with her makeup. She looked nice."

Sherlock had his concentrating face on. "This can't be right. This can't be it." He looked at me. "Do you know Irene Adler? What she looks like? Her room number?"

I didn't know what to say. I could hardly believe the strange, gregarious woman we'd met, so canny in teasing money out of us, had just shot Andy Warhol. "I know her from sight. We've met a time or two, when I was accidentally invited along to dinners, but I don't really know her. She wouldn't know me. I assume she'd be in the front on the second or third floor, where the nice rooms are."

He turned on his heel and strode to the counter. "Excuse me. I need to speak to Ms. Irene Adler. It's a matter of some urgency. Could you ring her room, please, or let me up?"

The desk clerk looked up, his ever-present cigarette dangling and burning. He muttered "Adler. Adler. Hm. What was your name, sir?" as he pulled out a slip of paper.

"Holmes. Sherlock Holmes. She may be in danger."

The clerk turned and looked at the keys on the wall behind him "Red tag. She's gone away for a while.

Sherlock stared at him. "Danger. She may be in serious danger. Can you tell me where she is, or anything useful?"

The clerk sighed and lit another cigarette, taking in Sherlock's lean frame and rumpled, but well-cut clothes. "Let me just have a look..." He thumbed through the guest ledger. "Says here she booked a taxi to LaGuardia. Gone at least a week, maybe longer. There's the forwarding address... now why would you go to Los Angeles in June? Surely you'd go in the winter?"

He closed the book with a thump and looked up at us, but Sherlock was already pulling at my arm.

"John. She's off to Los Angeles. What's happening there? We need newspapers, and time, and perhaps a little something to focus the mind..."

He led me away towards Union Square, muttering to himself. I listened, but could not make out very much. "Los Angeles... Irene Alder... Andy Warhol... The Factory... John!"

I was startled out of my reverie, walking along past Sherlock. "What is it?"

"You're around the Factory a lot. Has anything happened in the last few months? Anything peculiar?"

"Not that I can think of. People are always coming and going, at least a little. They fall in and out of favour according to Andy's whims."

"Would you know who was in and out?"

"I don't know. I don't particularly pay attention. I notice when people are gone for a while."

"What about Adler? She's the common thread."

"She was definitely in. Belle of the ball. She was in quite a few of Andy's films, Billy's films, too, two or three years back. Paul just loved her. She was starring in them. Andy even conceived of a series of films just about her. A series of series. She was the centre of the Factory's fleeting attention. She would take them all out; fifteen, twenty people. More, sometimes. They'd have champagne and oysters. Steak. And pills, Plenty of pills. She left, though, a while back. Peak of her stardom. People started talking about her afterwards. She'd been involved with a musician. She'd gotten pregnant. Couldn't handle the drugs. Bored. Lots of things."

"She's the key, John. She knows something. She was there. Somewhere. Important."

"I think she may be as crazy as Valerie."

"Right, John. The thing for this is to sharpen the senses. I want to know what's going on. Anything in those pockets to aid in focus? An upper?"

"I have some of the black beauties—cut with methaqulaone, though—Quaaludes, so maybe not so good for concentration, and some Obetrol—Andy Candy."

Sherlock took one of each and upped his pace, to get the blood flowing. I wasn't sure about the combination. Doubling up on the amphetamines, but, then, I was still a bit edgy from the blues, so I figured it couldn't hurt.

We headed to Midtown, East 47th Street, to the site of the original Factory, walking fast to get the pills into our bodies.

He stood in front of the scaffolding surrounding the pile of bricks, facing away, looking up and down the street.

"Sunlight. Grand Central. There's a YMCA nearby. Hmmm..."

He turned left and stalked away towards 3rd Avenue. I had trouble keeping up with his long, muscular legs, despite my own enhancement.

I was getting jittery, and the methaqualone was sending shivers down my spine as we strode down past Grand Central and towards the Chelsea.

Sherlock stopped in front of a newspaper stand and looked at the papers.

"Gum, please. Spearmint." He handed over his fifteen cents, scanning the headlines. "California Democratic primary. California. Los Angeles." He picked up a copy of the *New York Times*, and the *Los Angeles Times* for good measure. He handed me the *New York Times*. "Here, John. Back to Avenue B. We've got to get through these newspapers."

I was worried about him, but I thought that, back at Avenue B, we would have water and blankets and the comforts of home. I wasn't sure that we hadn't overdone it for a Monday evening, and I didn't expect we'd get any sleep tonight.

It was good that it was evening, because we were a giggling mess when we got back. We have had—still do, I suppose—our share of late-night or very early morning entries through the bakery, Mrs. Hendrix constantly reminding us that what we do is not her business, as long as the rent comes in on time.

"I'll take L.A., John, and you take New York. Systematic. Let's first spread the paper out in even numbers across the floor. We're looking for *patterns*. Something to do with the Presidential primary. Set aside advertising circulars and sports sections for now. Keep Arts and Culture."

I looked at him, peeling apart the newspaper, page by page, setting it down. "Sherlock, surely we'd be better off leafing through normally?"

"Nonsense, John. Trust me. Unless we can see the whole of it together, we can't see the patterns. Lay them out. Even pages up. Facing inwards so we can scan across the whole paper. Don't overlap the pages at all."

I laid them out, end to end, looking back at Sherlock crouched there, muttering at the pages as he read them. "We should have bought two copies of the papers, John. We could have them spread to see the entire pattern."

At last it was set out, and he walked back and forth in the centre of the room, looking at the newspapers spread there on the ground.

"Turn them, John. We need the odds, quickly."

We went through the laborious process of turning the papers over, one by one. Sherlock's fingers were crumpling the edges, twitching with overstimulation and speed. "Fuck it, John. I'm in a hurry. Just national and local news." He was stalking back and forth, wild-eyed, his own movements stirring the air to make the papers move around underneath his feet.

"Stop, Sherlock. Slow down. Listen to the sounds outside. New York at night, even on a Monday." Sirens whirred in the distance. Shouts came up, from the street and from the light-wells out back, one more scream. Laughter, and the tinkle of broken glass. "Take a breath. Let's have a glass of water. Maybe some wine."

He looked at me. "You're right, John, thanks. Get that."

I went upstairs to the third floor and our kitchenette. There was a jug of dry red wine that I poured into a couple of jelly jars and filled a coffee can with water from the tap, recoiling at the chlorine smell. I ran a handful of it over my hair, feeling the tingle of the water drops roll down my scalp and neck.

Another breath.

"I've got it, John!" Sherlock was shouting from downstairs. "We need the telephone. Long distance, direct to California."

I staggered down the staircase in a succession of freeze frames, like Duchamp's nude, glasses clattering in my hands, feet skittering over the steps one by one in a controlled fall, my heart bursting with fear and pride at the bottom. I hadn't fallen.

Sherlock was there, holding a piece of the *L.A. Times* in his hand, his pupils the size of quarters. "This is it, John. She's after Bobby Kennedy. We've got to tell someone."

"Sherlock, what the hell are you talking about? Valerie Solanas is after Bobby Kennedy? She's the subject of a citywide manhunt. She can't fly. That doesn't make sense. Here, let's sit down and have some wine. Settle, remember?"

"No, John. Don't mistake the pawn for the queen. Irene Adler, if that's even her name. She's played everyone. Had her revenge on Warhol for spurning her. Solanas is just an unpredictable bomb, tossed into the Factory. She'd hurt Andy somehow, but it's only chance that she's actually shot him."

He stops and thinks, looking at the ceiling.

"I can't figure it out. It would make sense, though, that she would focus her rage on Warhol himself, not just the hangers-on. That's who I'd go after. The leeches. The grovelling assholes who build egos out of propaganda and then think they're important. I understand Warhol and what he's built, but there are all these people around him, inserting themselves into his orbit. They don't have an original thought of their own, but they take delight in playing political games, talking down to people. Making fragile people like Valerie Solanas feel more isolated and alone."

He was spitting with anger, staring out the window, the sheets of newspaper crumpled in his hand, his forearms rippling with muscle. I stood behind him and put my arms around him, kissing him lightly behind the ear, rubbing his stomach through his shirt.

"It's okay, Sherlock. Really okay. They are shitheads. Everything they hate. I know. Andy, I think, knows."

He turned in my arms. "Maybe some of that wine?"

I handed him the wine. "I don't know if it's any good. It's just what was upstairs."

"I imagine our taste buds aren't working anyway. Just so long as it's not sweet. I can't stand sweet wine. Hippies and grassheads and those with no imagination. They should just drink Coke."

He put the papers down and took up the wine and toasted me, slipping his arm through mine for the sip. "You're good to me, John. Good *for* me."

I blushed and picked up the papers he'd put down.

"There's something there. I can see the whole thing, but I can't explain it all. My head is buzzing too much.

"Listen: Adler was been pushed out of the Factory six months or a year ago. Must have met Valerie at the same time. It doesn't make *sense* that she's a real socialite. She might have taken Warhol out in that case, but not all those people. The rich hang on to their money exactly by not giving it away. No. She wanted them to believe that she was wealthy. Buying her way into stardom? She had money, clearly, but the class? Breeding? I find it hard to believe.

"She met Solanas, and Solanas would have been the perfect bomb. Chaos incarnate. Delicate. Wounded. Fractured in places. If she could get Valerie angry enough, and directed, she'd go off in some unpredictable way. Hurt Warhol? Damage his reputation? Scare him? Could be anything.

"Why would she run, though? She didn't do anything. Introduced Valerie to Girodias and Warhol. Possibly stoked the coals of resentment, a bit, but nothing that would be out of the ordinary in the circles she ran in.

"But here's the thing: Valerie suddenly got set off. She turned from building up a head of steam to murderous in a few days. She was fine when we met her, just a couple of days ago. Solanas was a practice run, I'm sure of it. I don't have enough data, but she must have been grooming someone else, someone fragile and vulnerable. Someone poor. Getting her ready. Why would she go off now? Solanas has claimed friendship with Warhol on the most tenuous of links. There's no way the pigs would go after a rich socialite. Warhol is a distraction. Important, but something to get people to look at New York.

"The polls are opening any time in California for the Democratic Primary. Bobby Kennedy is the only candidate campaigning in Southern California. It's all there, John."

"I know, Sherlock. Just relax. It makes sense. It's plausible, but there's no way we can let anyone know now. I could possibly get one of Andy's groupies to trust me, but who would we call? The FBI? The LAPD? The NYPD? They're all pigs. One of the newspapers? They'd have us out as crank callers in a second. We can barely string sentences together."

He put his head in my lap. "I know. I know. I just... I'm sure of it."

"Could be the amphetamines or the 'ludes. We've had quite a lot."

We sat there for a few minutes, the morning sun bouncing off the windows of the building opposite, the smells from the bakery coming up and turning our stomachs. We drank the water, and the wine, and then Sherlock turned to me and kissed me again, and in his kiss was hunger and desperation. We made love on and on and it was like nothing I've experienced before or since. It—he—was filled with an intensity and urgency that was simply indescribable.

He was right, of course. Probably, anyway. Bobby Kennedy was shot just after midnight as the polls closed, and Nixon went on to win the election. It was the beginning of the end as well. The Factory stopped being so open. The hippies grew up. Irene Adler disappeared, and was forgotten by pretty much everyone. She would become a footnote in the Factory, a face flashing by in some of Warhol's films.

Sherlock was devastated.

He spent three days and the six blues that he had left wandering around the apartment, listless. He smoked cigarette after cigarette, shouting out the window into the night at the girls downstairs. He went down onto the street and bought bags of grass, then bags of brown powder later, cooking them up and, for want of a syringe, snorting the brown liquid.

I went out and bought a deadbolt and locked him into the bedroom on the top floor to let him dry out, leaving him newspapers, a carton of orange juice, some bananas, and water. After twenty-four hours, I went in to him, and he was sitting on the floor in the beam of the setting sun, holding his knees and rocking, my newspapers strewn all around him in a disordered mess, all the articles on the Kennedy and Warhol shootings arrayed around him, and a book open in his lap—Voltaire's writings after the revolution.

"It's my fault, John. I did it. I had it all figured out. I could have saved him, if I was able to speak. Knew who to speak to. Solanas was the practice run. Revenge on Warhol. She wasn't even really an heiress. She came in, flashing around money, acting the type, wanting something from Warhol, but her star fell too fast. Solanas was an opportunity, but Sirhan Sirhan was the long game. Irene Adler probably wasn't even her name.

He held up the Voltaire. "With power comes responsibility, John. I've got to make my work mean something. Save lives. Stop the corrupt.

"And for my diversions, and distractions, you and your magical tablets, those are for afterwards. When the lives are saved and the city is safe. To keep us from being bored."

Soon enough, we had a string of people coming in to 221 Avenue B, eating one of Mrs. Hendrix's cakes or bean pies, explaining to Sherlock and me their unsolvable riddles, which he'd go and unwind, rooting out evil and corruption across America.

Bored? We were never bored.

Sherlock got harder, colder. I think I was the only one who ever saw his sense of humour, and hardly ever again. He never spoke about our lovemaking, not after that one time. We were friends and associates. People suspected, sure, but they never found anything concrete. The times changed, the world got darker.

He never forgot Adler, though. She was always The Woman. I think he was a little in love with her. The only one to ever outsmart him, and to get away. He'd only find shreds, suggestions of her existence. A few lines in the Solanas transcripts. Scenes in Warhol's unwatchable films. Occasional cuttings from the newspaper.

She created him, in her own way. Would 221 Avenue B have given such hope to the hopeless? Would those we've caught have killed and stolen more? Would we have been something more than friends? Happier? Would New York be as safe, or any more—or less—interesting? Where would we have been without her?

ALL THE
SINGLE LADIES
GINI KOCH

A huge fan of Sherlock Holmes, Gini came into my life when she eavesdropped on me talking about this project at WorldCon. A few minutes' mutual enthusiastic gushing later, I was clutching a new business card and promising to get in touch with her about the anthology. And I'm very glad I did. 'All the Single Ladies' not only adds a frankly brilliant new Holmes to the canon—breezy and flippant where so many of her predecessors are haughty and insufferable—but offers a remarkable modernity by setting the story against the hysteria of a reality TV programme...

"I'M SORRY," MRS. Hudson said, sticking her head into my office. "But these detectives insist they need to speak to you, Doctor." She looked worried. I couldn't blame her. A visit from the police is rarely a good thing.

As I slid the file I'd been perusing into the top drawer of my desk, three people entered my office: two men and a woman. One man was at least a half a foot taller than the other, but the shorter man was the one who stepped forward. He had dark hair and eyes, with sharp features that reminded me just a bit of a rodent.

"Dr. John Watson?"

"Yes. What's this about?"

"I'm Detective Straude. This is Detective Saunders." He indicated the taller man, who was fair to Straude's dark, and who also looked as if he'd played football in school. "The lady is Sherlock Holmes. She's with us."

Holmes was between the two men in height; tall for a woman. Slender, but clearly well-muscled, with long, dark hair pulled back into a severe ponytail. She wore a grey turtleneck sweater, grey slacks and grey high-heeled boots, and had a grey wool coat draped over her arm. Apparently, grey was her color.

Holmes was what, about a hundred years ago, would have been called a *handsome* woman—not pretty, certainly not beautiful, but not unattractive, either. Like Straude, she had sharper features, but unlike him, she didn't resemble a rodent in any way. She reminded me more of an eagle, or even a wolf—a solitary, noble predator.

"Clearly, seeing as she came in with you." I tried to keep the sarcasm out of my tone, but didn't feel I'd been too successful.

Holmes hadn't been looking at me—she'd been examining the room, looking everywhere with seemingly great interest. I had no idea why—mine was a typically small office, with the standard diplomas and certificates on the walls. I didn't go in for much clutter, so the bookcases were filled with books helpful to my practice and some few mementos displayed on top. Otherwise, there wasn't much to see.

However, my sarcasm caught her attention. She turned to me and I realized why she was so committed to one color—her eyes were a piercing grey, and they radiated intelligence, more than I'd ever seen before, from anyone, man or woman. The resemblance to an eagle was even more pronounced.

She turned those eyes onto me and her lips quirked. "What a feat of deduction. Forgive Lee. He's the master of stating the obvious." She had an English accent, and a husky voice. She could make a fortune as a phone sex operator, but I knew without asking she wasn't interested in that kind of work.

"Sherlock, please," Straude said tiredly. "Not now."

"You're wasting your time," she said. Then turned away and went back to examining my unexciting office.

"Can I help you, detectives? And Mrs. Holmes?"

"Miz," she said, without turning towards me. "Not married, not divorced, not a sweet young thing, not looking, not interested, in you, your brother, or your sister."

"I see."

"I doubt it."

"Possibly you can help us, Dr. Watson," Straude said quickly. "I understand you're the school physician at New London College."

"Yes." New London was a small, private women's college, dedicated to the idea that young women learned better without the distraction of young men. That there were several other colleges and universities nearby, loaded with all those young men, and that much of the staff were male, never seemed to enter into consideration. "I see you're still set on stating the obvious, since the Dean's secretary brought you in, after all. To my office. On campus. Where I've answered questions from uniformed officers at least four times." I gave up on trying not to sound sarcastic.

Holmes was in profile to me and her lips quirked. She began moving through my office, taking special interest in the bookcases, but still giving the rest of my place a closer look as well.

"Where do you live, Dr. Watson?" Straude went on without any reaction.

"I'm between residences at the moment. I'm sleeping here, on campus, in the visiting professor's dorm room attached to the artist's wing."

"Why's that?" Saunders asked.

"Private colleges don't pay as well as rumor has it. And I'm not financially able to start my own practice, let alone afford any place close." I had no car. And in Southern California, that meant I had to live within walking distance of my job, because the bus system was deplorable at best. New London was in the Brentwood hills, meaning I couldn't afford to rent someone's tool shed, let alone a room or apartment.

"No friends to stay with?" Straude asked.

"Not any I want to burden, no."

"No family?"

"Not nearby."

"Where were you last night between nine p.m. and midnight?"

"Here, doing paperwork, and then in my room, watching TV."

"*Campus Queen* was on," Holmes said.

"Yes, it was. I don't care for reality TV, though. I watched an old movie, *Death Wish*."

"It's the number one reality show right now. *Campus Queen* is filming at New London this school year, isn't it?" Holmes asked.

"Since you appear to follow the show, why are you asking me? Yes, we have film crews here all the time. They practically live here." Some of them *were* living here, camped out to capture nighttime footage. Unlike me, they were allowed to be in the dorms, and didn't have to troop halfway down the high hill to get to their beds. Unlike them, I actually had some hope of sleeping in peace and quiet.

"Do you know why we're here?" Straude asked.

"I have no idea." This was a lie. By now, I had a very good idea. Bad news traveled fast, and until I'd taken this job, the police had never visited me before. At least not in America.

"Fifth rape and murder of one of the New London students in as many months and you don't know why we're here?" Saunders' tone was definitely snide.

"I do know that another one of our students was brutally murdered. I have no idea why you're here with me, however, unless it's to express condolences and assure me, as one of the many who work here, that you're doing all you can to find the murderer and bring him to justice."

"How is *Campus Queen* working the murders in?" Saunders asked. Straude shot Holmes a *why-me?* look. She looked like she was trying not to laugh.

"How would I know? I'm not part of the show, and I don't expect to get a 'secret letter announcing my potential royalty' any time soon."

Holmes was definitely trying not to laugh. "I thought you said you didn't watch the show."

"I work here. Some days it's all the girls talk about. It's good for the school, though." Hollywood on campus meant money coming into the school, plus the notoriety of being one of the colleges deemed worthy to have the next *Campus Queen* crowned. From what Mrs. Hudson had told me, applications for the next school year were up from the past five years, solely due to the show. I might hate *Campus Queen*, but it was helping my employer continue to employ me.

"Can anyone confirm your alibi?" Straude asked.

"Shockingly, I was alone, seeing as it's not exactly appealing to women to bring them back to a tiny room at an all-girl's school for a nightcap, reality TV show filming there or not. And before you ask, no, I didn't have a date last night, I was being sarcastic."

"Again," Saunders said.

"Sarcasm in the face of danger," Holmes said with a chuckle.

"Are the police dangerous to me?" I asked as mildly as possible.

Holmes looked at me over her shoulder. "Only if you're innocent."

I managed to control myself from laughing, and only achieved this because both detectives were glaring at me.

"Molly Parker saw you just last week, didn't she?" Straude asked.

"She did. I saw her the month before, too. Over the course of the school year, I'll end up seeing most of the student body, many of them more than once."

"Justine Clarke, Ramona Hernandez, Quannah Wells, and Susan Lewis all were your patients as well, were they not?" Straude asked.

"I've seen all of them, yes." I had. They were all nice girls. All different from each other. All dead now. Bright futures cut short. I tried not to think about it. Thinking about it created anger for which I had no safe outlet. "New London has a heavy emphasis on wellness and preventative care."

"Who was the doctor before you?" Holmes asked, as she examined the small statuettes of St. George slaying a dragon and St. Rita with a thorn in her forehead and a grapevine wrapped around her, both gifted to me by an old friend.

"I honestly have no idea. He or she left no notes or files. I'm sure Mrs. Hudson would know. Why am I being questioned?"

Straude opened his mouth but Holmes spoke before he could. "Save your breath, Lee." She was still looking at the statuettes. "Despite having gone to Oxford for medical school, which is both impressive and explains why he speaks properly, medicine is not Dr. Watson's life's calling, although he enjoys it. He's a veteran of Operation Enduring Freedom in Afghanistan and the War on Terror in Iraq, with his time in Iraq sandwiched between tours in Afghanistan. He hated war, but was a good soldier. He was wounded in battle, taking damage in his left shoulder and right hip. He's fully recovered, though wet weather makes him ache, hence why he moved to the Southwest instead of returning home to the Northeast, which is a wonderful excuse he uses for why he rarely visits his parents or siblings, whom he loves but doesn't really like. While he received an honorable discharge, that was because he was popular with his superior officers, since he killed a man in a protective rage. He does fit the profile, since he's highly intelligent, underachieving, and a loner. Sadly for you, Detectives, he's not our killer. However, once we find that man, should he be killed before trial, our good doctor should ensure he has an airtight alibi."

"None of that says he isn't our man," Saunders pointed out.

"True enough," Holmes said. "Regarding the man you killed in Afghanistan, how old was the woman he was attacking?"

"You seem to know so much about me; why don't you tell me why you've been investigating me and answer your own question at the same time?"

"Oh, Lee hates it when I do that." Holmes turned around and crossed her arms over her chest. "But it does save time." She looked at Straude.

Who shrugged. "I didn't ask you to come out from New York just for the weather. I'll let you work as you want, Sherlock."

"Fine. First off, I haven't investigated you, other than the time spent in this room. I was called to meet Lee and Will while they were en route to the college."

"You're saying you know all that about me from having been in this room ten minutes?"

"It's been nine minutes, but, yes."

"How?"

She shrugged. "You have your service medals framed and hung, but they sit on a side wall, meaning you have to stand where I am in order to see them—you're proud of them, but don't want to be reminded of your service. Presumably it's because you felt the horrors of war deeply and regret all you did there."

"That's quite true, yes. What about medicine? You insinuated I'm not happy being a doctor?"

"No, I said you enjoyed it but it wasn't where your heart lay. All your diplomas and certificates fill the wall behind you, but they're quite dusty. They need to be up and displayed to prove you're allowed to practice medicine, but you rarely think of them, meaning this wasn't your choice for a career. Before we joined you I verified with Mrs. Hudson that the medical practice is off limits to the regular cleaning staff. There's a service that picks up any hazardous materials, but otherwise, you're responsible for keeping the offices clean. It's part of your arrangement for living on campus."

There was a knock at the door, and Mrs. Hudson looked in. "Terribly sorry to interrupt, but Howard is here to collect your hazardous wastes."

"Speak of the devil. This needs to be done," I said to the police. Straude nodded and I went and opened the door all the way as Mrs. Hudson headed back to her desk.

Howard rolled his dolly in. He was a big man, not the sharpest knife in the drawer, but pleasant, thorough, and punctual. "Afternoon, Doctor," he said. He gave the detectives a nod, and Holmes a wide smile. "Miss, excuse me, don't want to run over your toes."

Holmes gave him an amused smile and moved out of his way. Howard collected the two hazardous bins and left two others in their places. "See you next month, Doctor." He shot Holmes another smile. "Hope to see you next month, too."

"You never know," Holmes said. Howard grinned, then left.

I shut the door behind him. "Sorry about that. Now, you were telling us how you know medicine isn't my heart's desire while rating my cleaning skills."

She lifted one of the statuettes. "There's no dust under these statuettes, nor on the bookcases. You're very thorough. And yet you rarely, if ever, think to dust your diplomas. But you haven't turned your hand to anything else. Meaning you enjoy it well enough, but it's not what you wanted to do, not really."

"I suppose you're right."

"Why did you go to school in England, when there are plenty of good medical universities in the States?"

"Family tradition. My parents immigrated here before they had children, and I'm the fifth in my line to graduate from

Oxford in medicine. Huge point of pride for my family. Speaking of whom, why do you think I don't like them?"

"The picture of your family is low on a wall you can't see— you love them enough to have their picture up, but you don't like them, which is why the picture isn't where you can see it easily. It also clearly shows architecture and landscape that's typical of the Northeastern United States. And I can understand the resentment, being forced into a role you do well with but didn't actually want. Why did you join the Army?"

"It seemed like... the right thing to do."

"Yes, and for at least one person, it made all the difference in the world. Which is why you went—to make a difference."

"How do you mean?"

"Your statuettes—they're cheaply made and inexpensive, yet you have them in a place of honor, where you can see them any time you look up from your desk. Saint George slew the dragon, Saint Rita is the patron saint of those wounded in battle. I doubt you bought those for yourself. They strike me as being gifted to you by the young woman whom you rescued."

"How do you know I saved a young woman?"

Holmes took a picture off the small wall opposite the one my medals hung upon. "She's about fourteen, based on her face, and Afghan, based on her clothing and location— somewhere in Kabul, if I'm any judge." She handed the picture to Straude. "She's also holding a sign that says 'to my hero' in Pashto, with a simple drawing of a man with blood on his left shoulder and right hip and a crown on his head. The photo is wrinkled, but you framed it anyway. It came with the Saint Rita statuette. You were injured after you rescued her. The Saint George statuette is older and shows signs of wear—she gave that to you before your injury and you kept it with you."

"Yes. To all of it. And she was being attacked by three men, one of whom was a relative of hers. I killed them all. They were insurgents, so my superior officers didn't mind. Her name is Anoosheh, it means—"

"Lucky," Holmes interrupted. "Or happy. And she was both, thanks to you." She took the photo back from Straude and hung it back up. "It's a rare thing for a man to save one girl from a brutal attack, in a situation where the authorities are unlikely to ever be involved, only to rape and murder five others in a country where the police are far more concerned, Lee."

Straude sighed. "We need to look at every possibility, Sherlock."

"I'll happily provide DNA if that's helpful."

"The killer uses a condom," Holmes said. "And he's very good about leaving nothing much for forensics to work with."

"Almost as if he's medically trained." Saunders shot me a look that said I was definitely still his favorite suspect. "He needs to be stopped. Whoever it is. It's why we called you in, Holmes."

"Four months too late," Holmes snapped.

Straude shrugged. "It took some convincing, Sherlock. You know I'd have had you out sooner if I could have."

Holmes didn't look appeased, but before anyone else could speak, there was a knock at my door and Mrs. Hudson stuck her head in. "I'm so sorry to interrupt yet again, but you're running late now, Doctor. Mr. Corey is here for your weekly order, and Alisa Brewer is waiting for her appointment as well. They've been chatting with me for a good ten minutes now, and Mr. Corey said he has to be off soon, and I know you don't like to miss him. And Alisa has a class starting at the top of the hour."

Straude and Saunders didn't look happy. "You two go to our next obvious suspects," Holmes said. "I'll stay here with the good doctor."

Straude heaved a sigh. "Fine, Sherlock. Meet up with us before you chase anything down, would you? Dr. Watson, don't leave town." With that, the two detectives left. The tension in the office went down to something normal.

"I'll see David first, Mrs. Hudson. Tell Alisa it'll just be a couple of minutes."

She ushered in my preferred pharmaceutical sales representative. Corey was a pleasant, unassuming man about my height, slender, with thinning blond hair, even though he wasn't quite out of his twenties. He shoved his glasses up as he came in, shot a shy look towards Holmes, then gave me a wry smile. "Guess I can't say you have the best job in the world today, can I, John?"

"I'll leave you to it," Holmes said as she stepped into the examining room. She closed the door, but not all the way.

Corey shook his head. "I heard about the latest. Terrible thing, John. I suppose drinks tonight is out. How are you holding up?"

"As well as can be expected. It wasn't my daughters who were raped and murdered, after all."

Corey shuddered. "Still, it's awful, and they were all your patients."

"True enough. And yes, I think our regular meet-up is out for this week. "

Corey dropped his voice. "John, I spoke to Howard on my way up. He said you had police in here, and those were police detectives I saw leaving. Are you... alright?"

"Hope so. Did the police question you?"

"No, and I don't think they've questioned Howard, either. I don't think we're here enough for them to care about us." He shot me a reassuring smile. "Well, for what it's worth, I know you didn't do it. Because there's no way my favorite customer is a lunatic." We both managed a chuckle, Corey gave me some new samples and I gave him my order. "John, I know your living arrangement isn't... ideal. I'm looking for a roommate. If you'd be interested, I'd like to offer it to you."

"Thank you, David, I appreciate that. Get me the information and I'll see if I can make it work."

Before Corey could leave, I heard raised voices from the hall, and my least favorite colleague burst into the room. My office was rarely this popular except during fraternity rush week, when all the girls came for help with 'difficult menstruation issues,' which was the nice girl code for wanting to get on birth control pills without upsetting their parents.

The head of the Physical Fitness Department, Frank LaBonte, slammed my door shut. "You little weasel, what have you done to my girls?" he roared at me. He was a big, muscular man, with a full head of thick hair and a walrus moustache. He seemed a century or so out of date, as if he belonged in the 1890s or 1920s, not now.

"What the hell are you talking about?"

"The police were here, questioning you. They know it was you who took my girls. I won't let you get Alisa, too!"

The one commonality the murdered girls had, in addition to being New London students, was that they were all on New London's track team. But this was close to the same as being a student, since track was the only competitive sport the college had, meaning any girl who had an ounce of athleticism in her was drafted onto the team. But it was a good program, and the team routinely medaled. That said, I didn't like how LaBonte claimed ownership of all the girls.

"Alisa's here to see her school physician," I said coldly. "And you're interrupting a business meeting."

"He undoubtedly wants the sick bastard doing this brought to justice. As in you, arrested."

Corey edged towards the door. "That's alright, John. I was just leaving. Sorry again about your loss. And, ah, Coach LaBonte, great job with the team. Hope one of them wins *Campus Queen*."

Corey fled. I couldn't blame him.

LaBonte glared at me. "You killed them."

"Hardly. You have more access to the girls than I do. You have them run through the trails in the hills behind the school. You're in a position of authority over them."

His face turned an interested shade of purple. "You're accusing *me* of hurting one of my girls? Of hurting *five* of them?"

"Oh, stop blustering." Holmes stepped out of the examination room. "I see Detectives Straude and Saunders have finished questioning you."

"For the fifth time," LaBonte shouted. "And yet they're no closer to finding the truth." He stabbed a thick finger at me. "He's the rapist, why isn't he under arrest?"

"I've heard that this country still enjoys little things like evidence and proof." Holmes got right up into LaBonte's face. "I said to stop blustering. You can calm down and leave, or I can make you leave. Your choice."

LaBonte glared at her. "Who the hell are you," he shook his finger at her, "to try to tell me—"

Holmes interrupted him with a lightning-fast jab to his throat, which shut him up. Then she grabbed the finger he'd waved in her face and bent it backwards. LaBonte was gasping and grimacing in pain, as well as on his knees on the floor in a moment. "I am Sherlock Holmes. I'm here, consulting for the L.A.P.D. I'm also adept in several forms of martial arts and am an excellent shot. And before you ask, I have a gun with me, and I'm truly not afraid to use it. Now, when I let you go, you'll have two choices. You can get up and leave, quietly, or I can beat the bloody crap out of you and you can leave on a stretcher. Choose wisely. If you're capable."

"I'd also apologize to her," I added. "Because you were extremely rude. I'm used to it, but Ms. Holmes is a visitor and you should represent New London better than you have so far."

To his credit, LaBonte stopped struggling. "I... apologize."

Holmes let him up and LaBonte stalked out of the room. "He's my top suspect," I said as Alisa peeked her head in.

"Maybe," Holmes said absently. "However, you'd do well to remember that just because you find someone reprehensible, it doesn't mean they're guilty. And the opposite is true as well."

She looked Alisa over. "Why are any of you girls going out alone?"

Alisa blinked. "Excuse me?"

"Since the second murder, the police have installed officers on campus, so it's presumably safe here. However, the five victims—they were all alone. None taken from their rooms, and their bodies weren't found on campus. Those with cars didn't drive them off school grounds, and all the girls were seen in the cafeteria at dinner the nights they were killed. As far as it's been determined, they left campus alone and were never seen alive again. Why, after the second murder, are any of you going out alone?"

"Most of us aren't. But some of the girls have jobs off-campus."

"None of the murdered girls, however." Holmes gave Alisa another piercing look. "Why, for instance, do you plan to go out tonight?"

"It's Friday night, and I'm done with homework and studying. Why shouldn't I go out? Molly was killed last night, and that's awful, but we weren't friends. The only thing we have in common is the track team, and we aren't in the same events. So I'm sorry, but..." She shrugged. "Besides, if it's a pattern, that means we're all safe for another month anyway."

"It's not been quite that regular," I said.

"Pretty close, though," Alisa argued. "Besides, I get the *Campus Queen* crew with me tonight, so what do I have to worry about?"

Holmes stared at her. "An excellent point. Are you a chosen contestant?"

"Not yet, but here's hoping."

"Indeed." Holmes nodded to me. "Go ahead and do your doctor-patient thing. I need to see your appointment book."

I handed it to her and took Alisa into the examination room. "She's strange," Alisa said.

"She's on to something." Although I had no idea of what.

*   *   *

ALISA TAKEN CARE of, I sent her on her way and rejoined Holmes. "What did you find?"

"It depends." She gave me a long look. "Did you know that the medical examiner has found steroids in all of the victims so far? Molly included."

"They weren't prescribed by me! But LaBonte likes winning. It wouldn't surprise me if he's encouraged the girls to dope themselves."

"How much of that statement is based on observation, or blood work you've done on the girls, and how much on the fact that the two of you obviously don't get along?"

"Honestly? I don't know."

"That's fair."

"I don't have blood work on all of them, but I did on Quannah and Molly. There were no steroids in their blood. So if Molly had steroids in her system, she started taking them after her appointment with me the month before last."

"The second-to-last appointment she had with you?"

"Yes. I drew no blood at her last visit."

"Interesting. Watch your back."

"Why?"

"You're the point of origin." Then she turned and left.

"That was abrupt," I said to the closed door. I waited a few seconds, then I left my office. Mrs. Hudson was able to act as my receptionist because the medical offices were on the main Administration floor, next door to the Dean's office. None of the police were there, and Holmes was walking down the long hallway. I nodded to Mrs. Hudson, then followed Holmes.

She didn't look behind her, just left the building. The school was quite beautiful and picturesque, and sat high on its hill, surrounded by foliage, mountains, and not much else. The visitors' level had a circular drive from which the main buildings radiated. The *Campus Queen* crew had taken over most of this area, using it for equipment storage and craft services. They let the girls and school staff eat from craft services, though I refused to on principle. I was, as far as I knew, the only person on campus who hadn't snuck at least a chocolate croissant and a latte.

I stopped at the main doors and looked out. Holmes was standing with Straude and Saunders and the men I knew to be the show's producer, director, and casting director—Tony Antonelli, Cliff Camden, and Joey Jackson—or, as I thought of them, the Unholy Three. Despite dressing in typically casual Southern California style, they gave off Mob vibes, but they were hugely successful in this realm. In addition to *Campus Queen*, they ran *Campus King*, *High School Confidential*, *The Real Families of Suburbia*, and *The Real Families of SoCal*. As moguls went, they were laid back, generous in many ways, and smarmy beyond belief.

Antonelli and Camden were having an animated conversation with the detectives, but Jackson was talking to Holmes. I got the impression he was suggesting that she try out for *Campus Queen*. Sometimes they asked faculty or staff to participate, to mix things up and keep the ratings high.

I wandered out. Beyonce's 'All the Single Ladies' was playing, courtesy of the show. It was the theme song for *Campus Queen* and, as such, seemed to be on constant repeat everywhere. Once, the first time I'd heard it, I'd enjoyed the song. Now I wondered if we were under some form of aural torture. As I neared them, Jackson shook his head. "Can't tell you that. It'll ruin the show."

"Oh, please?" Holmes asked, voice sweet as honey. "I'm such a big fan. And the soul of discretion, I promise you." She gave him a beaming smile.

Jackson smiled back. "Let me sleep on it."

Holmes winked at him, handed him what I thought was her

card, nodded to the detectives, then got into a silver sports car parked nearby and drove off. The detectives got into their far less interesting sedan and left as well, and two of the Unholy Three went back to whatever it was they did on our campus.

Jackson waved me over. "You're the school doctor, right? The one all the girls have a crush on?"

"Excuse me? I'm the doctor, but no one has a crush on me that I know of."

Jackson laughed. "Don't be coy. You're a war hero, young, good-looking, a doctor. You're catnip for the kittens."

"I'm not that young, and I don't date students."

"Then you have a baby face, which goes over well with the viewers. You could meet us down in Westwood. Alisa will be there—she's already told us she thinks you're hot. You two could casually knock into each other and spend the night getting to know each other off-campus."

"She's only nineteen." And now I was guaranteed to feel awkward the next time she needed medical attention.

"Okay, we'll find an older girl for you. But no problem if you don't want to show off your Casanova reputation on this show. We're going to be branching out—*Know Your Soldier*. More of a meaningful-month-in-the-life-of-a-returned-hero sort of thing." He nudged me. "You know, keeping the image up and giving some of the more patriotic something to be proud to watch."

"Good luck."

"Take my card." Jackson shoved his card at me.

I took it and backed away. "Thanks."

"Call me," he shouted, as I spun around and headed back into the Administration building. "We'll do lunch or have drinks."

I returned to my office and pulled out the file I'd been looking through when Holmes and the others arrived. For all her observational skills, it appeared she'd missed my slipping it away.

Or so I thought. As I opened the file, I saw a note, written in an unfamiliar hand. *You have a good case file started here. You're also making it very easy for the real culprit to incriminate you. Call me if you think of anything, or if anything out of the ordinary happens. And watch the show.* There was a card underneath this. The only thing printed on it was *Sherlock Holmes*, but there was a New York phone number written on the back in the same hand as the note. I slipped the card into my wallet.

NOTHING UNTOWARD HAPPENED for the next three and a half weeks. The entire campus was on edge, and some of the girls had been brought home by their parents, though none of the girls so far selected for *Campus Queen*. But no one else was attacked.

In addition to seeing patients and participating in what seemed like endless safety preparedness lectures for faculty, staff, and students, I did my best to avoid LaBonte, who glowered at me any time we were within eyeshot of each other.

It was impossible to avoid the Unholy Three, and apparently Jackson had shared his desire to 'cast' me with the other two, because they also spent time badgering me to 'bump into' various girls in various spots. I drew the line at their cameras entering the medical offices, but there were several times I was ambushed by some of the girls with cameras rolling.

Holmes was on campus frequently, as were Straude and Saunders, though she didn't drop in to see me. I tried not to allow it to hurt my feelings, with limited success. Why it bothered me I couldn't say, especially since she was cordial when we ran into each other in the halls. She spent quite a lot of time with Mrs. Hudson; they went to lunch together frequently.

Other than a couple of pleasant and unremarkable nights out with Corey, wherein, despite the protests of the Unholy Three to the contrary, we got no women to pay us any mind but did get to make each other laugh, I spent my spare time looking at my file and my appointment book. Holmes had seen something in them that had set her off and I wanted to figure out what.

Per the papers and my own experience, literally every New London student, member of the faculty and staff, including groundskeepers, delivery people, and all of the *Campus Queen* crew, had been questioned by now, not just by uniformed officers but the detectives in charge of the case. Some, like LeBonte, several times. Nothing.

The usual suspects at the other colleges and universities in the general area—the fraternities and similar groups—had also been investigated. After the second murder, the police had expanded to include all the colleges in the Los Angeles basin, of which there were many. But nothing had popped, and as near as forensics could tell, none of the murdered girls had gone too far from New London when they'd been taken.

LaBonte was still my number one suspect. The girls would trust him implicitly, meaning he could get them to leave campus alone to meet him somewhere. He was certainly strong enough to overpower them. And if drugs were involved in some way, they'd all be more likely to take them from their coach than anyone else.

I also, per Holmes' odd request, watched *Campus Queen*. The premise was that the show's staff spent time at a lucky college chosen at random. Their goal was to choose a set of 'beauties of all kinds' via an overly wrought Secret Invitation process which required total secrecy on the part of the recipient and bizarre stunts just this side of hazing in order to pass the show's approval stage. All filmed for the entertainment of the viewing public.

Once the girls had accepted the offer, and presumably signed all the consent forms, they were put into a competition with each other to see who would earn the title of Queen and a dream week in an exotic location with an attractive male celebrity chosen probably because he had a movie coming out.

Because the most popular portion of the show was the selection process, the crew followed more than just the girls given invitations, which was why there were on campus so much, capturing 'live' footage. They'd been at a college in New York prior to ours, and that was what this season was featuring. Other than making me hate everything about reality TV, there was nothing much of interest.

Corey and I had had drinks and dinner earlier, but he'd taken me back so he could get home in time to watch *Campus Queen*. He claimed to enjoy the show, which was the only thing about him I didn't like. But it allowed me to watch my assigned homework. This week's episode finally ended and, as I turned off the TV, my phone rang. The number had a New York prefix. "Hello, is this Sherlock?"

"Yes. Watson, your hazardous materials pickup is tomorrow, correct?"

"Ah, yes, I believe so. Why? And how did you get my number?"

"You believe or you know? I got your number from Lee. And, where are you?"

"I know. It's always the first Friday of the month. I'll complain about the police's invasion of my privacy later. And I'm at home. Just finished watching that Godawful program you told me to, though I have no idea why. Either why I'm watching or why you told me to. Or why you care about my wastes pickup."

"You're alone?"

"Yes. Why?"

She heaved an exasperated sigh. "Why do you think? The game's afoot and our serial killer is going to strike again. Tonight. If you have a gun, get it ready, and ensure you're in dark clothing. I'll be with you in ten minutes or less." She hung up before I could say anything and without answering any of my questions.

Wondering why I was doing what this woman told me to, I got my gun, ensured it had a full clip, shoved a few other clips into my jacket pocket and clipped my holster onto my waistband. There was a soft sound behind me just as I did so.

I spun around to see Holmes standing there, in a dark grey sweater and jeans, woman's pea coat—dark grey, of course—hair again pulled back into a ponytail. Like me, she had a gun clipped to the waist of her jeans. Unlike me, she seemed intent, almost excited. I managed not to jump or shout, but just barely. "How did you get in here?"

"Through the window. Which is how we're also going out. Lock up, but leave your lights on, as if you're home and having one of your many sleepless nights." She handed me a pair of goggles. "Night vision. Oh, and please assume we're in enemy territory and trying to avoid being captured."

"What? You literally don't speak to me for over three weeks and then just assume I'm going to head out on some weird adventure with you?" She put a pair of goggles on and I followed suit.

"So sensitive. I'll remember that. And I'm sorry I wounded your feelings. I was working, as were you. Unlike some people, I don't feel the need to see someone every waking moment to reassure myself of affinity." We crawled out the way she'd come in.

"How do you know I have insomnia? And yes, fine, I'll be stealthy. And stop complaining."

"Good. I could explain my cleverness," she said in a low voice, "but I know because I've been watching the school at night for the past three weeks. None of you has the first idea of what security actually means. There are twenty uniformed officers stationed all over, and yet the entire student body, all of the *Campus Queen* crew, and half of the staff are doing their level best to ensure that the police never see them coming or going. It's as if everyone *wants* to be the next victim."

"Well, you're having us avoid them, too; at least, I assume that's why we left via my rear window."

We were walking up the hill, towards the dorms, though we were off the paths or main road, moving through the foliage. I'd been trained in how to move without making noise or being seen, as well as how to speak softly enough to be heard by those right next to me and no one else, and I was good at it. The night vision goggles helped tremendously, of course, but if I was good, Holmes was a master. Barring us setting off a motion detector or stepping on an animal, no one would know we were around.

"I'm working *for* the police, and I'm trying to catch a killer. It's a tad different."

"Why are you having me back you up? I mean, I assume that's why I'm here."

"Why do you think?"

"The only thing I can come up with is that you trust me. While I appreciate that, I have no idea why you do."

She sighed. "You see, but you don't observe. That's the problem with most people, honestly. However, despite what you may think, we have a lot in common, you and I. We're both avoiding family we love but don't like, we're both loners who don't actually like being alone, and we're both protectors. Plus, you speak English properly and you have *no* idea how refreshing that is."

We reached the point where we should have turned to get to the dorms, but Holmes kept on going, towards the back of the school.

"Ah. Well, alright then. Speaking of which, shouldn't we be trying to protect whomever you think is the next intended victim? As in going into the dorms?"

"No. The idiot will come directly to him. By personal invitation."

"Then why are we skulking about?"

"Because I need our killer to firmly believe I'm nowhere around and that you're sitting home alone, making yourself the perfect patsy. You need a roommate."

"David's already suggested it. I don't have a car, however. And you think the killer is trying to frame me? Why?"

"I don't think, I know. And as for why? Because the killer is doing all of this to hurt *you*."

"That's insane."

"Most serial killers are."

"Why would you even think that?"

"Because after we remove the obvious connections of school and athletics, the only thing that the murdered girls have in common is that they all visited you and died a month later."

"If you know who it is, why isn't he under arrest?"

"Knowing and proving, Watson, are not the same thing. I've already searched and found nothing definitive. If I couldn't find it, the police won't, either, and a search warrant would just mean he goes to ground. Right now the only advantage we have is that he doesn't know that I suspect him."

"But you said you searched his home or wherever."

"I did. When I search, you don't know I've done so unless I want you to know."

"Ah. You've searched my rooms, haven't you?"

"Invading your privacy, one day at a time."

We reached the main trail that connected the school to the mountains behind. It was there for the fire department, and truly more of a dirt road. There was a main dump about a mile away, and those trucks occasionally used this part of the trail road as well. Sometimes hunters also accessed it. But mostly it was used by our track team for training.

"Are you going to tell me who you suspect?" I whispered, as Holmes once again kept us off the main track and in the foliage.

"I was rather hoping you'd figured it out," she replied in kind. "You have all the information I do. More, really."

"I haven't the faintest idea."

"Well, maybe that's not a surprise. He's a clever one, Watson, make no mistake. As clever as he is punctual. But we're going to be more clever."

Before I could respond to this, Holmes put her finger to her lips and pulled me down. I heard the sound of someone running. A girl jogged right past us on the path. She had something white in her hand.

I put my mouth to Holmes' ear. "That's Alisa."

She nodded, then nudged me. We followed Alisa, still staying off the main road. The trail forked and she went to the left, meaning she was heading for the dump. The goggles were a blessing—we were having to move quickly to keep her in view, and we wanted to remain unseen.

Alisa wasn't trying to go too fast, and we reached the dump in about six minutes. As she neared the entrance, car headlights flashed three times. Alisa headed for them.

"Hurry, Watson," Holmes said, as she took off running.

I'd been fine with all the exertion and the slow jog we'd been at. But my injury didn't allow me to sprint with ease. And Holmes was absolutely sprinting. If LaBonte wasn't the killer, he'd want to see if she'd be willing to take a course as a returning student just to get her onto the team.

I lost sight of Holmes, but could still see Alisa and the car she was heading for. The car door opened and someone got out, but he stayed behind the door and I couldn't tell who it was, only that, judging by his build, this wasn't LaBonte.

Alisa ran over to him and handed him the white thing she was holding. He stepped around the back of the car, went to the other side, and opened the passenger door. This side was near a pile of garbage that had what looked like a tarp against it.

As Alisa was between the door and the garbage, he grabbed her. I still couldn't tell who he was. Alisa's mouth opened to scream, but he stuffed something in it, backhanded her face, and shoved her down, hard, onto the tarp. He was on her in a moment.

And then Holmes was on him.

She body-slammed him off Alisa and they rolled, which put them into the glow of the car's headlights. They struggled for what seemed like forever, while I ran in what truly seemed like slow motion. He landed some good hits, but Holmes landed more, and she was clearly the more experienced grappler. He tried to hold onto her, but Holmes was able to shove him off and away. She scrambled to her feet and managed a good roundhouse to his head as he tried to stand up. He went down, but got back up again. And he had a gun in his hand. I looked—it was Holmes'.

I had no time to be shocked that she'd let her gun be taken away. I was too busy being shocked by who was in front of me.

There was no time to think, really. He wasn't going to grandstand. He was going to shoot Holmes dead with her own gun, wipe it, and then still rape and murder Alisa. So I didn't think. I did what I'd done before, in Afghanistan. I emptied the clip into him.

"NICELY DONE, WATSON, thank you," Holmes said a little breathlessly, as I reached them and she shoved her gun away from his hand and then retrieved it. "Can you please check on Alisa? I don't think he had time to drug her, but he did have time to hit her."

"I'm okay," Alisa said, sounding shaky, as she joined us. "I thought..."

"That you were the next *Campus Queen* contestant," Holmes said. "Yes, I know. You've had that invitation for a week, haven't you?"

Alisa nodded. "I got it last Friday."

"And you managed not to tell anyone, because if you had, it was goodbye to your shot on *Campus Queen*. It was brilliant, really. A *tour de force* example of utilizing all the elements available to you."

"He's a murdering rapist," Alisa snapped.

"Always appreciate intelligence, young lady. It will help you, in your later life. Which you're lucky to be able to look forward to having. And strictly speaking, he *was* a murdering rapist; now, he's a dead monster."

I flipped the man over, to be sure. I stared, still shocked. David Corey's glassy eyes stared back at me. "David? But... why? And how?"

Holmes was on her phone. "Yes. Yes, the pharmaceuticals rep. Right, the dump. Yes, thank you, the sooner the better." She hung up. "Lee's on his way. *Why* is simple, Watson. I already told you. He was doing this to hurt you."

"Why me?"

"You had what he wanted. A medical degree from an extremely impressive university, a job with all those lovely single ladies— none of whom were giving him the time of day, other than when they were waiting to see you—and a hero's reputation."

"But... he was my friend. He wanted to room together."

"No, he was a psychopath who'd created a dangerous and unnatural fixation on you. He *wanted* to ensure you didn't somehow take a roommate before he could complete his killing spree and frame-up, because you having an alibi would ruin his plans. Per Mrs. Hudson, Mr. Corey had applied for the position you ended up filling, but since his degree in medicine was from an unaccredited college, New London refused his application."

"He always visited me the day of my hazardous wastes pickup."

"Yes, and always took the time to speak to Howard, who is a nice man, though not a very observant one. The used condoms were therefore tossed into a hazardous waste bin, meaning they weren't going to be found."

"Did he bring all the girls to the dump to attack them?"

"Most likely. Because of *Campus Queen*, all the girls were prepared to get bizarre and highly suspicious invitations to go someplace remarkably dangerous alone and, also because of the show's secrecy policy, without telling a single living soul about it. In other words, he had an open field of choices and an easy way to fool them. Rape and murder her at the dump on a clean tarp, wrap her in heavy duty plastic when done, dispose of the tarp somewhere at the next dump area, transport the girl's dead body to a random site, and move on to the next."

"So forensics would only find the tarp traces, nothing else. What about the steroids?"

"That was done to implicate you and LaBonte both, just in case you had a clear alibi. LaBonte wants to win, and all the girls know it. It wouldn't take a lot to suspect he'd had them juicing, or used it as a way to get them to a secluded place alone. Corey here had access to drugs." She shrugged. "And for all we know, framing LaBonte was his backup plan. I'm sure he had one. At least one."

"This car, it isn't his."

"He only came to New London in his company car. This one is his personal car that he kept in a garage nowhere near his house. A garage that doesn't require a code for entry, by the way, just a key. And has no video surveillance."

"How did you find all this out? You'd had to have had suspicions earlier than today."

"I knew he was the killer when I met you," Holmes said. "Howard was a possibility, of course. Only those two were here only at the day and time when one of the murdered girls visited you. You pointed that out to me," she said to Alisa, as the sound of police sirens reached us. "So thank you."

"Oh, my God; no, thank *you*." Alisa heaved a shuddering sigh. "So, I'm not a *Campus Queen* candidate after all, am I?"

"You will be," Holmes said. "I've already arranged it. Under the circumstances, I can guarantee that Mister Jackson will have you."

"You have? Why?" Alisa sounded as shocked as I felt.

Holmes shrugged. "I'm something of a reality TV addict. You gave me the one clue I needed. I'd like to both thank you for that, and have someone I know personally to root for."

Alisa gaped, then flung her arms around Holmes. "You're so awesome!"

As they hugged, Holmes caught my eye. She was once again trying not to laugh. "Happier about landing a spot on the show than being alive. Ah, Southern California."

The police arrived before I could comment.

"Now what?" I asked Holmes, once we were done briefing Straude and a rather disappointed Saunders on what had happened. "I mean, when are you going back to New York or London?"

She looked around. "I rather like it here. Lee's convinced his superiors that I'm an asset the L.A.P.D. should be holding onto, and they've offered a very generous retainer while also allowing me to pursue cases on my own, which is better than the arrangement I had in New York. Did you know that Mrs. Hudson owns a duplex in Santa Monica? She lives in one half and rents the other. Each side has two bedrooms and two bathrooms, with shared kitchen, dining, and living rooms. On Baker Street. Nice little neighborhood, close to everything, but still private."

"No, I didn't. Santa Monica is rent-controlled. The waiting list must be extreme."

Holmes shrugged. "It depends on who you are. I quite like her, and she appears to have taken a shine to me, just as she has to you." She looked at me. "I can afford to rent it by myself, but I don't enjoy living alone. I lived with my brother in London, which is why I moved to New York. My... roommate in New York didn't work out, for a variety of reasons. However, I've never actually tried living with a friend. That's how most people do it, isn't it?"

"If I'm understanding your insinuation correctly, you realize I don't have a job anymore, don't you? I can't possibly stay here, not after all of this. The moment it comes out that David was doing this to harm me, I'll be asked to leave for the safety of the girls, just in case another lunatic fixates on me. I'll be the scapegoat to make New London safe for its students again. And the notoriety isn't going to help me land another position any time soon."

"That depends on what position you're looking for. And I think you're selling a campus that gleefully welcomed a reality TV show short." She shrugged. "However, you're open to leaving without a fight because you don't love medicine, Watson. People who love medicine don't keep files on murders and try to solve them, nor do they enthusiastically participate in the pursuit and capture of a dangerous serial killer."

"I suppose not."

"However, there are people who do that on a regular basis. We call them *detectives*." She smiled. It looked good on her. "And I'd like to offer you the position of partner. From what Lee tells me, I'm going to be very busy here. Your military and medical background will be most helpful to me. And... it's always good to have someone I can trust watching my back. Plus, it's just such a relief to hear someone, anyone, who doesn't murder the Queen's English every other sentence."

I couldn't help myself, I grinned. "Then, I'm your man."

"And, as you'll learn, Watson, I always get my man."

THE PATCHWORK KILLER

KASEY LANSDALE

Daughter of the celebrated horror author Joe Lansdale, Kasey's both an accomplished author and anthologist herself and a talented country musician. That she's also genuinely warm and unprepossessing can only be regarded as slightly unfair...

I'm frankly stumped where she finds the time for it all, negotiating and exchanging contracts, writing the story and wrangling edits with me, all in snatched email exchanges while on the road in the US and Europe. But I'm very glad she did, as she adds, in 'The Patchwork Killer,' a tone of creeping body horror to the collection, as well as finding a decidedly off-beat way to bring the famous detective into the modern world.

FOR SHERLOCK HOLMES, these matters were immaterial. Annoying, even. Not one for small talk or pleasantries, I only called upon him when I found myself in the greatest of need. Now you have likely heard the stories, but it is less likely that you have received the entire story. Everyone who knew him knew Sherlock was a genius, but at the same time, absolutely useless to carry on a conversation with the lay-person. Fast forward over one hundred years, and across the globe, and I can tell you with great confidence that nothing has changed.

The world has changed. The technology has changed. Holmes, however, is the same smug bastard as always. As my great-uncle (well, my great-great-uncle) used to say,

"For such a genius, he's a gormless sod."

Sure, I was American by all accounts, my great-uncle Dr. John H. Watson had immigrated to the States just before he died. (That's what he always told people. The truth was Holmes sent him here for a case, something about a chemist who was cloning other humans, and things had gone wrong. Terribly wrong. While investigating, he'd met a woman who worked at the lab he was there to investigate. His wife Mary had stayed behind, as it was supposed to be a short trip, but love works in mysterious ways.)

He would at first send word he was making progress and needed more time. It turned out he was actually making quite a bit of progress and nine months later came Cousin (once removed, I suppose; I never much understood all that) William. Aunt Caroline knew about John's other life—other wife, even—but she had decided at almost forty there was no room to be picky. She wanted a family, even if it was all a façade. Needless to say, my bloodline started off with lies and deception. Par for what has been my life.

My uncle was a military man, something I, too, became. I could imagine Sherlock standing over me now as I tell you this saying,

"Boring."

And he would be correct. My story was no different from that of dozens of other families who immigrated and began a new life.

Sherlock Holmes however, was never boring. Never dull. And most definitely, never ordinary.

Much of the original information I had about Holmes and the friendship he'd shared with my great-uncle came from shoddy, incomplete notes that had been passed down through the generations. Sherlock himself would later fill me in on their many great adventures.

You may wonder how that's so, but first things first, you see. Right now, I was staring at the mutilated, lifeless body of Darlene Jenkins, a local star in her own right. Her face had been slashed, and at one point during the brutal murder, the skin meticulously removed. Her body flat, drained of all its fluids, and—based on the resealed wound that traveled from navel to sternum—her insides harvested.

A thick, purplish bruise had formed around her throat, and though I hate to say it, none of that was the shocking part. The thing that had me stumped, and Detective Michaels besides, was the flesh of the body which had been removed, appeared to have been cut into squares and sewn back together with surgical precision. Several pieces were missing.

It made no sense why the murderer would take the time to kill her, cut her up, drain her, and then build her back together, save a few pieces.

It looked like something my grandmother might quilt for a baby gift, if she were in the business of gifting human skin. It didn't take long before the media had dubbed the murderer, 'The Patchwork Killer.'

A silly name, no doubt. But they never did ask for my input on those matters. I was called in only to assess the situation when Michaels was at a loss. It had become widely known that I was a go-to guy for strange events. I was not a doctor like my dear uncle, not in the traditional sense. I'd had medical training, but that which you get through dental school.

For the most part, people in town felt safe. It was a small community, and this appeared to be an isolated incident, one that Miss Jenkins likely brought on herself, being an entertainer and all.

Of course, no one said that out loud, but none had to. It was pretty clear that six months from now, no one would remember this or her, and if they did, they likely would not care.

Until it happened again.

This time to a young girl leaving her shift at the yogurt shop downtown near the Blue Moon Cabaret where Miss Jenkins worked.

This murder, executed in the same manner, brought everyone up in arms. This was no harlot who may or may not have had it coming; this was one of life's innocents.

No one was safe. No longer could they brush off Miss Jenkins' death as a lifestyle casualty. Someone who drew attention upon herself, so she must have surely been asking for it (I didn't agree with that, of course, but you might be surprised at how many around here did).

It was a mystery, alright. I reviewed my notes, tried to glean something about why these murders had occurred and by whom. The profile offered by the local police department was the same as it always was. Likely white, mid-forties, ill relationship with their mother. But that was almost everyone I knew. Several days later, with me no closer to any leads, the body of another victim was found. This time a man, throwing off some of my original theories.

Why a man, in broad daylight? A drifter, at that, found with nothing more than a lighter in his pocket. This didn't seem to fit.

He was discovered by a blind man, of all people, out on a morning stroll with his guide animal.

"The dog became intolerable. And he always obeys. That's how I knew something weren't right."

"The dog?"

"Correct, sir, something clearly weren't right. Even a blind man like myself could see that."

"What do you make of it?" Detective Michaels asked me.

"It is undoubtedly the same killer. This I'm certain. But again, this act of resealing the flesh has me puzzled. If he killed them at the location of their bodies, there's no way he would have the time to execute such clean lines, such amazing—"

"Doctor Watson, please. You sound more like an admirer than a doctor."

It was not the first time such an accusation had arisen, it had been a nightmare trying to explain to a room of detectives why I found it impressive that a kidnapper could abduct children in the light of day only feet away from their caregivers. Or how a delayed poisoning scheme was sheer brilliance. Holmes understood, of course, but he was a sociopath.

"It's just baffling. Usually if the skin is removed, it's for a souvenir or for something cannibalistic in nature. To just remove it for the fun of reassembling it, this makes no sense to me. It's as though the killer was just... curious. I shall think it over, Michaels, and report back my findings."

Detective Michaels was in his mid-forties, with greying orange hair and unruly brows. Sallow-faced, with a look of no good about him, save his piercing blue eyes.

He certainly didn't know my secret. In fact, only one person was aware, and even that had happened by accident.

Mrs. Hernandez, my landlady. She was a busybody and notorious neat freak. I knew only that her name was Maria because she would follow me around the house with a handy vac saying, "It's always Maria who must clean. Why does Maria get stuck with this? Who takes care of Maria?"

I had found her apartment through a client. I took great joy in asking my patients questions when they went under the gas, mouth full of utensils. It's quite a position of power, dentistry. That's what I told my lady friends, at least.

Anyhow, I had this fella who had quite a mouth full of work needed and he said in exchange for part of the cost, he could fix me up with a great rental apartment, since I'd mentioned I was looking. We arrived not long after at 221B Baker Street.

I found it to be quite suitable, and I never thought too much one way or another about why it was so affordable until once, by accident, a bit of mail addressed to Maria Turner appeared in our mailbox. This caused me to question some things, but I only did so to myself, never aloud. Based on the price of the rent and the way she moved her hips to the music as she cleaned, I was certain this was not her first life. I'd never mentioned this to Holmes, though I have no doubt he already knew. He was impossible about most things, but he had a soft spot for Mrs. Hernandez, or Turner, whoever she may be. Women were drawn to him in a way that even Sherlock Holmes could never understand. He dismissed their affections, all of them, save 'The Woman,' as he called her. She'd since passed years ago, and though he spoke of her rarely, it was always with great admiration. I never asked further.

Back in the confines of my quiet apartment, which overlooked a small patch of grass that masqueraded as a dog park, I locked the doors and pulled the shades closed. I waited until I heard the sound of the Mariachi blaring from Mrs. Hernandez' apartment and pulled out the small wooden box concealed inside my inner coat pocket. It was under number lock, but I never used it. I'd decided if anyone could get out of there what they thought they wanted, they could have it, and deal with the consequences.

There had been a case, several years back, where the services of a dental professional were required. Detective Michaels had, by sheer coincidence, chosen John Watson, D.D.S. from a random billboard sign near downtown where a jumper had been found.

Mysteriously, said jumper could not be identified through finger print analysis, so I was called in to access the dental records. Easy enough, and quite a standard procedure.

However, the lab tech who conducted the usual x-rays in my office was on holiday at that time, so I was reduced to the menial task of reviewing the slides and taking the photographs. Being careless, as I was in all honesty a bit snockered—I'd been called away mid-date with a gorgeous hygienist I'd met at a conference the weekend before—I examined and photographed the teeth for hours without wearing the proper gear, assuming my only risk was radiation.

Upon cleaning the lab and making my final notes, I placed everything into a manila envelope and filed it away under J, for Jane Doe, back in my office a few doors down. It was the only file there, save my own. The practice had begun to take a hit from the economy. I suppose people were more worried about the cost of food than what that food might do to their teeth. Just as I had convinced myself that I should have gone to school to be a medical doctor, I heard an unfamiliar noise.

"Anyone there?" I asked.

As though that ever truly worked. It was half past one in the morning, so I was most certain to be alone at this hour. The noise did not return, so I resumed my daydreaming until once again the unfamiliar sound from the lab rung out, louder than before. Now, certain it was more than the imagination of a middle aged-man who'd had one too many, I followed the sound down the narrow corridor and into the workroom.

"Who are you?" I asked.

There, in the far corner of the room, wearing only my dress jacket and a smile, was a tall, thin man with dark hair and a beak-like nose. He seemed alert, though dazed, and when I entered the room he glanced my way, then seemed to become disinterested just as quickly.

"I say again, sir, who are you? What are you doing in my office with my coat on?"

His eyebrows rose, as if surprised that I would dare ask such a question at all, let alone twice. I saw the wooden box that had been sealed and inside my coat pocket broken open and upside down on the floor, several feet away.

"What did you do to my uncle's box? How did you open it?"

The man skimmed me up and down, and a light presented itself in his eyes.

"That's it, I'm calling the police," I said.

As I turned, the man spoke.

"Dr. John Watson was your relative. He was your great-great-uncle, not your 'uncle' as you say, and I would recommend not drinking when you come into work so late."

"How did you—?"

"You made the correct decision, though, to leave your date, as she is married, and it would be nothing but trouble for you had you remained."

At this point, fear was no longer a factor.

"That's incredible; how did you know that?"

"It's fairly obvious, isn't it?"

I looked around, as he surely couldn't have been speaking to me.

"Not for me, it isn't."

"It must be dreadful to be you," he said.

The strangeness of it all was lessened by my intrigue and desire to know just who this man was. He took a step towards me, and I reached for my belt; though it had been years since the military, old habits die hard.

"Relax, Doctor, you are in no danger. Are you still having the nightmares?"

"Nightmares?"

He sighed, seemingly exasperated by this line of questioning.

"Yes, Doctor, the nightmares. Are you still having them?"

"Now and again," I said.

"Fascinating," he said.

"Is it?"

He didn't answer, and instead stepped closer in my direction. Though his appearance was a bit overbearing, I couldn't say I felt threatened. The man acted as though he was fascinated by everything around him, and yet his eyes said he was already over it. There was something familiar about him, but I couldn't quite put my finger on it.

"I feel like I know you. Like I've seen you before. Did my ex-wife send you? Are you her most recent fling that's now been flung?" I chuckled to myself, but was cut off by the sharp tone of the mystery man.

"Oh, you would like that, wouldn't you? An easy answer, something simple like yourself. Well it is quite simple actually, Doctor; quite simple indeed. I knew your great-great-uncle."

His accent was British, so it seemed plausible for a moment, until I realized that there was no way this gentleman could have been alive when my uncle was, based on his middle-aged appearance now.

"Whatever trick you are trying to pull, I think I've had enough. You've had your fun now. There's no money here, and you wouldn't make it far if you tried to sell the equipment. Everything has a serial number, and—"

"Oh, Dr. Watson, I'm not here to rob you. I'm here to help you."

YOU CAN IMAGINE how all of this must have looked to me, but I can assure you that whatever scenario you have drawn up in your mind would not be comparable to the confusion I felt. His voice was cold, articulate, and he sighed with exaggeration as each moment passed.

"There is no other answer, Dr. Watson. I knew your great-great-uncle—knew him quite well, actually—and the longer we waste here, the less we know about this jumper."

"Now, how did you know about that?" I asked.

"I've heard everything. Do you want me to explain why I am here, or do you want to catch a killer?"

BY THIS POINT, I had tweaked the technique, such that I did not require all of the equipment from my lab, only the portable x-ray unit, a few petri dishes, and a process similar to somatic cell nuclear transfer, but rather than needing a surrogate of sorts to fertilize the cells, a way was discovered to warm them using the radiation from the x-rays. This process was discovered by accident by my great-uncle Dr. John Watson. Apparently, he was working on something, when he'd refused to return from America—other than my great-aunt. That was what had been on those notes, and similar to the way he had discovered it, the right combination of radiation and lighting and all around odd luck had been exactly what had happened for me.

Though I would never have been able to recreate the process blind, as lightning tends to not strike twice, I was—through his spotty notes, and many failed attempts—able to decipher a process as close to human cloning as had been discovered. The ashes of Sherlock had been carefully preserved in that wooden box, and that was why my uncle had passed it down to me. I suppose he knew we were the same, he and I. Living a mundane life and in need of more than a military background and a boring medical practice, and that was how Sherlock Holmes came to be standing in my living room, looking over my notes on the Patchwork Killer case. He would at times disappear, usually when the days had been exceptionally long, but I could always find him again within that wooden box.

"This Miss Jenkins; what else do you know about her?" Holmes asked.

"Not much," I said. "She's a local celebrity of sorts, and not just for her performances down at the Blue Moon Cabaret."

"I see."

Sherlock continued scanning over the notes I had made while on scene as Mrs. Hernandez entered the room.

"Horchata, Dr. Watson?"

Mrs. Hernandez had both hands wrapped around the edge of a large, flowered metal tray that housed three glass tumblers filled with what at a distance looked like milk. Each glass had a stick of cinnamon peeking out from the top, and since it was clear she had gone to some trouble to make this presentation, I accepted and joined her at the small dining table several feet away.

"What about him?" she asked me.

"Just ignore him for now. He's thinking. This could go on for hours, days even."

Mrs. Hernandez, though visibly curious, refrained from any further questioning. Whatever was in her past life had taught her one thing: the less you knew, the safer you were.

We sat at the table drinking the ice-cold liquid and watched Holmes pace the floor, manic. He waved his arms overhead and mumbled to himself with each step.

"He looks like a crazy person," she said.

Though I agreed, and in his own way he was precisely that, I just nodded, and continued sipping my drink. Mrs. Hernandez had hung around as long as possible, brought snacks, more horchatas, even began sorting the dishes from the dishwasher, until from nowhere Sherlock yelled out.

"Get out!"

Mrs. Hernandez and I looked at one another, confused, but he yelled again and rushed in our direction like an ape whose ass had been lit on fire. Mrs. Hernandez grabbed up her tray and backed out of the kitchen. At the top of the stairs she called out,

"I'll stop by later to—"

"I said out!"

She made a final noise of indignation and disappeared below.

"Do you have to do that?" I asked.

"She's just curious. Imagine how you would feel if suddenly some strange person appeared in the living room from a box the size of your fist."

"You know my methods, Watson. We haven't much time."

And with that, he rushed out the door and down the dimly-lit corridor, onto the street, with me trailing closely behind.

* * *

AFTER HE HAD solved the mystery of why the jumper had no fingerprints in about ten minutes, which I relayed to Detective Michaels, the force started calling me in on all sorts of odd crimes. The jumper had, in fact, jumped. It was an open-shut case of suicide. A plastic surgeon known around town for her impeccable botox work and experimental drug trials. The fingerprints had been sheerly a coincidence. Something so bizarre and random only Sherlock was able to identify it. Adermatoglyphia. The extremely rare instance of someone being born without finger prints. Nothing more, nothing less.

"Sometimes, the easiest explanation is the correct one," he said.

Was it glamorous? No. But it was the only answer, and after the dental records were returned and the victim identified and family notified, the proof was further solidified by the suicide note that came three days later in the mail to the mother of the jumper.

The calls for help became more frequent, and eventually Detective Michaels hired me as the squad doctor. Though on paperwork it would appear I was doing dental consultations, I was, in fact, consulting on the murders when they were unable to reach a solution. Sherlock would tag along to each scene in one way or another; either in the wooden box in the inner pocket of my coat, or in person. He wore a ridiculous hat with a long grey trench coat which made him quite conspicuous, but everyone was always so caught up in the crime that he was usually able to get a first-hand look at the scene.

Eventually, I had to introduce him as my new assistant, training abroad, and trust me when I say he loathed the title, but it was my only choice when at one point he licked the body of a dead child to see if there was salt water residue. Something that, no matter how lenient, or how blind an eye one might turn, cannot be overlooked.

The onlookers watched, horrified, Detective Michaels gasped, and I—well, after I recovered from the mini stroke which had just occurred—said that he was with me officially, so as to avoid having to bail him out from jail as a child predator. I'd tried to keep his presence at a minimum and avoid any actions that might raise suspicion. The last thing I needed was the world to find out that I, a simple dentist, was doing human cloning of sorts in my illegally sublet apartment.

Sherlock had found nothing strange about what he had done, and thought that everyone had overreacted. I tried to explain how the mother of the child, how we as decent human beings, felt about what he had done, but it didn't register. Holmes was not one for softer passions, children, women, love; all things he admired as an onlooker, but would never involve himself in, especially when it came to a case.

We never spoke of his personal life, and when I spoke of mine, he seemed disinterested, annoyed. He once mentioned someone whom he called 'The Woman,' but he did not elaborate and I did not ask. He spoke of her the way one speaks of a rock star idol more than a lost lover. I was certain he felt no passionate feelings for The Woman, but he seemed to admire her a great deal, from what little he had said.

INSIDE THE BLUE Moon, it was dark, seedy, and not the sort of place you would want your mother to know you frequented. The women were scantily clad and the air was dank and smelled like stale sweat and fried potatoes. Some men gathered around green felt tables playing blackjack while the rest sat near the end of a small round stage where a young girl danced in fishnets. Too young, if you asked me.

Once the girl exited the stage, Sherlock approached her.

"Here, put this on."

"Are you serious?" the girl asked. "You think I'm going to make money looking like I'm wearing an old potato sack?"

"Just humor me. Watson, give me your wallet."

I had learned quite early on that to argue was useless, so I reached into my back pocket, and handed him my wallet. He reached inside, took out all of the cash I had and gave it to the girl. Her eyes beamed and her defensive demeanor melted.

"This is not what you think it is," Sherlock said. "This is for information."

The girl once again became skeptical, but with a wad of money pressed into her palm, she played along in case there was more where that had come from.

"Why would anyone want to kill Miss Jenkins?"

The girl, who had already appeared young and fraught, seemed to shrink even smaller. Her thin bleach-blonde hair fell over her eyes and she hunched down and hid her face.

"What is it, child?" I asked.

"I am not a child," she snapped back, but as soon as the last word left her mouth she returned to her defeated stance.

"I can't talk about this here," she said. "They're everywhere." She shifted her eyes upwards. From the dark corners of the room, a small red light came into focus. Cameras were set up throughout the building, and it was clear we would get nothing from her.

"Kiss me," Sherlock said.

"Sherlock!"

"It's not what you think. Just do it." The girl, accustomed to being told what to do, obliged.

I watched uncomfortably as the two proceeded to nuzzle and whisper to one another.

The door burst open onto the street and the light stung my eyes.

"What the hell was that about?" I asked.

"This," Holmes said.

Now once again wearing his coat, he reached his hand into the pocket and pulled out a slip of paper. On it was the number *303* and the name *Dave*.

"She told me that this Dave person had been harassing Miss Jenkins non-stop, and that the cabaret refused to do anything about it."

"You had to kiss her for that?"

"For the record, if you recall, we did no such thing. Merely pretended for the cameras. She's paranoid, but with good reason."

"Does she think this Dave person could be our Patchwork Killer?"

"She didn't seem to find it implausible."

"So what does this Dave guy have to do with the girl at the ice cream shop, or the drifter?"

"That's what we must find out."

Sherlock took stride once again and headed down the street in the direction of the city center. I followed in step, and hoped he was right.

THE NEXT DAY the papers were filled with 'Patchwork Killer' articles, each one framing its own theory of the murders. Someone in the department had let slip all the details of the cases save the fact that the drifter had a lighter in his pocket. I suppose *dead man has lighter* sells less papers than *lounge singer gets skin sewn back on*. The *Daily Sentinel* was puzzled, remarked that a crime this violent had not occurred here since the hangings of the early 1900s. I scanned each paper, looked for clues. The *Bugle* had an open call section where people could send in their thoughts on whatever local matter was at hand.

It was usually just a bunch of angry blue-hairs complaining about taxes and young people, but one letter caught my eye. It was a cry for help. A letter written by a woman desperately searching for her husband, who had gone missing a week before. He had, without warning, been called away to attend an urgent business matter and never returned. It was sad, but not a case for myself or Sherlock Holmes, so I read on.

I set aside any conjecture formed that might be of use, and over breakfast and iced horchatas, discussed the possibilities with Sherlock. Holmes seemed amused by the theories created by our locals.

"You would feel silly if one of these turned out to be correct," I said.

"You are right, I would feel considerably foolish, but lucky for me there's no chance of that, which you would know had you taken the time to read them."

"I did read them."

"Then you would know there is nothing here of interest."

Holmes reached across the table and retrieved one of the biscuits that Mrs. Hernandez had set out. Just as he was about to take a bite, he shot up from the table and walked out the door. That was my cue to follow.

SHERLOCK KNOCKED ON the door, and a moment later a young, attractive, thirty-something housewife peered through the screen door.

"Mrs. Peppard?"

"Yes?" she said.

"Your husband. Have you found him?" Holmes asked.

The woman turned red as an apple and shifted her glance downward.

"I did," she said. "It was a misunderstanding."

"Was it Mrs. Jenkins?"

The woman looked up at him, stunned, and through watery eyes nodded.

"That's all," Sherlock said, and turned around exiting the porch.

"Sorry, ma'am," I said. "Good luck."

"Don't you see, Watson? That's it. There's a connection here, I just can't see it. Tell me. Why would a serial killer take the time to remove the skin of their victims to just return it? And why for that matter would the murders cease altogether? It's been months now, and that can mean only that the killer has moved on, or that it wasn't a serial killer at all. Just someone who needed to get the attention of someone in particular. But who?"

"Well that's the great mystery, Sherlock. If I knew that, we wouldn't be here."

"But that's just it, Watson. There is no reason. None whatsoever. It was done for us. To distract us from what's really going on."

"Which is what?"

"That I don't know, but I would wager that Dave does."

DAVE PUSHED THE thick-rimmed glasses up onto the bridge of his nose, crossed his left leg over his right knee and took a sip of the bourbon he had poured himself.

"And you think I killed her?" Dave asked.

"It doesn't look good," I said.

Holmes, who'd stayed quiet, watching our exchange, leaned forward and said, "Then tell us what it was you were doing."

"Easy," said Dave. "She was showing up to work with tracks on her neck. Her face was swollen and it looked like she'd been hit more than once. I guess it had been going on for some time, and I hadn't noticed. But one day, she was late, stumbling all over herself, and it was clear she was on something. I know the Moon ain't the Ritz by no means, but if word gets out I hire junkies, no matter how famous they are locally, then the quality of the clientele is gonna plummet fast. And with that, the money follows. Maybe some things are off the books, but my girls are clean."

"Had she ever demonstrated a tendency for drugs before?" I asked.

"That was just it, Darlene was the last person I thought would get mixed up in that. But I saw it with my own eyes. She always seemed medicated and nervous. Even saw her meet a man in the back alley once. She kept looking over her shoulder all skittish."

"You saw her? You saw her take the drugs?"

"Well I didn't watch her put the needle in her arm, if that's what you're asking, but she was definitely up to something. I ducked back inside so she wouldn't know I was watching. I needed her to finish her shift. Hard to get a girl on short notice."

"So you made her work her shift, then fired her?"

"Listen, I'm an asshole, sure, a tax-evading asshole at that, but I ain't no killer. She was on something, and got caught up with the wrong people, and that's why she's dead."

"I NEED TO see the bodies again," Holmes said.

"Darlene?" I asked

"All of them, but it's my understanding the girl was cremated. The other two should still be in the morgue. Call Michaels, tell him to meet us there. And bring the letter."

"What letter?"

"Detective Michaels mentioned that the jumper—remember her?—had sent a letter to her mother. Have him bring that too."

"Why? That case has been closed for some time. I am not having him disturb a grieving mother so you can get some sort of sick satisfac—"

"There's something I just remembered, but I won't know for certain until I see the bodies and the letter. Now go, call him immediately."

"THIS BETTER BE good, Watson," Detective Michaels said as he entered the cold steel mortuary.

"Oh, it is, sir," I said, and hoped the same.

"Get him out," Sherlock said as he ran his fingers along the steel drawers.

"This guy again? What does he mean, 'out'? I am the head detective on this case, and I'll go where I damn well please."

"Listen, Michaels, he's peculiar, but I need him. He understands my methods, and believe it or not, in his own way, he's an actual genius. So long as he doesn't have to speak to anyone or deal with anything in normal human society, he's quite lovely. So please, the sooner we solve this, the sooner you can go back to whatever it is you do."

"Macrame," Holmes said.

Michaels looked over at Sherlock, clearly annoyed, but did as he was asked. He was skeptical, of course, but with the case still being open in the public eye, he bit his tongue. He set the letter down on the autopsy table and huffed as he left the room. By now, Sherlock had located both bodies and opened the drawers. He pulled a large magnifying glass from his pocket and began poking and prodding at the rotted flesh. He was now straddled over the remains of Miss Jenkins, and had anyone entered the room I was unsure if anything I told them would save us from being thrown under the jail.

"Holmes, what are you doing?"

"Look at this, Doctor."

I made my way to the body of Miss Jenkins and examined the area Sherlock had pointed to.

"What about it?"

"What do you see?"

"I see an earlobe; well, part of an earlobe and an earring hole. What of it, Sherlock?"

"Look again."

I looked again at the ear, then glanced at the other ear, and to my surprise, I saw it too.

"Her ear is only pierced on one side."

"That's because it isn't an ear piercing at all. It's a needle mark. A small scar had formed over it, which made it hard to recognize, but I see it now. It's clearly a needle prick from a repeated injection.

There's one here on the neck as well."

"How could I have missed that?" I asked. "And how did you know to look for it?"

"The letter. Bring it here. Do you remember what it said? Miss Jenkins wasn't on drugs; she was being injected with something, alright, but it wasn't narcotics."

I can't go on this way anymore. I have hurt too many people when all I wanted was to make our lives better. I'm sorry. Mother, I know I always said it was the coward's way out, but I had no choice. Sometimes things just become bigger than you ever intended.

"The man, look at him."

Holmes was now straddled over the drifter who had been found; rather than just a needle prick, there was a raised section on the earlobe. At first glance, it would appear to be just a result of the patchwork and flesh decay, but upon further inspection it was revealed that something was lodged beneath the skin. Something that the medical examiner had missed as well.

"What is that?" I asked.

Sherlock grabbed a metal instrument from a nearby table and poked at the nodule. On cue, the skin cracked and something shiny could be seen reflecting off the metal table. No bigger than a dime, there was a square USB drive embedded into the lobe.

"Incredible," I said. "You think the jumper is connected somehow?"

"I am sure of it. Grab Michaels and meet me back at Mrs. Peppard's."

"The woman with the missing husband? You heard her, it was a private matter, he returned home. I hardly think—"

"See you there," Holmes said, and with that, he was gone.

* * *

WE FOUND OURSELVES once again on Mrs. Peppard's doorstep. She seemed confused, but she let Michaels and me in. I hoped Holmes was right about this. Since he wasn't there, I would have to stall.

"Was there something you forgot earlier?" Mrs. Peppard asked. "To be honest, I sort of overreacted. Charley had a bad habit of wandering off at times, and without his medicine he gets confused. It was really just a mixup, hardly a police matter."

"Agreed," said Michaels, visibly annoyed.

"My assistant is on his way, just be patient, you two." I sipped the iced tea Mrs. Peppard had brought me and asked a few questions to pass time.

"So your husband was having an affair? And you two own a bio-tech lab together? That's not good for business."

"We do, and I don't think the other is your business. How did you know that?"

"The internet is full of amazing things. Healing Beauty, it's a good name."

"Oh, I know that place," said Michaels. "My wife had some work done there once. Was unnecessary, if you ask me, but women can be pretty stubborn once they get their minds set to something. Oh, sorry ma'am."

Then it hit me.

"Did you have another business partner?"

A panicked look came across her face and her eyes went wet.

"We did. Her name was Danielle Mackenroy. She passed away not too long ago. I'm sorry, it's all still pretty new."

Before I could inquire further, Holmes' silhouette appeared in the doorframe.

"Oh, it's new, alright," said Sherlock, "and murdering your husband's mistress can also be quite distressing."

Mrs. Peppard's tears vanished and a scowl stretched across her worn face.

"How dare you presume to know anything about me, about my marriage?"

"Oh, I know plenty, madam," Sherlock said.

Michaels, once again intrigued, stood and positioned himself near the kitchen exit in case Mrs. Peppard decided she was through with our questions.

"You discovered the affair between your husband and the cabaret singer, and not about to be bested by some local dollymop, took matters into your own hands. But how?" Sherlock's eyebrows rose, and he abruptly resumed his speech by answering his own question. "Ah, that was only part of it, wasn't it? Among your investigations of the affair, you discovered something more, didn't you? Something worth far more than that philandering husband of yours. This company was yours, built by your family." Sherlock pointed to a framed photo behind the fireplace that showed a young girl amongst a tall, double of a man in front of a *HEALING BEAUTY* banner. "Your father, he started this company; and you weren't about to let someone take that away from you."

"My father worked his whole life to build that company. When my mother got sick, he vowed to save her, cure her from her disease. He died trying to fulfill that promise. This is more than just some lab, it's his legacy."

"So what happened?" Sherlock asked. "You went to confide in your business partner, sweet unsuspecting Danielle, to lend you a sympathetic ear? She confessed something, though, didn't she? Something that could ruin you and your husband."

"If we divorced, he would get half of everything that my family has worked for."

"So why not kill him, then?" I asked. Michaels shot me a disapproving look. "Hypothetically, I mean."

"I'll tell you why," said Sherlock, "because it was too late, the wheels had already been set in motion."

"We were best friends," Mrs. Peppard said.

"You went to your friend, hoping for support, and instead she confessed that she had not only known about the affair, but amongst her digging, had discovered information far more valuable for blackmail."

"I suppose she had started out with the intention of telling me, but the idea of a payout had seemed too good, I guess. Science doesn't pay what it once did."

"You realized that she had found this," Sherlock said, and held up the small shiny object that had been unearthed from the drifter's lobe just hours before.

The color drained from Mrs. Peppard's face, and she said,

"She was going to sell it. My father's formula, *my* formula. She had done some useless botox treatments on that Jenkins woman and she, unknowing that we were friends, confessed to having slept with my husband, which is what got this whole thing started. Danielle was doing chemical trials on a homeless man she had met to cure muscular dystrophy, the same thing that had stolen the life of my mother. She had planned to use it, document the proof, and sell the formula to the highest bidder. She knew what that meant to me, what had happened to my mother. I had worked endlessly, and she was going to take everything away from me. I had already lost both my parents to that disease, in one way or another; I was not going to lose my research, too."

"So what? You confronted her? Told her you knew she had taken the formula?"

"It wasn't that hard, really. Everything from the work computer was automatically backed up to our home hard drive. I saw the photos, a woman always knows when something's not right, and I saw that the files had been recently accessed. I put two and two together and confronted her. She must have realized what had happened, because by the time I approached her, she had already hidden the drive. I searched everywhere for it; tore the office apart. I knew it had to be with her last patient, since it was nowhere in the office. I looked over the patient list and tracked down the last man who had come in. Danielle spent her professional career hiding things in plain sight, why would that drive be any different?"

"So why kill Miss Jenkins then if you knew she didn't have the drive?" I asked.

"I strangled Miss Jenkins because she was sleeping with my husband. I also thought she might know more than she let on, and I was certainly not going to allow some whore to gain one red cent from my family."

"Why cut her up?" Michaels interjected.

"Why not?" Mrs. Peppard said. "I had already killed that man in the hunt for the drive, dissected him in the hopes of finding it. I'm a scientist, after all, and there's nothing more scientific than hands-on experimentation. I liked watching the flesh as I peeled it strip by strip from their bodies."

"That's sick," I said.

"And anyway, it was fun watching the police chase their tails for a little while. Really got them going, thinking there was a bona fide serial killer on the loose."

"And the girl at the ice cream shop?" Michaels asked.

"Wrong place, wrong time." Sherlock said.

"Exactly. And I'd rather tell you all this now, be sure the facts are straight, than leave it up to some half-witted local media reporter to get even a minutia of the details correct. Healing Beauty will be famous by this time tomorrow. Mark my words."

"All of this for a drive smaller than my pinky nail," I said.

"It's not just the drive. It's about loyalty. Where is everyone's loyalty these days? You can find me on the internet, sure, but can you find a way to make a husband honor his marital vows? When I held that gun to the temple of my former best friend, she told me she had implanted it somewhere within that gentleman." Mrs. Peppard sighed. "I guess he was scheduled for a follow-up treatment, and was likely unaware of what he even had. A homeless man holding on to millions of dollars' worth of scientific research. Oh, how deliciously ironic. The sick, the downtrodden, they are ignored, disrespected." Mrs Peppard's eyes flashed and the hurt of a little girl echoed from within her. "Danielle got what she deserved, trying to extort money from my husband, and in turn, me."

"I think I've heard enough," Michaels said, unclasping the handcuff from his front belt loop. "You're coming with me, miss." Michaels slapped the cuffs around her petite, pale wrists and headed out the door with Mrs. Peppard latched in front. She released a guttural laugh, then began to sob.

"Watson, good work. And you"—he pointed at Sherlock— "you should consider another line of work besides dentistry. I think you have a knack for this."

I shot a pleading glance to Sherlock, knew full well he would love nothing more than to take this opportunity to talk about his grandeur, about all the cases he had solved, but instead he turned away, smiled, reached for his hat and coat, and said,

"We all have our secrets."

PARALLELS

JENNI HILL

A friend and fellow editor, Jenni's a wonderful new talent in the short fiction world, with a number of anthology credits to her name. I was hugely pleased to be able to get her on board. 'Parallels' takes the anthology's concept to its bleeding limit, not only wholly reinventing Holmes and Watson—as teenaged girls, no less—but giving us an alternate Holmes story itself full of alternate Holmes stories. It's almost frighteningly meta, and is a perfect finish to the anthology. Enjoy.

SUDDENLY, IT ALL *made sense to John Watson. Sherlock's true nature: the clues had all been there.*

His pale skin, his piercing grey eyes, the way he mesmerised John and others around him. Sherlock always had preferred the dark.

John thought of the many times they'd stayed awake all night, talking, smoking, following leads, chasing criminals through the gaslit streets of London. Had he ever seen Sherlock during daylight? He didn't think so.

As John watched Sherlock hold the unconscious Moriarty in his arms, teeth sunk into the master criminal's neck, crouching with his long black coat spread out behind him like the wings of some enormous bat, he faced the horrifying realisation: Sherlock Holmes was a vampire.

And John—trapped in the sewers with no way out, with dawn still hours away—John would be his next victim.

"It's good." Charlotte's words broke Jane out of her reverie. Watching over her friend's shoulder as the girl read her work, Jane had been lulled into a trance by the familiar paragraphs and the soft hum of the computers in the I.T. teaching room. It took a moment for her to process her friend's words.

"It's awful. I'm sorry you had to read it!"

Charlotte smiled. "These people don't seem to think so." She pointed to the feedback section at the bottom of the webpage. "Logically, awful writing probably wouldn't get you nine hundred hits in one week."

Jane shrugged.

"To put it in perspective, that's nearly three times the number of people who go to this school. Reading your fanfiction. Believe *them*, if you don't believe me."

"There's no accounting for taste," Jane mumbled, but she was pleased by the praise. Charlotte did not give compliments lightly.

"Your public loves you! Listen." Charlotte began to read the feedback out loud, putting on different voices for each comment, and Jane cringed, looking around to check they were alone in the computer room.

A trio of Year Fours gathered around a PC terminal playing the latest first-person shooter, but showed no signs of having noticed Charlotte's pantomime of fannish glee:

MrsWatson: Vamplock is my favourite flavour of Sherlock. Can't believe we have to wait another week to find out if Sherlock killed those girls! Or did Moriarty do it?

TeaAndJohnlock: Oh noes! I can't believe it ended here! Moar plz.

BakerStreetRegular: My new sexuality is Vampire Hunter Moriarty.

221Baby: I wish I could write fanfic like this! I wish the writers on the show could write like this. Plainjane, I love you.

Charlotte grabbed the smaller girl in an overdramatic hug at 'plainjane, I love you,' lanky limbs and long black hair flying everywhere, and Jane screeched in surprise.

"Oh, plainjane!" cried Charlotte. The Year Fours looked around accusingly at the noise, but seemed to dismiss this as typical sixth-form behaviour and went back to their shoot 'em up.

Jane disentangled herself from her friend, who always smelt faintly of coffee and cigarettes: Charlotte's two favourite vices. "Do you really have to read *all* my fanfic?"

"Can't your best friend take an interest in your hobbies? Anyway, how I am supposed to work out why Eric Sadler would take your notebook full of dirty fanfiction unless I study the subject?"

"He took it because he's a scumbag. My scumbag ex who wants to embarrass me horribly, a bit like what you're doing right now. And *hey!* Who said it was dirty?" Jane could feel herself blushing.

"Well, you won't tell me what's in it. What am I supposed to assume?"

"It's private, okay?" It was hard to say 'no' to Charlotte—the girl was a star student and proficient in five languages, but Jane often found herself wondering if Charlotte knew what 'no' meant in any of them.

"Spoilsport. Go on. We've known each other forever. What have you got to hide from me?"

"I just can't tell you." It was impossible to hide anything from Charlotte for long, but this time, Jane had to. She really had to.

"Please?" Charlotte actually fluttered her eyelashes.

"You don't have to know everything all the bloody time!"

Charlotte's face clouded, and she turned away, back to the words on the computer screen. Even as she said it, Jane knew she was making a mistake. If there was one thing Charlotte hated it was a mystery: she never let go until she had all the answers.

When Ms. McManus had given everyone detention because no-one would own up to the graffiti in the girls' bathrooms, Charlotte had worked out the culprit. When a masked flasher had turned up at the school disco, Charlotte had worked out his identity. (Mr. Harrison had been working out some issues after his divorce. The school had a new maths teacher now.)

If you had a problem to solve, a mystery to unravel, then Charlotte was your woman. She wouldn't be nice about it, but she'd find the answers. Such brutal honesty did not win her many friends.

Being seventeen years old and hanging out in the school computer labs writing fanfiction did not win you many friends either, which explained why Charlotte and Jane had remained so close.

It wasn't the only reason they were friends. In the years since they'd met, sitting next to each other in Harrison's maths lessons, Jane had come to appreciate Charlotte's intelligence, her energy, the way she always made life much more interesting.

What she didn't appreciate about Charlotte was how she sulked when her curiosity was denied.

"Do you want my help or not?" Dark eyebrows knitted together, Charlotte studied the screen, still not meeting Jane's eyes.

Why had Eric taken the notebook? What was he going to do with it? Where was he keeping it, and how could they get it back? Jane *needed* to get it back. Charlotte would solve this.

"Yes. I do want your help. But I still can't tell you what's in the notebook."

Charlotte sighed, and rolled her eyes. "Then either do something useful or let me study the problem in peace."

There was no talking to her when she was like this. Jane left Charlotte in the computer lab, reading around 'plainjane's' own unique corner of Sherlock Holmes fandom.

Holmes and Watson had always been beloved characters in pop culture, but recent reboots for TV and film had seen interest soar. The internet was full of fan forums, fanart, cosplay, fanfiction.

Quite a lot of the fan-created works focused on the two characters as each other's romantic interests—a dynamic some of the reboots did nothing to dispel. The reboots even played with the idea: emphasising Holmes' jealousy of Watson's wife, the awkwardness of their living arrangement, or the adulation of Sherlock shown in Watson's written accounts of their adventures.

Then again, as Jane was always quick to point out, quite a lot of fanfiction did not focus on this homoerotic dynamic. (Hers did.)

Jane herself specialised in alternate universes, or 'AUs' for short. AUs took the characters and situations from the original work, and placed them in different worlds, different stories. The characters might be aliens, barbarian warriors or rock stars, but at the end of the day they were still themselves.

Jane had written about Sherlock and Watson as vampires, serial killers, subversive radio hosts, WW2 super-soldiers; the list went on. Jane was, she had to admit, mildly internet-famous for her AUs.

It was a pity that 'mildly internet-famous' wasn't something that one could put on a university application, considering all the hours she'd spent writing fic when she could have been doing her homework, or even doing something her mother would call 'healthy,' like playing sports, spending time outdoors or kissing boys.

The fans loved her though—'plainjane' had quite a following. It fascinated Jane that even AUs where the characters had completely normal, mundane lives could win a huge readership if enough love and attention were put into the details, the characterisation, the dialogue. Coffee-shop AUs, for some reason, were quite trendy. Perhaps because young fans of the shows with plenty of writing time on their hands were more likely to be able to write their way around a coffee shop than an investment bank or a lawyer's office. Jane had lost count of the number of fics she'd written on her laptop at Starbucks.

Jane's own coffee-shop story, a multi-chapter epic titled 'Where the Barista Knows Your Name,' was one of her most popular works. She was genuinely proud of it, unlike so much of her other work she'd never quite got around to deleting online. That was the problem with being even mildly internet-famous. All your earliest mistakes stayed around to haunt you.

When Jane was about halfway down the road to the bus-stop home, she stopped as a sudden thought hit her.

Oh, God, she thought, *please don't let Charlotte find the Star Force fic.*

EXCERPT FROM 'WHERE *The Barista Knows Your Name' (subtitle: 'And Everything Else About You, Just By Looking At Your Shoes'), Chapter One, published by plainjane on fanfictionhouse. net, category: Literature: Sherlock Holmes: AUs, 12th July 2014.*

Keywords: coffee shop AU, character: Sherlock Holmes, character: John Watson, angst, fluff, John/Sherlock. **With thanks to beta readers singlecrow and ladymoonray! –plainjane**

THE NEW BARISTA was getting on John Watson's nerves.

He didn't smile, he didn't tell the patrons to 'have a nice

day!' but the customers loved him. They loved his party trick. John seemed to be the only patron it didn't impress.

"I'll have my usual; and what does she want?" asked one girl with pink hair and a nose piercing, pushing forward a blonde who smiled and blushed prettily.

The man (*Sherlock Holmes* was the name on his tag) studied her, but only for a moment before turning back to the espresso machine. "She'll have the double espresso Americano—the ink on her hands and the bags under her eyes show she's been up all night studying for something, probably... some kind of veterinary sciences exam, going by the cat, dog and yes, that is rabbit fur on her clothes. I'm adding a vanilla caramel shot. She wants a sugar boost, but prefers vanilla notes to citrus or cocoa, judging by her perfume. "

"He's good!" The girls giggled in triumph and ran to the end of the bar to await their coffees, making far too much noise, in John's hungover opinion.

He stared mournfully into his decaff latte. He'd wanted it caffeinated, but he hadn't wanted to prove the smug barista right. *He thinks he knows me,* thought John. *He's only just met me.*

Well not 'only just.' To be fair, they'd been dancing this dance for a whole week now. John would come in every day, first for his morning coffee, and then later, for a tomato mozzarella bagel and lunchtime caffeine hit. Before Sherlock's arrival, this had been the best coffee shop within ten minutes of the hospital where John worked.

Until the Battle of the Decaff Latte.

Until John had lied to the barista seven days ago, insisting that he did indeed want decaff, just to wipe the smug grin off the bastard's face. Oh, the man hadn't said anything about it at the time, but you could tell it bothered him. They'd barely exchanged any words since, but there had been a battle of wits going on...

On Wednesday, Sherlock the barista had played dirty. He'd brought over a regular latte to John's table, with just the right amount of foam, and with one of those plastic-wrapped, caramelised biscuits you get with coffee, that John adored but could never find in the supermarket.

John had never seen tables waited at the café in all his years as a customer, but the barista insisted (sir) that wasn't this his drink (sir) and actually apologised for messing up John's order, trying to take away John's decaff and replace it with the regular coffee.

John gritted his teeth as he remembered insisting that no, decaff was exactly what he wanted. He could swear the barista had waved the regular latte (which had smelled amazing) under his nose a few times, just to really rub it in.

At least in this seat next to the counter, he could enjoy the coffee aromas. Rich, dark, roasted—it smelled like freshly-brewed heaven. Here he could also hear the espresso machine singing its tempting siren wail. Oh, God, he was losing his mind...

One mozzarella bagel and one unsatisfying coffee later, John dropped his paper cup into the bin outside the cafe, and found himself looking up into grey smoke and darker, greyer eyes behind it. John was surprised to find himself thinking how beautiful these eyes were, but stopped when he realised who they belonged to.

The barista inhaled from a long, thin cigarette and, being tall, bent down to John's level. "Why did you lie to me?"

THE NEXT MORNING, with dawn still disappearing from the sky, Jane met Charlotte at the back gates of the school.

Jane had known Charlotte would be there—they did this every day before lessons started. And Charlotte wasn't the kind to hold grudges. Quick to anger, but quick to forgive—Jane found it refreshing. Eric had held onto grudges like they were his only friends. Always jealous of her time, he'd once fallen out with her when she'd helped Charlotte steal school records (crucial clues in the case of the School Disco Flasher) instead of going bowling with him, and he hadn't talked to her for nearly a month.

"I brought you a coffee." Jane held out the peace offering. Like the coffee, her breath steamed in the crisp morning air.

"Mmm, thanks." Charlotte fished a packet of Mayfairs out of her long black coat, and lit one with practised ease. "I brought you a culprit."

Charlotte gestured with the cigarette to where classrooms could be seen through the wrought iron fence. The lights were on inside and among other early arrivals Jane could see Eric quite clearly, sitting at his desk, probably finishing last night's homework. It was something he struggled with, now that he didn't have Charlotte and Jane to help him with the answers.

"We already have a culprit. That is the exact culprit we already have. He confessed, remember?"

"And what did he say, exactly? Tell me again."

"I confronted him, as he was the only person in the library with me when the notebook went missing. He actually admitted his guilt! I asked him what he was planning to do with my book and he told me he hadn't decided yet. What could he mean by that?"

Charlotte took out her phone and checked the time.

"Are you listening to me?"

"If he hasn't decided what to do with it yet, he's likely keeping it close by. Any move he makes against you is going to happen at school—you know how afraid he is of your mum—but he's unlikely to keep the book on his person in case we pay one of the rugby team to hold him upside down and empty his pockets."

"That's not fai—oh wait, yes we have done that." They'd found deciding evidence in the curious case of the Kidnapped School Tortoise.

Suddenly, a persistent, repetitive ringing noise started up from inside the school. Jane realised why it sounded unfamiliar—she had never heard the fire alarm from outside the school grounds before. It sounded muted and strange.

Charlotte put her phone away with a satisfied smile.

"That was you?"

"Those rugby boys will do anything on a dare."

They'll do anything for you, is more like it, thought Jane. In Jane's seventeen-year-old opinion, Charlotte was far too old to be doing the puppy-dog-eyes look at eighteen. But it worked. It was the hint of mischief behind the pleading grey eyes that Jane herself couldn't resist—she wondered if others saw it too.

"There, look!" Charlotte grabbed her and pointed at Eric's classroom. It was emptying fast as students made their way to the fire assembly point on the lawn, but Eric was skulking behind. As soon as he was alone he bent down in front of one of the filing cabinets and fished around the back of the unit.

"He must have known I'd break into his locker..." Charlotte muttered under her breath.

"You did what? For me? That's sweet."

Eric pulled out Jane's notebook—royal blue and designed like a British police public call box—and hid it under his jacket, before darting out the door to follow the other students.

"Yes!" Jane felt relief flooding through her body. Charlotte had pulled through—another of her moments, her brilliant flashes of cleverness. At moments like this, Jane wondered why she ever doubted her.

"Let's get him!" Jane was raring to go, but Charlotte pulled her back.

"We know his hiding place now. We can wait."

"Why? Let's do it now!"

"Be logical about this. Even if you really want to physically wrestle the book out of Eric's hands—"

"And give him a good sock on the nose to boot."

"—and give him a good sock on the nose to boot, scrapping over stolen property in view of the whole school, who will right now be assembling in fire-alarm formation on the front lawns, is likely to draw more attention to you and your secret notebook than you'd prefer, isn't it?"

Jane nodded.

"Speaking of the alarm, let's get out of here."

"Should we join the others?"

Charlotte turned her back on the alarms and started walking. "Nah, we've got time for another coffee before class. I can outline our next steps."

EXCERPT FROM 'ATTACK *of the Space Pirates,*' published by plainjane *on fanfictionhouse.net, category: crossovers, Sherlock Holmes/Star Force, 24th January 2012.*

Keywords: crossover, science fiction AU, character: Sherlock Holmes, character: John Watson, character: Irene Adler, John/ Sherlock, Irene/Sherlock, OCs

THE PROXIMITY ALARMS wailed throughout the ship, but too late. The enemy had boarded. First, the Krangon raiders had clamped their craft to the *Journey,* then they'd broken through its hull and pumped its life support systems full of sleep pollen, knocking out all the crew.

Lieutenant Sherlock Holmes dispatched another Krangon pirate with his laser pistol as he tried to think his way around the problem.

The ship's Chief Medical Officer, Doctor John Watson, knocked out another, freeing the pirate's hastily-grabbed hostages—two young ensigns in red shirts—and easing the girls' unconscious bodies safely to the floor.

He and Doctor Watson had been lucky, thought Sherlock. They had been... occupied in the medical bay when the attack hit. Sherlock had recognised the distinctive scent of the sleep pollen from Krang's opiate dens (he had not confessed the source of his knowledge to Watson, but he was sure John had his suspicions). Watson found the correct antidote (a powerful stimulant, to counteract the narcotic pollen) in his supply cupboards and injected them both just before the drug would have overpowered their senses. Although the Doctor's species was not as logical as his own, the Hephaestans, Sherlock had to credit the human with a modicum of quick thinking in that situation.

Now they were both on their way to the ship's air circulation systems with enough antidote to revive a dead space whale. If successfully revived, the ship's five hundred crew members were going to have trouble sleeping for a few nights, but at least they'd be alive and not flushed out into the vacuum of space, as was frequently the fate of any crew whose craft was taken by pirates.

There had recently been a number of ships stolen in this way in this part of the galaxy, both civilian and Star Force, merchant and military. Sherlock wondered if he'd discover how the Krangon pirates were getting so close undetected by the ships' defences, or if he'd go to his grave unknowing.

Dr Watson injected the ex-hostages with the antidote—Sherlock assumed this was John's annoying human sentimentality showing. It was hardly logical behaviour, as it wasn't as if two ensigns would help much in a fight. At least they had plenty of antidote to spare.

"Good girl, don't stand up too quickly. There now, how do you fancy coming with me and Lieutenant Holmes and saving the day?" Watson spoke soothingly to the two girls.

"I'm an ensign, not a child. You don't have to cajole me into doing my duty." The taller, dark haired girl spoke up and John and the shorter girl looked taken aback.

"She's right, John," observed Sherlock, taking a slim nicotine vaporiser out of his pocket and inhaling quickly. "You're speaking to Star Force officers, not frightened horses."

"Lieutenant Holmes?!" The two girls spoke in near unison.

"Clearly. And you are?"

"I'm Jane," said the shorter girl, breathlessly, "And this is Charlotte."

"She's read all your books, everything they had in the academy library and more," said Charlotte, with a wicked glint in her eye. "*Practical Deduction in the Field, An Elementary Introduction to Alien Psychology.* Even your biography." Jane, reddening, elbowed her in the ribs hurriedly, but was saved further embarrassment by a noise echoing from along the hallway.

"Ssh!" Sherlock thought it sounded like footsteps. The sound of someone walking in heels?

There was only one person he knew who went about on a starship in high heels.

A woman walked into view. *The* woman.

"Irene Adler. What are you doing here?" Sherlock asked. She looked as shocked to see him as he imagined he did to see her.

The merest moment's hesitation. A microexpression of guilt. Sherlock didn't want to believe it. Since her arrival one month ago, he'd had just cause to add Ambassador Adler to the list of crew whose company he actually enjoyed, rather than tolerated. John was getting a little jealous.

"Sherlock! John! I'm so glad to see you."

"How are you still awake?" asked John.

"I had a small amount of antidote stashed in my quarters." She smiled at Sherlock invitingly. "I always keep it handy for recreational use."

"Impossible, ma'am," said Charlotte. "Our transporter beam would have shown us if you were carrying any narcotics when you and your luggage were brought aboard. Same for anyone else who tried to bring it in without a medical license."

"The nerve!" said Irene. "She's lying, Sherlock."

"Ma'am, with all due respect, I work in the transporter room, and there's been no record of any such substance in the past year."

Sherlock noticed Irene checking the exits.

"What's more," continued Charlotte, "while we usually keep crew members' genetic make-up private, for good reason, I would deduce that the unusual markers the transporter showed in your DNA reveal a Krangon background. Krangons being famously immune to the narcotic pollen farmed on their planet."

"Irene, a Krangon agent? But that's absurd!" said John.

Sherlock thought of the other craft that had been taken by Krangon pirates in the last year. None while Irene had been aboard the *Journey*.

"Sir," said Jane, turning to Sherlock. "In your biography you said that when you have eliminated the impossible, whatever remains, however improbable, must be the truth..."

These girls were sharp. "Actually my dear, I must credit an ancestor of mine with that particular saying, but your point is a sound one. Irene, I'm placing you under arrest."

John was looking back and forth between Sherlock and Irene in puzzlement. He didn't see Irene go for the fallen Krangon's gun at her feet, until she was pointing it at him.

"Let me go, Sherlock, or your boyfriend gets it right between the eyes."

JANE STARED IN horror at the note in her hand. She was following the plan. She was following the plan to the letter.

So if she was following the plan, how had it all gone so horribly wrong? She'd let Charlotte distract Eric with a clandestine meeting on the school roof. She'd come to Eric's classroom, when she was sure it would be empty, and looked behind the filing cabinet, expecting to be reunited with her notebook and able to put the entire business behind her.

And instead, this.

> *Dear Plain Jane,*
>
> *Surprise! Not quite what you expected to find?*
>
> *Nice trick with the fire alarm, sweetie, but you're not going to get that notebook. It might have worked, if you hadn't already told me about the time Charlotte used the same trick on the headmistress.*
>
> *Charlotte, Charlotte, Charlotte. She was all you could talk about, even when we were together. No wonder you didn't want me. I had the wrong parts. No wonder you wouldn't put out! I thought you were frigid, but you're just bent.*
>
> *Admit it. She's the reason you left me. I never could live up to her, to her cleverness, to your adventures. You've got a crush, you dyke bint, and it isn't on me, or on the characters in your stupid little TV shows and your gay fanfiction. All the time you spent writing about the two of them, you were really writing about the two of you! It's pathetic.*
>
> *And now I've got proof. You won't be getting your notebook back, not until I've shown it to Charlotte. Next time she's alone I'll show her—it's not like you can spend every hour of the day with each other, no matter how hard you tried when we were dating.*
>
> *Let's see if she still wants you around when she knows how you feel.*
>
> *Be seeing you,*
> *—Eric Sadler*

The pit in Jane's stomach opened wide. What she was feeling—it was as awful as that time her dad caught Eric with his hand up her shirt, as bad as realising she had an exam she hadn't revised for, or being sent to the headmistress's office, but a hundred times worse.

Eric knew. Eric *knew*.

Next time she's alone I'll show her.

Eric knew and he had the notebook and he was alone with Charlotte and he was going to show it to her.

Jane broke into a run.

EXTRACT FROM JANE'S *notebook, unpublished work titled 'A High School AU: Ten Things John Watson Hated About Sherlock Holmes, and One Thing He Didn't.'*

MATHS LESSONS AT *the Baker Street School for Boys had to be a form of torture, John Watson was sure. Perhaps the U.N. would issue a decree against it.*

It wasn't just the maths itself. Or the teacher, Mr. Harrison, who sweated too much and had once put his hand on John's knee. No, it was sitting next to Sherlock Holmes every lesson, that was the worst part.

In the back of his exercise book, John was making a list of the ways Sherlock annoyed him. It was cathartic, and it was something to do—he'd already finished the trigonometry problems Harrison had set. Plus, John reasoned, if he ever did something rash, like, oh, maybe stabbing Sherlock through the heart with a biro for being such an annoying git, the list would help his manslaughter defence no end.

Number one on the list was 'he's a bloody know-it-all.' Sherlock was a genius, there was no way around it. The only reason Sherlock still had his head down working on maths problems was that he had finished the assigned work, and instead of slacking off like any normal sixth former was now ten pages ahead in the textbook, working on partial fractions instead of trigonometry.

He was such a know-it-all that it was impossible to hide anything from him. That was the second item for the list. When Big Jim and his gang had called John a 'poof' and worse, and given him a black eye, he had hidden his embarrassment by telling everyone he'd walked into a door at home. Even John's parents had accepted this. Sherlock was the only one who had questioned this explanation, applying logic where logic had no reason to be, asking where and how exactly he'd hit the door, and poking holes in the story until John had been forced to confess Big Jim's involvement.

Jim and his gang hadn't bothered John again. He wasn't sure why.

Sherlock turned the page of his textbook and began another sheet of problems. John couldn't explain it, but it was hard to take your eyes off Sherlock. John had always been the kind of student who got told off for gazing out of the window, but these days he found his gaze gravitating toward Sherlock instead. Whatever Sherlock was doing, be it excitedly explaining his theories as to why Mr. Harrison was the school disco flasher, eating his lunch or simply doing nothing at all, John found himself watching, head turning like a compass needle always pointing north. He'd noticed other students doing it too.

John wasn't quite sure how to articulate this particular annoyance, so he wrote 'attention whore' and stared at the big blue letters for a moment. He was aware this wasn't quite fair of him, but he couldn't work out how to say 'commands the attention of any room he's in' without sounding a bit, well, gay.

"You left out my amazing good looks."

It was true, Sherlock did have the kind of good looks that you expected to see on a poster pasted inside some girl's locker.

His hand started to write 'good looks' before his brain caught up and figured out what he was doing.

"Who said this was about you?" John thought he'd been clever by leaving the list untitled.

Sherlock smirked, and went back to his equations. (Impossible to hide anything from.)

John hid the list with his left hand, as Sherlock was on his left, and wrote 'SMUG GIT,' in sharp blue letters.

"So we're on for later, yeah?" asked Sherlock.

This was another problem with Sherlock, John mused. He was very difficult to say 'no' to.

"Sure." Damn it.

After class, John went to meet Sherlock at the bike sheds, where the students went if they wanted a sneaky smoke or a secret snog with one of the girls from the Catholic school.

Sherlock was waiting for him, lighting up one of his Mayfairs.

John hated the cool way that Sherlock smoked. And hated how good he looked in that black coat. If John had tried either of those things himself, he'd have had the same effect as a sparrow sticking raven feathers to its wings and pretending it was dark and interesting.

The problem was, thought John, the real problem was that he'd been perfectly happy assuming he was straight, before he'd met Sherlock. He'd liked girls, he'd liked the way they felt and the way they looked in tight clothes; still did, in fact, only now he was noticing the same things about Sherlock, too.

"You're too tall for this," John told him, reaching up to

Sherlock and locking his hands behind his neck, pulling the other boy down to his level.

Sherlock quirked one dark eyebrow. "Add it to your list."

One thing John liked about Sherlock, one thing he liked very much, was the way he kissed.

Here the legible part of the extract ends, as the author has scribbled deep, angry biro marks all over the pages, with notes such as 'stupid, stupid!' 'high school story = dead giveaway, idiot' and 'NEVER PUBLISH THIS' scrawled in the margins.

JANE WASN'T SURE what she expected to find when she reached the school roof, but it certainly wasn't Charlotte standing on the edge of the building. She had Jane's notebook in her hands and looked as if she were about to leap onto the pavement four floors below. Jane's heart jumped into her throat.

"Don't jump." She couldn't live with herself if Charlotte jumped, she couldn't live without—

"Wasn't planning on it."

"Oh, thank God." Eric was nowhere to be seen. Now Jane thought about it, Charlotte didn't seem so much like she were about to leap, more like she was watching something below. She had another horrible thought. "What did you do with Eric?"

Charlotte smirked, and gestured over the roof ledge.

"You didn't..."

"Nope. I threw his iPhone into the road."

"Good aim." Jane came forward, peering over ledge, into the playground and the school gates and the busy street beyond. "I hope he gets hit by traffic."

"But imagine some poor sod having to go to prison just because they'd hit *Eric Sadler*."

"Prison? He's a lower life form. It wouldn't even be like hitting someone's dog, more like hitting a squirrel."

"A mangy pigeon." Charlotte offered.

"A rat. A really disgusting one." The girls grinned, and then Jane broke Charlotte's gaze awkwardly. "So what did the rat say to you?"

"He said a lot of mean things about you, about me. There was truth in there too, but... nothing I hadn't already worked out for myself, over the last few days."

"He showed you the book?" Jane felt ill.

"Yes. But you didn't have to put us in a high school for me to realise who you were writing about, all this time." Charlotte looked angry.

The void was back in Jane's insides. This was starting to feel like the end of something: denial, maybe. Friendship, possibly.

"I'm sorry. I'll delete all the fics, I'll stop sitting next to you in class, I'll understand if you never want to talk to me again—"

"Why did you lie to me?"

Jane was taken aback. "Lie to you? I didn't lie, I—"

"You hid your feelings, you didn't tell me what you were going through. We could have talked about this. I might have understood. I could have helped!"

"You might have understood?"

Charlotte sighed, exasperated. "In all the time you've known me, have you ever known me to show any interest in boys?"

"No." Jane thought about it. "You've never shown any interest in girls, either."

"There is one girl I spend a lot of time with."

"Oh. Um."

The two girls were silent.

"So does that mean we can—" Jane left the question unspoken. Do what? Kiss, date, hook up? Pretend like Jane wasn't the creepiest creeper who ever creeped?

"I think... I think I need some time. You've made it weird, now. Studying me, how I dress, how I talk. Publishing it online all this time. We're not Sherlock and John, Jane, we're you and me."

Charlotte reached into her coat pocket for her Mayfairs, looked as if she were about to light one, saw Jane watching and put it back. "I'm going to have to change brands, aren't I."

"I'm really sorry, Charlotte." Jane felt tears pricking at the corner of her eye. "Really, really sorry. I can delete the fics, I mean it. All they were—it was a way to deal with how I felt. Writing it out on the page made it feel like fiction, something that wasn't really happening to me." Yes, there was a tear. She was actually crying now, and her face would go all red and blotchy and this was not what she needed. Jane cursed the way her tear ducts had betrayed her. "I couldn't talk about it with my parents, you know what they're like. They were heartbroken when I left Eric. I don't know how they'd take the news I was into girls..."

"Oh hey, look, don't cry." Charlotte hugged her tentatively. "And don't delete the fics, you've worked hard on them. You're internet famous. Well, you're a bit internet famous. A little bit."

Jane grinned the kind of soppy grin you make when someone makes you laugh through the tears, and they stayed hugging for a little too long.

There was some shouting from below, and they saw Eric pointing up at the roof, speaking to a teacher. As the girls made a quick break for the fire escape and the staircase leading below, Charlotte shouted, "I didn't know you liked *Star Force*."

"You read that one, then? Not my best work."

"There's a movie out next month." There was, it was one of the remakes with all the lens flare. "I'd been planning to see it. See how badly they get it wrong." Charlotte jumped a few more stairs, then said thoughtfully, "You want to come with me?

Jane almost stopped dead in her tracks. Charlotte wanted to see a movie. With her. They'd seen movies before, but did this mean she wanted to *see a movie* with her? Maybe they'd even go for dinner, too. Jane stopped herself—she knew that anything that happened between them now would have to happen slowly, if it happened at all. "Sure. I'd love to."

"It's a date," said Charlotte.

"Is it?"

"I think it could turn out to be, yeah."

ABOUT THE AUTHORS

Guy Adams (guyadamsauthor.com) has written far too many books. In recent years these have included: the *Heaven's Gate Trilogy* for Solaris; the *Deadbeat* books for Titan and the *Clown Service* series for Del Rey UK.

He has, as yet, not written far too many comics but he's working on it: he's written a number of strips for *2000 AD* including a reinvention of Grant Morrison's *Ulysses Sweet: Maniac for Hire*, scripted *The Engine* for Madefire and is the co-creator of *Goldtiger* with artist Jimmy Broxton.

A lifelong fan of Sherlock Holmes (once playing him, rather badly on stage) he has written two original novels, *The Breath of God* and *The Army of Dr Moreau*, as well as a couple of non-fiction books.

J. E. Cohen's (julie-cohen.com) life changed at age eleven, when she bought *The Complete Sherlock Holmes* because it was the biggest book in the shop. She joined the Baker Street Irregulars at sixteen, and at age twenty-two moved to England to study Arthur Conan Doyle's involvement in the Cottingley fairy photographs. Despite not being able to draw, she is an official cartoonist for *The Sherlock Holmes Journal*, with her feature "Overrun By Oysters." Under the name Julie Cohen she writes novels which have sold nearly a million copies worldwide. Tweet her @julie_cohen.

Joan De La Haye (joandelahaye.com) writes horror and some very twisted thrillers. She invariably wakes up in the middle of the night, because she's figured out yet another freaky way to mess with her already screwed up characters.

Joan is interested in some seriously weird stuff. That's probably also one of the reasons she writes horror.

Her novels, *Shadows* and *Requiem in E Sharp*, as well as her novella, *Oasis*, are published by Fox Spirit (foxspirit.co.uk).

You can find Joan on her website and follow her on Twitter @JoanDeLaHaye.

Ian Edginton is a *New York Times* bestselling author and multiple Eisner Award nominee.

His recent titles include the green apocalypse saga *The Hinterkind* for DC/Vertigo; *Steed and Mrs Peel* for BOOM, the steam- and clock-punk series *Stickleback*, *Ampney Crucis Investigates* and *Brass Sun* for the legendary UK science fiction weekly, *2000 AD*; game properties *Dead Space: Liberation* and *The Evil Within* for Titan Books and the audio adventure *Torchwood: Army of One* for the BBC.

He has adapted the complete canon of Sherlock Holmes novels into a series of graphic novels for Self Made Hero, as well writing several volumes of Holmes apocrypha entitled *The Victorian Undead*. He has also adapted H. G. Wells' *The War of the Worlds* as well as several highly acclaimed sequels, *Scarlet Traces* and *Scarlet Traces: the Great Game*.

He lives and works in England. He keeps a Bee.

Kelly Hale (kellyhale.blogspot.com) lives in the magical city of Portlandia where the streets are paved with espresso beans and the garbage recycles itself. She is the author of many short stories, three novels in progress, a play, a novella, some overwrought poetry, a co-authored TV tie-in novel of the *Doctor Who* variety, and her award winning novel *Erasing Sherlock*. She is the proud mother of a stand-up comic, a tall ship sailor, and grandmother to geeks in process. You can watch her flail, struggle and ultimately triumph on her blog "Mistress of the Jolly Dark."

Although she's best known for science fiction, paranormal, horror, and fantasy, **Gini Koch's** (ginikoch.com) first literary love is mystery and suspense, and her first literary crush, at the tender age of 7, was on Sherlock Holmes. Gini writes the fast, fresh and funny *Alien*/Katherine "Kitty" Katt series for DAW Books, the *Necropolis Enforcement Files* series, and the *Martian Alliance Chronicles* series for Musa Publishing, and as G. J. Koch she writes the Alexander Outland series. Gini's made the most of multiple personality disorder by writing under a variety of other pen names as well, including Anita Ensal, Jemma Chase, A. E. Stanton, and J. C. Koch. Her dark secret is that pretty much everything she writes has a mystery in it—because mysteries are the spice of literary life.

Jenni Hill has written short stories for several anthologies and is also working on a sci-fi novel.

She lives in London with her husband and their several million books, but you can find her on Twitter @Jenni_Hill.

First published at the tender age of 8, Kasey **Lansdale** is the author of numerous short stories as well as editor to several anthology collections. Her most recent project, *Impossible Monsters*, was released from Subterranean Press summer of 2013. A full time singer/songwriter, she has also just completed her first novel. She is the daughter of acclaimed author, Joe R. Lansdale.

James Lovegrove (jameslovegrove.com) was born on Christmas Eve 1965 and is the author of more than 40 books. His novels include *The Hope*, *Days*, *Untied Kingdom*, *Provender Gleed*, the *New York Times* bestselling *Pantheon* series—so far *The*

Age Of Ra, The Age Of Zeus, The Age Of Odin, Age Of Aztec, Age Of Voodoo and *Age Of Shiva*, plus a collection of three novellas, *Age Of Godpunk*—and *Redlaw* and *Redlaw: Red Eye*, the first two volumes in a trilogy about a policeman charged with protecting humans from vampires and vice versa. He has produced two Sherlock Holmes novels, *The Stuff Of Nightmares* and *Gods Of War*.

James has sold well over 40 short stories, the majority of them gathered in two collections, *Imagined Slights* and *Diversifications*. He has written a four-volume fantasy saga for teenagers, *The Clouded World* (under the pseudonym Jay Amory), and has produced a dozen short books for readers with reading difficulties, including *Wings*, *Kill Swap*, *Free Runner*, *Dead Brigade*, and the *5 Lords Of Pain* series.

James has been shortlisted for numerous awards, including the Arthur C. Clarke Award, the John W. Campbell Memorial Award, the Bram Stoker Award, the British Fantasy Society Award and the Manchester Book Award. His short story 'Carry The Moon In My Pocket' won the 2011 Seiun Award in Japan for Best Translated Short Story.

James's work has been translated into twelve languages. His journalism has appeared in periodicals as diverse as *Literary Review*, *Interzone* and *BBC MindGames*, and he is a regular reviewer of fiction for the *Financial Times* and contributes features and reviews about comic books to the magazine *Comic Heroes*.

He lives with his wife, two sons and cat in Eastbourne, a town famously genteel and favoured by the elderly, but in spite of that he isn't planning to retire just yet.

Glen Mehn (glen.mehn.net) was born and raised in New Orleans, and has since lived in San Francisco, North Carolina, Oxford, Uganda, Zambia, and now lives in London. He's previously been published by Random House Struik and Jurassic London, and is currently working on his first hopefully publishable novel. When not writing, Glen designs innovation programmes that use technology for social good for the Social Innovation Camp and is head of programme at Bethnal Green Ventures. Glen holds a BA in English Literature and Sociology from the University of New Orleans and an MBA from the University of Oxford.

Glen has been a bookseller, line cook, lighting and set designer, house painter, IT director, carbon finance consultant, soldier, dishwasher, and innovation programme designer. One day, he might be a writer. He lives in Brixton, which is where you live if you move from New Orleans to London. He moved country five times in two years once, and happy to stick around for a while.

David Thomas Moore has been a plague on time and space, stealing the Mona Lisa days after completion, crashing the great Bankotron 5000 central finance system in the year 2213 and snatching six irreplaceable scrolls from the Library of Alexandria and setting fire to it to cover his retreat. He was finally brought to ground in Shanghai in 1901 by Job-raked-out-of-the-ashes Holmes, a seventeenth-century crime-fighting preacher from the colony of Virginia, and his companion John-on-Watts, a grizzled tribal medic from the nuclear wastelands of the twenty-fifth century. Now reformed, David lives in Berkshire in twenty-first-century England with his wife Tamsin and daughter Beatrix. *Two Hundred and Twenty-One Baker Streets* is his first anthology as editor.

Emma Newman (enewman.co.uk) lives in Somerset, England and drinks far too much tea. She writes dark short stories and post-apocalyptic, science fiction and urban fantasy novels. Emma's *Split Worlds* urban fantasy series was recently published by Angry Robot Books and the first in the series, *Between*

Two Thorns, was shortlisted for the BFS Best Novel and Best Newcomer awards. Emma is a professional audiobook narrator and also co-writes and hosts the Hugo nominated podcast *Tea and Jeopardy*, which involves tea, cake, mild peril and singing chickens. She is represented by Jennifer Udden at DMLA. Her hobbies include dressmaking and playing RPGs. She blogs, rarely gets enough sleep and refuses to eat mushrooms.

Adrian Tchaikovsky (shadowsoftheapt.com) is the author of the acclaimed *Shadows of the Apt* fantasy series, from the first volume, *Empire In Black and Gold*, in 2008 to the final book, *Seal of the Worm*, in 2014, with a new series and a standalone science fiction novel scheduled for 2015. He has been nominated for the David Gemmell Legend Award and a British Fantasy Society Award. In civilian life he is a lawyer, gamer and amateur entolomogist.

Bram Stoker nominee and Shirley Jackson Award winner **Kaaron Warren** (kaaronwarren.wordpress.com) has lived in Melbourne, Sydney, Canberra and Fiji. She's sold many short stories, three novels (the multi-award-winning *Slights*, *Walking the Tree* and *Mistification*) and four short story collections. *Through Splintered Walls* won a Canberra Critic's Circle Award for Fiction, an ACT Writers' and Publisher's Award, two Ditmar Awards, two Australian Shadows Awards and a Shirley Jackson Award. Her story 'Air, Water and the Grove' won the Aurealis Award for Best SF Short Story and will appear in Paula Guran's *Year's Best Dark Fantasy and Horror*. Her latest collection is *The Gate Theory*. Kaaron Tweets @KaaronWarren.

After a misspent adulthood pursuing a Music Education degree, **Jamie Wyman** (www.jamiewyman.com) fostered several interests before discovering that being an author means never having to get out of pajamas. She has an unhealthy addiction to chai, a passion for circus history, and a questionable hobby that involves putting a flaming torch into her mouth. When she's not traipsing about with her imaginary friends, she lives in Phoenix with two hobbits and two cats. Jamie is proud to say she has a deeply disturbed following at her blog.

Jamie's debut novel *Wild Card* (Entangled Edge, 2013) is available wherever ebooks are sold. You can also find her short story 'The Clever One' in the anthology *When The Hero Comes Home 2* (Dragon Moon Press, August 2013). Look for *Unveiled*, the follow-up to *Wild Card*, in November 2014.